PIRANESI

PIRANESI

SUSANNA CLARKE

THORNDIKE PRESS
A part of Gale, a Cengage Company

LIBRARY OF CONGRESS CIP DATA ON FILE.
CATALOGUING IN PUBLICATION FOR THIS BOOK
IS AVAILABLE FROM THE LIBRARY OF CONGRESS.

ISBN-13: 978-1-4328-8657-8 (hardcover alk. paper)

Published in 2021 by arrangement with Bloomsbury Publishing.

Printed in Mexico
Print Number: 01   Print Year: 2021

For Colin

'I am the great scholar, the magician, the adept, who is *doing* the experiment. Of course I need subjects to do it *on.*'

The Magician's Nephew,
C. S. Lewis

'People call me a philosopher or a scientist or an anthropologist. I am none of those things. I am an anamnesiologist. I study what has been forgotten. I divine what has disappeared utterly. I work with absences, with silences, with curious gaps between things. I am really more of a magician than anything else.'

Laurence Arne-Sayles,
interview in *The Secret Garden,*
May 1976

CONTENTS

PART 1: PIRANESI. 11

PART 2: THE OTHER. 33

PART 3: THE PROPHET 119

PART 4: 16 175

PART 5: VALENTINE KETTERLEY . . 239

PART 6: WAVE. 255

PART 7: MATTHEW ROSE
   SORENSEN 315

■ ■ ■ ■

PART 1
PIRANESI

■ ■ ■ ■

When the Moon rose in the Third Northern Hall I went to the Ninth Vestibule
ENTRY FOR THE FIRST DAY OF THE FIFTH MONTH IN THE YEAR THE ALBATROSS CAME TO THE SOUTH-WESTERN HALLS

When the Moon rose in the Third Northern Hall I went to the Ninth Vestibule to witness the joining of three Tides. This is something that happens only once every eight years.

The Ninth Vestibule is remarkable for the three great Staircases it contains. Its Walls are lined with marble Statues, hundreds upon hundreds of them, Tier upon Tier, rising into the distant heights.

I climbed up the Western Wall until I reached the Statue of a Woman carrying a Beehive, fifteen metres above the Pavement. The Woman is two or three times my own height and the Beehive is covered with

13

marble Bees the size of my thumb. One Bee — this always gives me a slight sensation of queasiness — crawls over her left Eye. I squeezed Myself into the Woman's Niche and waited until I heard the Tides roaring in the Lower Halls and felt the Walls vibrating with the force of what was about to happen.

First came the Tide from the Far Eastern Halls. This Tide ascended the Easternmost Staircase without violence. It had no colour to speak of and its Waters were no more than ankle deep. It spread a grey mirror across the Pavement, the surface of which was marbled with streaks of milky Foam.

Next came the Tide from the Western Halls. This Tide thundered up the Westernmost Staircase and hit the Eastern Wall with a great Clap, making all the Statues tremble. Its Foam was the white of old fishbones, and its churning depths were pewter. Within seconds its Waters were as high as the Waists of the First Tier of Statues.

Last came the Tide from the Northern Halls. It hurled itself up the middle Staircase, filling the Vestibule with an explosion of glittering, ice-white Foam. I was drenched and blinded. When I could see again Waters were cascading down the Statues. It was then that I realised I had made a mistake in calculating the volumes of the Second and Third Tides. A towering Peak of Water swept up to where I crouched. A great Hand of Water reached out to pluck me from the Wall. I flung my arms around the Legs of the Woman carrying a Beehive and prayed to the House to protect me. The Waters covered me and for a moment I was surrounded by the strange silence that comes when the Sea sweeps over you and drowns its own sounds. I thought that I was going to die; or else that I would be swept away to Unknown Halls, far from the rush and thrum of Familiar Tides. I clung on.

Then, just as suddenly as it began, it was over. The Joined Tides swept on into the surrounding Halls. I heard the thunder and crack as the Tides struck the Walls. The Waters in the Ninth Vestibule sank rapidly down until they barely covered the Plinths of the First Tier of Statues.

I realised that I was holding on to something. I opened my hand and found a marble Finger from some Faraway Statue that the Tides had placed there.

The Beauty of the House is immeasurable; its Kindness infinite.

A description of the World

I am determined to explore as much of the World as I can in my lifetime. To this end I have travelled as far as the Nine-Hundred-and-Sixtieth Hall to the West, the Eight-Hundred-and-Ninetieth Hall to the North and the Seven-Hundred-and-Sixty-Eighth Hall to the South. I have climbed up to the Upper Halls where Clouds move in slow procession and Statues appear suddenly out of the Mists. I have explored the Drowned Halls where the Dark Waters are carpeted with white water lilies. I have seen the Derelict Halls of the East where Ceilings, Floors — sometimes even Walls! — have collapsed and the dimness is split by shafts of grey Light.

In all these places I have stood in Doorways and looked ahead. I have never seen any indication that the World was coming to an End, but only the regular progression of Halls and Passageways into the Far Distance.

No Hall, no Vestibule, no Staircase, no Passage is without its Statues. In most Halls they cover all the available space, though

16

here and there you will find an Empty Plinth, Niche or Apse, or even a blank space on a Wall otherwise encrusted with Statues. These Absences are as mysterious in their way as the Statues themselves.

I have observed that, while the Statues of a particular Hall are more or less uniform in size, there is considerable variation between Halls. In some places the figures are two or three times the height of a Human Being, in others more or less life-size and in yet others, only reach as high as my shoulder. The Drowned Halls contain Statues that are gigantic — fifteen to twenty metres high — but they are the exception.

I have begun a Catalogue in which I intend to record the Position, Size and Subject of each Statue, and any other points of interest. So far I have completed the First and Second South-Western Halls and am engaged on the Third. The enormity of this task sometimes makes me feel a little dizzy, but as a scientist and an explorer I have a duty to bear witness to the Splendours of the World.

The Windows of the House look out upon Great Courtyards; barren, empty places paved with stone. The Courtyards are generally four-sided, although now and then you will come upon one with six sides, or eight, or even — these are rather strange and gloomy — only three.

Outside the House there are only the Celestial Objects: Sun, Moon and Stars.

The House has three Levels. The Lower Halls are the Domain of the Tides; their Windows — when seen from across a Courtyard — are grey-green with the restless Waters and white with the spatter of Foam. The Lower Halls provide nourishment in the form of fish, crustaceans and sea vegetation.

The Upper Halls are, as I have said, the Domain of the Clouds; their Windows are grey-white and misty. Sometimes you will see a whole line of Windows suddenly illuminated by a flash of lightning. The Upper Halls give Fresh Water, which is shed in the Vestibules in the form of Rain and flows in Streams down Walls and Staircases.

Between these two (largely uninhabitable) Levels are the Middle Halls, which are the Domain of birds and of men. The Beautiful Orderliness of the House is what gives us Life.

This morning I looked out of a Window in the Eighteenth South-Eastern Hall. On the other side of the Courtyard I saw the Other looking out of a Window. The Window was tall and dark; the Other's noble head with its high forehead and neatly trimmed beard was framed in one Corner. He was lost in thought as he so often is. I waved to him. He did not see me. I waved more extravagantly. I jumped up and down with great energy. But the Windows of the House are many and he did not see me.

A list of all the people who have ever lived and what is known of them

ENTRY FOR THE TENTH DAY OF THE FIFTH MONTH IN THE YEAR THE ALBATROSS CAME TO THE SOUTH-WESTERN HALLS

Since the World began it is certain that there have existed fifteen people. Possibly there have been more; but I am a scientist and must proceed according to the evidence. Of the fifteen people whose existence is verifiable, only Myself and the Other are now living.

I will now name the fifteen people and give, where relevant, their positions.

First Person: Myself

I believe that I am between thirty and thirty-five years of age. I am approximately 1.83 metres tall and of a slender build.

Second Person: The Other

I estimate the Other's age to be between fifty and sixty. He is approximately 1.88 metres tall and, like me, of a slender build. He is strong and fit for his age. His skin is a pale olive colour. His short hair and moustache are dark brown. He has a beard that is greying, almost white; it is neatly trimmed and slightly pointed. The bones of his skull are particularly fine with high, aristocratic cheekbones and a tall, impressive forehead. The overall impression he gives is of a friendly but slightly austere person devoted to the life of the intellect.

He is a scientist like me and the only other living human being, so naturally I value his friendship highly.

The Other believes that there is a Great and Secret Knowledge hidden somewhere in the World that will grant us enormous powers once we have discovered it. What this Knowledge consists of he is not entirely sure, but at various times he has suggested that it might include the following:

1. vanquishing Death and becoming immortal
2. learning by a process of telepathy what other people are thinking
3. transforming ourselves into eagles

and flying through the Air
4. transforming ourselves into fish and swimming through the Tides
5. moving objects using only our thoughts
6. snuffing out and reigniting the Sun and Stars
7. dominating lesser intellects and bending them to our will

The Other and I are searching diligently for this Knowledge. We meet twice a week (on Tuesdays and Fridays) to discuss our work. The Other organises his time meticulously and never permits our meetings to last longer than one hour.

If he requires my presence at other times, he calls out 'Piranesi!' until I come.

Piranesi. It is what he calls me.

Which is strange because as far as I remember it is not my name.

Third Person: The Biscuit-Box Man

The Biscuit-Box Man is a skeleton that resides in an Empty Niche in the Third North-Western Hall. The bones have been ordered in a particular way: long ones of a similar size have been collected and tied together with twine made from seaweed. To the right is placed the skull and to the left is a biscuit box containing all the small bones — finger bones, toe bones, vertebrae etc. The biscuit box is red. It has a picture of biscuits and bears the legend, *Huntley Palmers* and *Family Circle.*

When I first discovered the Biscuit-Box Man, the seaweed twine had dried up and fallen apart and he had become rather untidy. I made new twine from fish leather and tied up his bundles of bones again. Now he is in good order once more.

Fourth Person: The Concealed Person

One day three years ago I climbed the Staircase in the Thirteenth Vestibule. Finding that the Clouds had departed from that Region of the Upper Halls and that they were bright, clear and filled with Sunlight, I determined to explore further. In one of the Halls (the one positioned directly above the Eighteenth North-Eastern Hall) I found a half-collapsed skeleton wedged in a narrow space between a Plinth and the Wall. From the current disposition of the bones I believe it was originally in a sitting position with the knees drawn up to the chin. I have been unable to learn the gender. If I took the bones out to examine them, I could never get them back in again.

Persons Five to Fourteen: The People of the Alcove

The People of the Alcove are all skeletal. Their bones are laid side by side on an Empty Plinth in the Northernmost Alcove of the Fourteenth South-Western Hall.

I have tentatively identified three skeletons as female and three as male, and there are four whose gender I cannot determine with any certainty. One of these I have named the Fish-Leather Man. The skeleton of the Fish-Leather Man is incomplete and many of the bones are much worn away by the Tides. Some are scarcely more than little pebbles of bone. There are small holes bored in the ends of some of them and fragments of fish leather. From this I draw several conclusions:

1. The skeleton of the Fish-Leather Man is older than the others

2. The skeleton of the Fish-Leather Man was once displayed differently, its bones threaded together with thongs of fish leather, but over time the leather decayed

3. The people who came after the Fish-Leather Man (presumably the People of the Alcove) held human life in such reverence that they

<blockquote>patiently collected his bones and laid him with their own dead</blockquote>

Question: when I feel myself about to die, ought I to go and lie down with the People of the Alcove? There is, I estimate, space for four more adults. Though I am a young man and the day of my Death is (I hope) some way off, I have given this matter some thought.

Another skeleton lies next to the People of the Alcove (though this does not count as one of the people who have lived). It is the remains of a creature approximately 50 centimetres long and with a tail the same length as its body. I have compared the bones to the different kinds of Creatures that are portrayed in the Statues and believe them to belong to a monkey. I have never seen a live monkey in the House.

The Fifteenth Person: The Folded-Up Child

The Folded-Up Child is a skeleton. I believe it to be female and approximately seven years of age. She is posed on an Empty Plinth in the Sixth South-Eastern Hall. Her knees are drawn up to her chin, her arms clasp her knees, her head is bowed down. There is a necklace of coral beads and fishbones around her neck.

I have given a great deal of thought to this child's relationship to me. There are living in the World (as I have already explained) only Myself and the Other; and we are both male. How will the World have an Inhabitant when we are dead? It is my belief that the World (or, if you will, the House, since the two are for all practical purposes identical) wishes an Inhabitant for Itself to be a witness to its Beauty and the recipient of its Mercies. I have postulated that the House intended the Folded-Up Child to be my Wife, only something happened to prevent it. Ever since I had this thought it has seemed only right to share with her what I have.

I visit all the Dead, but particularly the Folded-Up Child. I bring them food, water and water lilies from the Drowned Halls. I speak to them, telling them what I have been doing and I describe any Wonders that I have seen in the House. In this way they know that they are not alone.

Only I do this. The Other does not. As far as I know he has no religious practices.

The Sixteenth Person

And You. Who are You? Who is it that I am writing for? Are You a traveller who has cheated Tides and crossed Broken Floors and Derelict Stairs to reach these Halls? Or are You perhaps someone who inhabits my own Halls long after I am dead?

My Journals

I write down what I observe in my notebooks. I do this for two reasons. The first is that Writing inculcates habits of precision and carefulness. The second is to preserve whatever knowledge I possess for you, the Sixteenth Person. I keep my notebooks in a brown leather messenger bag; the bag is generally stored in a hollow place behind the Statue of an Angel caught on a Rose Bush in the North-Eastern Corner of the Second Northern Hall. This is also where I keep my watch, which I need on Tuesdays and Fridays when I go to meet the Other at 10 o'clock. (On other days I try not to carry my watch for fear that Sea Water will get inside and damage the mechanism.)

One of my notebooks is my Table of Tides. In it I set down the Times and Volumes of High and Low Tides and make calculations of the Tides to come. Another notebook is my Catalogue of Statues. In the others I keep my Journal in which I write my thoughts and memories and make a record of my days. So far my Journal has filled nine notebooks; this is the tenth. All are numbered and most are labelled with the dates to which they refer.

No. 1 is labelled *December 2011 to June 2012*

No. 2 is labelled *June 2012 to November 2012*

No. 3 was originally labelled *November 2012*, but this has been crossed out at some point and relabelled *Thirtieth Day in the Twelfth Month in the Year of Weeping and Wailing, to the Fourth Day of the Seventh Month in the Year I discovered the Coral Halls*

Both No. 2 and No. 3 have gaps where pages have been violently removed. I have puzzled over the reason for this and tried to imagine who might have done it, but as yet have reached no conclusion.

No. 4 is labelled *Tenth Day of the Seventh Month in the Year I discovered the Coral Halls, to the Ninth Day of the Fourth Month in the Year I named the Constellations*

No. 5 is labelled *Fifteenth Day of the Fourth Month in the Year I named the Constellations, to the Thirtieth Day of the Ninth Month in the Year I counted and named the Dead*

No. 6 is labelled *First Day of the Tenth Month in the Year I counted and named the Dead, to the Fourteenth Day of the Second Month in the Year that the Ceilings in the Twentieth and Twenty-First North-Eastern Halls collapsed*

No. 7 is labelled *Seventeenth Day of the Second Month in the Year that the Ceilings in the Twentieth and Twenty-First North-Eastern Halls collapsed, to the last Day of the same Year*

No. 8 is labelled *First Day of the Year I travelled to the Nine-Hundred-and-Sixtieth Western Hall, to the Fifteenth Day of the Tenth Month of the same Year*

No. 9 is labelled *Sixteenth Day of the Tenth Month in the Year I travelled to the Nine-Hundred-and-Sixtieth Western Hall, to the Fourth Day of the Fifth Month in the Year the Albatross came to the South-Western Halls*

This Journal (No. 10) was begun on the Fifth Day of the Fifth Month in the Year the Albatross came to the South-Western Halls.

One of the drawbacks of keeping a journal is the difficulty of finding important entries again and so it is my practice to use one notebook as an index to all the others. In this notebook I have allocated a certain number of pages to each letter of the alphabet (more pages for common letters, such as A and C; fewer for letters that occur less frequently, for example Q and X). Under each letter I list entries by subject and where in my Journals they are to be found.

Reading over what I have just written, I have realised something. I have used two systems to number the years. How could I not have noticed this before?

I am guilty of bad practice. Only one system of numbering is needed. Two introduces confusion, uncertainty, doubt and muddle. (And is aesthetically unpleasing.)

In accordance with the first system I have named two years 2011 and 2012. This strikes me as deeply pedestrian. Also I cannot remember what happened two thousand years ago which made me think that year a good starting point. According to the second system I have given the years names like 'The Year I named the Constellations' and

'The Year I counted and named the Dead'. I like this much more. It gives each year a character of its own. This is the system I shall use going forward.

Statues

ENTRY FOR THE EIGHTEENTH DAY OF THE FIFTH MONTH IN THE YEAR THE ALBATROSS CAME TO THE SOUTH-WESTERN HALLS

There are some Statues that I love more than the rest. The Woman carrying a Beehive is one.

Another — perhaps *the* Statue that I love above all others — stands at a Door between the Fifth and Fourth North-Western Halls. It is the Statue of a Faun, a creature half-man and half-goat, with a head of exuberant curls. He smiles slightly and presses his forefinger to his lips. I have always felt that he meant to tell me something or perhaps to warn me of something: *Quiet!* he seems to say. *Be careful!* But what danger there could possibly be I have never known. I dreamt of him once; he was standing in a snowy forest and speaking to a female child.

The Statue of a Gorilla that stands in the Fifth Northern Hall always catches my eye. He is depicted squatting on his Lower Limbs, leaning forward and propping himself up on his Powerful Arms and Fists. His Face fascinates me. His Great Brow overshadows his Eyes and in a human person this expression would be called a scowl, but in the Gorilla it seems to mean the exact opposite. He represents many things, among them Peace, Tranquillity, Strength and Endurance.

There are many others that I love — the Young Boy playing the Cymbals, the Elephant carrying a Castle, the Two Kings playing Chess. The last I will mention is not exactly a favourite. Rather it is a Statue, or, to be more exact, a pair of Statues, that never fails to arrest my attention whenever I see it. The two Statues flank the Eastern Door of the First Western Hall. They are approximately six metres tall and have two unusual features: firstly, they are much larger than the other Statues in the First Western Hall; secondly, they are incomplete. Their Trunks emerge from the Wall at their Waists; their Arms reach back to push mightily; their Muscles swell with the effort and their Faces are contorted. They are not comfortable to contemplate. They seem to be in pain, struggling to be born; the struggle may be fruitless and yet they do not give up. Their Heads are extravagantly horned and so I have named them the

Horned Giants. They represent Endeavour and the Struggle against a Wretched Fate.

Is it disrespectful to the House to love some Statues more than others? I sometimes ask Myself this question. It is my belief that the House itself loves and blesses equally everything that it has created. Should I try to do the same? Yet, at the same time, I can see that it is in the nature of men to prefer one thing to another, to find one thing more meaningful than another.

Do trees exist?

ENTRY FOR THE NINETEENTH DAY OF THE FIFTH MONTH IN THE YEAR THE ALBATROSS CAME TO THE SOUTH-WESTERN HALLS

Many things are unknown. Once — it was about six or seven months ago — I saw a bright yellow speck floating on a gentle Tide beneath the Fourth Western Hall. Not understanding what it could be, I waded out into the Waters and caught it. It was a leaf, very beautiful, with two sides curving to a point at each end. Of course it is possible that it was part of a type of sea vegetation that I have never seen, but I am doubtful. The texture seemed wrong. Its surface repelled Water, like something meant to live in Air.

■ ■ ■ ■

PART 2
THE OTHER

■ ■ ■ ■

Batter-Sea

This morning at ten o'clock I went to the Second South-Western Hall to meet the Other. When I entered the Hall he was already there, leaning on an Empty Plinth, tapping at one of his shining devices. He wore a well-cut suit of charcoal wool and a bright white shirt that contrasted pleasingly with the olive tones of his skin.

Without looking up from his device he said, 'I need some data.'

He is often like this: so intent on what he is doing that he forgets to say Hello or Goodbye or to ask me how I am. I do not mind. I admire his dedication to his scientific work.

'What data?' I asked. 'Can I assist you?'

'Certainly,' he said. 'In fact, I won't get far if you don't. Today the subject of my research is' — at this point he looked up from what he was doing and smiled at me — 'you.' He has a most charming smile when he remembers to use it.

'Really?' I said. 'What are you trying to find out? Do you have a hypothesis about me?'

'I do.'

'What is it?'

'I can't tell you that. It might influence the data.'

'Oh! Yes. That is true. Sorry.'

'That's OK,' he said. 'It's natural to be curious.' He placed his shining device on the Empty Plinth and turned around. 'Sit down,' he said.

I sat on the Pavement, cross-legged, and waited for his questions.

'Comfortable?' he said. 'Good. Now tell me. What do you remember?'

'What do I remember?' I asked, confused.

'Yes.'

'As a question it lacks specificity,' I said.

'Nevertheless,' he said. 'Try to answer it.'

'Well,' I said. 'I suppose the answer is everything. I remember everything.'

'Really?' he said. 'That's rather a large claim. Are you sure?'

'I think so.'

'Give me some examples of the things you remember.'

'Well,' I said, 'suppose you were to name a Hall many days journey from here. Providing that I had visited it before, I could immediately tell you how to get there. I could name every Hall you would need to travel through. I could describe the notable Statues you would see on the Walls, and, with a reasonable degree of accuracy, I could tell you their positions — which Wall they stood against, whether North, South, East or West — and how far along the Wall they stood. I could also enumerate all the . . .'

'What about Batter-Sea?' asked the Other.

'Um . . . What?'

'Batter-Sea. Do you remember Batter-Sea?'

'No . . . I . . . Batter-Sea?'

'Yes.'

'I do not understand . . .'

I waited for the Other to explain, but he said nothing. I could see that he was observing me closely and I was sure that this question was crucial to whatever research he was conducting, but as to how I was supposed to answer it, I had not the least idea.

'Batter-Sea is not a word,' I said at last. 'It has no referent. There is nothing in the

World corresponding to that combination of sounds.'

Still the Other said nothing. He continued to gaze at me intently. I gazed back, troubled.

Then: 'Oh!' I exclaimed, light suddenly dawning. 'I see what you are doing!' I started to laugh.

'What am I doing?' asked the Other, smiling.

'You need to find out if I am telling the truth. I just said that I can describe the way to any Hall that I have previously visited. But you have no way of judging the truth of my claim. For example, if I were to describe the Path to the Ninety-Sixth Northern Hall, you would not know if my directions were accurate because you have never been there. So you have asked me a question with a nonsense word in it — Batter-Sea. Very cunningly you have chosen a word that sounds like a place. A place that is battered by the Sea. Now if I were to say that I remembered Batter-Sea and then described the way there, you would know I was lying. You would know I was simply boasting. You have put this in as a control question.'

'That's it exactly,' he said. 'That's exactly what I am doing.'

We both laughed.

'Have you more questions for me?' I asked.

'No. All done.' He was about to turn away to enter the data in his shining device, but something about me caught his attention and he gave me a puzzled sort of look.

'What is it?' I asked.

'Your glasses. What happened to them?'

'My glasses?'

'Yes,' he said. 'They look slightly . . . odd.'

'What do you mean?'

'The arms are wrapped round and round with strips of something,' he said. 'And the ends hang down at the sides.'

'Oh! I see,' I said. 'Yes! The arms of my glasses keep breaking off. First the left. And then the right. The salt-laden Air corrodes the plastic. I am experimenting with different methods of mending them. On the left arm I have used strips of fish leather and fish glue and on the right arm I have used seaweed. That is less successful.'

'Yes,' he said. 'I imagine it would be.'

In the Halls beneath us the incoming Tide struck a Wall. *Boom.* It withdrew, surged forward through the Doors and struck the Wall of the Next Chamber. *Boom. Boom. Boom.* Withdrew again; surged forward again. *Boom.* The Second South-Western Hall thrummed like the plucked string of

39

an instrument.

The Other looked anxious. 'That sounded really close,' he said. 'Oughtn't we to be getting out of here?' He does not understand the Tides.

'There is no need,' I said.

'OK,' he said. But he was not reassured. His eyes widened and his breathing became more shallow and rapid. He kept glancing from Door to Door as though expecting to see Water pouring in at any second.

'I don't want to get caught,' he said.

Once the Other was in the Eighth Northern Hall. A strong Tide from the Northern Halls rose in the Tenth Vestibule, followed moments later by an equally strong Tide from the Eastern Halls in the Twelfth Vestibule. Vast quantities of Water poured into the surrounding Halls, including the one where the Other was. The Waters plucked him up and carried him away, sweeping him through Doors and battering him against Walls and Statues. Several times he was completely immersed, and he expected to drown. Eventually the Tides cast him up on the Pavement of the Third Western Hall (a distance of seven Halls from where he began). That is where I found him. I fetched him a blanket and hot soup made of seaweed and mussels. As soon as he was able to walk, he took himself off without a word. I do not know where he went. (I never really know.) This happened in the Sixth Month of the Year I named the Constellations. Since then the Other has been afraid of the Tides.

'There is no danger,' I told him.

'Are you sure?' he said.

Boom. Boom.

'Yes,' I said. 'In five minutes, the Tide will reach the Sixth Vestibule and mount the Staircase. The Second Southern Hall — two Halls east of here — will be flooded for an hour. But the Water will be no more than ankle deep and it will not reach us.'

He nodded, but his anxiety levels remained high and he left a short while after.

In the early evening I went to the Eighth Vestibule to fish. I was not thinking about my conversation with the Other; I was thinking of my supper and of the beauty of the Statues in the Evening Light. But as I stood, casting my net into the Waters of the Lower Staircase, an image rose up before me. I saw a black scribble against a grey Sky and a flicker of bright red; words drifted towards me — white words on a black background. At the same time, there was a sudden blare of noise and a metallic taste on my tongue. And all of the images — no more than fragments or ghosts of images really — seemed to coalesce around the strange word, 'Batter-Sea'. I tried to get hold of them, to bring them into sharper focus, but like a dream they faded and were gone.

A white cross

ENTRY FOR THE THIRTIETH DAY OF THE FIFTH MONTH IN THE YEAR THE ALBATROSS CAME TO THE SOUTH-WESTERN HALLS

If you examine my previous Journal (Journal no. 9) you will see that I wrote very little in the final month of last year and the first month and a half of this one. (This sometimes happens for a reason that I will explain below.) During this period an event took place, which I have been meaning to write about. I shall do so now.

It was the very depths of Winter. Snow was piled on the Steps of the Staircases. Every Statue in the Vestibules wore a cloak or shroud or hat of snow. Every Statue with an outstretched Arm (of which there are many) held an icicle like a dangling sword or else a line of icicles hung from the Arm as if it were sprouting feathers.

There is a thing that I know but always forget: Winter is hard. The cold goes on and on and it is only with difficulty and effort that a person keeps himself warm. Every year, as Winter approaches, I congratulate Myself on having a plentiful supply of dry seaweed to use as fuel, but as the days, weeks and months stretch out I become less certain that I have sufficient. I wear as many of my clothes as I can cram onto my body. Every Friday I take stock of my fuel and I calculate how much I can permit Myself each day in order to make it last until Spring.

In the Twelfth Month of last year the Other suspended his work on the Great and Secret Knowledge and cancelled our meetings because he said it was too cold to stand about talking. My fingers were numb with cold — which caused my handwriting to deteriorate. Eventually I stopped writing in my Journal altogether.

About the middle of the First Month a Wind came up from the South. It blew for days without ceasing and though I tried hard not to complain about it, I found it something of a trial. It blew stinging Snow into the Halls. It blew on me at night in my bed in the Third Northern Hall. It howled in the Vestibules, catching up handfuls of loose snow and making them into little ghosts.

Not everything about the Wind was bad. Sometimes it blew through the little voids and crevices of the Statues and caused them to sing and whistle in surprising ways; I had never known the Statues to have voices before and it made me laugh for sheer delight.

One day I rose early and went to the Forty-Third Vestibule. The Halls that I passed through were grey and dim, with just a suggestion of Light in the Windows — the idea of Light, more than Light itself.

My intention was to gather seaweed, both for food and fuel. Normally I must wait until Spring, Summer and Autumn to dry seaweed. Winter is too cold and wet. But it had occurred to me that if I could hang the seaweed up (perhaps across a Doorway) then the Wind would dry it quickly. The only difficulty would be in securing the seaweed so that it did not blow away. I had thought of three different ways to do this and was eager to try all of them to see which would prove the most efficient.

As I crossed the Eleventh Western Hall, the Wind knocked me from one Paving Stone to another as if I were a chess piece on a board. (I made some highly original moves!)

I descended the Staircase in the Forty-

44

Third Vestibule and entered the Lower Hall, the one that lies directly beneath the Thirty-Seventh South-Western Hall. One effect of the Wind was that the High Tides were much higher and more violent than usual; the Low Tides were conversely lower. It was Low Tide just then and the Sea had drawn back so far that the Hall was entirely empty of Water (which hardly ever happens). It was strewn with remnants of the Tide: seaweed, which streamed in the Wind like little banners, and pebbles, starfish and shells, which rattled across the Stone Pavement as the Wind chased them.

It was early, a handful of moments after Dawn. I could see the pale golden Sky reflected in some of the Windows in the Courtyard. Ahead of me the grey, restless Waters were framed in the Doorway that led to the next Hall. The wildness of the Water contrasted with the severity of the lines of the Doorway.

I bent down and began to gather the cold, wet seaweed. Even this simple task was made more difficult by the Wind, since so much of my energy had to be expended on staying in the same place. The Wind also caught the strands of seaweed; they lashed my hands and made them cold and sore.

After a while I straightened Myself to ease

my back. Once again, I raised my eyes to the Doorway that led to the next Hall.

I saw a vision! In the dim Air above the grey Waves hung a white, shining cross. Its whiteness was a blazing whiteness; it far outshone the Wall of Statues behind it. It was beautiful but I did not understand it. The next moment brought enlightenment of a sort: it was not a cross at all but something vast and white, which glided rapidly towards me on the Wind.

What could it be? It must be a bird, but if I could see it at such a great distance, then it must be a bird of much greater size than the birds I was accustomed to. It swept on, coming directly towards me. I spread my arms in answer to its spread wings, as if I was going to embrace it. I spoke out loud. *Welcome! Welcome! Welcome!* was what I think I meant to say, but the Wind took my breath from me and all I could manage was: 'Come! Come! Come!'

The bird sailed across the heaving Waves, never once beating its wings. With great skill and ease it tipped itself slightly sideways to pass through the Doorway that separated us. Its wingspan surpassed even the width of the Door. I knew what it was! An albatross!

Still it continued, straight towards me, and

the strangest thought came to me: perhaps the albatross and I were destined to merge and the two of us would become another order of being entirely: an Angel! This thought both excited and frightened me, but still I remained, arms outstretched, mirroring the albatross's flight. (I thought how surprised the Other would be when I flew into the Second South-Western Hall on my Angel Wings, bringing him messages of Peace and Joy!) My heart beat rapidly.

The moment that he reached me — the moment that I thought we would collide like Planets and become one! — I gave out a sort of gasping cry — *Aahhhh!* In the same instant, I felt some sort of pent-up tension go out of me, a tension I did not know I had until that moment. Vast, white wings passed over me. I felt and smelt the Air those wings brought with them, the sharp, salty, wild tang of Faraway Tides and Winds that had roamed vast distances, through Halls I would never see.

At the last moment the albatross swung over my left shoulder. I fell to the Pavement. He flapped his wings in a frantic, panicked sort of way, stuck out his wiry pink legs and tumbled out of the Air into a sort of heap on the Pavement. In the Air he was a miraculous being — a Heavenly Being —

but on the Stones of the Pavement he was mortal and subject to the same embarrassments and clumsiness as other mortals.

We picked ourselves up. Now that he was on the dry Pavement he seemed bigger than ever: his head reached almost to my breastbone.

'I am very glad to see you,' I said. 'Welcome. I am the Inhabitant of these Halls. One of the Inhabitants. There is another, but he is not fond of birds and so you will probably not see him.'

The albatross spread his wings wide and stretched out his throat towards the Ceiling. He made a sort of clacking, whirring sound in his throat, which I took to be his way of greeting me. The backs of his wings were dark, almost black, with a white shape like a star on each one.

I returned to my work of gathering seaweed. The albatross walked about the Hall. His greyish-pinkish feet made loud slapping sounds on the Pavement. From time to time he came and looked at what I was doing as if it interested him.

The next day I returned. The albatross had come up the Staircase and was examining the Forty-Third Vestibule. But more than that: imagine my joy when I found that the Vestibule now sheltered two albatrosses!

His wife had joined him! (Or perhaps the original albatross was female and this was her husband. I did not have enough information to be certain on this point.) The new albatross had a different patterning on the back of her (or possibly his) wings: a patterning of white flecks, like a silver rain falling. The two albatrosses spread their wings; they danced around each other; they pointed their beaks at the Ceiling and made a joyful shrieking, screeching sound; they tapped their long pink beaks together to express their happiness.

A few days later I visited them again. This time they seemed quieter and there was an air of despondency and discouragement in the Vestibule. The albatross that I thought of as male (the one with stars on his wings) had fetched up a quantity of seaweed from the Lower Hall. He picked up lumps of it in his beak and made a heap of them. A few minutes later he became dissatisfied with this arrangement and collected the lumps of seaweed again and tried them in a different spot. He performed this action perhaps a dozen times.

'I think I see your problem,' I said. 'You have come here to build a nest. But you cannot find the materials you need. There is only cold, wet seaweed and you need something drier to make a cosy nest for your egg. Do not worry. I will help you. I have a supply of dry seaweed. Speaking as a non-avian, I feel sure that this would be a highly suitable building material. I will go and fetch it immediately.'

The starred albatross spread his wings and stretched his neck; he pointed his beak at the Ceiling and made the raucous clacking sound. This, I thought, was an expression of enthusiasm.

I returned to the Third Northern Hall. I lined a fishing net with heavy-gauge plastic. Inside I placed what I thought was the right amount of nesting material for two such enormous birds. It approximated to three days' fuel. This was no insignificant amount and I knew that I might be colder because I had given it away. But what is a few days of feeling cold compared to a new albatross in the World? I made two other additions to the pile of seaweed: some clean, white feathers that I had found and kept for no better reason than because I liked them, and an old woollen jumper that was in so many holes it was of scarcely any use as a garment, but which might do very well as a lining for a precious egg.

I dragged the fishing net to the Forty-Third Vestibule. I was immediately rewarded by the interest which the male albatross showed in the contents; he seized a beakful of dry seaweed and began trying it out in different places.

Shortly thereafter the albatrosses built a tall nest approximately a metre wide at its base and laid an egg in it. They are excellent parents; they were devoted to their egg and are now equally diligent in caring for their chick. The chick grows slowly and has shown no sign of being ready to fledge.

I have named this year the Year the Albatross came to the South-Western Halls.

The birds sit silent in the Sixth Western Hall

ENTRY FOR THE THIRTY-FIRST DAY OF THE FIFTH MONTH IN THE YEAR THE ALBATROSS CAME TO THE SOUTH-WESTERN HALLS

Ever since the Ceilings of the Twentieth and Twenty-First North-Eastern Halls collapsed two years ago, the Weather in this Region of the House has changed. Clouds drift down through the Broken Ceilings and into the Middle Halls where normally they would not go. It makes the World chill and grey.

This morning I awoke cold and shivering. A Cloud had penetrated the Third Northern Hall where I sleep. The Statues were delicate white images painted on white Mist.

I rose quickly and busied Myself with my daily tasks. I gathered seaweed in the Ninth Vestibule and made Myself a breakfast of nourishing, warming soup; then I set off for the Third South-Western Hall to continue my work on the Catalogue of Statues.

The House was peculiarly silent. No birds flew; no birds sang. Where had they all gone? It seemed they found the Cloud-haunted World as oppressive as I did. In the Sixth Western Hall I found them at last. They were gathered there, perched on the Shoulders and Heads of every Statue, on Plinths and on Columns, sitting silently, waiting.

The Drowned Halls

ENTRY FOR THE EIGHTH DAY OF THE SIXTH MONTH IN THE YEAR THE ALBATROSS CAME TO THE SOUTH-WESTERN HALLS

East of the First Vestibule the House is Derelict. Masonry and Statues from the Upper Halls have fallen through Broken Floors into the Middle and Lower Halls, blocking Doorways. There is an Area covering perhaps as many as forty or fifty Halls where the Tides cannot penetrate. Over time the Sea Water has drained away and these Halls have filled up with Rain, making dark, still, freshwater Lakes. Their Windows are half-submerged in Water or blocked by Masonry, making them dim and shadowy. Cut off from the Tides, they are unusually silent.

These are the Drowned Halls.

On the Periphery of this Region the Waters are shallow, tranquil and covered with water lilies, but in the centre they are deep and treacherous, full of broken Masonry and drowned Statues. The majority of the Drowned Halls are inaccessible, but some can be entered from the Upper Level.

They contain giant Statues of Men with curly Heads and Beards that strain and struggle out of the confines of the Walls, extending their Upper Bodies over the Dark Waters. There is one in particular who leans out so far that his broad, muscular Back forms an almost horizontal platform half a metre or so above the level of the Water, making an excellent place from which to fish.

Night fishing is best, when the fish are drawn to play in spots of bright Moonlight and are easy to see.

The Clouds above the Nineteenth Eastern Hall

ENTRY FOR THE TENTH DAY OF THE SIXTH MONTH IN THE YEAR THE ALBATROSS CAME TO THE SOUTH-WESTERN HALLS

It used to be that I dared not live too close to the Tides. When I heard their Thunder, I ran and hid Myself. In my ignorance, I feared to be caught in their Waters and drowned.

As far as possible I kept to the Dry Halls where the Statues are not clothed in rags of seaweed or armoured with encrustations of shellfish, where the Air is not scented with the Tides: Halls, in other words, that have not been flooded in recent Times. Water was not a problem; most Halls contain Falls of Fresh Water (sometimes you will see a Statue almost bisected by the Water that has splashed onto it for centuries). Food was a different matter; for that I had to brave the Tides. I would go to the Vestibules and descend the Staircases to the Lower Halls, to the Rim of the Ocean. But the Force of the Waves frightened me.

Even then I knew that the Tides were not random. I saw that if I could record and document them, I might be able to predict their appearance. That was the beginning of

54

my Table. But, though I grasped certain things about the movements of the Tides, I had no understanding of their Natures. I thought one Tide was pretty much the same as all the others. It astonished me when I went to meet a Tide expecting plentiful fish and sea vegetation, only to find it bright, clean, empty.

I was often hungry.

Fear and hunger forced me to explore the House and I discovered that fish were plentiful in the Drowned Halls. Their Waters were still and I was not so afraid. The difficulty here was that the Drowned Halls were surrounded by Dereliction on all sides. To reach them it was necessary to go up to the Upper Halls and then descend by means of the Wreckage through the great Rents and Gashes in the Floor.

Once, when I had not eaten for two days, I determined to go to the Drowned Halls to find some food. I ascended to the Upper Halls. This in itself was not easy for someone in my enfeebled condition. The Staircases, though they vary in size, are mostly built on the same noble scale as the rest of the House and each Step is almost twice the height that is comfortable for me. (It is as though God had originally built the House intending to people it with Giants before inexplicably changing His Mind.)

I passed into one of the Upper Halls, the one that stands directly above the Nineteenth Eastern Hall. From there I intended to descend to the Drowned Halls, but to my dismay I found that the Hall was full of Clouds: a chill, grey, wet blank. I had my Journal with me. Consulting it, I discovered that I had been in this Vicinity once before and had in fact made detailed notes of the Hall beyond this one; the Hall above the Twentieth Eastern Hall. I had described the character and condition of the Statues and had even made a sketch of one of them. But of this Hall — the Hall on whose Threshold I now stood, the Hall that was full of Clouds — of this Hall I had recorded nothing whatsoever.

Today I would consider it madness to journey through a Hall I cannot see properly and of which I have no record, but today I do not allow Myself to get as hungry as I was then.

Adjoining Halls usually share some characteristics. The Hall immediately to my rear was approximately 200 metres in length and 120 metres wide and so the chances were good that the Hall before me was the same. It did not seem an impossible distance; I was more concerned about the Statues. From what I could see, these depicted Human or Demi-Human figures, all two or three times my own stature and all in the throes of violent action: Men fighting, Women and Men being carried off by Centaurs or Satyrs, Octopuses tearing People apart. In most Regions of the House the expressions of the Statues are joyful or tranquil or possessed of a distant calm; but here the Faces were distorted in screams of rage or anguish.

I resolved to go carefully. To bash oneself on an outstretched marble limb is painful.

I entered the Cloud and slowly made my way along the Northern Side of the Hall. Statues appeared, one by one, out of the pale Cloud. They covered the Walls so thickly and were twisted into such tortuous forms that it was like walking under the dripping branches of a great forest of Arms and Bodies.

One Statue had toppled from the Wall and was lying shattered on the Floor. This ought to have been a warning to me.

I came to a place where a Statue thrust itself a long way out from the Wall. It depicted a Man, his vast Body flailing backwards, stretched over the Pavement, his Arms thrown over his Head as a Centaur trampled on him. The Palms of his great Hands faced upwards and his Fingers were curled in agony. I took a step away from the Wall to circumvent him and my foot met with . . .

. . . nothing.

No Floor! No Stone Pavement beneath me! I was falling! I lunged in terror towards the Wall. Immediately, I was caught! I lay suspended over the Empty Air, too terrified to move, my mind deadened by fear and shock. By some miracle I had fallen into the Trampled Man's Hands. The Hands were dripping with wet and horribly slippery; any movement on my part threatened to loose his hold on me and send me tumbling into the Void. Whimpering with fear and clinging to the Trampled Man with every atom of my strength, I inched up his Arms to his Head; from his Head to his Chest and so to his Lap where I wedged myself in. The Body of the Attacking Centaur formed a sort of Ceiling two or three centimetres over my head. The Cloud was so dense that I could not see where the Floor began again.

I stayed there all day and all night, hungry, almost dead from cold but deeply grateful to the Trampled Man for saving me. In the morning the Wind came and carried the Cloud westwards. I peered out at the great

Gash in the Floor and I saw the dizzying drop — 30 metres or more — to the still Waters of the Drowned Hall beneath.

A conversation

As well as my regular meetings with the Other and the quiet, consolatory presence of the Dead, there are the birds. Birds are not difficult to understand. Their behaviour tells me what they are thinking. Generally it runs along the lines of: *Is this food? Is this? What about this? This might be food. I am almost certain that this is.* Or occasionally: *It is raining. I do not like it.*

While ample for a brief neighbourly exchange, such remarks do not suggest a broad or deep intelligence. Yet it has occurred to me that there may be more wisdom in birds than appears at first sight, a wisdom that reveals itself only obliquely and intermittently.

Once — it was an evening in Autumn — I came to the Doorway of the Twelfth South-Eastern Hall intending to pass through the Seventeenth Vestibule. I found that I was unable to enter it; the Vestibule was full of

59

birds and the birds were all aflight. They circled and spiralled, creating a whirling dance. They filled the Vestibule like a column of smoke, which grew darker and denser in places and the next moment lighter and airier. I have witnessed this dance on several occasions, always in the evening and in the later months of the year.

Another time I entered the Ninth Vestibule and found it full of little birds. They were of different kinds, but mostly sparrows. I had not taken more than a few steps into the Vestibule when a large group of them took to the Air. They flew together in one great swoop up to the Eastern Wall, then in another swoop to the Southern Wall and then they turned and flew around me in a loose spiral.

'Good morning,' I said. 'I hope that you are well?'

Most of the birds scattered to different perches, but a handful — maybe as many as ten — flew to the Statue of a Gardener in the North-West Corner. They remained there for perhaps thirty seconds and then, still together, they ascended to a higher Statue on the Western Wall: the Woman carrying a Beehive. The birds remained on the Statue of the Woman carrying a Beehive for a minute or so and then they flew away.

I wondered why out of the thousand or so Statues in the Vestibule the little birds had chosen these two to perch on. It occurred to me — it was no more than an idle thought — that both these Statues might be said to represent Industriousness. The Gardener is old and bent, and yet he digs faithfully in his garden. The Woman is pursuing her profession of beekeeping and the Beehive that she carries is full of bees who are also patiently carrying out their tasks. Were the birds telling me that I ought to be industrious too? That seemed unlikely. After all I was already industrious! I was at that very moment on my way to the Eighth Vestibule to fish. I carried fishing nets over my shoulder and a lobster trap made from an old bucket.

The warning of the birds — if that was what it was — seemed on the face of it nonsensical, but I decided nonetheless to follow this unusual line of reasoning and see where it took me. That day I caught seven fish and four lobsters. I threw none of them back.

That night a Wind came from the West, bringing an unexpected Storm. The Tides were made turbulent and the fish were driven away from their customary Halls far out to Sea. For the next two days there were no fish at all and if I had not attended to the birds' warning I would have had hardly anything to eat.

This experience led me to form a hypothesis: perhaps the wisdom of birds resides, not in the individual, but in the flock, the congregation. I have tried to think of an experiment that would test this theory. The problem, as I see it, is that it is impossible to know in advance when such events will occur; and so the only viable course of action is months — more likely years — of careful observation and meticulous record keeping. Unfortunately, this is not possible just now since so much of my time is taken up by my work with the Other (I refer of course to our search for the Great and Secret Knowledge).

However, it is with this hypothesis in mind that I record something which happened this morning.

I entered the Second North-Eastern Hall and, as had happened in the Ninth Vestibule, I found it full of small birds of different sorts. I called a cheerful Good morning! to them.

Immediately twenty or so flew in a great rush to the Northern Wall and alighted on the High Statues. Then they flew in a swoop to the Western Wall.

I recalled that on the previous occasion this behaviour had been the preface to a message.

'I am paying attention!' I called to them. 'What is it that you wish to say to me?'

I watched very carefully what they did next.

The birds separated into two groups. One group flew to the Statue of an Angel blowing a Trumpet; the other group flew to the Statue of a Ship that travels on little Waves.

'An angel with a trumpet and a ship,' I said. 'Very well.'

The first group flew to a Statue of a Man reading from a large Book; the second group flew to a Statue of a Woman displaying a large Dish or Shield; upon the Shield is a representation of Clouds.

'A book and clouds,' I said. 'Yes.'

Finally the first group flew to the Statue of a little Child bowing its Head to gaze at a Flower, which it holds in its Hand; the Child's Head is covered with such exuberant Curls they are themselves like the petals of a flower; the second group of birds flew to a Statue of a Sack of Grain being devoured by a Horde of Mice.

'A child and mice,' I said. 'Very good. I see.'

The birds dispersed to different places in

the Hall.

'Thank you!' I called to them. 'Thank you!'

Supposing my hypothesis to be correct, this is certainly the most elaborate communication that the birds have offered me. What is the meaning?

An angel with a trumpet and a ship. An angel with a trumpet suggests a message. A joyful message? Perhaps. But an angel might also bring a stern or solemn message. Therefore the character of the message, whether good or bad, remains uncertain. The ship suggests travelling long distances. *A message coming from afar.*

A book and clouds. A book contains Writing. Clouds hide what is there. *Writing that is somehow obscure.*

A child and mice. The child represents the quality of Innocence. The mice are devouring the grain. Little by little it is diminished. *Innocence that is worn down or eroded.*

So this, as far as I can tell, is what the birds told me. *A message from afar. Obscure Writing. Innocence eroded.*

Interesting.

I will allow some time to elapse — say a few months — and then I will examine this communication again to see if the intervening events can shed any light upon it (and vice versa).

Addy Domarus

ENTRY FOR THE FIFTEENTH DAY OF THE SIXTH MONTH IN THE YEAR THE ALBATROSS CAME TO THE SOUTH-WESTERN HALLS

This morning in the Second South-Western Hall the Other said, 'I'm going to be working on the ritual today so you may not want to stick around.'

The Ritual is a piece of ceremonial magic by which the Other intends to free the Great and Secret Knowledge from whatever holds it captive in the World and to transfer it to ourselves. So far, we have performed it four times, each time in a slightly different version.

'I've made some changes,' he continued, 'and I want to hear how they sound, *in situ* as it were.'

'I will help you,' I said, eagerly.

'Fine,' he said. 'Just as long as you don't get too chatty. I need focus. Clarity.'

'Absolutely,' I said.

Today the Other was wearing a suit of mid-grey with a white shirt and black shoes. He laid his shining device upon the Empty Plinth. 'This is a summoning, and in summonings, the seer ought to face east,' he said. 'Which way's east?'

I pointed.

'Right,' he said.

'Where shall I stand?'

'Wherever you like. It doesn't matter.'

I took up a position two metres South of the place where he was standing and decided that I would face North — that is, towards him. I have no real insight or knowledge concerning rituals, but this seemed to me an appropriate position for an acolyte, subservient yet connected to the Interpreter of Mysteries.

'What shall I do?' I asked.

'Nothing. Just keep quiet like I told you.'

'I will concentrate on lending you the strength of my Spirit,' I said.

'Fine. Good. You do that.' He returned briefly to his shining device to check something. 'OK,' he said. 'This first part of the ritual is where I've made most changes. Up to now I've been simply invoking the knowledge and asking it to come to me and bestow itself upon me. That doesn't seem to have got me anywhere so instead I'm going to summon the spirit of Addy Domarus.'

'Who or what is Addy Domarus?' I asked.

'A king. Long dead. Someone who possessed the knowledge. Or some of it at any

66

rate. I've had success calling on him for aid in other rituals, notably for . . .' He stopped abruptly and for a brief moment looked confused. 'I've had success calling on him in the past,' he finished.

The Other assumed the noble posture of an Interpreter of Mysteries. He straightened his back, pulled back his shoulders and lifted up his head. He put me in mind of the Statue of a Hierophant in the Nineteenth Southern Hall.

Suddenly the significance of what he had said struck me.

'Oh!' I exclaimed. 'You have never said before that you knew one of the names of the Dead! Do you know which one he is? Please tell me if you do! I would very much like to call him by his name when I take him offerings of food and drink!'

The Other stopped what he was doing and frowned. 'What?' he said.

'The Dead,' I went on, eagerly. 'If you do indeed know one of their names, then please tell me to which of them it belongs.'

'Sorry? You've lost me. Which of the what was what?'

'You said that in times gone by one or more of the Dead possessed the Knowledge. Then they lost it. So I wanted to know which of them it was. The Biscuit-Box Man?

The Concealed Person? Or was it one of the People of the Alcove?'

The Other gazed at me blankly. 'Biscuit box . . . What are you talking about? Oh, wait. Is this something to do with those bones you found? No. No-no-no-no-no. Those aren't . . . That's not . . . Oh, for God's sake! Didn't I just say that I need to focus? Didn't I just say that? Can we not do this now? I'm trying to get this ritual sorted.'

Immediately I felt ashamed. I was impeding the Other's important work. 'Yes, of course,' I said.

'I don't have time to answer irrelevant questions,' he snapped.

'Sorry.'

'If you could just be quiet, that would be wonderful.'

'I will,' I said. 'I promise.'

'Fine. Good. OK. Where was I?' said the Other. He took a deep breath and stood very erect again, rearing up his head. He raised his arms and in sonorous tones he called on Addy Domarus several times and in several different ways to *Come! Come!*

In the ensuing silence he gradually let his arms fall to his sides, and relaxed. 'OK,' he said. 'For the real thing I'll maybe have a brazier. Some incense burning. We'll see. Then after the invocation comes the enumeration. I name the powers I seek: the vanquishing of Death, the penetration of lesser minds, invisibility etc., etc. It's important to visualise each power and so, as I name them, I imagine myself living forever, reading someone else's thoughts, becoming invisible and so on.'

I raised my hand politely. (I did not want to be accused of asking irrelevant questions again.)

'Yes?' he said, sharply.

'Shall I do that too?'

'Yes. If you like.'

In the same sonorous voice the Other recited the list of powers that the Knowledge bestows, and when he intoned, *I name the power of flight!,* I pictured Myself transformed into an osprey, flying with the other ospreys over the Surging Tides. (Of all the powers that the Other talks about, this is my favourite. To be perfectly honest, I am largely indifferent to the rest. What use would invisibility be to me? Most days there is no one here to see me except the birds. Nor do I have any desire to live forever. The House ordains a certain span for birds and another for men. With this I am content.)

The Other reached the end of his list. I could see that he was thinking about the parts of the ritual he had just performed and that he was not satisfied with them. There was a scowl on his face, and he stared off into the distance. 'I feel like I should be addressing all this to some sort of — some kind of energy, something vital and alive. It is power that I seek and therefore I should be speaking these words to something that is already powerful. Does that make sense?'

'Yes,' I said.

'But there isn't anything powerful. There isn't even anything alive. Just endless dreary rooms all the same, full of decaying figures covered with bird shit.' He fell into an unhappy silence.

I have known for many years that the Other does not revere the House in the same way I do, but it still shocks me when he talks like this. How can a man as intelligent as him say there is nothing alive in the House? The Lower Halls are full of sea creatures and vegetation, many of them very beautiful and very strange. The Tides themselves are full of movement and power so that, while they may not exactly be alive, neither are they not-alive. In the Middle Halls are birds and men. The droppings (of which he complains) are signs of Life! Nor is he correct to say that the Halls are all the same. They vary a great deal in the style of their Columns, Pilasters, Niches, Apses,

70

Pediments etc., as well as in the number of their Doors and Windows. Every Hall has its Statues and all the Statues are unique, or if there are any repetitions they must occur at vast distances as I have yet to see one.

There was, however, no point in saying any of this. I knew that it would only irritate him further.

'What about a Star?' I said. 'If we perform the Ritual at night, you can address the Invocation to a Star. A Star is a source of power and energy.'

A moment's silence, then: 'That's true,' he said. He sounded surprised. 'A star. That's actually not a bad idea.' He thought some more. 'A fixed star would be better than a wandering one. And it would need to be bright — appreciably brighter than the surrounding stars. What would be best would be to find somewhere in the labyrinth, some point or place that's unique — and to perform the ritual there, facing the brightest star!' For a moment he was full of excitement. Then he sighed and all the energy seemed to drain out of him again. 'But that's not very likely, is it?' Then he said again that every Hall was exactly like every other Hall, except that he called them 'rooms' and used an epithet meant to denigrate them.

I felt a surge of anger and for a moment I thought I would not tell him what I knew. But then I thought that it was unkind to punish him for something he cannot help. It is not his fault that he does not see things the way I do.

'Actually,' I said, 'there is one Hall different from the others.'

'Oh?' he said. 'You never said anything about it. In what way is it different?'

'It has only one Doorway and no Windows. I only saw it once. It has a strange atmosphere that is difficult to describe precisely. It is majestic, mysterious and at the same time, full of Presence.'

'You mean like a temple?' he said.

'Yes. Like a temple.'

'Why didn't you tell me about this before?' he demanded, his anger and irritation rising again.

'Well, it is some distance from here. I thought that you were unlikely to . . .'

But he was not interested in my explanation. 'I need to see this place. Can you take me? How far is it?'

'It is the One-Hundred-and-Ninety-Second Western Hall and it is 20 kilometres from the First Vestibule,' I said. 'It takes 3.76 hours to reach it, not including rest periods.'

'Oh,' he said.

I knew that I could scarcely have said anything more discouraging to him (though that was not my intention). He has no desire to explore the World. I do not believe that he has ever travelled more than the length of four or five Halls from the First Vestibule.

He said, 'What I need to know is what stars can be seen from the door of this room. Have you any idea?'

I thought. Had the One-Hundred-and-Ninety-Second Western Hall been oriented along an East/West axis? Or was it a South-East/North-West axis? I shook my head. 'I do not know. I cannot remember.'

'Well, can't you go back and find out?' he demanded.

'Go to the One-Hundred-and-Ninety-Second Western Hall?'

'Yes.'

I hesitated.

'What's the problem?' he asked.

'The Path to the One-Hundred-and-Ninety-Second Western Hall lies through the Seventy-Eighth Vestibule, a Region subject to frequent flooding. Just now it will be dry, but the Tides bring up Debris from the Lower Halls and scatter it throughout the surrounding Halls. Some of the Debris has jagged edges, which can cut a person's

73

feet. It is not good to have bleeding feet. There is a danger of infection. A person must pick their way carefully through the Broken Marble. It is possible, but laborious. It will take time.'

'OK,' said the Other. 'So there's debris. But I'm still not really understanding what the problem is. You must have passed through this place where the debris is before and you didn't come to any harm then. What's changed?'

A blush rose to my face. I fixed my eyes on the Pavement. The Other was so neat, so elegant in his suit and his shining shoes. I, on the other hand, was not neat. My clothes were ragged and faded, rotten with the Sea Water I fished in. I hated drawing his attention to this contrast between us, but nevertheless he had asked me and so I must answer. I said, 'What changed was that I used to have shoes. Now I have none.'

The Other gazed in astonishment at my naked brown feet. 'When did this happen?'

'About a year ago. My shoes fell apart.'

He burst out laughing. 'Why didn't you say something?'

'I did not want to trouble you. I thought I could make some shoes out of fish leather. But I have not found the time to do it. I have only myself to blame.'

'Honestly, Piranesi,' said the Other. 'What an idiot you are! If that's all that's preventing you going to the . . . the . . . whatever you call this room . . .'

'The One-Hundred-and-Ninety-Second Western Hall,' I interjected.

'Yes. Whatever. If that's all it is, I'll get you the shoes tomorrow.'

'Oh! That would be . . .' I began, but the Other put up his hand.

'No need to thank me. Just get me the information I need. That's all I ask.'

'Oh, I will!' I promised. 'Once I have shoes there will be no problem. I will reach the One-Hundred-and-Ninety-Second Western Hall in three-and-a-half hours. Four at the most.'

Shoes

ENTRY FOR THE SIXTEENTH DAY OF THE SIXTH MONTH IN THE YEAR THE ALBATROSS CAME TO THE SOUTH-WESTERN HALLS

On the way to the Third South-Western Hall this morning I passed through the Second South-Western Hall. On top of the Empty Plinth where the Other leans was a small cardboard box. It was a deep grey colour. On the lid was a picture of an octopus in a paler shade of grey and some

75

orange writing. The writing said: AQUAR-IUM.

I opened it. At first sight it appeared to contain nothing except thin white paper, but when I lifted the paper I found a pair of shoes. They were made of canvas of a blue-green colour that reminded me of the Tides of the Southern Halls. The rubber soles were thick and white and they had white laces. I removed them from the box and put them on. They fitted perfectly. I tried walking about in them. My feet felt beautifully cushioned and bouncible.

All day long I have been running and dancing for the sheer pleasure of feeling my feet in their new shoes.

'Look!' I said to the crows in the First Northern Hall when they flew down from the High Statues to see what I was doing, 'I have new shoes!'

But the crows only cawed and flew back to their perches.

A list of things the Other has given me

ENTRY FOR THE SEVENTEENTH DAY OF THE SIXTH MONTH IN THE YEAR THE ALBATROSS CAME TO THE SOUTH-WESTERN HALLS

I have made a list of all the things that the Other has given me, so that I will remember to be grateful and thank the House for sending me such an excellent friend!

In the Year I named the Constellations, the Other gave me:

- a sleeping bag
- a pillow
- 2 blankets
- 2 fishing nets made of a synthetic polymer
- 4 large sheets of heavy-gauge plastic
- a torch. I have never used this and cannot now remember where I put it.
- 6 boxes of matches
- 2 bottles of multivitamins

In the Year I counted and named the Dead, he gave me:

- a cheese and ham sandwich

In the Year that the Ceilings in the Twentieth and Twenty-First North-Eastern Halls collapsed, he gave me:

- 6 plastic bowls. I use them to catch Fresh Water as it flows through Cracks in the Ceilings and down the Faces of the Statues. One of the bowls is blue, two are red and three are cloud coloured. The cloud-coloured ones are troublesome. They are almost exactly the same whitey-grey colour as the Statues. Whenever I put them somewhere to catch Water they immediately fade into their surroundings and I lose sight of them. One disappeared last year and I have yet to find it.

- 4 pairs of socks. For two Winters my feet have been warm and cosy, but now the socks are all in holes. Unfortunately, it has not occurred to the Other to give me new ones.
- a fishing rod and line
- an orange
- a slice of Christmas cake
- 8 bottles of multivitamins
- 4 boxes of matches

In the Year I travelled to the Nine-Hundred-and-Sixtieth Western Hall, he gave me:

- a new battery for my watch
- 10 new notebooks
- various assorted items of stationery, including 12 large sheets of paper to make Star Maps, envelopes, pencils, a ruler and some rubbers
- 47 pens
- more multivitamins and matches

78

This year (the Year the Albatross came to the South-Western Halls), he has given me so far:

- 3 more plastic bowls. These are the best ones, being brightly coloured and therefore easy to see. One is orange and two are different shades of green.
- 4 boxes of matches
- 3 bottles of vitamins
- a pair of new shoes!

I owe so much to the Other's generosity. Without him I would not sleep snug and warm in my sleeping bag in Winter. I would not have notebooks in which to record my thoughts.

That being said, it occurs to me to wonder why it is that the House gives a greater variety of objects to the Other than to me, providing him with sleeping bags, shoes, plastic bowls, cheese sandwiches, notebooks, slices of Christmas cake etc., etc., whereas me it mostly gives fish. I think perhaps it is because the Other is not as skilled in taking care of himself as I am. He does not know how to fish. He never (as far as I know) gathers seaweed, dries it and stores it to make fires or a tasty snack; he does not cure fish skins and make leather out of them (which is useful for many things). If the House did not provide all these things for him, it is quite possible that he would die. Or else (which is more likely) I would have to devote a great deal of my time to caring for him.

None of the Dead claim the name Addy Domarus

ENTRY FOR THE EIGHTEENTH DAY OF THE SIXTH MONTH IN THE YEAR THE ALBATROSS CAME TO THE SOUTH-WESTERN HALLS

It has been some weeks since I visited the Dead and so today I did so. It is no small undertaking to visit them all in the space of one day since they lie several kilometres distant from each other. I brought each one an offering of water and food, and water lilies that I had gathered in the Drowned Halls.

At each of the Niches and Plinths I whispered the name *Addy Domarus.* I hoped that one of them — the one to whom the name belongs — would somehow communicate his acceptance of it. But that did not happen. Rather, as I knelt at each Niche or Plinth, I felt a faint sense of repudiation, as if the name were being pushed away.

A journey

I spent today working at my usual tasks: fishing, gathering seaweed, working on my Catalogue of Statues. In the late afternoon I gathered some supplies and set out to walk to the One-Hundred-and-Ninety-Second Western Hall.

On the way the House showed me many wonders.

In the Forty-Fifth Vestibule I saw a Staircase that had become one vast bed of mussels. One of the Statues that lined the Wall of the Staircase was all but engulfed in a blue-black carapace of mussels with only half a staring Face and one white, out-flung Arm left free. I made a sketch of it in my Journal.

In the Fifty-Second Western Hall I came upon a Wall ablaze with so much golden Light that the Statues appeared to be dissolving into it. From there I passed into a little Antechamber with few Windows, where it was cool and shadowy. I saw the Statue of a Woman holding out a wide, flat Dish so that a Bear Cub could drink from it.

81

As I approached the Seventy-Eighth Vestibule, the Pavements were strewn with Rubble. At first, I saw only a scattering here and there, but by the time I drew close to the Vestibule I was walking over an uneven and treacherous Floor of Jagged Stones. In the Vestibule itself a thin sheet of Water still ran beneath the Rubble. Broken Statues were heaped in the Corners.

I walked on. In the Eighty-Eighth Western Hall the Pavement was free from Debris, but I found another problem. A colony of herring gulls had built their nests in this Hall and my intrusion among them was met with fury. They squawked indignantly and flew at me, beating their wings and attempting to peck at me with their beaks. I waved my arms and shouted to ward them off.

I reached the One-Hundred-and-Ninety-Second Western Hall. I stood at the Single Door and peered inside. The surrounding Halls were full of a soft blue Twilight but this particular Hall — which, as I have already said, has no Windows — was dark, its Statues invisible. A faint draught — like a cold breath — emanated from it.

I am not accustomed to Absolute Darkness. There are very few Dark Places in the House; perhaps here and there you will find the Shadowy Corner of an Antechamber or an Angle of the Derelict Halls where the Light is blocked by Debris; but generally, the House is not dark. Even at night the Stars blaze down through the Windows.

I had imagined that all I would need to do to answer the Other's question — What Stars can be seen from the door of the Hall? — was to ascertain the exact orientation of the Hall and then consult my Star Maps. But now that I was actually at the Door, I realised that this plan was wildly optimistic. The Door was approximately four metres wide and eleven metres high, which is huge for a Door but minuscule when compared to the vastness of the Sky. I would not be able to tell which Stars would be framed in the Doorway unless I spent the night in the Hall and saw for Myself.

I did not find this prospect appealing.

I remembered how I climbed a Staircase to the Upper Hall above the Nineteenth Eastern Hall and found it filled with Cloud. I remembered how that Hall was full of gigantic Figures in the throes of violent action, how every Face was distorted by screams of rage or anguish.

Suppose (I thought) this happened again? Suppose I went into the Darkness of the One-Hundred-and-Ninety-Second Western Hall and I lay down to sleep, only to wake and find Myself surrounded by horrors?

I became angry at Myself, disgusted at my own timidity. This was no way to think! Had I walked for four hours to reach this Hall only to be too afraid to go in? How ridiculous! I told Myself that the fear I had experienced in that Upper Hall was highly unlikely to be repeated anywhere else. I had, after all, entered the One-Hundred-and-Ninety-Second Western Hall before. If the Statues had been particularly violent or frightening, I would surely have remembered. Besides, I had an obligation to the Other. He needed to know what Stars were visible from the Door.

But still the Darkness unnerved me. I put off entering it for a while. I sat down outside and ate and drank and wrote this entry in my Journal.

The One-Hundred-and-Ninety-Second Western Hall

ENTRY FOR THE TWENTIETH DAY OF THE SIXTH MONTH IN THE YEAR THE ALBATROSS CAME TO THE SOUTH-WESTERN HALLS

Having completed the previous entry in my Journal I entered the One-Hundred-and-Ninety-Second Western Hall. Dark and Cold enveloped me. A little way in (I estimate about twenty metres) I turned to face the Single Door that aligned perfectly with a Window in the Corridor outside. I sat down and wrapped Myself in my blanket.

At first I was acutely conscious of the Darkness at my back and the stares of the Unknown Statues. It was very quiet. The Hall where I usually sleep — the Third Northern Hall — is full of birds and at night I hear the little sounds as they shift and flutter on their perches; but as far as I could tell there were no birds in the One-Hundred-and-Ninety-Second Western Hall. They apparently found it as unsettling as I did.

I made Myself focus on the one thing familiar to me: the sound of the Sea in the Lower Halls, the Water lapping the Walls in a thousand, thousand Chambers. It is a sound that accompanies me all my days. I fall asleep to it every night, just as a child might fall asleep, safe on its mother's breast, listening to her heartbeat. And indeed, this is what must have happened now, because the next thing I knew was that I was waking suddenly out of sleep.

A Full Moon stood in the centre of the Single Doorway, flooding the Hall with Light. The Statues on the Walls were all posed as if they had just turned to face the Doorway, their marble Eyes fixed on the Moon. They were different from the Statues in other Halls; they were not isolated individuals, but the representation of a Crowd. Here were two with their Arms about each other; here one had his Hand on the Shoulder of one in front, the better to pull himself forward to see the Moon; here a Child held on to its Father's Hand. There was even a Dog that — having no interest in the Moon — stood on its Hind Legs, its Front Paws on its Master's Chest, pleading for attention. The Rear Wall was a mass of Statues — not neatly arranged in Tiers, but a jumbled, chaotic Crowd. Foremost among them was a Young Man, who stood bathed in the Moonlight, elation in his Face, a Banner in his Hand.

I almost forgot to breathe. For a moment I had an inkling of what it might be like if instead of two people in the World there were thousands.

The Eighty-Eighth Western Hall

SECOND ENTRY FOR THE TWENTIETH DAY OF THE SIXTH MONTH IN THE YEAR THE ALBATROSS CAME TO THE SOUTH-WESTERN HALLS

The Full Moon declined westwards, the Light in the Hall diminished and the Constellations grew brighter in the Window opposite the Doorway. I made notes of what Constellations and Stars I saw. At Dawn I slept for a few hours and then I began the journey home.

As I walked, I was thinking about the Great and Secret Knowledge, which the Other says will grant us strange new powers. And I realised something. I realised that I no longer believed in it. Or perhaps that is not quite accurate. I thought it was possible that the Knowledge existed. Equally I thought that it was possible it did not. Either way it no longer mattered to me. I did not intend to waste my time looking for it any more.

This realisation — the realisation of the Insignificance of the Knowledge — came to me in the form of a Revelation. What I mean by this is that I knew it to be true before I understood why or what steps had led me there. When I tried to retrace those steps my mind kept returning to the image of the One-Hundred-and-Ninety-Second Western Hall in the Moonlight, to its Beauty, to its deep sense of Calm, to the reverent looks on the Faces of the Statues as they turned (or seemed to turn) towards the Moon. I realised that the search for the Knowledge has encouraged us to think of the House as if it were a sort of riddle to be unravelled, a text to be interpreted, and that if ever we discover the Knowledge, then it will be as if the Value has been wrested from the House and all that remains will be mere scenery.

The sight of the One-Hundred-and-Ninety-Second Western Hall in the Moonlight made me see how ridiculous that is. The House is valuable because it is the House. It is enough in and of Itself. It is not the means to an end.

This thought led on to another. I realised that the Other's description of the powers that the Knowledge will grant has always made me uneasy. For example: he says that we will have the power to control lesser minds. Well, to begin with there are no lesser minds; there are only him and me and we both have keen and lively intellects. But, supposing for a moment that a lesser mind existed, why would I want to control it?

Abandoning the search for the Knowledge would free us to pursue a new sort of science. We could follow any path that the data suggested to us. The thought of all this made me excited and happy. I was eager to return to the Other and explain it to him.

I was walking through the Halls, thinking

of these things, when I heard the raucous cries of birds and I remembered that the Eighty-Eighth Western Hall was full of herring gulls. I wondered whether or not to take a different Path, but, estimating that any diversion would add seven or eight Halls (1.7 kilometres) to my journey, I decided against it.

I had got halfway across the Hall when I noticed a scattering of white shapes lying on the Pavement. I picked them up. They were pieces of torn paper with writing on them. They were crumpled and so I smoothed them out and tried putting them together. Two — no, three — of the scraps fitted perfectly, forming part of a small sheet of paper with one jagged side. It appeared to be a page torn from a notebook.

I could see that, even when reconstructed, the page would be difficult to decipher. The writing was atrocious — like a tangle of seaweed. After some minutes of peering at it I thought I could make out the word 'minotaur'. A line or two above I thought I saw the word 'slave' and a line or two below the phrase 'kill him'. The rest was completely impenetrable. But the reference to a 'minotaur' intrigued me. The First Vestibule contains eight massive Statues of Minotaurs, each one different from the others. Perhaps the person who had written this had visited my own Halls?

I wondered whose writing it could be. Not the Other's. Aside from the fact that I was sure he had never ventured as far as the Eighty-Eighth Western Hall, I knew his writing to be neat and precise. One of the Dead then. The Fish-Leather Man? The Biscuit-Box Man? The Concealed Person? Potentially this was a discovery of great historical importance.

Now that I knew what I was looking for I could see more white shapes lying on the Pavement. I set about gathering them up. Beginning in the South-Western Corner I worked my way systematically over the Pavement of the entire Hall, covering every part of it. At first the herring gulls made raucous objection to my doing this, but when they saw that I did not come near their eggs or young, they lost interest. I found forty-seven pieces of paper, but when I knelt and tried to fit them all together it became clear that many more were still missing.

I looked around. Herring gull nests were perched on the Shoulders of Statues and crammed onto Plinths; there was one tucked between the Legs of the Statue of an Elephant and another balanced in the Crown of an Elderly King. Peeking out of the nest in the Crown I could see two white fragments. Cautiously I approached and climbed up a neighbouring Statue to examine it. Immediately two gulls attacked me, screaming their indignation and dashing at me with wings and beaks. But I was equally determined. With one arm I hauled Myself up the Statue and with the other I beat back the birds.

The nest was a ramshackle, untidy thing built of dry seaweed and fishbones; woven into its structure were five or six scraps of paper with writing on them. I dismounted and retreated to the middle of the Hall away from the Walls, the nests and the attacking gulls.

I considered what I ought to do. There was no possibility of retrieving the missing pieces now. The herring gulls would never permit me to dismantle their nests — nor did I want to. No, I must wait until late summer — or, even better, early autumn — when the gulls had abandoned the nests and the young were grown. Then I could come back and get all the missing pieces.

I placed the forty-seven pieces carefully in my pack and continued my journey home.

The Other explains that he has said all this before

ENTRY FOR THE TWENTY-SECOND DAY OF THE SIXTH MONTH IN THE YEAR THE ALBATROSS CAME TO THE SOUTH-WESTERN HALLS

This morning I took my Star Maps to the Second South-Western Hall.

I found the Other leaning back against the Empty Plinth, his ankles crossed and his elbows resting on the Plinth. He looked relaxed. He wore an immaculate suit of a dark navy colour and a brilliant white shirt. He gave me a friendly smile. 'How're the shoes?' he asked.

'Excellent!' I said. 'Brilliant! Thank you! But what I value even more than the shoes themselves is the proof they give of our friendship! I consider the possession of such a friend as you to be one of the greatest happinesses of my Life!'

'I do my best,' said the Other. 'So tell me. How have you been getting on? Now that you've got the shoes.'

'I have already visited the One-Hundred-and-Ninety-Second Western Hall!'

'OK. And did you see what stars there were? Did you make notes?'

'I did make notes,' I said. 'But I have not

brought them with me since I remember everything I have to tell you.'

Then I told him what I had seen in the One-Hundred-and-Ninety-Second Western Hall. 'The Statues are its most remarkable feature. I mean other than the Single Door and the No-Windows. The Moonlight picked out one Statue in particular — the image of a Young Man. He seemed to me to represent the Virtues of —'

'Don't bother with all that. You know I'm not interested in statues. Tell me about the stars,' said the Other. 'What could you see?'

'I will show you.' I opened one of my Star Maps and placed it on the top of the Empty Plinth. He came and stood by me. 'I saw the Rose, the Good Mother and the Lamppost. Towards morning these were followed by the Shoemaker and the Iron Snake.' (These were some of the names I had given the Constellations.)

The Other examined the Map carefully. Then he picked up his shining device and made some notes.

'Are any of these stars particularly bright?' he asked.

'Yes. This Star here. It forms part of the Good Mother. It is the tip of her extended arm, so to speak. It is one of the brightest Stars in the Sky.'

'Perfect,' said the Other. 'The brightest star to symbolise the greatest knowledge. Well, while you've been doing all that I've come to a decision. I've decided that I will go to this room and perform the ritual there. Obviously it's much further into the labyrinth than I've ever been before, so there are risks . . .' He paused for a moment and looked very determined, as if steeling himself to something. '. . . but balancing the risks against the rewards — well, the rewards are potentially immense. This information you've brought me is invaluable and what I need you to do now is to go back there and establish what constellations can be seen at different times of year.'

Now was the time for me to explain my Revelation concerning the Great and Secret Knowledge.

'As to that,' I said, 'I too have something to say. Something has been revealed to me that I must now share with you, something that has far-reaching implications for all our future research. We must cease our search for the Knowledge! When we began, we believed that it was a worthy endeavour, deserving all our attention, but it turns out that it is not. We should abandon it straightaway and, in its place, establish a new programme of scientific research!'

The Other was not paying attention. He was making notes on his shining device. 'Mmm? What?' he said.

'I am speaking of our search for the Knowledge,' I said, 'and of how the House has revealed to me that we should abandon it.'

The Other stopped tapping. He took a moment to process what I had just said. Then he put the device down on the Empty Plinth, covered his face with his hands, made a sort of groaning noise and massaged his eyes. 'Oh, God! Not this again,' he said.

He uncovered his eyes. He turned away and stared off into the distance. 'Don't say anything,' he said (though I had not uttered another word). 'I need to think.'

There was a long silence at the end of which he seemed to come to a decision. 'Sit down,' he said.

We sat down together on the Pavement of the Hall. I sat cross-legged and he sat with his knees bent, his back against the Empty Plinth.

There was a sort of glowering darkness in his face. He seemed to be finding it difficult to look at me. By these signs I knew that he was angry but struggling not to show it.

He coughed. 'OK,' he said in a controlled

voice. 'There are three reasons — three — why you shouldn't stop looking for the knowledge. I'm going to go through all of them now and at the end, I think you'll see I'm right. I just need you to listen to me. You can do that, can't you?'

'Of course,' I said. 'Tell me the three reasons.'

'OK, the first reason is this. It may seem to you that what I'm doing is rather selfish — trying to get the knowledge for myself. But the reality is quite different. This search that you and I are embarked on, it's a truly great project. Momentous. One of the most important in humanity's history. The knowledge we seek isn't something new. It's old. Really old. Once upon a time people possessed it and they used it to do great things, miraculous things. They should have held on to it. They should have respected it. But they didn't. They abandoned it for the sake of something they called progress. And it's up to us to get it back. We're not doing this for ourselves; we're doing it for humanity. To get back something humanity has foolishly lost.'

'I see,' I said. (This did indeed put things in a slightly different light.)

'And personally,' continued the Other, 'I think that this search is so important, so absolutely vital that I have to keep going. No matter what. I don't have any choice. If your decision is to stop looking — well, in that case I suppose we'd no longer be colleagues. Our meetings on Tuesdays and Fridays — we'd no longer have them. Because what would be the point? I'd be pursuing my researches and you'd be off' — he gestured vaguely — 'doing whatever it is that you do. This isn't what I want of course, let me be very clear about that, but it is the way things would have to be. So that's the second reason.'

'Oh!' I said. It had never occurred to me that he and I would cease to be colleagues. 'But working with you is one of the great pleasures of my life!'

'I know,' said the Other. 'And of course, I feel the same way.' He paused. 'Now I need to tell you the third reason. But before I do that, I need you to hear something else.' He gazed intently and searchingly into my face. 'This is the most vital thing I have to say. Piranesi, this isn't the first time you've told me that you want to stop the search for the knowledge. This isn't the first time I've explained why that's not the right course of action. Everything we've just said? *We've said it all before.*'

'I . . . What?' I said. I blinked at him in

97

astonishment. 'What? . . . No. No. That is not correct.'

'Yes, I'm afraid it is. You see, the labyrinth plays tricks on the mind. It makes people forget things. If you're not careful it can unpick your entire personality.'

I sat dumbfounded. 'How many times have we said it?' I said at last.

He thought for a moment. 'This is the third time. There's a pattern. The idea of stopping the search for the knowledge seems to occur to you roughly once every eighteen months.' He glanced at my face. 'I know. I know,' he said, sympathetically. 'It's hard to take in.'

'But I do not understand,' I protested. 'I have an excellent memory. I remember every Hall I have ever visited. There are seven thousand, six hundred and seventy-eight of them.'

'You never forget anything about the labyrinth. That is why your contribution to my work is so valuable. But you do forget other things. And, of course, you lose time.'

'What?' I said, startled.

'Time. You're always losing it.'

'What do you mean?'

'You know. You get days and dates wrong.'

'I do not,' I said, indignant.

'Yes, you do. It's a bit of a pain, to be honest. My schedule's always so packed. I come to meet you and you're nowhere to be seen because you've lost a day again. I've had to put you right numerous times when your perception of time has got out of sync.'

'Out of sync with what?'

'With me. With everyone else.'

I was astonished. I did not believe him. But neither did I disbelieve him. I did not know what to think. But in all my uncertainty one thing was clear, one thing remained that I could absolutely rely on: the Other was honest, noble and industrious. He would not lie. 'But why do *you* not forget?' I asked.

The Other hesitated for a moment. 'I take precautions,' he said carefully.

'Could I not take them too?'

'No. No. That wouldn't work. Sorry. I can't go into the whys and wherefores. It's complicated. I'll explain it to you one day.'

This was not very satisfactory but just then I did not have the energy or mental capacity to pursue it. I was too busy thinking about what I might have forgotten.

'From my point of view this is very worrying,' I said. 'Suppose I forget something important, like the Times and Patterns of the Tides? I might drown.'

'No, no, no,' said the Other, soothingly.

'There's no need to worry about that. You never forget anything like that. I wouldn't let you go wandering about if I thought you were in the slightest danger. We've known each other for years now and in that time your knowledge of the labyrinth has grown exponentially. It's extraordinary, really. And as for the rest, anything important you forget, I can remind you. But the fact that you forget while I remember — that's why it's so vital that I set our objectives. Me. Not you. That's the third reason we should stick to our search for the knowledge. Do you see?'

'Yes. Yes. At least . . .' I was silent a moment. 'I need time to think,' I said.

'Of course. Of course,' said the Other. He patted me consolingly on the shoulder. 'We'll discuss it again on Tuesday.'

He rose to his feet and went over to the Empty Plinth and examined the little shining device lying there. 'In any case,' he said, 'I need to get going. I've been here almost fifty-five minutes.' Without another word he turned and set off in the direction of the First Vestibule.

The World does not bear out the Other's claim that there are gaps in my memory

ENTRY FOR THE TWENTY-THIRD DAY OF THE SIXTH MONTH IN THE YEAR THE ALBATROSS CAME TO THE SOUTH-WESTERN HALLS

The World (so far as I can tell) does not bear out the Other's claim that there are gaps in my memory.

While he was explaining it to me — and for some time afterwards — I did not know what to think. At several points I experienced a feeling akin to panic. Could it really be the case that I had forgotten whole conversations?

But as the day went on, I could find no evidence of memory loss to support the Other's claim. I busied Myself with my ordinary, everyday tasks. I mended one of my fishing nets and worked on my Catalogue of Statues. In the early evening I went to the Eighth Vestibule to fish in the Waters of the Lower Staircase. The Beams of the Declining Sun shone through the Windows of the Lower Halls, striking the Surface of the Waves and making ripples of golden Light flow across the Ceiling of the Staircase and over the Faces of the Statues. When night fell, I listened to the Songs that the Moon and Stars were singing and I sang with them.

The World feels Complete and Whole, and I, its Child, fit into it seamlessly. Nowhere is there any disjuncture where I ought to remember something but do not, where I ought to understand something but do not. The only part of my existence in which I experience any sense of fragmentation is in that last strange conversation with the Other. And so I have to ask Myself: whose memory is at fault? Mine or his? Might he in fact be remembering conversations that never happened?

Two memories. Two bright minds which remember past events differently. It is an awkward situation. There exists no third person to say which of us is correct. (If only the Sixteenth Person were here!)

As for the Other's claim that I lose time and muddle days, I do not see how this can possibly be true. I invented the calendar I use, so how could it get 'out of sync' as he put it? There is nothing for it to get out of sync with.

I wonder now if this is why he asked me that strange question three and a half weeks ago? I mean the question with a strange word in it. Turning back the pages of my Journal I see that the strange word was 'Batter-Sea'.

And then, in an instant, the solution presents itself! All I have to do is read through my Journals and discover if there are any discrepancies, any events recorded there that I no longer recall. Yes! This will certainly decide the matter. In fact, the only drawback with this idea is that it will take a substantial amount of time — my writings being lengthy — which I cannot just now spare from other projects.

I am resolved to read through my Journals at some point in the coming months and in the meantime shall proceed on the assumption that it is the Other's memory, and not mine, which is incorrect.

I write a letter

ENTRY FOR THE TWENTY-FOURTH DAY OF THE SIXTH MONTH IN THE YEAR THE ALBATROSS CAME TO THE SOUTH-WESTERN HALLS

The following is a transcript of the letter that I inscribed in chalk on the Pavement of the Second South-Western Hall.

DEAR OTHER
ALTHOUGH I CANNOT ANY LONGER REGARD THE SEARCH FOR THE GREAT AND SECRET

KNOWLEDGE AS A LEGITIMATE
SCIENTIFIC ENDEAVOUR, I HAVE
DETERMINED THAT THE COR-
RECT COURSE OF ACTION IS TO
CONTINUE TO HELP YOU AND
GATHER ANY DATA YOU RE-
QUIRE. IT IS NOT RIGHT THAT
YOUR   SCIENTIFIC   WORK
SHOULD SUFFER SIMPLY BE-
CAUSE I HAVE LOST CONFI-
DENCE IN THE HYPOTHESIS. I
HOPE THAT THIS IS ACCEPTABLE
TO YOU.

YOUR FRIEND

The Other warns me about 16

ENTRY FOR THE TWENTY-SIXTH DAY OF THE
SIXTH MONTH IN THE YEAR THE ALBATROSS
CAME TO THE SOUTH-WESTERN HALLS

This morning I went to the Second South-
Western Hall to meet the Other. I confess
that I was a little anxious about how the
meeting would go. Sometimes when I am
anxious, I talk a lot, and so I immediately
launched on a long speech, elaborating
quite unnecessarily on the letter I had
chalked on the Pavement.

It did not matter. Halfway through I realised that the Other was not listening. His

head was bent in thought and he was absent-mindedly turning over some small metallic objects in the pocket of his jacket. Today he wore a suit of a dark charcoal colour and a black shirt.

'You haven't seen anyone else in the labyrinth, have you?' he said suddenly.

'Someone else?' I said.

'Yes.'

'Someone new?' I said.

'Yes,' he said.

'No,' I said.

He studied my face intently as though for some reason he doubted the truth of what I had just said. Then he relaxed and said, 'No. No. How could you? There's only us.'

'Yes,' I agreed. 'There is only us.'

A short silence.

'Unless,' I added, 'there are other people in other Parts of the House. In Far Distant Places that you and I have not seen. I have often wondered about that. As a hypothesis it is impossible to prove one way or the other — unless one day I come across signs of human activity, signs that cannot reasonably be attributed to our own Dead.'

'Mmmmm,' he said. He was deep in thought again.

Another silence.

It occurred to me that I might already

have come across such signs. The fragments of paper with writing on them that I had found in the Eighty-Eighth Western Hall! They might belong to our own Dead or they might belong to Someone as yet unknown to us. I was about to tell the Other all about it when he began speaking again.

'Listen,' he said. 'I want you to promise me something.'

'Of course,' I said.

'If you ever see someone in the labyrinth — someone you don't know — I want you to promise me that you won't try to speak to them. Instead you must hide. Keep out of their way. Don't let them see you.'

'Oh, but think what an opportunity will be lost if I do that!' I said. 'The Sixteenth Person will almost certainly possess knowledge that we do not. He will be able to tell us about the Distant Regions of the World.'

The Other looked blank. 'What? What are you talking about? The sixteenth person?'

I explained about the Thirteen Dead and the Two Living, and how someone new would be the Sixteenth Person. (I have explained this many times. The Other can never seem to keep this important information in his head.)

'I agree that "the Sixteenth Person" is rather a cumbersome designation,' I said.

'We could, if you prefer, call him "16" for short. My point is that 16 has information about the World that we do not and therefore . . .'

'No-no-no-no-no,' said the Other. 'You don't understand. It's really important that we keep as far away from this person as we can.' He paused and then said, 'You see, Piranesi, I've met this person. This person you call "16".'

'What? No!' I exclaimed. 'Then there really is a Sixteenth Person in the World? Why did you never tell me this before? This is wonderful! This is a cause for celebration!'

'No.' He shook his head dolefully. 'No, Piranesi. I know that this means a great deal to you and I'm sorry to have to break it to you. But this is not a cause for celebration. It's entirely the reverse. This person — 16 — means me harm. 16 is my enemy. And so, by extension, yours too.'

'Oh!' I said and fell silent.

What terrible news. Of course I understand the concept of enmity: there are many Statues in which one Figure struggles with Another. But I had never experienced it at first hand before. A random thought came to me — the phrase *kill him* on one of the scraps of paper from the Eighty-Eighth Western Hall. The person who had written that had had an enemy.

'Is there any possibility that you are mistaken?' I said. 'Perhaps it is all a misunderstanding. When 16 arrives, I can talk to him and explain that you are a Good Person with many Admirable Qualities. I can demonstrate to him that the attitude of hostility he holds towards you has no reasonable foundation.'

The Other smiled. 'How like you, Piranesi, to try and find the good in the situation. Unfortunately in this case it can't be done. This is why I didn't want to tell you about 16. You imagine that 16 can be reasoned with. But unfortunately, that's not the case. 16 is opposed to everything we are, everything you and I think is valuable and precious. And that includes reason. Reason is one of the things that 16 wants to tear down.'

'How dreadful!' I said.

'Yes.'

We lapsed into silence again. There seemed nothing more to say. I was shocked by his description of 16's wickedness. To be opposed to Reason itself!

After a moment the Other continued. 'But I'm probably stressing us both out for no reason. There's really only a very small likelihood of 16 coming here.'

'Why is the likelihood small?' I asked.

'16 doesn't know the way,' said the Other. He smiled at me. 'Try not to let it worry you.'

'I will try,' I said. A new thought struck me. 'When did you meet 16?'

'Mmm? Oh, the day before yesterday.'

'You have visited the Far-off Places where 16 lives? You never said so before. Tell me about them!'

'What do you mean?'

'You said you met 16. But you also said 16 does not know the way here. Meaning that you must have met him in his own Halls or, at any rate, in some Remote Region. This surprises me because I do not believe that you have undertaken any long journeys since I have known you.'

I smiled at the Other, awaiting his answer, which I fully expected would be very interesting.

He looked blank. Blank and slightly horrified.

A long silence.

'Actually . . .' he began, then seemed to change his mind about what he was going to say. 'Actually, it's not important where we met. And I don't have time to go into all that now. I'm needed . . . I mean I can't stay today. I just wanted to warn you. You know, about 16.' Then he nodded briskly at me, picked up his shining devices and walked away towards the First Vestibule.

'Goodbye!' I called to his retreating back. 'Goodbye!'

I update my information about 16

ENTRY FOR THE TWENTY-SEVENTH DAY OF THE SIXTH MONTH IN THE YEAR THE ALBA-TROSS CAME TO THE SOUTH-WESTERN HALLS

I am very interested in the fact that the Other has met 16 and it is a great pity that he is so disinclined to say anything about it. I would like to know much more about the circumstances and location. But I suppose that the Other does not wish to dwell on a meeting with a wicked person.

The entry which I made in my Journal six weeks ago (See *A list of all the people who have ever lived and what is known of them*) is now outdated, so this morning I appended a note there directing the reader to this page.

The Sixteenth Person

The Sixteenth Person resides in a Far-off Region of the House, possibly in the North or South. I have never seen him, but the

Other reports that he is a malevolent person, hostile to Reason, Science and Happiness. The Other believes that 16 may attempt to come here in order to disrupt our Peaceful Existence and he has warned me that if I should ever see 16 in these Halls, I should hide Myself.

The First Vestibule

ENTRY FOR THE FIRST DAY OF THE SEVENTH MONTH IN THE YEAR THE ALBATROSS CAME TO THE SOUTH-WESTERN HALLS

Today I decided to visit the First Vestibule. It is, oddly enough, a place I hardly ever go. I say 'oddly' because when I set up my System of Numbering the Halls several years ago I chose this Vestibule as the starting point, the place from which everything else is reckoned. Knowing Myself as I do, I do not think I would have chosen it had I not felt some sort of strong connection with it; yet I no longer remember what that connection was. (Is the Other right? Am I forgetting things? It is an unpleasant thought and I push it away.)

The First Vestibule is an impressive place, larger than the majority of Vestibules and more gloomy. It is dominated by eight massive Statues of Minotaurs, each one approximately nine metres high. They loom over the Pavement, darkening the Vestibule with their Bulk, their Massive Horns jutting into the Empty Air, their Animal Expressions solemn, inscrutable.

The temperature of the First Vestibule is different from that of the surrounding Halls. It is several degrees colder and there is a draught that blows from somewhere, bringing with it a smell of rain, metal and petrol. I have noticed this many times before, but somehow I always seem to forget about it immediately afterwards. Today I concentrated my attention on the scent. It was neither pleasant nor unpleasant, but extremely interesting. I followed its path. I passed along the Southern Wall of the Vestibule until I came to the two Minotaurs that flank the South-Eastern Corner. Here I noticed something. The Shadows between the two Statues were producing a sort of optical illusion. I could almost imagine that they extended backwards a long way and that I was in fact gazing into a corridor leading to a distant point where there was a patch of misty light. This patch of light contained other lights that seemed to flicker and move. It was from there that both the draught and the scent seemed to emanate. I could hear faint sounds — a sort of vibration and a dashing noise, like the Waves but less regular.

Suddenly I heard footsteps, followed by a voice, loud and indignant: '. . . not what I was hired to do and I said to him, "You have to be joking. You have to be fucking joking, mate." '

Another, glummer voice said: 'People have no shame. I mean what goes through their heads when . . .' The footsteps died away.

I leapt back from the South-Eastern Corner as if I had been stung.

What had just happened? Cautiously, I approached the Statues again and peered between them. The Shadows now looked unremarkable. I could sort of see how they might suggest the shape of a corridor, but that was all. The cold draught played around my ankles and I could still smell rain, metal and petrol, but the lights and the noises had vanished.

As I stood thinking of these things, four old crisp packets blew along the Pavement, one after the other. I made a sound of exasperation; this was a problem I thought I had dealt with. At one time I was forever finding crisp packets scattered about the First Vestibule. I also found old fish finger packets and sausage-roll wrappings. I gathered them up and burnt them so that they did not mar the Beauty of the House. (I do not know who it was that ate all the crisps and the fish fingers and the sausage rolls, but I cannot help wishing that he or she had been more tidy!) I also found a sleeping bag under the marble Sweep of the Staircase. It was very dirty and evil-smelling, but I washed it thoroughly and it has served me well.

I ran after the four crisp packets and picked them up. The fourth crisp packet was not a crisp packet at all. It was a crumpled-up piece of paper. I smoothed it out. On it was written the following:

All I am asking you to do is to give me directions to the statue you were telling me about — the one of an elderly fox teaching some young squirrels and other creatures. I would like to see it for myself. This task is not difficult and should be well within your capabilities. Write the directions in the space below. I have left a biro next to your lunch.

Eat it while it is hot — the lunch, not the biro.

Laurence

P.S. Please try to remember to take your multivitamin.

Underneath the message there was a large blank space for the recipient to write in but as it was still blank, I deduced that he or she had not given the writer the information they requested.

I would have liked to have kept the paper. It was evidence of two of the People who have lived: firstly, a person called Laurence and secondly, a person to whom Laurence had written and whose lunch and multivitamin he had provided. But who were they? I considered and immediately discounted the possibility that either of them was 16. The Other had said that 16 did not know the way here and clearly both Laurence and his friend had been familiar with these Halls at one time. They might well belong to my own Dead. But there was another possibility: that they were inhabitants of the Far-Distant Halls. If Laurence was still alive and waiting for the information about the Statue, then it would be wrong to take the paper.

I got out my own pen and wrote the following in the empty space.

Dear Laurence

The Statue of the Dog-Fox teaching two Squirrels and two Satyrs is in the Fourth Western Hall. From this Place go through the Western Door. In the next Hall go through the Third Door on the right. You will be in the First North-Western Hall. Follow the Southern (left-hand) Wall and again take the Third Door you come to. You will find yourself in a Corridor at the end of which is the Fourth Western Hall. The Statue is in the North-Western Corner. It is one of my favourites too!

1. If you are alive then my hope is that you will find this letter and that the information I have given will be useful to you. Perhaps one day we will meet. You may find me in any of the Halls North, West and South of here. The Halls to the East are derelict.

2. If you are one of my own Dead (and if your Spirit passes through this Vestibule and reads this paper) then I hope you already know that I visit your Niche or Plinth regularly to talk with you and bring you offerings of food and drink.

3. If you are dead — but not one of my own Dead — then please know that I travel far and wide in the World. If ever I find your remains I will bring you offerings of food and drink. If it seems to me that no one living is caring for you then I will gather up your bones and bring them to my own Halls. I will put you in good order and lay you with my own Dead. Then you will not be alone.

May the House in its Beauty shelter us both.

Your Friend

I placed the paper at the foot of one of the Minotaurs — the one nearest to the South-Eastern Corner of the Vestibule — and I weighted it down with a small pebble.

■ ■ ■ ■

PART 3
THE PROPHET

■ ■ ■ ■

The Prophet

From the Windows of the First North-Eastern Hall great shafts of Light descended. Within one of the shafts a man was standing with his back to me. He was perfectly still. He was gazing up at the Wall of Statues.

It was not the Other. He was thinner, and not quite so tall.

16!

I had come on him so suddenly. I had entered by one of the Western Doors and there he was.

He turned to look at me. He did not move. He said nothing.

I did not run away. Instead I approached

121

him. (Perhaps I was wrong to do this, but it was already too late to hide, too late to keep my promise to the Other.)

I walked slowly round him, taking him in. He was an old man. His skin was dry and papery, and the veins were thick and clotted in his hands. His eyes were large, dark and liquid, with magnificently hooded eyelids and arched eyebrows. His mouth was long and mobile, red and oddly wet. He wore a suit in a Prince of Wales check. He must have been thin for a long time because, although it was an old suit, it fitted him perfectly — which is to say that it was wrinkled and saggy because the fabric was old and worn, not because the cut was wrong.

I felt oddly disappointed; I had imagined that 16 would be young like me.

'Hello,' I said. I was curious to hear what his voice sounded like.

'Good afternoon,' he said. 'If, in fact, it is afternoon where we are. I never know.' He had a haughty, drawling, old-fashioned way of speaking.

'You are 16,' I said. 'You are the Sixteenth Person.'

'I don't follow you, young man,' he said.

'There exist in the World two Living, thirteen Dead and now you,' I explained.

'Thirteen dead? How fascinating! No one ever told me there were human remains here. Who are they, I wonder?'

I described the Biscuit-Box Man, the Fish-Leather Man, the Concealed Person, the People of the Alcove and the Folded-Up Child.

'You know, it's the most extraordinary thing,' he said. 'But I remember that biscuit box. It used to stand on a little table next to the mugs in the corner of my study at the university. I wonder how it got here? Well, I can tell you this. One of your thirteen dead is almost certainly that dishy young Italian that Stan Ovenden was so keen on. What was his name?' He looked away, thought for a moment, shrugged. 'No, it's gone. And I imagine that another is Ovenden himself. He kept coming here to see the Italian. I told him he was asking for trouble, but he wouldn't listen. You know, guilt and so forth. And I wouldn't be surprised if one of the others is Sylvia D'Agostino. I never heard anything of her after the early nineties. As to who I am, young man, I can see how you might conclude that I am "16". But I am not. Charming as it is here . . .' He glanced round. '. . . I do not intend to stay. I am only passing through. Someone told me you were here. No.' He checked himself. 'That is not quite right. Someone told me what they thought had happened to you and *I* concluded you were here. This person showed me a photograph of you and since you were clearly a bit of a dish, I thought I would come and take a look at you. I'm glad I did. You must have been well worth looking at before, you know . . . before everything happened. Ah, well! Old age happened to me. And this happened to you. And now look at us! But to return to the matter in hand. You mentioned two people living. I suppose the other one is Ketterley?'

'Ketterley?'

'Val Ketterley. Taller than you. Dark hair and eyes. Beard. Dark complexion. His mother was Spanish, you see.'

'You mean the Other?' I said.

'The other what?'

'The Other. The Not-Me.'

'Ha! Yes! I see what you mean. What an excellent name for him! The other. No matter what the situation he is only ever "the other". Someone else always takes precedence. He is always second fiddle. And he knows it. It eats him up. He was one of my students, you know. Oh, yes. Complete charlatan, of course. For all the grand intellectual manner and the dark, penetrating stare, he hasn't an original thought in his head. All his ideas are second-hand.' He paused a moment and then added, 'Actually all his ideas are mine. I was the greatest scholar of my generation. Perhaps of any generation. I theorised that this . . .' He opened his hands in a gesture intended to indicate the Hall, the House, Everything. '. . . existed. And it does. I theorised that there was a way to get here. And there is. And I came here and I sent others here. I kept everything secret. And I swore the others to secrecy too. I've never been very interested in what you might call morality, but I drew the line at bringing about the collapse of civilisation. Perhaps that was wrong. I don't know. I do have a rather sentimental streak.'

He fixed one bright, hooded, malevolent eye on me.

'We all paid a terrible price in the end. Mine was prison. Oh, yes. That shocks you, I imagine. I wish I could say that it was all due to a misunderstanding, but I did all the things they said I did. To be perfectly honest I did quite a lot more that they never knew about. Although — do you know? — I rather liked prison. One met such fascinating people.' He paused for a moment. 'Did Ketterley tell you how this world was made?'

he asked.

'No, sir.'

'Would you like to know?'

'Very much, sir,' I said.

He looked gratified by my interest. 'Then I will tell you. It began when I was young, you see. I was always so much more brilliant than my peers. My first great insight happened when I realised how much humankind had lost. Once, men and women were able to turn themselves into eagles and fly immense distances. They communed with rivers and mountains and received wisdom from them. They felt the turning of the stars inside their own minds. My contemporaries did not understand this. They were all enamoured with the idea of progress and believed that whatever was new must be superior to what was old. As if merit was a function of chronology! But it seemed to me that the wisdom of the ancients could not have simply vanished. Nothing simply vanishes. It's not actually possible. I pictured it as a sort of energy flowing out of the world and I thought that this energy must be going somewhere. That was when I realised that there must be other places, other worlds. And so I set myself to find them.'

'And did you find any, sir?' I asked.

'I did. I found this one. This is what I call a Distributary World — it was created by ideas flowing out of another world. This world could not have existed unless that other world had existed first. Whether this world is still dependent on the continued existence of the first one, I don't know. It's all in the book I wrote. I don't suppose you happen to have read it?'

'No, sir.'

'Pity. It's terribly good. You'd like it.'

All the time that the old man was speaking, I was listening with great attention and trying to understand who he was. He had said that he was not 16, but I was not so naive as to believe him without further evidence. The Other had said that 16 was wicked, so it was possible that 16 would lie about who he was. But as the old man talked, I became more and more certain that he was telling the truth. He was not 16. My reasoning was this: the Other had described 16 as being opposed to Reason and to Scientific Discovery. This description did not fit the old man. The old man was as passionately fond of science as we were. He knew how the World was made and was eager to pass that knowledge on to me.

'Tell me,' he said, 'does Ketterley still

think that the wisdom of the ancients is here?'

'Do you mean the Great and Secret Knowledge, sir?'

'Exactly that.'

'Yes.'

'And is he still searching for it?'

'Yes.'

'How amusing,' he said. 'He'll never find it. It's not here. It doesn't exist.'

'I was beginning to wonder if that might be the case,' I said.

'Then you are a good deal brighter than him. The idea that it's hidden here — I'm afraid he got that from me too. Before I had seen this world, I thought that the knowledge that created it would somehow still be here, lying about, ready to be picked up and claimed. Of course, as soon as I got here, I realised how ridiculous that was. Imagine water flowing underground. It flows through the same cracks year after year and it wears away at the stone. Millennia later you have a cave system. But what you don't have is the water that originally created it. That's long gone. Seeped away into the earth. Same thing here. But Ketterley is an egotist. He always thinks in terms of utility. He cannot imagine why anything should exist if he cannot make use of it.'

'Is that why there are Statues?' I asked.

'Is what why there are Statues?'

'Do the Statues exist because they embody the Ideas and Knowledge that flowed out of the other World into this one?'

'Oh! I never thought of that!' he said, pleased. 'What an intelligent observation. Yes, yes! I think that highly likely! Perhaps in some remote area of the labyrinth, statues of obsolete computers are coming into being as we speak!' He paused. 'I must not stay long. I am all too well aware of the consequences of lingering in this place: amnesia, total mental collapse, etcetera, etcetera. Though I must say that *you* are surprisingly coherent. Poor James Ritter could barely string a sentence together by the end and he wasn't here half as long as you. No, what I really came here to tell you is this.' He wrapped his cold, bony, papery hand round my hand; then he jerked me sharply towards him. He smelt of paper and ink, of a finely balanced perfume of violet and aniseed, and, beneath these scents, a faint but unmistakeable trace of something unclean, almost faecal. 'Someone is looking for you,' he said.

'16?' I asked.

'Remind me what you mean by that.'

'The Sixteenth Person.'

He put his head on one side to consider. 'Yeh-e-es . . . Yes. Why not? Let us say that it is, in fact, "16".'

'But I thought that 16 was looking for the Other,' I said. '16 is the Other's enemy. That was what the Other said.'

'The other . . . ? Ah, yes, Ketterley! No, no! 16 is not looking for Ketterley. You see what I mean about him being an egotist? Thinks everything's about him. No, it's you 16 is looking for. 16 has asked me how to find you. Now while I have no particular wish to oblige 16 — I have no particular wish to oblige anybody — I'm all in favour of doing Ketterley an ill turn. I hate him. He's spent the last twenty-five years slandering me to anyone who would listen. So I shall give 16 copious directions to get here. Minute instructions.'

'Sir, please do not do that,' I said. 'The Other says that 16 is a malevolent person.'

'Malevolent? I wouldn't say so. No more than most people. No, I'm sorry, but I simply must tell 16 the way. I want to put the cat among the pigeons and there's no better way to do it than to send 16 here. Of course, there's always the possibility — a very strong possibility really — that 16 will never get here. Very few people can come here unless someone shows them the way.

In fact, the only person I ever knew who managed it — apart from myself — was Sylvia D'Agostino. She seemed to have a talent for slipping in between, if you follow me. Ketterley was absolutely dreadful at it, even after I had shown him numerous times. He could never get here without equipment — candles and uprights to represent a door and a ritual and all sorts of nonsense. Well, you saw all that when he brought you here, I suppose. Sylvia on the other hand could just slip away at any moment. Now you see her. Now you don't. Some animals have the facility. Cats. Birds. And I had a capuchin monkey in the early eighties who could find the way any time. I shall tell 16 the way and after that it all depends on how talented 16 is. What you need to remember is that Ketterley is afraid of 16. The closer 16 gets, the more dangerous Ketterley will become. In fact I shouldn't be at all surprised if he doesn't resort to violence of some kind. You might like to head off the danger by killing him or something.' (He pronounced 'off' as 'orrf'.) He smiled at me. 'I'm going now,' he said. 'We shan't meet again.'

'Then, sir, may your Paths be safe,' I said, 'your Floors unbroken and may the House fill your eyes with Beauty.'

He was silent for a moment. He seemed

to contemplate my face and as he did so, a last thought occurred to him. 'You know I don't regret refusing to see you when you asked me before. That letter you wrote to me. I thought you sounded an arrogant little shit. You probably were then. But now . . . Charming. Quite charming.'

He picked up a raincoat that was lying in a heap on the Pavement. Then he walked in an unhurried manner to the Doorway leading to the Second Eastern Hall.

I consider the words of the Prophet

ENTRY FOR THE TWENTY-FIRST DAY OF THE SEVENTH MONTH IN THE YEAR THE ALBA-TROSS CAME TO THE SOUTH-WESTERN HALLS

Naturally I was very excited about this unexpected meeting. I went immediately and fetched this Journal and wrote it all down. I titled the entry *The Prophet,* because that is what he must have been. He explained the Creation of the World and told me other things that only a Prophet could have known.

I took time to study his words carefully. There was a great deal I did not understand though this, I expect, is usual with prophets, their minds being very great and their thoughts following strange paths.

I do not intend to stay. I am only passing through.

From this I understood that he inhabited Far Distant Halls and intended to return there immediately.

I can see how you might conclude that I am '16'. But I am not.

I had already determined this statement to be true. Perhaps (I hypothesised freely) the Prophet believed that the fifteen people who inhabited my Halls should be counted as one set of People, while in the Far Distant Halls there lived another set and he ought to be counted as one of them. Perhaps among his own People he was the Third Person or the Tenth. Perhaps he was even some dizzyingly high number like the Seventy-Fifth Person!

But I digress into what is surely fantasy.

I came here and I sent others here.

Could the Prophet have sent some of my own Dead to these Halls? The Fish-Leather Man or the Folded-Up Child? This was pure speculation. Like so many of the Prophet's statements, it remained, for the time being, impenetrable.

We all paid a terrible price in the end. Mine was prison.

I could make nothing of this.

. . . that dishy young Italian . . . Stan Oven-
den . . . Sylvia D'Agostino . . . poor James
Ritter . . .

The Prophet mentioned four names. Or, to be more accurate, three names and a designation ('that dishy young Italian'). This was a great addition to my knowledge of the World. If the Prophet had said no more than this, then his words would still have been priceless. The Prophet indicated that three of the names belonged to the Dead (Stan Ovenden, Sylvia D'Agostino and 'that dishy young Italian'). The status of 'poor James Ritter' was unclear to me. Did the Prophet mean that he was to be counted among the Dead too? Or was he one of the Prophet's own people in the Far Distant Halls? I could not tell. So many questions!

So many things I wished that I had asked him. But I did not reproach Myself. His appearance had been so sudden. I had been completely unprepared for it. Only now, in solitude and peace, could I process the information he had given me.

. . . does Ketterley still think that the wisdom of the ancients is here? . . . He'll never find it. It's not here. It doesn't exist.

I was delighted to have this confirmation that I was right. Perhaps it was a little conceited of me, but I could not help it.

The consequences for my future work and collaboration with the Other I have yet to decide.

It was clear from many things the Prophet said that he and the Other had known each other at one time. The Prophet called the Other 'Ketterley' and said he was his student. Yet the Other has never spoken of the Prophet. I have talked to him on several occasions about the fifteen people the World contains, but he has never said to me, 'Fifteen is an incorrect number! I know of one more!' Which is strange (especially when you consider how much he likes to contradict me whenever an opportunity arises). But the Other has never been interested in finding out the number of people who have lived. It is one of the areas where our scientific interests diverge.

The closer 16 gets, the more dangerous Ketterley will become.

I have never known the Other show the least predisposition to violence.

You might like to head off the danger by killing him or something.

The Prophet, on the other hand, was clearly a violent person.

You know I don't regret refusing to see you when you asked me before. That letter you wrote to me. I thought you sounded an ar-

rogant little shit. You probably were then.

This was the most baffling of all the Prophet's utterances. I never wrote him a letter. How could I when I only discovered yesterday that he existed? Perhaps one of the Dead wrote him a letter — Stan Ovenden or poor James Ritter — and the Prophet is confusing me with that person. Or perhaps prophets perceive Time differently from other people. Perhaps I will write him a letter in the future.

The Other describes the circumstances under which it will be right to kill me

ENTRY FOR THE TWENTY-FOURTH DAY OF THE SEVENTH MONTH IN THE YEAR THE ALBATROSS CAME TO THE SOUTH-WESTERN HALLS

Naturally I was anxious to tell the Other all about my meeting with the Prophet. It was vital that he know as soon as possible of the Prophet's intention to tell 16 the way to our Halls. Between Friday (the day I met the Prophet) and today (the day I was due to meet the Other) I looked everywhere for the Other, but I did not find him.

This morning I entered the Second South-Western Hall. The Other was already there and I saw immediately that he was in a state of some agitation. His hands were thrust into his pockets, he was pacing up and down and his face was dark with suppressed anger.

'I have something important to tell you,' I said.

He made a motion with his hand to brush away my utterance. 'It'll have to wait,' he said. 'I need to talk to you. There's something I haven't told you about 22.'

'Who?' I said.

'My enemy,' said the Other. 'The one who is coming here.'

'You mean 16?'

A pause.

'Oh, yes. Right. 16. I can't keep them straight, the bizarre names you give things. Well, there's something I haven't told you about 16. It's you that 16 is really interested in.'

'Yes!' I exclaimed. 'Strangely enough I already know. You see . . .'

But the Other interrupted me. 'If 16 comes here,' he said, 'and I'm beginning to think now that it's a real possibility — then it'll be you that 16 will be looking for.'

'Yes, I know. But . . .'

The Other shook his head. 'Piranesi! Listen to me! 16 will want to say things to you — things that you will not understand, but if you allow this to happen, if you allow

16 to speak to you, then those words will have a terrible effect. If you listen to what 16 says then the consequences will be awful. Madness. Terror. I've seen it happen before. 16 can unravel your thoughts just by speaking to you. 16 can make you doubt everything you see. 16 can make you doubt *me*.'

I was appalled. This was a level of wickedness that I had never imagined. It was frightening. 'How can I protect Myself?' I asked.

'By doing what I've already told you. By hiding. By not letting 16 see you. Above all by not listening to 16's words. I can't stress enough how absolutely vital that is. You have to understand that you're particularly vulnerable to this . . . this power that 16 has, because you're already mentally unstable.'

'Mentally unstable?' I said. 'What do you mean?'

A flicker of annoyance crossed the Other's face. 'I told you,' he said. 'You forget things. You repeat yourself. We spoke about it a week ago. Don't tell me that you've forgotten already.'

'No, no,' I said. 'I have not forgotten.' I wondered whether to tell him my theory that it was he, not me, whose memory was at fault, but, what with one thing and another, now did not seem the time.

'Well, then,' said the Other. He sighed. 'There's more. There's something else I need to say and I want you to understand that this is as painful for me as it is for you. If I find that you've listened to 16 and that 16 has infected you with this madness, then that puts me at risk. You see that, don't you? There's a danger you might attack me. In fact it's very likely that you would. 16 will almost certainly try to manipulate you into hurting me.'

'Hurting you?'

'Yes.'

'How terrible.'

'Quite. And then there's the whole question of your dignity as a human being. You would be in this degraded, mad condition. It would be very humiliating for you. I can't imagine that you would want to go on like that, would you?'

'No,' I said. 'No, I do not think that I would.'

'Well,' he said and took a deep breath. 'In those circumstances, if I find you are mad, then I think it's best if I kill you. For both our sakes.'

'Oh!' I said. This was rather unexpected.

There was a short silence.

'But perhaps, given time and help, I might recover?' I suggested.

'It's unlikely,' said the Other. 'And in any case I really couldn't take the chance.'

'Oh,' I said.

There was a longer silence.

'How will you kill me?' I asked.

'You don't want to know that,' he said.

'No. I suppose not.'

'Don't think like that, Piranesi. Do what I've told you. Avoid 16 at all costs, then we won't have a problem.'

'Why have you not gone mad?' I asked.

'What?'

'You have spoken to 16. Why have you not gone mad?'

'I told you before. I have certain ways to protect myself. Besides,' he said with a rueful screwing up of his mouth, 'it's not as if I'm completely immune to it. God knows I feel half-mad with everything at the moment.'

We fell into silence again. We were both in a state of shock, I think. Then the Other put on a slightly forced smile and made an effort to appear more normal. A thought struck him. 'How did you know?' he asked.

'What?' I said.

'I thought you said . . . You seemed to be saying that you already knew that 16 was looking for you. You in particular. But how could you? How could you know that?' I could see by his face that he was trying to work it out.

Now was the time to tell him about the Prophet. It was on the tip of my tongue to do so. I hesitated. I said, 'It was revealed to me. By the House. You know how I have these revelations?'

'Oh. Right. That. And what was it that you wanted to say to me? You said you had something important to tell me.'

Another short pause.

'I saw an octopus swimming in the Lower Halls that are reached from the Eighteenth Vestibule,' I said.

'Oh,' said the Other. 'Did you? That's nice.'

'It was nice,' I agreed.

The Other took a deep breath. 'So! Keep away from 16! And don't go mad!' He smiled at me.

'You may be certain that I will keep away from 16,' I said. 'And I will not go mad.'

The Other clapped me on the shoulder. 'Excellent,' he said.

My reaction to the Other's declaration that he may, under certain circumstances, kill me

I had had a lucky escape! I had almost told the Other about the Prophet! And then he (the Other) would have said, 'Why did you speak to an Unknown Person when you promised me you would not? Did you not think that it might be 16?'

And what would I have answered? Because I *did* think that he was 16 when I spoke to him. I did break my promise to the Other. There is no excuse for it. Thank the House I had not told him! At best he would have thought me an untrustworthy person. At worst it would have inclined him all the more to kill me.

And yet I cannot help thinking that if the situation was reversed and if it were the Other's sanity that was threatened by 16, I would not resort to killing him quite so quickly. To be honest I do not think that I would ever want to kill him — the idea of it is abhorrent to me. Certainly I would try other things first, like finding a cure for his

142

madness. But the Other is rather inflexible in his character. I would not go so far as to say it is a fault, but it is a definite tendency.

I change my appearance in anticipation of the coming of 16

ENTRY FOR THE FIRST DAY OF THE EIGHTH MONTH IN THE YEAR THE ALBATROSS CAME TO THE SOUTH-WESTERN HALLS

Just now I am practising hiding from 16.

Imagine, (I say to Myself) *that you have just seen someone — 16! — in the Twenty-Third South-Eastern Hall. Now hide Yourself!*

Then I run swiftly and silently to a Wall and I spring into the Gap between two Statues. I press Myself into it and remain still and silent. Yesterday a buzzard flew into the Hall where I was hiding, looking for smaller birds to eat. He circled the Hall and perched on the Statue of a Man and a Boy mapping Stars. He remained there for half an hour but did not perceive me.

My clothes are perfect for camouflage. When I was younger my shirts and trousers were different colours: blue, black, white, grey, olive brown. One shirt was a very nice cherry red colour. But they have all faded to mere ghosts of colours. All are now an undistinguished and indistinguishable grey, which fades into the greys and whites of the marble Statues.

However my hair is a different matter. Over the years, as it has grown longer, I have interlaced it with pretty things that I have found or made: seashells, coral beads, pearls, tiny pebbles and interesting fish-bones. Many of these little ornaments are bright, shiny and have eye-catching colours. All of them rattle when I walk or run. So last week I spent an afternoon extricating them all. It was not easy and sometimes it was painful. I have placed my ornaments in the beautiful box with the octopus on it, which previously contained my shoes. When 16 returns to his own Halls, I shall put them back — I feel oddly naked without them.

The Index

ENTRY FOR THE EIGHTH DAY OF THE EIGHTH MONTH IN THE YEAR THE ALBATROSS CAME TO THE SOUTH-WESTERN HALLS

It is my practice to index my Journal entries every other week or so. I find that this is more efficient than indexing them straight away. After some time has passed it is easier to separate the important from the ephemeral.

This morning I sat down cross-legged on

the Pavement of the Second Northern Hall with my Journal and Index. A great deal has happened since I last performed this task.

I made an entry in the Index:

Prophet, appearance of: Journal no. 10, pages 148–152

I made another entry:

Prophecies concerning the coming of 16: Journal no. 10, pages 151–152

Then I read over what the Prophet had said concerning the identities of the Dead and made an entry:

Dead, the, some tentative names for: Journal no. 10, pages 149, 152

I began to make entries for the individual names. Under the letter 'I', I wrote:

Italian, dishy, young: Journal no. 10, page 149

I was halfway through writing Stan Ovenden's name (under the letter O) when my eye was caught by an entry higher up.

Ovenden, Stanley, student of Laurence

Arne-Sayles: Journal no. 21, page 154.
See also The disappearance of Maurizio
Giussani, Journal no. 21, pages 186–7

I was stunned. Here he was. Stanley Ovenden. Already in the Index. Yet his name,
when the Prophet spoke it, had not been in
the least familiar.

I read the index entry again.

I paused. I knew as I looked at it that there
was something very strange here. But the
strange thing was *so* strange, so entirely
incomprehensible that I found it difficult to
form coherent thoughts about it. I could
see the strangeness with my eyes, but I
could not think it with my mind.

Journal no. 21.

I had written Journal no. 21. Why in the
World had I done that? It made no sense
whatsoever. The Journal I am writing in now
is (as I have already explained) Journal no.
10. There is no Journal no. 21. There never
could have been a Journal no. 21. What did
it mean?

I cast my eyes over the rest of the page.
Most of the entries under O were about the
Other. There were a great many of those,
which is only to be expected seeing as he is
the only other human being apart from
Myself — and, of course, the Prophet and

16, but about them I know very little. I saw that there were earlier entries for other subjects. These were as strange as the entry for Stanley Ovenden. As I focussed on them, I experienced the same reluctance to register what my eyes saw. Nevertheless, I forced my eyes to see it; I forced my mind to think it.

Orkney, planning for summer 2002: Journal no. 3, pages 11–15, 20–28

Orkney, archaeological dig: Journal no. 3, pages 30–39, 47–51

Orkney, Ness of Brodgar: Journal no. 3, pages 40–47

Observational uncertainty: Journal no. 5, pages 134–35

O'Keeffe, Georgia, exhibition: Journal no. 11, pages 91–95

Outsider psychiatry, see R. D. Laing

Outsider philosophy: Journal no.17, pages 19–32; see also J.W. Dunne (Serialism), Owen Barfield, Rudolf Steiner

Outsider ideas, how different systems of knowledge and belief treat them: Journal no. 18, pages 42–57

Outsider literature, see Fan fiction

Outsider, The, Colin Wilson: Journal no. 20, pages 46–51

Outsider mathematics: Journal no. 21,

pages 40–44; see also Srinivasa Ramanujan
Outsider art: Journal no. 21, pages 79–86

Here were references to more Journals
that did not exist! Journals 11, 17, 18 and
20. Journals 3 and 5 did exist of course, so
those entries were sound. Except . . .
except . . . The more I looked at them, the
more I suspected that these entries did not
refer to *my* Journals 3 and 5, but to different ones. The entries were written with a
pen I did not recognise. The ink was thinner and more fluid and the nib of the pen
was broader than any pen I possess. Added
to this was the writing itself. It was my
handwriting — no doubt about that — but
it was subtly different from the writing I
currently employ. It was slightly rounder
and fatter — in a word, younger.

I went to the North-Eastern Corner and
climbed up to the Statue of an Angel caught
on a Rose Bush. I fetched out my brown
leather messenger bag. I took all my Journals
out of it. There were nine of them. Just nine.
I did not find twenty others that I had
inexplicably overlooked until this moment.

I examined the Journals carefully, paying
particular attention to the covers and the
numbers written on them. My Journals are

black and I number each one with a white gel pen at the bottom of its spine. To my astonishment I discovered that the first three Journals had originally been numbered differently. They had been numbered 21, 22 and 23, but someone had scratched out the initial numeral '2', transforming them into 1, 2 and 3. The scratching out had not been done perfectly (gel ink is difficult to remove) and I could still make out the ghostly form of the '2'.

I sat for a while, trying to comprehend this, but I could make nothing of it.

If Journal no. 1 (my Journal no. 1) had originally been Journal no. *21,* then it ought to contain the two entries on Stanley Ovenden. I picked it up, opened it and turned to page 154. There he was. The entry was dated 22 January 2012. It was titled: *Biography of Stanley Ovenden.*

Stanley Ovenden. Born 1958, Nottingham, England. Father, Edward Francis Ovenden, owned a sweet shop. Mother's name and occupation unknown. Studied mathematics at the University of Birmingham. Began postgraduate research in 1981. The same year he attended one of Laurence Arne-Sayles's famous lectures: *The Forgotten, the Liminal, the Transgressive and the Divine.* Shortly afterwards Ovenden abandoned mathematics and began a PhD in anthropology at the University of Manchester under Arne-Sayles's supervision.

The first entry finished here, so next I turned to page 186, to the entry entitled: *The disappearance of Maurizio Giussani.*

In the summer of 1987 Laurence Arne-Sayles rented a farmhouse called the Casale del Pino, twenty kilometres from Perugia. His most favoured students (the inner circle) went with him: Ovenden, Bannerman, Hughes, Ketterley and D'Agostino.

Tensions had begun to appear within the group. Arne-Sayles had become highly sensitive to any remark or question that showed the speaker was insufficiently committed to his 'great experiment'. Anyone who dared to question him was subjected to a savage raking-over of all their failings, personal and academic. Consequently most of the group maintained a diplomatic silence, but Stanley Ovenden, who had a sort of tone-deafness when it came to other people's personalities, continued to express doubts about what they were doing. When Tali Hughes defended Ovenden to Arne-Sayles she also came in for a generous share of his spleen. The atmosphere at Casale del Pino became increasingly tense and, as a result, Ovenden and Hughes began spending more and more time away from the others. They became friendly with a young man, Maurizio Giussani, a philosophy student at the University of Perugia. This new friendship seems to have seriously alarmed Arne-Sayles.

On the evening of 26 July, Arne-Sayles invited Giussani and his fiancée, Elena Marietti, to a dinner party at Casale del Pino. During dinner Arne-Sayles talked about the other world (a place where architecture and oceans were muddled together) and how it was possible to get there. Elena Marietti thought that Arne-Sayles was talking metaphorically or else that he was describing some sort of Huxleyan psychedelic experience.

Marietti had to work the following day. (Like Giussani she was a postgrad student, but during the summer she worked as a paralegal in her father's law firm in Perugia.) At about 11 o'clock she said goodnight and got into her car and drove home and went to bed. The others were still talking. The English party had promised that one of them would drive Giussani home.

Maurizio Giussani was never seen again. Arne-Sayles claimed that he had gone to bed shortly after Marietti left and knew nothing about what had happened. The others (Ovenden, Bannerman, Hughes, Ketterley, D'Agostino) said that Giussani had refused the offer of a lift and that he had begun to walk home a little after midnight. (The night was moonlit and warm; Giussani lived about 3 kilometres away.)

Ten years later when Arne-Sayles was convicted of kidnapping another young man, the Italian police reopened the case of the missing Giussani, however . . .

I stopped reading and stood up, breathing hard. I had a strong urge to fling the Journal away from me. The words on the page — (in my own writing!) — looked like words, but at the same time I knew they were meaningless. It was nonsense, gibberish! What meaning could words such as 'Birmingham' and 'Perugia' possibly have? None. There is nothing in the World that corresponds to them.

The Other was right after all. I had forgotten many things! Worse still, at the very point at which the Other has declared he will kill me if I become mad, I have discovered that I am mad already! Or, if not mad now, then certainly I have been mad in the past. I was mad when I wrote those entries!

I did not fling the Journal away. I dropped it on the Pavement and walked away. I wanted to put some physical distance between Myself and these evidences of my madness. The nonsense words — Perugia, Nottingham, university — echoed in my mind. I felt a great pressure there as if a whole host of half-formed ideas were about to break through into my consciousness, bringing with them more madness or else understanding.

I walked rapidly through several Halls, not knowing or caring where I went. Suddenly I saw in front of me the Statue of the Faun, the Statue that I love above all others. There was his calm, faintly smiling face; there was his forefinger gently pressed to his lips. In the past I have always thought he meant to warn me of something with that gesture: *Be careful!* But today it seemed to mean something quite different: *Hush! Be comforted!* I climbed up on to his Plinth and flung Myself into his Arms, wrapping my arm around his Neck, intertwining my fingers with his Fingers. Safe in his embrace, I wept for my lost Sanity. Great, heaving sobs rose up, almost painfully, from my chest.

Hush! he told me. *Be comforted!*

I resolve to take better care of Myself

ENTRY FOR THE NINTH DAY OF THE EIGHTH MONTH IN THE YEAR THE ALBATROSS CAME TO THE SOUTH-WESTERN HALLS

I left the Embrace of the Faun and wandered miserably through the House. I believed that I was mad — or that I had been mad — or else that I was becoming mad now. Whichever way it was, it was a terrifying prospect.

After a while I decided that this way of going on did no good at all.

I forced Myself to return to the Third Northern Hall where I ate a little fish and drank some water. Then I revisited all my favourite Statues: the Gorilla, the Young Boy playing the Cymbals, the Woman carrying a Beehive, the Elephant carrying a Castle, the Faun, the Two Kings playing Chess. Their Beauty soothed me and took me out of Myself; their noble expressions reminded me of all that is good in the World.

This morning I am able to reflect more calmly on what has happened.

I accept that I have been very ill in the past. I must have been ill when I wrote those entries in my Journal or else I would not have filled them with outlandish words such as 'Birmingham' and 'Perugia'. (Even now, as I write the words, I begin to feel anxious again. A crowd of images stirs in my mind — strange, nightmarish, but at the same time oddly familiar. The word 'Birmingham', for example, brings with it a blare of noise, a flash of movement and colour and the fleeting image of towers and spires against a heavy grey sky. I try to catch hold of these impressions, to examine them further, but instantly they fade.)

Despite all this I believe that I was precipitate to dismiss these two entries as gibberish. Some of the words — 'university' is an example — do seem to possess meaning of a sort. I believe that if I set my mind to it, I could write a clear definition of 'university'. I have given some thought as to what might be the explanation of this. I understand 'scholar' because scattered around the House are Statues of Scholars with books and papers in their hands. Perhaps I extrapolated the idea of a 'university' (a place where scholars congregate) from these? This does not seem a very satisfactory hypothesis, but it is the best I can do for the moment.

The entries also include the names of people whose existence is confirmed by other evidence. The Prophet spoke about Stanley Ovenden, so clearly this was a real person. The Prophet also tried to think of the name of the dishy young Italian but could not do so. Perhaps it was Maurizio Giussani. Lastly both entries mentioned someone called 'Laurence Arne-Sayles' and I found a letter from 'Laurence' in the First Vestibule.

In other words, mixed in with the nonsense of these entries there does seem to be actual information. In my quest to learn all I can about the people who have lived I would be wrong to ignore this important source.

It has become clear that I have forgotten many things and — it is best to face these things squarely — I now have evidence of periods of serious mental derangement. My first and most important task is to hide these defects from the Other. (While I do not think he would go so far as to kill me because of them, he would certainly regard me with even more suspicion than he already does.) Almost as important is the need to guard Myself against the return of illness. To this end I have resolved to take better care of Myself. I must not become so absorbed in my scientific work that I forget to fish and end up with nothing to eat. (The House provides much food for the active and enterprising person. There is no excuse for going hungry!) I must devote more of my energies to mending my clothes and making coverings for my feet, which are often cold. (Question: is it possible to knit socks from seaweed? Doubtful.)

I have considered the renumbering of my Journals and have concluded that I must have done it Myself. Which means that twenty Journals (twenty!) are missing — a highly alarming thought! And yet, at the same time, it makes sense that there are missing Journals. I am (as I have previously stated) approximately thirty-five years of age. The ten Journals I possess cover a period of five years. Where are the Journals of my earlier life? And what did I do in those years?

Yesterday I thought that I never wanted to read or look up entries in my Journals again. I pictured Myself throwing all ten Journals and the Index into a raging Tide, and I imagined how relieved I would feel to be free of them. But today I am calmer. I am less at the mercy of fear and panic. Today I can see that there are sound reasons for studying my Journals carefully, even the mad parts — perhaps especially the mad parts. First, I have always longed to know more about the people who have lived and, incomprehensible as it is, the Journals do seem to contain actual information about them, however bizarrely presented. Second, I need to learn as much as I can about my own madness, specifically what triggers it and how I can guard against it in the future.

Perhaps by studying the past in the pages of my Journal I will be able to make sense of these things. In the meantime it is important to recognise that reading the Journal is in itself a triggering activity, giving rise to many painful emotions and nightmarish thoughts. I must proceed cautiously and only read small portions at a time.

The Other and the Prophet have both stated that the House itself is a source of madness and forgetfulness. They are scientists and men of intellect. When two such impeccable authorities are in agreement then I believe I must accept their conclusions. The House is the cause of my forgetting.

Do you trust the House? I ask Myself.

Yes, I answer Myself.

And if the House has made you forget, then it has done so for good reason.

But I do not understand the reason.

It does not matter that you do not understand the reason. You are the Beloved Child of the House. Be comforted.

And I am comforted.

Sylvia D'Agostino
ENTRY FOR THE TWENTIETH DAY OF THE EIGHTH MONTH IN THE YEAR THE ALBATROSS CAME TO THE SOUTH-WESTERN HALLS

I am very curious about the other people that the Prophet mentioned, so I decided to begin my study with Sylvia D'Agostino and poor James Ritter, but I did not look them up straightaway. In accordance with my plan of looking after Myself, I allowed a week and a half to elapse before I read the Journal again. I passed the intervening time in ordinary, soothing activities. I fished; I made soup; I washed clothes; I composed music on the flute that I made from the bone of a swan. Then this morning I brought my Journals and the Index to the Fifth Northern Hall. This Hall contains the Statue of the Gorilla and I thought the sight of Him would lend me Strength.

I sat down, cross-legged on the Pavement opposite the Gorilla. I turned to the letter D in my Index. There she was.

D'Agostino, Sylvia, student of Arne-Sayles:
Journal no. 22, pages 6–9

I turned to page 6 of Journal no. 22 (which was my Journal no. 2).

Biography of Sylvia D'Agostino

Born 1958 in Leith, Scotland, the daughter of Eduardo D'Agostino, the poet.

Photographs show a woman of a slightly androgynous appearance, attractive, even beautiful, with thick dark brows, dark eyes, a strong nose and emphatic jawline. She had a mass of dark hair usually tied back. According to Angharad Scott, D'Agostino made no concessions to conventional ideas of femininity and only intermittently cared what she wore.

When she was a teenager D'Agostino told a friend that she wanted to go to university to study Death, Stars and Mathematics. Inexplicably the University of Manchester didn't offer such a course, so she settled for Mathematics. At the university she quickly stumbled upon Laurence Arne-Sayles and his lectures; that encounter shaped the remainder of her life.

Arne-Sayles's talk of communing with ancient minds and glimpses into other worlds answered all her cosmic longings — the 'Death and Stars' part of her. As soon as her Mathematics degree had concluded, she switched to Anthropology with Arne-Sayles as her supervisor.

Of all Arne-Sayles's students and acolytes D'Agostino was by far the most devoted. He assigned her a room in his house in Whalley Range where she became his unpaid housekeeper and secretary. She had a car (Arne-Sayles did not drive) and part of her duties consisted of driving him wherever he wanted to go, including to Canal Street on Saturday nights to pick up young men.

In 1984 she gained her doctorate. She did not seek out academic or teaching work, but stayed at Arne-Sayles's side, taking a string of menial jobs to support herself.

She was an only child and had always been very close to her parents, particularly her father. At some point in the mid-80s Arne-Sayles instructed her to quarrel with her parents. According to Angharad Scott, this was a test of loyalty. D'Agostino cut off all contact with her parents and they never saw her again.

Scott describes her as a poet, an artist and a film-maker and lists the magazines in which her poems were published: *Arcturus, Torn Asunder* and *Grasshopper.* (To date I haven't been able to find any copies of these magazines.) The editor of *Grasshopper* — a man called Tom Titchwell — was also a friend of Eduardo D'Agostino. He (Titchwell) kept in touch with Sylvia and relayed news of her back to her parents.

Two of her films survive: *Moon/Wood* and *The Castle. Moon/ Wood* is a unique and atmospheric piece of film-making admired by critics and fans outside the usual circle of Arne-Sayles conspiracy theorists. It is 25 minutes long and was filmed on moors and in woods around Manchester. It was shot on Super 8 in colour, but the feel of it is almost entirely monochrome — black woods, white snow, grey sky etc. — with occasional splashes of blood-red. In the film a hierophant of ancient times holds a small community in thrall. He dispenses cruelty to the men and abuses the women. One woman opposes him. To show his power and to punish her, the hierophant casts a spell. The woman crosses a stream. She takes a step and her foot comes down in the moon's reflection. She is caught in the stream; she cannot move from the moon's reflection. The hierophant comes and beats her where she stands helpless. Still she cannot move. Left alone, she asks a wood of birch trees to help her. As the hierophant passes through the wood, he becomes caught in the tangle of birch trees; they bind him and pierce him. He cannot move and eventually dies. The woman is released from the moon's reflection. *Moon/Wood* contains very little speech and what there is is incomprehensible. The woman and the hierophant speak their own language which has nothing to do with ours. The true language of *Moon/Wood* is simple, stark imagery: moon, darkness, water, trees.

D'Agostino's other surviving film is even odder. It is untitled, but usually referred to as *The Castle.* It is shot on Betamax and the quality is very poor. The camera meanders around various enormous rooms, presumably in different castles or palaces (we cannot be seeing one building; it is simply too vast).The walls are lined with statues and puddles of water crowd the floor. According to the people who believe such things, this is a record of one of Arne-Sayles's other worlds, possibly the one described in his 2000 book, *The Labyrinth.* Other people have tried to establish the locations in order to prove that it is not a film of another world, but to date none of them has been conclusively identified. Notes in D'Agostino's handwriting were found with *The Castle,* but these are in the same peculiar code as her last diary and remain impenetrable.

D'Agostino seems to have kept a diary most of her adult life. The early volumes (1973–1980) were kept at her parents' house in Leith; these are written in English. Another diary, current at the time of her disappearance (spring 1990) was found in the doctor's surgery where she worked. This diary employs a weird mixture of hieroglyphs and descriptions of images (possibly dream imagery?) in English. Angharad Scott made several attempts to decipher it but got nowhere.

In early 1990 D'Agostino was working as a receptionist in a doctor's surgery in Whalley Range. She struck up a friendship with one of the doctors there, a man about her own age called Robert Allstead. At this point she seems to have been distinctly less enamoured of Laurence Arne-Sayles than before. She told Allstead that her life was one of drudgery, but that she would always be grateful to Arne-Sayles because he had opened the way to a more beautiful world and she was happy there. Allstead did not know what to make of this. He later told police that he was certain she was not on drugs. If she had been, he would never have allowed her to work in the surgery.

When Arne-Sayles learnt about her friendship with Allstead he threw one of his peculiar jealous fits and demanded that she leave the job. This time D'Agostino refused.

In the first week of April she failed to turn up for work. After she had been missing for two days Dr Allstead called the police. She was never seen again.

Poor James Ritter

SECOND ENTRY FOR THE TWENTIETH DAY OF THE EIGHTH MONTH IN THE YEAR THE ALBA-TROSS CAME TO THE SOUTH-WESTERN HALLS

There were two entries for James Ritter both in Journal no. 21: page 46 and page 122. The first one was titled: *The disgrace of Laurence Arne-Sayles.*

Arne-Sayles's career, always controversial, ended abruptly in April 1997, when a woman employed to clean his house found something: a brown liquid that seemed to ooze out from beneath a wall in one of the rooms. The room was a bedroom and, according to Arne-Sayles, not used. But the cleaner could see that it was being used, hence her cleaning it. She sponged up the liquid. Then she smelt it. Urine and faeces. A little more liquid seeped out from under the wall. She pushed the wall, it gave slightly. She put her ear to it. Then she called the police. Behind the wall — the fake wall — the police found a room in which was a young man, very ill and entirely incoherent.

Arne-Sayles's academic career was over. Following a trial (widely reported) he was sent to prison initially for three years; however, while in prison he was convicted of inciting other inmates to violence and riots. In the end he served four and a half years and was released in 2002.

Arne-Sayles did not testify at his trial and never offered any explanation as to why he'd imprisoned James Ritter.

I found this entry to be disappointing; there was very little information as to who poor James Ritter was. I turned to the second entry. This looked more promising.

Biography of James Ritter

Born 1967 in London. In his youth Ritter was very good-looking. He worked as a model, a waiter, a barman, an actor and occasionally as a prostitute. Throughout his adult life he suffered prolonged periods of mental illness. He was sectioned at least twice between 1987 and 1994, once in London, once in Wakefield. He was sometimes homeless.

After he was found behind the fake wall in Arne-Sayles's house he was taken to hospital where he was treated for pneumonia, malnutrition, dehydration and bipolar disorder. The police tried to discover how long Arne-Sayles had kept him prisoner, but Ritter was incapable of giving any sort of coherent answer. So the police talked to people who knew him — drug addicts, social workers, people who ran hostels for the homeless. All that they (the police) were able to establish was that Ritter had been seen in and around Manchester in the early part of 1995, so it was possible — though by no means definite — that he had been imprisoned for as long as two years.

Ritter's own story, as he gradually became able to tell it, served to make matters more obscure. He insisted that he had only been at Arne-Sayles's house in Whalley Range for brief periods; most of the time he had been at a different house, a house that contained statues and where many of the rooms were flooded by the sea. Most of the time he appeared to think that he was still there. On several occasions while he was in hospital he became very agitated, saying that he needed to go back to the minotaurs because the minotaurs would have his dinner. Despite being put on medication to control his delusions, he continued to insist on this story of a house with a flooded basement and statues.

Quite what Arne-Sayles was trying to achieve by keeping Ritter prisoner is still a matter for debate. Two theories have been put forward.

The first is that Arne-Sayles brainwashed Ritter in order to lend credence to his claims that other worlds not only existed, but that he and other people had been there. Certainly, Ritter's description of the house is similar to the vast, empty rooms in Sylvia D'Agostino's film, *The Castle;* it is also similar to Arne-Sayles's own description of the other world in the book he wrote in prison: *The Labyrinth.* (Of course, it is perfectly possible that Arne-Sayles simply elaborated on Ritter's hallucinations.) But if that was Arne-Sayles's aim — to manufacture evidence of another world — then why did he choose a man with a history of delusional illness as his witness?

The second theory was that the kidnapping had less to do with Arne-Sayles's Other World theories than with his outré sexual tastes. (This was the line the prosecution took at the trial in October 1997.) But in that case why was Ritter babbling about houses with seas in the basement?

Angharad Scott attempted to interview Ritter for her biography of Arne-Sayles, but Ritter had taken offence that no one believed him about the house with the ocean imprisoned in it and he refused to speak to her. In 2010 a *Guardian* journalist — Lysander Weeks — tracked him down for a retrospective piece on the Arne-Sayles scandal. At this point Ritter was working as a caretaker for Manchester Town Hall. Weeks described him as calm, self-possessed, almost Zen-like. Ritter claimed to have been drug-free for a decade. Nevertheless the story he told Weeks was the same one he had told the police: that for about eighteen months between 1995 and 1997 he had inhabited a large house where the sea flooded the basement and sometimes rose up to the ground floor. Ritter said he had slept in a sort of white, translucent cave beneath the marble sweep of a great staircase. Ritter said that working at Manchester Town Hall was what had saved him; it too was a vast building with great rooms and statues and staircases. The resemblance to the other house — the one Arne-Sayles had taken him to — calmed him.

Journal entries on Sylvia D'Agostino and poor James Ritter: some initial thoughts

ENTRY FOR THE TWENTY-FIRST DAY OF THE EIGHTH MONTH IN THE YEAR THE ALBATROSS CAME TO THE SOUTH-WESTERN HALLS

The last entry on poor James Ritter was the one I found the most intriguing. It was just as full of nonsense words as the others, but the part about the Minotaurs was a clear reference to the First Vestibule. I also recognised Ritter's description of the white, translucent cave beneath a Staircase. The First Vestibule contains just such a Staircase with just such a cave-like space beneath it. And it was in that cave-like space that I had

170

found much of the rubbish that had so annoyed me. James Ritter was clearly the person who had eaten crisps and fish fingers in the First Vestibule. (This insight alone justifies my decision to continue reading my Journal!)

Sylvia D'Agostino's entry was less informative, but judging by the description of her film, *The Castle,* she too had visited these Halls.

The word 'university' occurs three times in the entry about Sylvia D'Agostino and three times in the entries about Stanley Ovenden. Two weeks ago I hypothesised that I was able to ascribe a meaning to this seemingly nonsense word because I have seen Statues of Scholars in the House. At the time I was inclined to dismiss this theory as weak, but it seems more plausible now. It occurs to me that there are many other ideas that I understand perfectly, even though no such things exist in the World. For example I know that a garden is a place where one can refresh oneself with the sight of plants and trees. But a garden is not a thing that exists in the World nor is there any Statue representing that particular idea. (Indeed I cannot quite imagine what a Statue of a garden would look like.) Instead, scattered about the House are Statues in

which People or Gods or Beasts are surrounded by Roses or Strands of Ivy, or
shelter under the Canopies of Trees. In the
Ninth Vestibule there is the Statue of a
Gardener digging and in the Nineteenth
South-Eastern Hall there is a Statue of a
different Gardener pruning a Rose Bush. It
is from these things that I deduce the idea
of a *garden.* I do not believe this happens
by accident. This is how the House places
new ideas gently and naturally in the Minds
of Men. This is how the House increases
my understanding.

This realisation is very encouraging and I
no longer feel quite so alarmed when a
nonsensical word in my Journal gives rise to
a mental image that I cannot account for.
Do not be anxious, I tell Myself. *It is the
House. It is the House enlarging your understanding.*

All the Journal entries contain names. I
have made a list of those I have found so
far. There are fifteen of them. Assuming that
'Ketterley' belongs to the Other and that
another belongs to the Prophet, then thirteen remain. This is the exact number of
the Dead in my Halls. A coincidence? After
careful consideration I am inclined to think
it might be. While fifteen people are *named,*
several more seem to be implied in the text:

people such as the friend to whom D'Agostino said that she wished to study 'Death, Stars and Mathematics'; 'the police' (who are mentioned in all the texts); the woman who cleaned Laurence Arne-Sayles's house; and the young men whom Laurence Arne-Sayles picked up on Saturday nights. It is impossible to say at this juncture how many of these people there are.

■ ■ ■ ■

PART 4
16

■ ■ ■ ■

I retrieve the scraps of paper from the Eighty-Eighth Western Hall

ENTRY FOR THE FIRST DAY OF THE NINTH MONTH IN THE YEAR THE ALBATROSS CAME TO THE SOUTH-WESTERN HALLS

I had not forgotten the scraps of paper that I found in the Eighty-Eighth Western Hall, nor the ones that remained there, woven into herring gull nests.

Two days ago I gathered together supplies for the journey: food, blankets, a small saucepan in which to heat water and some rags. I set off and reached the Eighty-Eighth Western Hall about the middle of the afternoon. The gulls must have been out searching for food because there were none in the Hall, though fresh deposits of excrement on the Statues showed that it was still their roosting place.

Immediately I began work extricating the

scraps of paper from the nests. The ease with which this could be accomplished varied. In some nests the seaweed was dry and fell apart at the first tug, but in others the paper scraps were cemented to the seaweed by the gulls' droppings. I made a fire using dry seaweed from the old nests; I heated water in the saucepan; then I dipped a rag into the water and applied it gently to the paper that was stuck in the nests. It was delicate work: too little hot water and the hard droppings would not soften; too much and the paper itself would dissolve. It took me many hours of labour, but by the evening of the second day I had recovered seventy-nine scraps from thirty-five nests. I examined every nest again and satisfied Myself that no more remained.

This morning I returned to my own Halls.

I spent some time trying to assemble the writing. Eventually, after an hour, I had part of a page — perhaps as much as half — and a few smaller sections of other pages.

The writing was very bad, full of crossings out. I read:

. . . that he has done to me. How could I have been so stupid? I will die here. There is no one coming to save me. I will die here. The silence *[piece missing]* no sound, only the pounding of the sea in the rooms below. There is nothing to eat. I rely on him to bring me food and water — which only underlines my status as a prisoner, a slave. He leaves the food in the room with the minotaur statues. I indulge myself in long fantasies of killing him. In one of the destroyed rooms I found a jagged piece of marble about the size of a roof tile. I have thought about crushing his head with it. This would give me great satisfaction . . .

This was the writing of a very angry and unhappy person. I wondered who it had been? I wished that I could reach through his writing to comfort him, to show him the fish that abounds in every Vestibule, the beds of shellfish just waiting to be gathered, how with only a little foresight he need never go hungry, how the House provides for and protects its Children. I wondered about his persecutor, the man who had made him a slave. I felt very sad to think that there had existed such antagonism between two human beings, perhaps even between two of my own Dead. Had the Concealed Person tormented the Biscuit-Box Man? Or the other way round?

Very carefully I turned over the scraps and

examined the reverse. The writing here was even worse.

> I forget. I forget. Yesterday I could not think of the word for lamp-post. This morning I thought that one of the statues spoke to me. I passed some time (about half an hour I think) talking to it. I am LOSING MY MIND. How horrible, how terrible to be in this dreadful place and MAD. I am DE-TERMINEDTO KILL him before this happens. Before I forget why I HATE HIM.

I sighed when I unravelled this. I took three envelopes the Other gave me once. In the first I placed the scraps that I had succeeded in putting together. On the outside of the envelope I carefully wrote a copy of the two transcriptions. In the second envelope I placed some scraps that fitted together, making fragments of sentences. In the third envelope I placed the scraps I had not managed to fit to any others.

A problem

ENTRY FOR THE SECOND DAY OF THE NINTH MONTH IN THE YEAR THE ALBATROSS CAME TO THE SOUTH-WESTERN HALLS

One overriding problem concerns me at the moment: whether or not to ask the Other about Stanley Ovenden, Sylvia D'Agostino, poor James Ritter and Maurizio Giussani. The Prophet called the Other 'Ketterley'. In the entry about the disappearance of Maurizio Giussani the name 'Ketterley' appears in close proximity to the names D'Agostino and Ovenden, and to Giussani itself. From this I conclude that the Other knew these people. I long to know more of them and several times it has been on the tip of my tongue to ask him. But always at the last moment I have hesitated. Supposing he said: *Where did you hear of these people? Who told you?*, I would not know what to say. He must not know that I have spoken to the Prophet. He must not know about the entries in my Journal.

He is full of suspicion. He thinks of nothing but the approach of 16. Two months ago he declared his intention to go to the One-Hundred-and-Ninety-Second Western Hall and perform the ritual, which he believes will summon the Great and Secret Knowledge, but at present all that is forgotten.

Lemon

ENTRY FOR THE FIFTH DAY OF THE NINTH MONTH IN THE YEAR THE ALBATROSS CAME TO THE SOUTH-WESTERN HALLS

This morning I was on my way from the Third Northern Hall to the Sixteenth Vestibule. I passed out of the First Northern Hall and into the First Vestibule. I took a step or two, then stopped.

Something had just happened. What was it? What had just happened?

I took a couple of steps back into the Doorway and breathed in. There it was again! A scent. A perfume of lemons, geranium leaves, hyacinths and narcissi.

It was quite strong in this one spot. Someone — a person wearing a beautiful perfume — had stood for a while in the Doorway, perhaps looking out at the Long Vista of Receding Halls. I returned to the First Northern Hall but could find no trace of it there. I went back to the First Vestibule and passed southwards along the Wall under the looming Statue of a Minotaur. Yes, the scent was discernible here too. I traced the person's path as far as a point between the Doorway to the First Western Hall and the Doorway to the Corridor leading to the First South-Western Hall. There I lost it.

Who was the person who had passed this way? Not the Other. I knew the perfume he wore: a spicy scent of coriander, rose and sandalwood. The Prophet? I remembered his perfume very well. Again, quite different

— violet had been the dominant note, with hints of cloves, blackcurrant and rose.

No, this was someone new.

16 had come. 16 was here.

My heart started beating faster. I looked around the Vestibule. The great space was darkened by the velvet Shadows of the Minotaurs with splinters of golden Light between. 16 did not step out from a hiding place to begin making me mad. Yet he had been there and perhaps no more than an hour before.

It was surprising to me that someone like 16, someone so wedded to Destruction and Madness, should wear a perfume so lovely, so redolent of Sunshine and Happiness. But then I told Myself that I was foolish to think like that. *Treat this as a warning,* I said. *Be on your guard. 16 will not wear his ill intentions in his face. It is very likely he will be pleasing to the eyes. His manners will be friendly and insinuating. That is how he intends to destroy you.*

More people to kill
ENTRY FOR THE SEVENTH DAY OF THE NINTH MONTH IN THE YEAR THE ALBATROSS CAME TO THE SOUTH-WESTERN HALLS

This morning I told the Other about the

perfume in the First Vestibule. To my surprise he took the news quite calmly.

'Yes, well, I'm beginning to think that it's better to get it over with,' he said, 'rather than hanging about, waiting for it to happen. And besides, perhaps it isn't such a bad thing after all.'

'But I thought you said that 16 is a great threat to us,' I said. 'I thought you said that he threatens your safety and my sanity?'

'That's true.'

'Then how can it possibly be good if he comes here?'

'Because the threat to us is so great that our only option is to eliminate 16 entirely.'

'How do we do that?'

For an answer, the Other put two fingers to his head in imitation of a gun and made the sound: *Boom!*

I was stunned. 'I do not think that I could kill someone however wicked they are,' I said. 'Even the wicked deserve Life. Or if they do not, then let the House take it from them. Not me.'

'You're probably right,' he said. 'I'm not sure I could kill someone with my hands.' He examined his own thoughtfully, spreading the fingers and turning them over. 'Though it would be interesting to try. Tell you what. I'll get a gun. That'll make it easier, whichever of us has to do it. Which reminds me, there's a possibility — a small possibility — that someone else might come here. If you ever see an old man . . .'

'. . . an old man?' I said, startled.

'. . . yes, an old man. If you see him, tell me straightaway. He's not quite so tall as me. Very thin. Pale. With hooded eyes and a red, wet mouth.' The Other gave an involuntary shudder, then said, 'I don't know why I'm describing him to you. It's not as if hordes of old men are going to start turning up.'

'Why? Are you going to kill him as well?' I asked anxiously. I had no doubt that the Other was talking about the Prophet.

'Well, no,' he said. He paused. 'Although now that you mention it, it's about time that somebody did. It was always amazing to me that no one killed him while he was in prison. Anyway, tell me if you see him.'

I nodded in as non-committal a manner as I could manage. The Other had asked me to tell him if I saw the Prophet in the future, not if I had seen him in the past, so I was not exactly lying. The one good thing about this new development is that the Prophet has gone back to his own Halls and he said quite definitely that he did not intend to return.

185

I find writing made by 16

For five days a steady, grey, drenching rain fell in all the Vestibules. The World was damp and chill and puddles formed on the Stone Pavements at the Doors to the Vestibules. The Halls were full of the chatter of birds who came there to shelter.

I kept as busy as I could. I mended my fishing nets and practised my music. But all the while at the back of my mind was the thought that 16 was here and intended to make me mad. I had no idea when the crisis would come, and it was not a pleasant feeling.

Today it stopped raining. The World became light of Heart again.

I made my way to the Sixth North-Western Hall, which is home to a flock of rooks. The moment they saw me they descended from their perches on the High Statues, wheeling and flapping and calling to each other. I scattered scraps of fish to feed them. Two alighted on my shoulders. One pecked at my ear, hoping to discover if I was good to eat. It made me laugh. Standing in the middle of the rattle and whirl of black wings, I was not paying attention to my surroundings and I did not at first see that on a Door to my right, there was a mark, a slash of bright yellow chalk. Then I did see it. I shrugged the birds away and went to look.

Long ago I used to mark Doors and Floors with chalk in this manner because I was afraid of losing my way. I had not done it for years, but as I looked at this yellow mark I thought at first that it must be one of my marks, which had somehow survived Flood, Tide, Wind, Rain, Mist. Yet at the same time I knew that I have never possessed any yellow chalk. I have some white chalk, some blue chalk and a small amount of pink chalk. But yellow chalk? No, I have never had such a thing.

Then I saw that on the Pavement by the Door were more chalk marks, this time in white.

Words! Not the Other's words. He rarely ventures this far from the First Vestibule. No, these were someone else's words. 16! I stood for a moment trying to take this in. This had never occurred to me: that 16 might leave written words to make people mad! (I had to applaud his ingenuity. I am not sure it would have occurred to me.)

But would they in fact make me mad? All

the Other's warnings had been against my speaking to 16, against my listening to him. Was it not probable that the danger resided in some quality of 16's voice? Perhaps the written word was safe? (I realised that the Other had been annoyingly unspecific.)

My eyes turned cautiously downwards. I read:

13TH ROOM FROM THE ENTRANCE. THE WAY BACK IS AS FOLLOWS. GO THROUGH THIS DOOR AND TURN LEFT IMMEDIATELY. GO THROUGH THE DOOR IN FRONT OF YOU AND THEN TURN RIGHT. KEEP TO THE RIGHT WALL. MISS TWO DOORS AND THEN . . .

Directions. It was only directions.

This did not seem too dangerous. I paused and examined Myself for signs of imminent madness or tendencies to self-destruction. Finding none, I read further.

They were directions from the Sixth North-Western Hall to the First Vestibule. Although the Path itself was somewhat meandering, the directions were clear, precise, efficient and the letters themselves square, upright and pleasing.

Using these directions, I traced 16's path back as far as the First Vestibule. Each

Doorway I passed through was carefully marked with yellow chalk. The marks were somewhat below my eye-level. (I estimate that 16 is between 12 and 15 centimetres shorter than me.) Beneath each Doorframe he had written his directions again so that if any were destroyed by a Tide or a mishap, he would still have the others. How methodical he was!

I went to the Second Northern Hall and got some blue chalk. Then I returned to the Sixth North-Western Hall where I had first seen 16's directions. (This seemed to be as far as he had gone.) Underneath his writing I wrote:

DEAR 16
THE OTHER HAS WARNED ME OF HOW YOU INTEND TO MAKE ME MAD. BUT IN ORDER TO MAKE ME MAD, YOU MUST FIRST FIND ME AND HOW WILL YOU DO THAT? THE ANSWER IS YOU WILL NOT. I KNOW EVERY NICHE OF THESE HALLS, EVERY APSE, EVERY PLACE TO HIDE. RETURN TO YOUR OWN HALLS, 16, AND REFLECT ON YOUR WICKEDNESS.

Writing this letter lessened the hunted

feeling I had been experiencing. I felt much more in control of the situation — almost as much as 16. My only difficulty was that I did not know how to sign the letter. I could not write 'YOUR FRIEND' as I did when I wrote to the Other or to Laurence (the person who had wanted to see the Statue of an Elderly Fox teaching some Squirrels). 16 and I were not friends. I tried putting 'your enemy' but this seemed unnecessarily confrontational. I considered 'the one who will never submit to being driven mad by you' but that was rather long (and not a little pompous). In the end, I simply put:

PIRANESI

This being what the Other calls me.
(But I do not think that it is my name.)

I ask the Other about 16's writing
ENTRY FOR THE FOURTEENTH DAY OF THE NINTH MONTH IN THE YEAR THE ALBATROSS CAME TO THE SOUTH-WESTERN HALLS

I met the Other this morning in the Second South-Western Hall. He was wearing a suit of medium-grey wool and an impeccable shirt of a darker grey. His mood was calm, serious and focussed. When I told him about the words that I had found chalked on the Pavement of the Sixth North-Western Hall, he simply nodded.

'Can 16 impart madness through the medium of the written word?' I asked. 'Ought I not to have read it?'

'16's words are dangerous whatever form they take,' he said. 'It would've been better not to read it. But I don't blame you. It took you by surprise. You weren't expecting a written message. Quite frankly that hadn't occurred to me as a possibility either. But this is a critical time. We need to be more careful.'

'I will be. I promise,' I said.

He gave my shoulder a couple of encouraging pats. 'There's good news too,' he said, 'well, sort of. I've managed to get hold of a gun. It was nowhere near as difficult as I thought it would be. But — and this I suppose is the bad news . . .' He made a rueful face. '. . . it turns out I'm a dreadful shot. I just don't seem to be able to hit anything at all. I'll have to practice, I suppose. Not quite sure how I'll manage that, but anyway . . . The thing is, Piranesi, try not to worry. One way or another this nightmare will soon be over.'

'Oh, please!' I begged. 'Let us not kill 16!'

He laughed. 'And what's the alternative? To allow ourselves to be driven mad? I don't think so.'

I said, 'But when 16 sees his plan does not work, when he sees how we avoid him, he may return to his own Halls.'

The Other shook his head. 'There's not a chance of it, Piranesi. I know this person. 16 is relentless. 16 will keep on coming.'

Light in the Darkness
ENTRY FOR THE SEVENTEENTH DAY OF THE NINTH MONTH IN THE YEAR THE ALBATROSS CAME TO THE SOUTH-WESTERN HALLS

Three days passed. I kept watch for signs that 16 had been in our Halls, but I found none. Then in the middle of the third night I awoke suddenly. Something had woken me, but I did not know what it was.

I sat up. I looked around. The Stars blazed bright in all the Windows. The Thousand Statues of the Third Northern Hall, faintly lit by the Stars, looked out upon the Hall as if they blessed it. Everything was as it always was; and yet I could not rid Myself of the feeling that something was happening.

It was very cold. I put on my shoes and a woollen jumper, and I walked to the Second North-Western Hall. All was empty; all was quiet; all was peaceful.

I passed through a Door on my right into

another Hall. Here I heard a faint sound. The sound repeated at irregular intervals and, as I walked on, it grew louder. It was like the distant bellow of an animal.

A faint blossoming of light emanated from a Door at the other end of the Hall. I had only just observed this when the light changed and brightened until it became a beam that sliced through the Darkness and illuminated the Statues on the Opposite Wall! Then, just as suddenly, it faded again.

I walked to the Door and peered inside.

There was someone in the next Hall — someone with a torch who was rapidly casting the beam from Wall to Wall, from Corner to Corner, searching the Darkness for something or someone. (This was the reason that the light had suddenly grown stronger and faded again.) The person was shouting: 'Raphael! Raphael! I know you're here!'

It was the Other.

'Raphael!' he shouted again.

Silence.

'You should never have come here!' he shouted.

Silence.

'I know every inch of this place! You can't escape! I'll find you in the end!'

Silence.

I slipped into the Hall, an action I performed with the utmost economy of movement. Nevertheless the Other must have glimpsed it out of the corner of his eye because he swung around and shone the torch on the Door I had just passed through, but he moved too suddenly, the torch jerked out of his hand and skittered across the Pavement. The light extinguished itself.

'Shit!' exclaimed the Other.

Darkness returned to the Hall. The Tides moved in the Halls below. The Other cast about, searching for his torch, muttering to himself.

My eyes, which had seen little when dazzled by the torch, began to adjust to the Starlight again. At first, I saw nothing but the quiet Hall, but then a flicker of movement passed along the Southern Wall, East to West. It was the merest suggestion of a grey shadow against the faintly gleaming Statues and I could almost have believed that I was imagining it. But I was not. It passed through a Door leading to the Fifth North-Western Hall.

16!

The Other had found the torch. He made it give out its beam again. Then he exited the Hall by one of the Northern Doors.

I waited until he had gone and then I ran rapidly, silently, after 16. I hid Myself in the

194

Door to the Fifth North-Western Hall.

16 was standing in the Hall. Like the Other, he had a beam of light; but unlike the Other, he was not casting it around aimlessly. He shone it steadily on the Walls of the Hall. The strong, silvery white light illuminated the beautiful Statues and gave to each one a strange new shadow, so that the Walls appeared to be thickly covered in immense black feathers. 16 moved the torch slowly, making the feather-shadows elongate, shrink, swoop and spin. But as for 16 himself, I could see nothing of him. He was a mere blot behind the dazzle of the light.

16 contemplated the Statues for several minutes. Then he turned the light away from the Walls and walked to a Door that led to the Sixth North-Western Hall. He checked the Jamb to reassure himself that the chalk mark he had made was still there and he passed through. I followed and hid Myself in the next Doorway.

In the Sixth North-Western Hall, 16 was shining his torch on the message that I had written. He stood motionless for a long moment. I had told him to reflect on his wickedness. Was that what he was doing? Suddenly he knelt and began to write rapidly.

No one has ever written to me before.

16 wrote for a long time, which in some obscure way pleased me. But then I thought: *Why are you pleased? Why does it matter if the message is long or short? You know you may not read it. If you read it, you will go mad.* Part of me (a very foolish part) felt that it would almost be worth going mad in order to read the message.

The Darkness in front of 16 coalesced into two wild black shapes that flapped and beat the Air. Startled, 16 leapt up with a cry of alarm.

It was only two rooks who had been awakened by the unusual activity and had come to see what was happening.

'Piss off!' cried 16. 'Piss off! Go away! I'm busy!'

16's voice was not at all what I was expecting.

I departed as silently as I had come. I made my way back to the Third Northern Hall and lay down on my bed. But my mind was too full for sleep.

I erase a message from 16

SECOND ENTRY FOR THE SEVENTEENTH DAY OF THE NINTH MONTH IN THE YEAR THE ALBATROSS CAME TO THE SOUTH-WESTERN HALLS

As soon as the Sun rose I fetched my Index

and my Journals. I opened the Index at R, but there was no entry for 'Raphael'.

I quickly ate some food and thanked the House for its Beneficence. I had a question that I needed to put to the Other but today was not one of the days when the Other and I meet, so I knew my question must wait.

I set off for the Sixth North-Western Hall. The rooks greeted me noisily, but I had no time to talk to them today. 16's message covered an area of the Pavement approximately 60 centimetres by 80 centimetres.

My heart beat fast in my chest. I glanced down:

I saw the words:

MY NAME IS . . .

I saw the words:

. . . LAURENCE ARNE-SAYLES . . .

I saw the words:

. . . ROOM WITH THE STATUES OF MINOTAURS . . .

What should I do? I knew that as long as the message existed I would experience a strong urge to read it. I decided that my only option was to destroy it.

I ran back to the Third Northern Hall and fetched an old shirt and some chalk. I say 'shirt'; in fact, the garment was so ragged that it scarcely deserved the name. I tore it in two. Then I ran back to the Sixth North-Western Hall. I tied one half of the shirt around my eyes as a blindfold. Holding the other half in my hand, I knelt down and began to sweep it over the surface of the Pavement, erasing 16's words.

After a couple of minutes, I removed the blindfold and looked. Bits of the message remained here and there.

COMPREHENSIBLE? MY
NAME
      LICE OFFI   READ THE FILES ON
YOUR DIS   IS VALENTINE
KETTER

      RTAINLY
GROOMED OTHER POTENTIAL VICTIMS AND I
    A DISCIPLE OF THE OCCULTIST LAURENCE
ARNE-SAY
  NK HE KNOWS THAT I HAVE PENETRATED TH
    EN HERE FOR ALMOST SIX YEARS, DID YO
      WAY OUT IS
LOCATE
      NED ME THAT YOU MAY BE SUFFERING
FROM

As none of this made much sense — at least at first glance — I was hopeful that it would not affect me. (So far I feel fine.) I knelt down and wrote a reply.

DEAR 16
AS LONG AS YOU REMAIN IN OUR HALLS THEN THE OTHER WILL TRY TO KILL YOU. HE HAS A GUN!

I HAVE ERASED YOUR MESSAGE WITH-OUT READING IT. YOUR WORDS HAVE NOT TOUCHED ME. YOU HAVE NOT MADE ME MAD. YOUR PLAN HAS FAILED.

PLEASE! RETURN TO THE FAR-DISTANT HALLS WHENCE YOU CAME!

PIRANESI

I question the Other

ENTRY FOR THE EIGHTEENTH DAY OF THE NINTH MONTH IN THE YEAR THE ALBATROSS CAME TO THE SOUTH-WESTERN HALLS

Today at ten o'clock I went to the Second South-Western Hall to meet the Other.

He was standing by the Empty Plinth. He wore a suit of dark brown wool and a shirt of dark olive. His gleaming shoes were a chestnut colour.

'I want to ask you something,' I said.

'OK.'

'Why have you not been honest with me?'

The Other put on a cold look. 'I am always honest with you,' he said.

'No,' I said. 'You are not. Why did you not tell me that 16 is a woman?'

The expression on the Other's face flickered from haughty denial, to irritation, to reluctant acquiescence in the space of about half a second. 'OK,' he conceded. 'I suppose that's fair enough. But I never said that she wasn't a woman.'

I rolled my eyes at this extraordinarily weak defence. 'I have been referring to 16 as "he" for months,' I said, 'and you have not corrected me — not once. Why not?'

The Other sighed. 'OK. The reason I didn't say anything is that I know you, Piranesi. You're a romantic. Oh, you talk about being a scientist and a disciple of reason — and most of the time you are. But you're also a romantic. I knew it was going to be hard enough as it was to convince you of the threat that 16 poses. But I thought it would be even harder once you knew she was a woman. You would be so much more interested in a woman. I thought you might even fall in love with her. I certainly didn't think you'd be able to stop yourself from talking to her. I know you may find this difficult to believe but I was actually looking out for you. It was so important that you didn't trust 16, because 16 is fundamentally untrustworthy. Do you see?'

There was a pause.

'Well,' I said. 'Thank you for looking out for me. I do not believe I would be so easily swayed in favour of a woman as you seem to suggest. Please do not keep things from me in future.'

'Fair enough,' said the Other. He frowned. 'Anyway, how did you know?' His voice became sharp with alarm. 'You haven't spoken to her, have you?'

'No. I saw her in the Sixth North-Western Hall and I heard her voice. She did not see me.'

'You heard her?' The Other was even more alarmed. 'Who was she speaking to?'

'The rooks.'

'Oh.' Pause. 'How bizarre.'

I decide to look up Laurence Arne-Sayles in the Index

ENTRY FOR THE NINETEENTH DAY OF THE NINTH MONTH IN THE YEAR THE ALBATROSS CAME TO THE SOUTH-WESTERN HALLS

The Other is right about one thing. I am not as rational as I thought. I used to smile (secretly) at the Other whenever I saw him acting out of self-love or arrogance or pride. My own actions were, I was sure, guided solely by Reason. But I was only deceiving Myself. A rational person would never have spoken to the Prophet in the First North-Eastern Hall. A rational person would have kept on cleaning the Pavement of the Sixth North-Western Hall until every trace of 16's message was erased.

It is not the fact 16 is a woman that fascinates and excites me — or at least, not entirely; it is the fact that she is another human being. I want to learn everything I can about her — or as much as I can learn without going mad. (That is the tricky part.)

I have not told the Other about the message that 16 wrote. Nor have I told him that after I erased it there were little half phrases and sentences remaining and that I left these untouched.

. . . IS VALENTINE KETTER(LEY) . . . This refers to the Other. The Prophet said that the Other's name is Val Ketterley. It is not surprising that 16 writes about the Other since, according to the Other, 16 is obsessed with him and wants to destroy him.

... (CE)RTAINLY GROOMED OTHER POTENTIAL VICTIMS AND I ... Is 16 boasting of her victims? Of the harm she has done and intends to do? Unclear.

... A DISCIPLE OF THE OCCULTIST LAURENCE ARNE-SAY(LES) ... Everything keeps leading back to this one same person, Laurence Arne-Sayles, who I believe is identical with the Prophet.

... (BE)EN HERE FOR ALMOST SIX-YEARS, DID YO(U) ... Unclear what this refers to.

WAY OUT IS LOCATE(D) ... A puzzling fragment. 16 appears to want to tell me about an exit. But I know these Halls, all their entrances and exits. She does not.

I have looked up 16 in my Index, using the name the Other called her. She is not there. So I shall look up Laurence Arne-Sayles.

Laurence Arne-Sayles

SECOND ENTRY FOR THE NINETEENTH DAY OF THE NINTH MONTH IN THE YEAR THE ALBATROSS CAME TO THE SOUTH-WESTERN HALLS

Once again I took my Index and Journals to the Fifth Northern Hall and sat down opposite the Statue of the Gorilla. May his

Strength and Resolution give me courage! I opened the Index at A.

There were twenty-nine entries for Laurence Arne-Sayles. Some of these were only a line or two; others ran to several pages. I skim-read about half of them, but was no wiser. The information they contained varied wildly: lists of publications, biography, quotations, descriptions of people Arne-Sayles had met in prison. I came across one entitled: *Laurence Arne-Sayles: pros and cons of writing a book,* and, since the idea of writing a book appeals to me strongly, I read this with interest.

Possible project: a book about Arne-Sayles, exploring the idea of transgressive thinkers — people whose ideas go beyond what is thought acceptable within a discipline (or even possible). Heretics.

Not sure whether this is a good use of my time or not. Pros and cons.

- Angharad Scott did a passable job with her book, *A Long Spoon: Laurence Arne-Sayles and His Circle.* (Con)
- That said, Scott's strength is biography, not analysis. She would be the first to admit this. (Pro? Neutral?)
- Scott herself is gracious, encouraging,

willing to help. She would like to see another book written. Gave me quite a lot of background information and has indicated that there's more to come. See notes of phone call with Angharad Scott, page 153. (Pro)

- Arne-Sayles is quite a sexy subject? Major scandal, trial, prison sentence etc. (Pro)
- Arne-Sayles is the perfect example of a transgressive thinker — transgressive in more ways than one — morally, intellectually, sexually, criminally. (Pro)
- The extraordinary effect he had on his followers, getting them to believe that they had seen other worlds etc. (Pro)
- Arne-Sayles refuses to speak to academics/writers/journalists. (Con)
- His close associates — the people who knew him at the time he claimed to be passing to and fro between this world and others — are few. Of that number several have disappeared and most of the others won't talk to journalists. (Con)
- Tali Hughes was the only student of Arne-Sayles's who was willing to talk to Angharad Scott. According to Scott, Hughes is emotionally unstable and

possibly delusional. James Ritter spoke to a journalist (Lysander Weeks) in 2010. Might be worth a conversation? According to Weeks, Ritter works as a caretaker in Manchester Town Hall. Worth checking if Weeks himself is working on a book? (Neither pro nor con — neutral)

- Mystery of the people connected to Arne-Sayles who disappeared: Maurizio Giussani, Stanley Ovenden, Sylvia D'Agostino. (This is a strong pull for readers and therefore a definite pro. Unless I disappear myself, in which case, con.)
- Spending a long time writing about a deeply unpleasant man could be emotionally taxing. It's universally agreed that Arne-Sayles is malicious, vindictive, manipulative, spiteful, arrogant, a complete and utter prick. (Con)

Not sure where this comes out. Very slightly con?

This told me very little about Laurence Arne-Sayles himself. It was the last entry of all that was the most informative. It was called:

Notes for a talk to be given at Torn and Blinded: a Festival of Alternative Ideas, Glastonbury, 24–27 May 2013

Laurence Arne-Sayles began with the idea that the Ancients had a different way of relating to the world, that they experienced it as something that interacted with them. When they observed the world, the world observed them back. If, for example, they travelled in a boat on a river, then the river was in some way aware of carrying them on its back and had in fact agreed to it. When they looked up to the stars, the constellations were not simply patterns enabling them to organise what they saw, they were vehicles of meaning, a never-ending flow of information. The world was constantly speaking to Ancient Man.

All of this was more or less within the bounds of conventional philosophical history, but where Arne-Sayles diverged from his peers was in his insistence that this dialogue between the Ancients and the world was not simply something that happened in their heads; it was something that happened in the actual world. The way the Ancients perceived the world was the way the world truly was. This gave them extraordinary influence and power. Reality was not only capable of taking part in a dialogue — intelligible and articulate — it was also persuadable. Nature was willing to bend to men's desires, to lend them its attributes. Seas could be parted, men could turn into birds and fly away, or into foxes and hide in dark woods, castles could be made out of clouds.

Eventually the Ancients ceased to speak and listen to the World. When this happened the World did not simply fall silent, it changed. Those aspects of the world that had been in constant communication with Men — whether you call them energies, powers, spirits, angels or demons — no longer had a place or a reason to stay and so they departed. There was, in Arne-Sayles's view, an actual, real disenchantment.

In his first published work on the subject (*The Curlew's Cry,* Allen & Unwin, 1969) Arne-Sayles said that these powers of the Ancients were irretrievably lost, but by the time he wrote his second book (*What the Wind Has Taken,* Allen & Unwin, 1976) he was not so sure. He had experimented with ritual magic and now thought it might be possible to get some of the powers back, providing you had a physical link with a person who had once possessed them. The best sort of link would be actual remains — the body or part of the body of the person in question.

In 1976 Manchester Museum had in its collection four preserved bog bodies, dated between 10 BCE and 200 CE, and named after the peat bog in which they had been found: Marepool in Cheshire. They were:

- Marepool I (a headless body)
- Marepool II (a complete body)
- Marepool III (a head, but not one that belonged to Marepool I)
- and Marepool IV (a second complete body).

Arne-Sayles was most interested in Marepool III, the head. Arne-Sayles said that he had performed a divination that had identified the head as belonging to a king and a seer. The knowledge the seer had possessed was exactly what Arne-Sayles needed to further his own researches. Combined with his own theories, it would result in a watershed moment for human understanding. In May 1976 Arne-Sayles wrote a letter to the director of the museum, asking to borrow the head so that he could perform a magical rite of his own invention, transfer the seer's knowledge to himself and so usher in a New Age for Mankind. To Arne-Sayles's astonishment, the director refused. In June Arne-Sayles persuaded fifty or so students to demonstrate outside the museum against this blinkered and outdated thinking. The students carried placards that said 'Free the Head'. Ten days later there was a second demonstration, during which a window was broken and there was a scuffle with the police. After this, Arne-Sayles seemed to lose interest in the bog bodies.

At the end of December the museum closed for Christmas. When it re-opened in the New Year, the staff discovered there had been a break-in. There was evidence of people having camped inside the museum. Food crumbs, biscuit packets and other litter were scattered about. There was a smell of cannabis. 'Free the Head' appeared again painted on a wall, and burnt stubs of candles were stuck to the floor. The candles formed a circle. Nothing appeared to have been taken but the cabinet in which Marepool III was displayed had been broken and the head had been handled. Some candle wax and fragments of mistletoe adhered to it.

The police and the museum staff naturally suspected Arne-Sayles. Arne-Sayles however had an alibi; he had spent the Midwinter festival with some wealthy neo-pagans at a farmhouse in Exmoor. The neo-pagans (people called Brooker) confirmed this. The Brookers revered Arne-Sayles as an extraordinary genius and a sort of pagan saint. The police did not think their testimony was reliable but had no means of refuting it.

No one was charged with the break-in at the museum, but in his next book (*The Half-Seen Door,* Allen & Unwin, 1979) Arne-Sayles talked about a Romano-British seer called Addedomarus who had been able to walk a path between worlds.

In 2001, while Laurence Arne-Sayles was in prison, a man called Tony Myers walked into a police station in London and asked to make a statement. He said that while a student at Manchester University he had broken into the museum on Christmas Day 1976.He had smashed a window, climbed in and then opened the doors to let other people in. He had witnessed Arne-Sayles performing a ritual with two other men. He thought that the two men were Valentine Ketterley and Robin Bannerman, but it was a long time ago and he could not be sure.

Myers said that at one point he had seen the lips of Marepool III move but he had not heard any words.

Myers was not prosecuted.

Arne-Sayles himself never wrote about the ritual he used with Marepool III. In the late seventies he was in any case changing his ideas. He was less concerned with the content of lost beliefs and powers and more interested in where they had gone. Based on his earlier idea that the lost beliefs and powers constituted a sort of energy, he said this energy could not have simply winked out of existence; it must have gone somewhere. This was the beginning of his most famous idea, the Theory of Other Worlds. Simply put, it said that when knowledge or power went out of this world it did two things: first, it created another place; and second, it left a hole, a door between this world where it had once existed and the new place it had made.

Picture it, said Arne-Sayles, like rainwater lying on a field. The next day the field is dry. Where has the rainwater gone? Some has evaporated into the air. Some has been drunk by plants and animals. But some has seeped down into the earth. This happens over and over again. For decades, centuries, millennia, the water, seeping down, makes a crack in the rock under the earth; then it wears the crack into a hole; then it wears the hole into a cave entrance — a kind of door in fact. Beyond the door the water keeps flowing and it hollows out caverns and carves out pillars. Somewhere, said Arne-Sayles, there must be a passage, a door between us and wherever magic had gone. It might be very small. It might not be entirely stable. Like the entrance to an underground cave it might be in danger of collapse. But it would be there. And if it was there, it was possible to find it.

In 1979 he published his third, most famous book, *The Half-Seen Door,* in which he discussed these ideas of other worlds and described how, after a certain amount of struggle, he entered one of them.

Extract from *The Half-Seen Door* by Laurence Arne-Sayles

Once you have found the door, it is always with you. You simply look for it and there it is. Finding it the first time is where the difficulty lies. Following the insights that Addedomarus had given me, what I eventually concluded was that it was necessary to cleanse one's vision in order to see the door. To do this one must return to the place, the geographical location where one last believed the world to be fluid, responsive to oneself. In short one must return to the last place in which one had stood before the iron hand of modern rationality gripped one's mind.

For me this was the garden of the house where I grew up in Lyme Regis. Unfortunately by 1979 the house had gone through several hands. The then-owners (dull exemplars of the prevailing mediocrity) were unsympathetic to my request to be allowed to stand in the garden for several hours performing an Ancient Celtic ritual. No matter. I discovered from a friendly milkman when they would be taking their holiday, returned at that time and 'broke in'.

The day I entered the garden was cold, rainy, grey. I stood on the lawn in the pouring rain, surrounded by the roses my mother had planted (though now forced to share their beds with flowers of insufferable vulgarity). Behind the rain were masses of colour — white, apricot, pink, gold and red.

I focussed on my memory of being a

child in that garden, of the last time when both the world and my mind had been unfettered. I had stood before the roses in my blue wool romper suit. I gripped a metal soldier in my hand, his paint somewhat peeling.

To my surprise I discovered that the act of remembering was extremely potent. My mind was immediately freed, my vision cleansed. The long, complicated ritual that I had prepared became completely unnecessary. I no longer saw or felt the rain. I was standing in the clear, strong sunlight of early childhood. The colours of the roses were supernaturally bright.

All around me doors into other worlds began appearing but I knew the one I wanted, the one into which everything forgotten flows. The edges of that door were frayed and worn by the passage of old ideas leaving this world.

The door was perfectly visible now. It was in a gap between the *Antoine Rivoire* and the *Coquette des Blanches.* I stepped through.

I was standing in a vast chamber with stone floor and walls of marble. I was surrounded by eight massive statues, each one different, each depicting a minotaur. A great marble staircase rose up to a great height and descended to an equally disorientating depth. A strange thundering — as of a sea — filled my ears . . .

I remain calm

The description of Laurence Arne-Sayles's theories contained in my Journals corresponds closely to what the Prophet himself said. (More evidence that they are one and the same person!) I was pleased to rediscover the name Addedomarus, and to have its correct spelling. This was the name that the Other called on in his ritual three months ago! I feel certain that the Other learnt of Addedomarus from Laurence Arne-Sayles. ('All his ideas are mine,' the Prophet said.)

One sentence puzzles me: *The world was constantly speaking to Ancient Man.* I do not understand why this sentence is in the past tense. The World still speaks to me every day.

I believe I am better at reading these Journal entries than I was at first. I remain calm even when faced with the most obscure

216

language. Words and phrases that pulsate with mysterious energy — words such as 'Manchester' and 'police station' — no longer discompose me. I seem, almost unconsciously, to have fallen into a habit of treating these entries as if they were the writings of an oracle or seer, someone in a frenzied or inspired state who imparts knowledge, albeit in a strange and not easily processed form.

Perhaps I was indeed in an altered state of consciousness when I wrote them? I find this theory persuasive, but it leaves several questions unanswered. What did I do to achieve this altered state? And why, when I have always thought of Myself as a scientist, did I begin this practice in the first place?

There will be a Great Flood

ENTRY FOR THE TWENTY-FIRST DAY OF THE NINTH MONTH IN THE YEAR THE ALBATROSS CAME TO THE SOUTH-WESTERN HALLS

One of my regular tasks is to maintain a Table of Tides. In order to do this I rely on my observations and on a set of equations that I have invented. Every few months I perform my calculations and make sure that there are no Extraordinary Occurrences in the coming weeks. I have been so occupied recently that I have rather neglected this work. This morning I sat down to apply Myself to it and immediately discovered something Highly Alarming — a Conjunction of Four Tides in less than a week's time!

I was shocked to think how close I had come to missing this event altogether! My last set of calculations were for a period that ended more than two weeks ago. I had neglected my duties and put Myself and the Other in mortal danger!

In my agitation I leapt up and walked rapidly up and down the Hall. *Oh, fuck! Fuck! Fuck! Fuck! Fuck!* I muttered to Myself. *Fuck! Fuck! Fuck! Fuck!* After a minute or two of walking uselessly to and fro, I spoke to Myself sternly, telling Myself that it was no good bewailing the Past; what was needed now was to plan for the Future.

I sat down again and set Myself to doing further calculations in order to understand more accurately what was likely to happen. Depending on the Force and Volume of the Waters — which are difficult to predict with exactness — between forty and a hundred Halls will be flooded.

Fortunately today was a Friday, one of the days when I have my regular meetings with the Other. I arrived in the Second South-Western Hall almost half an hour early, so anxious was I to speak with him.

The moment he appeared I said, 'I have something to tell you.'

He frowned and opened his mouth to protest; he does not like me to take charge of the meeting but on this occasion I overrode him. 'There will be a Great Flood!' I declared. 'If we do not prepare ourselves properly, there is a very real danger that we will be swept away and drowned.'

Immediately he was all attention. 'Drowned? When?'

'In six days' time. On Thursday. The Flood will begin to rise approximately half an hour before midday. A High Tide from the Eastern Halls will be followed by . . .'

'Thursday?' He relaxed again. 'Oh, that's OK. I won't be here on Thursday.'

'Where will you be?' I asked, surprised.

'Somewhere else,' he said. 'It's not important. Don't worry about it.'

'Oh, I see,' I said. 'Well, that is good. The Flood will be centred around a point 0.8 kilometres to the North-West of the First Vestibule. It is vital that you are out of the Path of the Waters.'

'I'll be fine,' said the Other. 'Will you be OK?'

'Oh, yes,' I said. 'Thanks for asking. I shall walk to the Southern Halls.'

'That's good.'

'That only leaves 16,' I said without thinking. 'I need to . . .' I stopped. 'That is . . .' I began and stopped again.

There was a pause.

'What?' said the Other, sharply. 'What are you talking about? What's any of this got to do with 16?'

'I only mean that 16 is not a native of these Halls,' I said. 'She will not know that a Great Flood is coming.'

'No, I suppose not. So what?'

'I do not want her to drown,' I said.

'Trust me, Piranesi. That would solve all sorts of problems. But, in any case, it doesn't really matter one way or the other. You've no way of getting in contact with 16 and so you couldn't warn her even if you wanted to.'

There was a silence.

'That's right, isn't it?' said the Other. 'You haven't spoken to her?' He gave me a sharp, appraising look.

'I have not,' I said.

'Not now? Not in the past?'

'Not now. Not in the past.'

'Well, there you are then. Whatever happens it's not your responsibility. I wouldn't worry about it.'

Another pause.

'Well,' said the Other at last. 'I expect you've got things to do.'

'Many things to do.'

'Preparing for this inundation and so forth.'

'Oh, yes.'

'Well, I'll leave you to it then.' He turned and walked towards the First Vestibule.

'Goodbye,' I called. 'Goodbye!'

ARE YOU MATTHEW ROSE SORENSEN?

SECOND ENTRY FOR THE TWENTY-FIRST DAY OF THE NINTH MONTH IN THE YEAR THE ALBATROSS CAME TO THE SOUTH-WESTERN HALLS

My course of action was clear. I must go immediately to the Sixth North-Western Hall and write a message to 16 warning her of the coming Flood!

As I walked I thought about the last message I had left her — the one begging her to leave these Halls. Perhaps in the intervening time she had replied. Perhaps the reply would be something like:

Dear Piranesi
You are right. Today I will return to my own Halls.

Sincerely
16

If that was the case I could stop worrying about her drowning in the Flood.

But deep down I hoped that she had not gone back to her own Halls. Strange as it may seem, I knew that I would miss her if she had. Other than 16, there is only Myself and the Other in the World and (it may surprise you to read this) the Other is not always the best of company. I was looking forward to seeing if 16 had written me another message, even though I would not dare read it. I suppose that what I really hoped for was that she would write something like:

Dear Piranesi
Reading your useful and informative messages, I have come to realise that if only I were to cast off my wickedness then we could be friends. Let us meet and talk. I promise not to make you

mad. In return will you teach me how to be not-wicked?

Hopefully

16

I arrived at the Sixth North-Western Hall. The rooks greeted me noisily. On the Pavement I found the remnants of 16's last message and my own message. But there was nothing new. 16 had not written to me. I was disappointed, but I told Myself that this was only to be expected; if I kept erasing 16's messages without reading them it was hardly likely that she would keep writing.

I got out my chalk and knelt down. Beneath my last message I wrote:

DEAR 16
IN SIX DAYS' TIME A GREAT FLOOD WILL RISE IN THESE HALLS. EVERYWHERE WILL BE UNDER WATER TO A DEPTH GREATER THAN YOUR HEIGHT OR MINE.

ACCORDING TO MY ESTIMA-TIONS THE PERILOUS REGION-WILL STRETCH AS FAR AS:

SIX HALLS WEST OF HERE

FOUR HALLS NORTH OF HERE

FIVE HALLS EAST OF HERE

SIX HALLS SOUTH OF HERE

THE FLOOD WILL LAST THREE TO FOUR HOURS AFTER WHICH IT WILL BEGIN TO SUBSIDE.

PLEASE ABSENT YOURSELF FROM THESE HALLS AT THIS TIME OR YOU WILL BE IN DANGER. THERE WILL BE <u>STRONG CURRENTS</u>. SHOULD YOU FIND YOURSELF CAUGHT BY THE FLOOD, THEN CLIMB QUICKLY! THE STATUES ARE GRACIOUS AND WILL PRO-TECT YOU.

PIRANESI

I considered the message carefully. It was as clear as I could make it except for one thing. 'In six days' time' was only meaningful if 16 knew the day on which I had written the message and how would she know that?

I could write today's date, but that was according to a calendar of my own invention and it seemed unlikely that 16 had invented the same calendar as me.

POSTSCRIPT: TODAY IS THE SECOND DAY OF THE NEW MOON. THE DAY OF THE FLOOD WILL BE THE FIRST DAY OF THE QUARTER MOON.

All I could hope for was that 16 had not stopped visiting this Hall altogether and that she saw this warning.

Before the Flood comes I need to gather up all my plastic bowls — the ones I use to collect Fresh Water — so that they are not carried off by the Waters. I knew that there were two not far from the Sixth North-Western Hall, in the Eighteenth North-Western Hall on the other side of the Twenty-Fourth Vestibule. I thought I might as well get them now as I was in the Vicinity.

I walked to the Twenty-Fourth Vestibule. This Vestibule is notable for a shallow, sloping bank of white marble pebbles, which partially blocks the Mouth of the Staircase leading to the Lower Halls. The pebbles have been deposited here over time by the Tides. They have smooth, rounded shapes, delightful to the touch; they are a pure white colour with a beautiful, glowing translucency. I have climbed over this bank many times to fish and gather shellfish. Always I dislodge a few pebbles, but never so many that it alters the overall shape of the bank.

The first thing that I saw today was that some of the pebbles had been removed. There was a hollow in the side of the bank where no hollow had been before. I was astonished by this. Who could have done it? I have seen rooks and crows take small stones to break open shellfish, but birds do not move a great number of stones for no reason.

I looked around. Something white was scattered over the Pavement in the North-Eastern Corner of the Vestibule.

I approached. Too late I realised that the pebbles formed shapes. Words! Words made by 16! Before I had time to tear my eyes away I had read the entire message! In letters approximately 25 centimetres high it said:

ARE YOU MATTHEW ROSE SO-RENSEN?

Matthew Rose Sorensen. A name. Three words that make up a name.

Matthew Rose Sorensen . . .

An image rose up in front of me, like a

memory or a vision.

. . . I seemed to be standing at the junction of many streets in a city. Dark rain poured down on me from a dark sky. Lights, lights, lights sparkled everywhere! The lights were many coloured and all were mirrored in the wet tarmac. Buildings rose up on every side. Cars rushed past. Words and images were inscribed on the buildings. Dark forms filled the streets; I thought at first that they were statues, but they moved and I saw they were people. Thousands upon thousands of people. More people than I had ever conceived of before. Too many people. The mind could not contain the thought of so many. And everything smelt of rain, and metal, and staleness. This vision had a name and its name was . . .

But, just as the word trembled on the brink of conscious thought, it vanished and so too did the image. I was in the Real World again.

I staggered and almost fell. I felt dizzy, parched, breathless.

I looked up at the Statues on the Walls of the Vestibule. 'I need water,' I told them hoarsely. 'Bring me a drink of water.'

But they were only Statues and they could not bring me water. They could only look down on me with Calm Nobility.

227

I am . . .

16 had found a way to fulfil her dark purpose and make me mad! I had erased her last message and what happened? She had constructed a message I could not possibly erase without reading it!

Are you Matthew Rose Sorensen?

I am . . . I stuttered. *I am . . .*

At first I could get no further than this.

I am . . . I am the Beloved Child of the House.

Yes.

Immediately I felt calmer. Was any other identity even necessary? I did not think that it was. Another thought struck me.

I am Piranesi.

But I knew that I did not really believe this. Piranesi is not my name. (I am almost certain that Piranesi is not my name.)

I once asked the Other why he called me Piranesi.

He laughed in a slightly embarrassed way. *Oh, that* (he said). *Well, originally it was a sort of joke I suppose. I have to call you something. And it suits you. It's a name as-*

sociated with labyrinths. You don't mind, do you? I'll stop if you don't like it.

I do not mind, I said. *And, as you say, you have to call me something.*

The Silence of the House feels charged with expectation as I write these words. It seems to be waiting for something extraordinary to happen.

Are you Matthew Rose Sorensen?

How could I possibly answer this question when I had no idea who Matthew Rose Sorensen was? Perhaps the thing to do was to look up Matthew Rose Sorensen in the Index?

I went to the Eighteenth North-Western Hall and had a long drink of water. It was delicious and refreshing (it had been a Cloud only hours before). I rested a moment. Then I made my way to the Second Northern Hall where I fetched out my Index and Journals.

Are you Matthew Rose Sorensen?

The fact that Matthew Rose Sorensen had three names made him tricky to locate in the Index. I looked for him first under S. Nothing. I looked for him under R. There were three entries.

Rose Sorensen, Matthew: publications 2006–2010, Journal no. 21, page 6

Rose Sorensen, Matthew: publications
2011–12, Journal no. 22, pages 144–45
Rose Sorensen, Matthew, bio for Torn and
Blinded: Journal no. 22, page 200

The last entry looked most promising.

Matthew Rose Sorensen is the English
son of a half-Danish, half-Scottish father
and a Ghanaian mother. He originally
studied mathematics, but his interest soon
migrated (via the philosophy of mathematics and the history of ideas) to his current
field of study: transgressive thinking. He is
writing a book about Laurence Arne-
Sayles, a man who transgressed against
science, against reason and against law.

I found it interesting that Matthew Rose
Sorensen believed that Laurence Arne-
Sayles had denied Science and Reason. In
this he was not correct. The Prophet was a
scientist and a lover of Reason. I spoke out
loud to the Empty Air.

'I do not agree with you,' I said.

I was trying to summon up Matthew Rose
Sorensen, to trick him into revealing himself. If he really was some forgotten part of
Myself, then he would not like to be contra-
dicted; he would argue his position.

But it did not work. He did not rise up

from some shadowy recess of my mind. He remained an emptiness, a silence, an absence.

I turned to the other two entries.

The first was simply a list.

' *"Now, here, now, always": J. B. Priestley's Time Plays'*, Tempus, *Volume 6: 85–92*

Embrace/Tolerate/Vilify/Destroy: How Academia treats Outsider Ideas, *Manchester University Press, 2008*

'Sources of outsider mathematics: Srinivasa Ramanujan and the Goddess', Intellectual History Quarterly, *Volume 25:204–238*, Manchester University Press

The second entry was just more of the same.

'Timey-Wimey: Steven Moffat, Blink and J.W. Dunne's theories of Time', Journal of Space, Time and Everything, *Volume 64: 42–68*, University of Minnesota Press

' *"The circles that you find in the windmills of your mind": The Importance of Labyrinths in Laurence Arne-Sayles's Exploitation of his Adherents'*, Review of Psychedelia and the Counterculture, *Volume 35, issue 4*

231

'The Gargoyle on the Cathedral Roof: Laurence Arne-Sayles and Academia', Intellectual History Quarterly, *Volume 28: 119–152*, Manchester University Press
Outsider Thinking: A Very Short Introduction, *OUP, pub. 31 May 2012*
'Time-travelling Architecture': article on Paul Enoch and Bradford for the Guardian, *28 July 2012*

I let out a long snort of frustration. This was utterly useless! Other than the fact that Matthew Rose Sorensen was interested in Laurence Arne-Sayles (which in no way differentiated him from everyone else in the World) I had learnt nothing. I felt a strong urge to shake my Journal, as if I could somehow shake more information out of it.

I sat for a long time thinking.

There was one person that I had not yet looked up in the Index and that was the Other. I had not thought of it until now. But perhaps if I read about the Other and found Matthew Rose Sorensen mentioned there, then . . . I paused. Then what? Then perhaps I would be able to judge whether the Other knew Matthew Rose Sorensen, and ultimately whether Matthew Rose Sorensen was me.

There did not seem to be any harm in trying. In fact, of all the names in the World that I might look up, the Other seemed the safest. He and I had been friends for years. I opened the Index under O. I counted seventy-four entries for the Other. I had written far more about the Other than about any other subject. In fact, I had already been obliged to reallocate two pages from the letter P to accommodate them all.

I found:

Other, the, Rituals performed by
Other, the, Discourses on the Great and
    Secret Knowledge
Other, the, lends me a camera so that I
    can take pictures of the Drowned Halls
Other, the, asks me to make him a map
    of the Stars
Other, the, asks me to draw a map of the
    Halls immediately surrounding the First
    Vestibule
Other, the, proposes that the Statues
    form a sort of code, which we might be
    able to decipher

and on and on and on. Until I reached the most recent entries:

Other, the, uses the nonsense word

I skim-read a few entries. I read how the Other had performed various Rituals at which I had assisted. I read how clever the Other was, how scientific, how insightful, how handsome. I read detailed descriptions of his clothes. This was mildly interesting, but in no way helped me with my present problem. Unlike the entries on Stanley Ovenden, Maurizio Giussani, Sylvia D'Agostino and Laurence Arne-Sayles, none of the entries on the Other was new to me. They contained no arcane words or phrases that seemed to pulsate with hidden meaning (words such as 'Whalley Range' and 'doctor's surgery'). All the events were ones I remembered clearly. And nowhere did the name Matthew Rose Sorensen appear.

I remembered that the Prophet had called the Other, Ketterley. So I turned to K.

There were eight entries. The first was on page 187 of Journal no. 2 (previously Journal no. 22).

Dr Valentine Andrew Ketterley. Born 1955 in Barcelona. Brought up in Poole, Dorset. (The Ketterleys are an old Dorsetshire family.) Son of Colonel Ranulph Andrew Ketterley, soldier and occultist.

Valentine Ketterley was a student of Laurence Arne-Sayles and afterwards a research fellow in Social Anthropology at Manchester. Married Clémence Hubert 1985. Divorced 1991. Two children. In 1992 Ketterley left Manchester and took up a teaching post at UCL. In June of the same year he wrote a letter to *The Times* in which he publicly repudiated Arne-Sayles, accusing him of deliberately misleading and manipulating students, feeding them pseudo-mysticism and stories of other worlds. Ketterley called on the University of Manchester to dismiss Arne-Sayles. (The university did not do so until 1997 when Arne-Sayles was arrested for false imprisonment.)

In recent years Ketterley has refused to answer any questions about Arne-Sayles.

Question: is it worth getting in touch with Ketterley to see if he will talk to me? Lives somewhere near Battersea Park.

Action point: make a list of questions for Dr Ketterley.

I was back on familiar ground. The entry was the usual mishmash of words that held a clear meaning and words whose meaning was obscure — always presuming that they meant anything at all. I noted with interest the re-emergence of the mysterious word 'Battersea' (and saw that it ought not to be hyphenated).

I returned to the Index to find the location of the next entry and it was then that I noticed something rather strange. The remaining entries — there were seven of them — were all on consecutive pages. The last ten pages of Journal no. 22 and the first thirty-two pages of Journal no. 23 were all about Ketterley.

I opened Journal no. 2 (previously Journal no. 22). The last ten pages — the very pages that I wanted — were missing; just a few torn edges remained in the spine. I opened Journal no. 3 (previously Journal no. 23) and found the same thing. The thirty-two pages with information about Ketterley were gone.

I sat back, mystified.

Who could have done this? Could it have been the Prophet? I knew that he detested Ketterley. Perhaps his hatred would cause him to destroy writing about his enemy? Or could it have been 16? 16 hated Reason. Perhaps she also hated Writing, a medium by which Reason can pass from one Person to another. But that made no sense. 16 had employed Writing to leave me a long message. And in any case how could the Prophet or 16 find my Journals? They are kept (as I have explained) in my messenger bag, which is hidden behind the Statue of an Angel caught on a Rose Bush in the North-Eastern Corner of the Second Northern Hall. It is one Statue among thousands, among millions. How would either of them know where to look?

I sat for a long time and thought. I had no recollection of tearing out the pages. But realistically who else could have done it? And I have known for some time that many things have happened of which I have no recollection. I have *done* many things of which I have no recollection (such as write these mysterious entries). Which meant I could have torn out the pages.

But if I had torn out the pages, what had happened to them? Where had they gone?

I fetched the scraps of paper that I found in the Eighty-Eighth Western Hall. I took out a few and spread them out so that I could examine them. One — a corner piece — bore the numeral 231. It was a page number from Journal no. 2.

Quickly — almost feverishly — I began to put the pieces together. There were approximately thirty entries covering a period that I had designated 15 November 2012 to 20 December 2012. The longest entry was titled: *The events of 15 November 2012.*

■ ■ ■ ■

PART 5
VALENTINE
KETTERLEY

■ ■ ■ ■

The events of 15 November 2012

I visited him in mid-November. It was just after four, a cold blue twilight. The afternoon had been stormy and the lights of the cars were pixelated by rain; the pavements collaged with wet black leaves.

When I got to his house I heard music playing. A requiem. I waited for him to answer the door to an accompaniment of Berlioz.

The door opened.

'Dr Ketterley?' I said.

He was between fifty and sixty, tall and slender. A handsome man. He had an ascetic-looking head with high cheekbones and forehead. His hair and eyes were dark and his skin was olive-coloured. His hair was receding, but only a little, and he had a neatly trimmed, slightly pointed beard with more grey in it than his hair.

'Yes,' he said. 'And you are Matthew Rose

Sorensen.'

I agreed that I was.

'Come in,' he said.

I remember how the smell of rain that pervaded the streets did not die away as I entered, but somehow intensified; inside the house there was a smell of rain, clouds and air, a smell of limitless space. A smell of the sea.

Which made no sense at all in a Victorian terraced house in Battersea.

He led me to a sitting room. The Berlioz was playing. He turned down the volume but it still played in the background of our conversation, the soundtrack of catastrophe.

I placed my messenger bag on the floor. He brought coffee.

'You're an academic, I understand,' I said.

'I *was* an academic,' he explained with a slight weariness. 'Until about fifteen years ago. I'm in private practice as a psychologist now. Academia was never very welcoming to me. I had the wrong sort of ideas and the wrong sort of friends.'

'I suppose the Arne-Sayles connection didn't do you any favours?'

'Well, quite. People still think I must have known about his crimes. I didn't.'

'Do you still see him?' I asked.

'God, no! Not for twenty years.' He looked

242

at me speculatively. 'Have *you* spoken to Laurence?'

'No. I've written to him of course. But so far he's refused to see me.'

'Sounds about right.'

'I thought perhaps he didn't want to talk to me because he feels ashamed of the past,' I said.

Ketterley gave a short, sharp, humourless laugh. 'Hardly. Laurence has no shame. He's just perverse. If someone says white, he'll say black. If you say you want to see him, then he won't want to see you. That's just the way he is.'

I lifted my messenger bag on to my lap and fetched out my journal. As well as my current journal I also had with me the previous volume of my journal (which I referred to almost every day); the index to my journals; and a blank notebook that would form the next volume of my journal (I was very close to the end of the current one).

I opened my current journal and began to write.

He watched with interest. 'You use physical pen and paper?'

'I use a journal system for all my notes. I find that it's much the best way for keeping track of information.'

'And are you a good record keeper?' he

asked. 'On the whole?'

'I'm an excellent record keeper. On the whole.'

'Interesting,' he said.

'Why? Do you want to offer me a job?' I asked.

He laughed. 'I don't know. Maybe.' He paused. 'What is it that you're actually after?'

I explained that I was chiefly interested in transgressive ideas, in the people who formulate them, and how they are received by the various disciplines — religion, art, literature, science, mathematics and so forth. 'And Laurence Arne-Sayles is the transgressive thinker *par excellence*. He crossed so many boundaries. He wrote about magic and pretended it was science. He convinced a group of highly intelligent people that there were other worlds and he could take them there. He was gay when it was still illegal. He kidnapped a man and to this day no one knows why.'

Ketterley said nothing. His face was a discouraging blank. He looked more bored than anything.

'I realise that all of this happened a long time ago,' I offered with a stab at empathy.

'I have an excellent memory,' he said coldly.

'Oh. Well, that's good. Just at the moment I'm trying to build up a picture of what it was like at Manchester in the first half of the eighties. Working with Arne-Sayles. What the atmosphere was like. What sort of things he was saying to you. What sort of possibilities he was conjuring up. That kind of thing.'

'Yes,' mused Ketterley, speaking apparently to himself, 'people always use words like that about Laurence. *Conjuring.*'

'You object to the word?'

'Of course I object to the fucking word,' he said irritably. 'You're suggesting that Laurence was some sort of stage magician and we were all his wide-eyed dupes. It wasn't like that at all. He liked you to argue with him. He liked you to put the rationalist point of view.'

'And then . . . ?'

'And then he demolished you. His theories weren't just smoke and mirrors. Far from it. He'd thought everything through. It was perfectly coherent as far as it went. And he wasn't afraid to merge intellect with imagination. His description of the thinking of Pre-Modern Man was more persuasive than anything else I've come across.' He paused. 'I'm not saying that he wasn't manipulative. He was certainly that.'

'But I thought you just said . . . ?'

'On a personal level. In his relationships he was manipulative. On an intellectual level he was honest, but on a personal level he was as manipulative as hell. Take Sylvia for example.'

'Sylvia D'Agostino?'

'Strange girl. Devoted to Laurence. She was an only child. Very close to her parents, particularly her father. She and her father were both gifted poets. Laurence told her to manufacture a quarrel with her parents and break off all contact with them. And she did. She did it because Laurence instructed her to do it and because Laurence was the great magus, the great seer who was about to guide us all into the next Age of Man. There was absolutely no advantage to him in cutting her off from her family. It didn't benefit him in the slightest. He did it because he could. He did it to cause anguish for her and her parents. He did it because he was cruel.'

'Sylvia D'Agostino was one of the people who disappeared,' I said.

'I don't know anything about that,' said Ketterley.

'I don't think you can claim he was intellectually honest. He said he'd been to other worlds. He said other people had been there too. That's not exactly honest, is it?' There may have been a slight edge of superciliousness in my voice, which I suppose I would have done better to suppress but I have always liked winning arguments.

Ketterley scowled. He seemed to struggle with something. He opened his mouth to say something, changed his mind, and then: 'I don't like you very much,' he said.

I laughed. 'I can live with that,' I said.

There was a silence.

'Why a labyrinth, do you suppose?' I asked.

'What d'you mean?'

'Why do you think he described the other world — the one he said he went to most often — as a labyrinth?'

Ketterley shrugged. 'A vision of cosmic grandeur, I suppose. A symbol of the mingled glory and horror of existence. No one gets out alive.'

'OK,' I said. 'But what I still don't quite understand was how he convinced you of its existence. The labyrinth-world, I mean.'

'He had us perform a ritual that was supposed to bring us there. There were aspects of the ritual that were . . . evocative, I suppose. Suggestive.'

'A ritual? Really? I thought Arne-Sayles's position was that rituals were nonsense.

247

Didn't he say something like that in *The Half-Seen Door*?'

'That's right. He claimed that he personally was able to access the labyrinth-world simply by making an adjustment to his frame of mind, by returning to a child-like state of wonder, a pre-rational consciousness. He claimed to be able to do this at will. Unsurprisingly, most of us — his students — got absolutely nowhere with this, so he created a ritual that we were to perform in order to access the labyrinth. But he made it clear that this was a concession to our lack of ability.'

'I see. Most of you?'

'What?'

'You said most of you couldn't enter the labyrinth without the ritual. It seemed to imply that some of you could.'

A slight pause.

'Sylvia. Sylvia thought she could get there in the same way that Laurence did. With this return to a state of wonder. She was a strange girl, as I've said. A poet. She lived very much inside her head. Who knows what she thought she saw.'

'And did you ever see it? The labyrinth?'

He considered. 'Mostly I had what you might call intimations, a sense of standing in a huge space — not just wide, but immensely tall too. And — this is quite hard to admit — but yes, I did see it once. I mean I thought I saw it once.'

'What did it look like?'

'Very much like Laurence's description. Like an infinite series of classical buildings knitted together.'

'And what do you think it meant?' I asked.

'Nothing. I don't think it meant anything at all.'

A short silence. Then he suddenly said, 'Does anyone know you're here?'

'Sorry?' I said. It seemed an odd question.

'You said that the Laurence Arne-Sayles connection dogged my career in academia. Yet here you are, an academic, asking questions about it all, dragging it all up again. I just wondered why you weren't being more careful. Aren't you afraid it will tarnish your brilliant career?'

'I don't think anyone is going to take issue with my approach,' I said. 'My book on Arne-Sayles is part of a wider project on transgressive thinking. As I think I've already explained.'

'Oh, I see,' he said. 'So you've told lots of people that you were coming here today to see me? All your friends.'

I frowned. 'No, I haven't told anyone. I don't usually tell people what I'm doing.

But that's not because . . .'

'Interesting,' he said.

We looked at each other with a sort of mutual dislike. I was about to rise and go, when he suddenly said, 'Do you really want to understand Laurence and the hold he had over us?'

'Yes,' I said. 'Of course.'

'Then in that case we should perform the ritual.'

'The ritual?' I said.

'Yes.'

'The one to . . .'

'The one to open the path to the labyrinth. Yes.'

'What? Now?' I was a bit startled by the suggestion. (But I wasn't afraid. What was there to be afraid of?) 'You still remember it?' I said.

'Oh, yes. As I said, I have an excellent memory.'

'Oh, well, I . . . Will it take long?' I asked. 'Only I have to . . .'

'It takes twelve minutes,' he said.

'Oh! Oh, OK. Sure. Why not?' I said. I stood up. 'I don't have to take any drugs, do I?' I said. 'Because that's not really . . .'

He laughed that rather contemptuous laugh again. 'You've had a cup of coffee. I think that'll be sufficient.'

He lowered the blinds of the windows. He took a candle in a candlestick from the mantelpiece. The candlestick was an old-fashioned brass one with a square base. It didn't really match the rest of the furnishings in the house, which were modern, minimalist, European.

He got me to stand in the sitting room, facing the door that led to the hall. This area had been left free from furniture.

He picked up my messenger bag — the bag containing my journals, my index and my pens — and placed it on my shoulder.

'What's that for?' I asked, frowning.

'You're going to need your notebooks,' he said. 'You know. When you get to the labyrinth.'

He had an odd sense of humour.

(Writing this, I feel a sort of terror descend on me. I know now what is coming. My hand is shaking and I must stop writing for a moment to try to control it. But at the time I felt nothing, no presentiment of danger, nothing.)

He lit the candle and placed it on the floor of the hall, just beyond the door. The floor of the hall was the same as the floor of the sitting room: a solid wood flooring in oak. I noticed a blotch where he put the candlestick, as if the oak there had been repeatedly stained with candlewax, and within the dark stain was an unstained lighter square into which the candle-stick base fitted precisely.

'You need to focus on the candle,' he said. So I did.

But at the same time, I was thinking about that pale square in the dark patch and the candlestick fitting into it. And that was the point at which I realised that he was lying. The candle had stood in that precise spot many, many times and he had performed this ritual over and over again. He still believed. He still thought he could reach the other world.

I wasn't afraid, only incredulous and amused. And I started going over in my mind what questions I could ask him after the ritual in order to expose his dishonesty.

He turned out the lights in the house. It was dark except for the candle burning on the floor and the orange haze from the streetlights outside that penetrated the blinds.

He stood slightly behind me and instructed me to keep my eyes upon the candle. Then he began to chant in a language I'd never heard before. I surmised, from the similarities to Welsh and Cornish, that it was Brittonic. I think if I had not already found out his secret, I would have guessed it then. He chanted with conviction, with fervour, like he believed absolutely in what he was doing.

I heard the name 'Addedomarus' several times.

'Close your eyes now,' he said.

I did so.

More chanting. My amusement at discovering his secret sustained me for a while, but then I began to grow bored. He abandoned language altogether and seemed to drag out of himself a sort of animal growl that started in his stomach, impossibly deep, and grew higher, wilder, louder, more extraordinary.

Everything switched.

It was as if the world had somehow just stopped. He fell silent. The Berlioz was cut off mid-chorus. My eyelids were still closed but I could tell that the quality of the darkness had changed; it was greyer, cooler. The air felt colder and much damper, as if we'd been plunged into a fog. I wondered if somewhere a door had been thrown open; but that made no sense because at the same time the hum of London ceased. There was a sound of vast emptiness, and all around me waves were hitting walls with a dull thud. I opened my eyes.

The walls of a vast room rose up around me. Statues of minotaurs loomed over me, darkening the space with their bulk, their massive horns jutting into the empty air, their animal expressions solemn, inscrutable.

I turned in utter incredulity.

Ketterley was standing in his shirtsleeves. He was completely at his ease. He was looking at me and smiling as if I was an experiment that had gone surprisingly well.

'Forgive me for not saying anything before now,' he smiled, 'but I really am delighted to see you. A young, healthy man is just what I wanted.'

'Put it back!' I screamed at him.

He began to laugh.

And he laughed, and laughed, and laughed.

■ ■ ■ ■

PART 6
WAVE

■ ■ ■ ■

I was mistaken!

I was sitting cross-legged with my Journal in my lap and the fragments in front of me. I turned away slightly, not wanting to soil any of them, and vomited on the Pavement. I was shaking.

I fetched Myself a drink of water, as well as a rag and some more water to wipe up the vomit.

I was mistaken. The Other is not my friend. He has never been my friend. He is my enemy.

I was still shaking. I had the cup of water in my hand, but I could not hold it steady.

I had known once that the Other was my enemy. Or rather Matthew Rose Sorensen

257

had known it. But when I had forgotten Matthew Rose Sorensen, I had forgotten this as well.

I had forgotten, but the Other remembered. I could see now that he was apprehensive in case one day I remembered. He called me Piranesi so he would not need to use the name Matthew Rose Sorensen. He tested me by speaking words such as 'Battersea' to see if they sparked any memories. I had been incorrect when I said that Battersea was nonsense. It was not nonsense. It was a word that meant something to Matthew Rose Sorensen.

But why was the Other able to remember when I was not?

Because he did not stay in the House but went back to the Other World.

Revelations came thick and fast now. My head seemed to shudder with the weight of them. I clasped my head in my hands and groaned.

I must not stay long, the Prophet had said, *I am all too well aware of the consequences of lingering in this place: amnesia, total mental collapse, etcetera, etcetera.* Like the Prophet, the Other never lingered. He never allowed our meetings to last longer than an hour and at the end of them he walked away; and when he did that he was walking away into the Other World.

But how could I make sure that I did not forget again? I pictured Myself forgetting and becoming the Other's friend again and running about the House taking measurements and photos and collecting data for him, while all the time he was laughing at me! No-no-no-no-no-no-no-no-no-no! I could not bear the thought of it! I pressed my head between my hands as if I could physically keep the memories from escaping.

I will learn from 16 and collect marble pebbles from the Vestibules and form letters with them. I will write in letters a metre high! *REMEMBER! THE OTHER IS NOT YOUR FRIEND! HE TRICKED MATTHEW ROSE SORENSEN INTO COMING INTO THISWORLD FOR HIS OWN ADVANTAGE!* If necessary, I will fill Hall after Hall with immense writing!

. . . for his own advantage . . . Yes, yes! That was the key to it. That was why he had brought Matthew Rose Sorensen here. The Other had needed someone — a slave! — to live in these Halls and collect information about them; he dares not do it himself in case the House makes him forget.

Furious, hot anger rose up inside me.

Why, why had I told him about the Flood?

If only I had learnt all this before I knew about the Flood! Then I could have kept it a secret. I could have waited until Thursday came and I could have climbed up to a High Place, safe from the Waters and I could have watched him Destroyed. Yes! That is what I want now! Perhaps it is not too late! I will go back to the Other. I will smile and look as usual and I will deceive him as he has deceived me. I will say I made a mistake about the Flood. No Flood is coming. Be here on Thursday! Be in the very middle of these Halls!

But of course, the Other has said that he will not be here on Thursday. He is never here on Thursdays. He will be safe in the Other World. That does not matter! Anger makes me resourceful! On Tuesday the Other will come to meet me — it is our regular meeting day. I will snatch him and bind him with fishing nets. With these hands I will do it! I have two fishing nets. They are made of a synthetic polymer and very strong. I shall bind him to the Statues in the Second South-Western Hall. For two days he will be bound. He will be in torment, knowing the Flood is coming. Perhaps I will give him water to drink. Perhaps I will not. Perhaps I will say to him: 'Soon you will have plenty of Water!' And on Thursday he will watch the Tides pouring in through the Doors and he will scream and scream. And I will laugh and laugh. I will laugh as long and as loud as he laughed at Matthew Rose Sorensen when he brought him here . . .

This is where I lost Myself.

I lost Myself in long, sick fantasies of revenge. I did not think to rest. I did not think to eat. I did not think to drink water. Hours passed — I do not how many. I wandered about and over and over in my imagination the Other died in the Flood or he fell from a great Height. And sometimes I raved at him and accused him; and sometimes I was cold and silent, and he begged me to tell him why I had turned against him, but I did not. And always I could have saved him, but I never did.

These imaginings left me ravaged. I do not think I could have felt more exhausted if I really had murdered someone a hundred times over. My thighs ached, my back ached, my head ached. My eyes and throat were sore with weeping and shouting.

When night came, I made my way back to the Third Northern Hall. I collapsed on my bed and slept.

It is 16 that is my friend and not the Other

I awoke this morning exhausted from the excesses of the day before. I went to the Ninth Vestibule to gather seaweed and mussels to make a broth for my breakfast. I felt dull and empty with no appetite for further anger. Yet, despite this emotional blankness, from time to time a sob or cry would escape my lips — a little sound of desolation.

I did not believe it was Myself that cried out. It was, I thought, Matthew Rose Sorensen who reposed in a state of unconsciousness somewhere inside Myself.

He had suffered. He had been alone with his enemy. It had been more than he could bear. Perhaps the Other had taunted him. Matthew Rose Sorensen had torn into pieces the description of his enslavement that he had written in his Journal and he had scattered the pieces in the Eighty-Eighth Western Hall. Then the House in its Mercy had caused him to fall asleep — which was by far the best thing for him — and it had placed him inside me.

But the sight of his name written in

262

pebbles in the Twenty-Fourth Vestibule had caused him to stir uneasily and the revelation of what the Other had done had only made matters worse. I worried in case he woke up completely and his anguish began all over again.

I placed my hand on my chest. *Hush now!* I said, *Do not be afraid. You are safe. Go back to sleep. I will take care of us both.*

It seemed to me that Matthew Rose Sorensen fell asleep again.

I thought of all those Journal entries that I had read — the ones about Giussani, Ovenden, D'Agostino and poor James Ritter. I had thought that I was mad when I wrote them. But I could now see that this conclusion was incorrect. I had not written the entries at all; *he* had written them. And, what is more, he had written them in a different World where, no doubt, different Rules, Circumstances and Conditions applied. As far as I can tell, Matthew Rose Sorensen was in his right mind when he wrote them. Neither he nor I had ever been mad.

Another revelation came to me: it was the Other who wanted me to be mad, not 16. The Other had lied when he said 16 was trying to drive me insane.

I made my seaweed-and-mussel broth and drank it. It was important to keep up my strength. Then I took up my Journal again. I turned back to the message that 16 had written and which I had erased leaving only fragments.

IS VALENTINE
KETTER(LEY)
(CE)RTAINLY
GROOMED OTHER POTENTIAL VICTIMS AND I
A DISCIPLE OF THE OCCULTIST LAURENCE
ARNE-SAY(LES)

I saw now that this whole passage was about Ketterley. The victims 16 talked about were not 16's own, but (most likely) Ketterley's. Had he tricked others into coming into this World? Or was Matthew Rose Sorensen the only victim? The word 'potential' suggested that 16 believed me to be the only one.

(THI)NK HE KNOWS THAT I HAVE
PENETRATED TH(E)

This too referred to Ketterley. 16 was saying that Ketterley knew that she had arrived in these Halls. (Which he knew because I had told him. Inwardly I cursed my own stupidity.)
So why had 16 come?
Because she was looking for Matthew

Rose Sorensen. Because she wanted to rescue him from the slavery of the Other. I saw it clearly now. It is 16 that is my friend and not the Other.

Tears sprang into my eyes at the thought. My only friend and I had hidden from her!

'I am here! I am here!' I shouted to the Empty Air. 'Come back! I will hide no longer!'

So many times I could have found her. I could have spoken to her that night when she knelt to write to me in the Sixth North-Western Hall. I could have waited by the trail of her perfume in the First Vestibule. Perhaps she had given up looking for me! Perhaps she had been disgusted when she saw how I hid from her, how I erased her message.

But no. She had formed that sentence in the Twenty-Fourth Vestibule: *ARE YOU MATTHEW ROSE SORENSEN?* It would have taken a long time to arrange those pebbles. 16 was patient, resolute and ingenious. 16 was still looking for me.

Perhaps by now she had found my message warning her of the Flood. Perhaps she had written something in return. I washed my bowl and the saucepan I had made my soup in; I put my possessions in order; then I set out for the Sixth North-Western Hall.

The rooks made a fuss at my approach. *Yes, yes. I am glad to see you too,* I told them. *Only I have things to do today and cannot stop for a long conversation.*

There was no new message from 16. But something very worrying had happened. My message warning her of the Flood had vanished. All our other messages were here, but not that one. I gazed at the empty Pavement in perplexity. What had happened? I know that I have forgotten many things; have I now started to remember things that have not happened? Had I, in fact, never written that message at all?

I passed from the Sixth North-Western Hall into the Twenty-Fourth Vestibule where 16 had constructed the message: *ARE YOU MATTHEW ROSE SORENSEN?* The pebbles that had formed the words were scattered far and wide over the Pavement. The words were utterly destroyed.

The Other. The Other had done this. I was quite sure of it.

I went back to the Sixth North-Western Hall and examined the Pavement carefully. I could see the faint traces of chalk where my warning had been. The Other had erased this message too.

Why?

He had scattered the pebbles in order to

prevent me finding out about Matthew Rose Sorensen: that much was clear. But why erase the message to 16? In the hope that she would accidentally wander into the Perilous Region and be destroyed by the Flood? No. The Other does not hope; he plans and acts. He wanted her to drown and he would try to ensure it.

Three months ago, when the Other had first told me about 16, he said that he had spoken to her; but when I asked him where this conversation had taken place, he had become confused and would not tell me. That was because it had happened in the Other World, the existence of which the Other wanted to keep hidden from me.

The Other would contact 16 in the Other World and convince her to come to these Halls at the Hour of the Flood. Perhaps he had already done it. 16 was in danger.

I knelt down and quickly and efficiently restored the message the Other had erased. If 16 comes here between now and Thursday she will see the message and receive the warning of the Flood. And yet . . . Only five days remain between now and Thursday. Supposing she does not come in this period? This seems to me perfectly possible; now that I know she comes from somewhere else (another World) it seems to me that her visits are irregular and unpredictable. There is a risk she will not see it and so I am in a state of some anxiety concerning her. My thoughts return constantly to her and her safety, yet I cannot think of anything else I can do to protect her.

Preparations for the Flood

ENTRY FOR THE TWENTY-SIXTH DAY OF THE NINTH MONTH IN THE YEAR THE ALBATROSS CAME TO THE SOUTH-WESTERN HALLS

With the exception of the Concealed Person, all the Dead stand in the Path of the Flood Waters. On Sunday I began the work of carrying them to safety.

I took a blanket and transferred all the Biscuit-Box Man's bones into it — all except for the ones inside the biscuit box. I tied up the blanket with seaweed twine, making it into a sort of sack, and I carried it to the Second Vestibule and up the Staircase to the Upper Halls. There I emptied out the blanket and placed the bones on the Plinth of a Statue of a Shepherdess with a Lamb in her Arms. Then I went back for the biscuit box.

I did the same for the People of the Alcove and the Folded-Up Child, carrying each of them up a Staircase — whichever Staircase was nearest to their usual Habitation — and storing them carefully in one of the Upper Halls. I did not empty out the Fish-Leather Man but kept him wrapped up in the blanket (he has so many tiny fragments of bone that I am afraid of losing some). Similarly, I left the Folded-Up Child snuggled in a blanket, but that was more because I wanted her to feel safe in an unfamiliar Place.

It took me the best part of three days to complete the task. The bones of each individual Dead Person weigh between 2.5 and 4.5 kilograms and the Staircases are 25 metres high. Yet I found that it was good to do hard, physical work; it prevented me from continually obsessing over the injuries the Other has done me and my fears concerning 16.

I had not forgotten the albatross chick (now a very large bird!). I did a series of calculations to find out how the Forty-Third Vestibule would be affected by the flood and was relieved to discover that there would be, at most, only a thin skin of Water. The albatrosses consider me a friend, but I did not think they would allow me to carry their chick up a Staircase — and in any struggle between us they would surely win!

Yesterday was Tuesday, the day that I would normally go to my meeting with the

Other. I did not go. Was he suspicious, I wonder? Or did he simply think that I was too busy preparing for the Flood?

The Statue of an Angel caught on a Rose Bush (behind which I keep my Journals and Index) is approximately 5 metres from the Floor; a height likely sufficient to keep them safe from the Flood. But, since my Journals and Index are almost as dear to me as my Life, I have placed them all in my brown leather messenger bag, wrapped the messenger bag in heavy-gauge plastic and carried it up to the Upper Halls and placed it beside the Biscuit-Box Man. I have stowed all my fishing gear, sleeping bags, pots and pans, bowls, spoons and other possessions in High Places out of the reach of the Flood. My last task was to gather up the remaining plastic bowls (the ones I use to collect Fresh Water).

I had just collected the last ones from the Fourteenth South-Western Hall and was carrying them back to the Third Northern Hall. On my way I passed through the First Western Hall. This is the Hall that contains the Statues of the Horned Giants, those Vast Figures that emerge, struggling powerfully and with contorted Faces, from the Walls on either side of the Eastern Door.

I observed something near the North-

Eastern Corner of the Hall and went to look at it. It was a bag made of some grey fabric and, lying beside it, two objects made of black canvas. The bag was approximately 80 centimetres long, 50 centimetres wide and 40 centimetres deep. It had two handles made of canvas, also grey. I picked it up; it was very heavy. I put it down again. It was fastened with two canvas straps that were held in place by metal buckles. I undid the buckles and opened the bag. I took out all the contents. They were as follows:

- a Gun
- a quantity of folded material made of a dense, heavy plastic. This was by far the largest object in the bag; it filled most of the bag and was coloured blue, black and grey.
- a small cylindrical container with a secure lid. This contained other small objects the purpose of which was unclear.
- a thing like a slice of a larger cylinder cut down at an angle, with a yellow hose coming out of it
- two black plastic rods extendable to a length of approximately 2 metres
- 4 black paddle-shapes

After studying these items for a minute or two I saw that the paddle-shapes could be attached to the ends of the black rods. I unfolded the material; it became a long flat shape, which was pointed at both ends. It was a boat. The thing like a slice of a cylinder was a bellows or pump. You pumped Air into the long flat shape and it would inflate and become a boat about 4 metres long and 1 metre wide.

I examined the two black canvas objects that had lain beside the bag. They had a number of straps hanging from them. I concluded that they must belong to the boat, but beyond this I could not ascertain their purpose.

Why had a boat appeared suddenly in the House on the eve of the Flood? Had the House sent it to me to keep me safe? I considered this proposition. There had been other Floods in the past and no boat had appeared; also, although I could imagine that the House might send me a boat, I could not imagine any circumstances in which it would send me a Gun. No, the Gun proclaimed the bag's ownership; it was the Other's.

I folded up the boat and packed everything neatly back in the bag. Everything except the Gun. I picked it up and held it for some time, thinking. I could take it and descend the Great Staircase in the First Vestibule to the Lower Halls. I could throw it into the Tides.

I replaced the Gun in the bag and did up the closures. I returned to the Third Northern Hall.

Wave

Today was the day of the Flood. I woke at my usual time. I was keyed up with nerves and my stomach was clenched tight.

The day felt cold and I could tell by the touch of the Air on my skin that it was already raining in the Vestibules.

I had no appetite, but nevertheless I heated a little soup and forced Myself to drink it. It is important to keep the body well nourished. I washed up my pan and bowl and stowed the last of my possessions behind High Statues. I put on my watch.

It was a quarter to eight.

My most important task was to find 16 and ensure her safety. But as to the best way to accomplish it, that was far from

273

clear. I was certain that the Other had set a trap for 16. Most likely he had promised to meet her in a certain Hall at a certain time and to tell her how to find Matthew Rose Sorensen. This meant that the most reliable way to find 16 was to look for the Other, but I did not want to go near the Other if I could avoid it. I remembered the words of the Prophet:

The closer 16 gets, the more dangerous Ketterley will become.

My hope was that I could find 16 before she reached the Other.

I went to the First Vestibule. I stood in the grey Rain and waited, hoping that she would appear. Between nine o'clock and ten o'clock I searched the adjacent Halls. Nothing. At ten o'clock I returned to the First Vestibule.

At half-past ten I began to walk between the First Vestibule and the Sixth North-Western Hall; I followed the Path laid down in 16's directions. I trod this Path six times, but I did not find her. I was growing extremely anxious.

I returned to the First Vestibule. It was now half-past eleven. Two Halls West and North of here, in the Ninth Vestibule, the first Tide was already ascending the Easternmost Staircase. A delicate Wash of Water was scuttling over the Pavements of the surrounding Halls.

There was nothing for it. I must look for the Other. I had only just come to this decision, when upon the instant he appeared in front of me. (Why could 16 not do that?) He walked briskly across the First Vestibule, East to West. His head was ducked down against the Rain. His clothes were strikingly different from what he usually wore: jeans, an old jumper and sneakers, and over his jumper an odd sort of harness. *Life-jacket,* I thought. (Or rather Matthew Rose Sorensen thought it inside my head.)

He did not see me. He passed into the First Western Hall. Silently I followed him and hid Myself in a Niche near the Door.

The Other went immediately to the bag containing the inflatable boat and began to unpack it. I waited, watching constantly for 16. The Other's attention was elsewhere and there might still be enough time to intercept her if she entered the Hall.

Some distance behind the Other, at the Western End of the Hall, I could see the glitter of Light on the Pavement: a film of Water was washing through the North-Western Doors. I glanced at my watch. Five Halls South and West of here, in the Twenty-Second Vestibule, another Tide was already rising, tumbling up the Staircase.

The Other unrolled his boat. He attached his little pump to it and began to pump with his foot. The boat began to inflate in an efficient manner.

Water was filling up the Second and Third South-Western Halls; I could hear the dull thud of the Waves hitting their Walls.

Then it came to me. 16 was clever. She was at least as clever as me, perhaps even more so. She knew nothing about the Flood but she would not trust the Other. She would wait and watch, as I was doing, hoping that Matthew Rose Sorensen would appear. Suddenly I had a mental image of both 16 and Myself hiding in the First Western Hall, both waiting for the other one to appear. I could not afford to remain hidden any longer: I stepped down from the Niche and walked towards the Other.

He glanced up and scowled as I approached. He did not pause in pumping up his boat. About two metres to his left was the grey bag, now empty, and beside it, resting on the Pavement, was the silver Gun.

'Where the Hell have you been?' he said in a voice of displeasure and anger. 'Why weren't you there on Tuesday? I looked for you everywhere. I can't remember if you said that ten rooms will be flooded or a hundred.' His foot on the pump was slowing; the inflatable boat was almost full of Air and his foot was meeting with more resistance. 'I've had to change my plans. It's a pain, but there it is. Raphael is coming here and, like it or not, we're going to finish this. So no nonsense from you, all right? Because I swear, Piranesi, I've just about had enough from everyone.'

'I visited him in mid-November,' I said. *'It was just after four, a cold blue twilight.'*

He stopped pumping. The boat was now a plump shape with a taut, rounded skin. 'We attach the seats next,' he said. 'They're those black things over there. Pass them to me, will you?' He pointed to the two contraptions whose purpose I had not divined. 'When the room floods, you and I will get into this kayak. If Raphael tries to get into it with us, or to hang on to it, use your paddle to strike at her hands and head.'

'The afternoon had been stormy,' I said, *'and the lights of the cars were pixelated by rain; the pavements collaged with wet black leaves.'*

He was fiddling with the valves where the Air had gone in. 'What?' he asked, irritably. 'What are you talking about? Can you hurry up and pass me those seats? We need to get a move on. She'll be here any moment now.'

'When I got to his house I heard music playing,' I said. 'A requiem. I waited for him to answer the door to an accompaniment of Berlioz.'

'Berlioz?' He stopped what he was doing, straightened and looked at me properly for the first time. He frowned. 'I don't . . . Berlioz?'

I said: *'The door opened. "Dr Ketterley?" I said.'*

He froze at the sound of his own name. His eyes widened. 'What are you talking about?' he asked again in a voice made hoarse with fear.

'Battersea,' I said. 'You asked me once if I remembered Battersea. And now I do.'

Boom! . . . . . . Boom! . . . . . . The Tide from the Twenty-Second Vestibule was growing stronger; it was hitting the Walls of the Second and Third South-Western Halls with more force.

'You saw her message,' he said.

'Yes,' I said.

A thin Ripple of Water raced across the Pavement and hit my feet. It was followed immediately by another one.

He laughed suddenly, an odd sound: hysteria masquerading as relief. 'No, no!' he said. 'You don't get me that easily. Those aren't your words. They're someone else's.

278

You don't really remember. Raphael put you up to this. Really, Matthew, how stupid do you think I am?'

He dived suddenly to the right, towards the Gun that was lying on the Pavement. But I had chosen my position with care and I was nearer to it than he was. I gave it a good, sharp kick with my foot. It skittered across the marble Pavement and came to rest by the Northern Wall about fifteen metres away. More Ripples — deeper now — were coursing past our feet. They flowed after the Gun, as if we were all playing a game with the Gun and they intended to catch it.

'What . . . ? What are you going to do?' asked the Other.

'Where is 16?' I asked.

He opened his mouth to say something, but at that moment a voice was heard. 'Ketterley!' it cried. A woman's voice. 16 was here!

From the sound I judged that she was hidden in one of the Southern Doors. The Other, who is not accustomed to the way in which the echoes reverberate in the Halls, looked around him in a confused manner.

'Ketterley,' she shouted again. 'I've come for Matthew Rose Sorensen.'

He grabbed me by my right arm. 'He's

here!' he shouted. 'I have him! Come and get him.'

The Booming of the Tides was growing louder. The whole Hall reverberated with the Force of it. Water was flowing freely in through all the Southern Doors.

'Take care!' I shouted. 'He means you harm. He has a Gun!'

A small, slight figure stepped out of the Door that leads to the First Southern Hall. She wore jeans and a green jumper. Her dark hair was pulled back into a ponytail.

The Other let go of me with his right hand (though he still had hold of me by his left). Then he made a fist of his right hand and he swung his arm and body back, intending to get some momentum to hit me; but I swung with him, overbalancing him. He half-fell to the Floor. I pulled free from him and began to run towards 16.

As I ran, I shouted: 'A Flood is coming! We must climb!'

I do not know how much of my words she heard, but she understood the urgency in my voice. I seized her hand. Together we ran towards the Eastern Wall.

The Statues of the Horned Giants were in front of us on either side of the Eastern Door, but we could not climb them; their bodies emerged from the Wall two metres above the Floor and there were no hand- or footholds until that point. Next to the Giant on the left was the Statue of a Father seated with his little Son in his Arms; the Father was plucking a thorn from his Son's Foot. I climbed into their Niche and then onto their Plinth. I mounted onto the Father's lap and by holding onto one of the Columns at the side, and using the Arm, Shoulder and Head of the Father as footholds, I climbed onto the Top of the triangular Pediment that surmounted the Niche. 16 tried to follow me, but she was not so tall as me and, I suspect, not accustomed to climbing. She got as far as the Statue's lap but seemed at a loss what to do next. Quickly I climbed down again and lifted her up; with my help, she heaved herself up onto the Pediment.

It was noon. In the Tenth and Twenty-Fourth Vestibules the last two Tides were rising, filling the surrounding Area with tempestuous, raging Waters.

Half a metre above the Pediment was a Deep Cornice or Shelf that ran the whole length of the Hall. We scaled the slope of the Pediment and hoisted ourselves onto the Cornice above. We were now about seven metres above the Floor. 16 was pale and shaking (she clearly did not love climbing), but she had a fierce, determined expression.

The Air was suddenly rent by sharp, cracking sounds — perhaps four of them — one after the other. For one terrifying moment I thought that the Weight and Vibrations of the Waters were causing the Hall to collapse. I looked out into the Hall and I saw that the Other had not yet got into his boat (where he would be safe); instead he had run to the Northern Wall to retrieve his Gun. He was firing at us.

'Get in the boat!' I shouted to him. 'Get in the boat before it is too late!'

He fired again, hitting a Statue above our heads. I felt a sharp pain in my forehead. I cried out. I put my hand up and brought it away covered in blood.

The Other started to wade through the running Waters towards us — presumably with the idea of firing his Gun at us more effectively.

I shouted at him again, something to the effect that the Tides were almost here! — but there was a Great Roar of Waters from every direction and I doubt that he heard me.

If there had not been someone firing a Gun at us, we could have stayed on the Cornice. (Then, if the Waters rose higher than I expected, we could have climbed up again.) But, as matters stood, we were exposed, without protection.

A metre or so below us the Back and Upper Arms of the Horned Giant emerged from the Wall. There was a Space between his Back and the Wall, a sort of marble pocket. I jumped; it was a distance of approximately two metres sideways, one metre down; I managed it with ease. I looked up at 16. Her eyes were wide with apprehension. I held out my arms. She jumped. I caught her.

We were now shielded from the Other's Gun by the Giant's Body. I heaved Myself up his marble Back to look over his Shoulder.

The Other had turned away from us and was trying to reach the boat. But he had left it too late. The Waters were as high as his knees and the contending Waves were dragging at him. As he struggled, he seemed to grow heavier; the boat by contrast grew lighter, freer. It danced on the Waters, spun from one Part of the Hall to another; one moment it was by the Northern Wall, the next it was halfway to the Western Wall. The Other kept changing direction to follow it, but by the time he had taken a few arduous steps, the boat was somewhere else entirely.

Suddenly it was as if the boat remembered the purpose for which it had been brought here; it seemed to make up its mind to save him. It turned and sailed directly towards him. He held out his arms and leant forwards to catch it. It was barely half a metre from his grasp. For an instant I think he had his hand on its bow; then it twirled around and was gone, borne away to the Western End of the Hall.

'Climb! Climb!' I shouted. It was too late to catch the boat, but I thought that if he climbed, he might still save himself. But he could not hear me above the Sound of the Waters pouring into the Hall. He continued to wade desperately, uselessly, after the boat.

There was a Great Rush and a Great Roar in the next Hall; a Weight of Water hit the other side of the Northern Wall. *Boom!!!* And then I was grateful that we had climbed down to the Horned Giant. If we had still been standing on the Cornice, we would have been flung off the Wall. But the Horned Giant held us fast.

Spray as high as the Ceiling exploded through all the Northern Doors. The Spray caught the Sun; it was as if someone had suddenly thrown a hundred barrelfuls of diamonds into the Hall.

Great Waves surged through the Northern

284

Doors. One plucked up the Other and threw him against the Southern Wall. He crashed into the Statues at a point about fifteen metres from the Floor. I imagine that that was when he died.

The Wave drew back; he disappeared into it.

Meanwhile the little inflatable boat whirled about on the Waters, sometimes engulfed by them for a moment or two, but always reappearing immediately. If he could only have reached it, it would have saved him.

Raphael

SECOND ENTRY FOR THE TWENTY-SEVENTH DAY OF THE NINTH MONTH IN THE YEAR THE ALBATROSS CAME TO THE SOUTH-WESTERN HALLS

Waves crashed against the Southern Wall; explosions of white Spray filled the Hall. The Waters covered the Bottom Tier of Statues; the colour of the Waters was a stormy grey and their Depths were black. Several times Waves passed over our heads, but they fell back the next instant. We were drenched, we were numbed, we were blinded, we were deafened; but always we were saved.

Time passed.

The Waves sank down and the Waters became peaceable. They began to drain away into the Staircases and the Lower Halls. The Heads of the Bottom Tier of Statues reappeared above the Surface of the Waters.

In all this time 16 and I had not spoken to each other. The Roar of the Waves would have made it impossible for us to hear each other and in any case, we had been intent on saving ourselves and each other; we had had no thought for anything else. Now we turned and looked at each other.

16 had large dark eyes and an elfin face. Her expression was solemn. She was a little older than me — about forty, I thought. Her hair was black with wet.

'You are Six . . . You are Raphael,' I said.

'I'm Sarah Raphael,' she said. 'And you are Matthew Rose Sorensen.'

And you are Matthew Rose Sorensen. This time she framed it as a statement, rather than a question. This was surely premature. It would have been better to keep it as a question. But then again, if she *had* framed it as a question, I would not have known how to answer it.

'Did he know you?' I asked.

'Did who know me?' she said.

'Matthew Rose Sorensen. Did Matthew Rose Sorensen know you? Is that why you came here?'

She paused, taking in what I had just said. Then she said carefully, 'No. You and I have never met.'

'Then why?'

'I'm a police officer,' she said.

'Oh,' I said.

We fell back into silence. We were both still dazed by what had happened. Our eyes were still full of images of the Violent Waters; our ears were still full of their Sounds; our minds were still full of that moment when the Other was flung by the Wave against the Wall of Statues. We had nothing at that moment to say to each other.

Raphael turned her attention to practical matters. She examined the injury to my forehead and said that it was not very deep. She did not think that I had been hit by one of the Other's bullets; more likely I had been grazed by a shard of splintered marble.

The Level of the Waters continued to fall. When they came no higher than the Plinths of the Bottom Tier of Statues, I began to consider how we would get down from the Horned Giant. We could not return the way we had come since that would involve a leap upwards onto the Cornice. I did not think that Raphael could manage it. (Indeed, I was not sure that I could either.)

'I'll go and fetch something to help you climb down,' I told her. 'Don't be anxious. I'll return as quickly as I can.'

I lowered Myself from the Giant's Torso and dropped down. The Waters reached as high as my thighs. I waded to the Third Northern Hall and climbed up the Statues to the places where I keep my belongings. Everything was wet from the Spray, but nothing was drenched. I retrieved my fishing nets, a bottle of Fresh Water and some dried seaweed. (It is important to keep the body hydrated and nourished.)

I returned to the First Western Hall. The Waters had already dropped some more and only came up as high as my knees. I climbed back up the Horned Giant. I gave Raphael some water and made her eat a little of the dried seaweed (though I do not think she liked it). Then I tied my fishing nets together and fastened them to one of the Giant's Arms. They hung down to a point about half a metre above the Pavement. I showed Raphael how to use the fishing nets to climb down.

We waded to the First Vestibule and ascended the Great Staircase so that we were out of the reach of the Waters. We sat down. Our clothes were plastered to our bodies with wet. My hair — which is dark and curly — was as full of droplets as a Cloud. I rained every time I moved.

The birds found us there. Many different kinds — herring gulls, rooks, blackbirds and sparrows — gathered on the Statues and Banisters and chattered at me in their different voices.

'It'll be gone soon,' I told them. 'Don't worry.'

'What?' asked Raphael, startled. 'I don't understand.'

'I was talking to the birds,' I said. 'They're alarmed by the great quantities of Water that are everywhere. I'm telling them that it'll soon be gone.'

'Oh!' She said. 'Do you . . . Do you do talk to the birds often?'

'Yes,' I said. 'But there's no need to look surprised. You talked to the birds yourself. In the Sixth North-Western Hall. I heard you.'

She looked even more surprised at that. 'What did I say?' she asked.

'You told them to piss off. You were writing a message to me and they were being a nuisance, flying in your face and over your writing, trying to find out what you were doing.'

She thought a moment. 'Was that the message that you wiped out?' she asked.

'Yes.'

'Why did you do that?'

'Because the Oth . . . Because Dr Ketterley told me you were my enemy and that reading what you had written would make me go mad. So I erased the message. But at the same time, I wanted to read it, so I didn't erase all of it. I wasn't being very logical.'

'He made things very hard for you.'

'Yes. I suppose he did.'

There was a silence.

'We're both soaking wet and cold,' said Raphael. 'Perhaps we should go?'

'Go where?' I said.

'Home,' said Raphael. 'I mean we can go to my house and get dry. And then I can take you home.'

'I am home,' I said.

Raphael looked around at the sombre grey Waters lapping the Walls and the dripping Statues. She didn't say anything.

'It's usually a lot drier than this,' I said quickly in case she was thinking that my Home was inhospitable and damp.

But that wasn't what she was thinking.

'There's something I have to tell you,' she said. 'I don't know if you remember this, but you have a mum and a dad. And two sisters. And friends.' She gazed at me intently. 'Do you remember?'

I shook my head.

'They've been looking for you,' she said. 'But they didn't know the right place to look. They've been worried about you. They've been . . .' She looked away again to find the right words to express her thought. 'They've felt pain because they didn't know where you were,' she said.

I considered this. 'I'm sorry that Matthew Rose Sorensen's mum and dad and sisters and friends feel pain,' I said. 'But I don't really see what it has to do with me.'

'You don't think of yourself as Matthew Rose Sorensen?'

'No,' I said.

'But you have his face,' she said.

'Yes.'

'And his hands.'

'Yes.'

'And his feet and his body.'

'All that is true. But I haven't got his mind and I haven't got his memories. I don't mean that he's not here. He is here.' I touched my breast. 'But I think he's asleep. He's fine. You mustn't worry about him.'

She nodded. She was not a contentious person as the Other had been; she did not

291

argue and contradict everything I said. I liked that about her. 'Who are you?' she asked. 'If you're not him.'

'I am the Beloved Child of the House,' I said.

'The house? What is the house?'

Such a strange question! I spread my arms to indicate the First Vestibule, the Halls beyond the First Vestibule, Everything. 'This is the House. Look!'

'Oh. I see.'

We were silent a moment.

Then Raphael said, 'I need to ask you something. Would you be prepared to come with me to Matthew Rose Sorensen's parents and sisters — to let them see his face again? It would help them a lot to know he is alive. Even if you had to go away again — I mean even if you had to return here, it would help them. What do you think about that?'

'I can't do it now,' I said.

'OK.'

'I have to consider the needs of the Biscuit-Box Man — and the Folded-Up Child — and the People of the Alcove. They only have me to take care of them. They are in unfamiliar surroundings and may feel disconcerted. I have to return them to their appointed places.'

'There are other people here?' asked Raphael, in surprise.

'Yes.'

'How many?'

'Thirteen. The ones I have just said and also the Concealed Person. But the Concealed Person resides in one of the Upper Halls and has not been affected by the Flood so there was no need to move him or her.'

'Thirteen people!' Raphael's dark eyes were wide with astonishment. 'My God! Are they all right?'

'Yes,' I said. 'They're fine. I take good care of them.'

'But who are they? Can you take me to them? Is Stanley Ovenden here? What about Sylvia D'Agostino? Maurizio Giussani?'

'Oh, it is highly probable that one of them is Stanley Ovenden. Certainly the Proph . . . Certainly Laurence Arne-Sayles thought so. Another may be Sylvia D'Agostino and another Maurizio Giussani. Unfortunately, I have no idea which is which.'

'What do you mean? Have they forgotten who they are? What do they say?'

'Oh, they don't say much really. They're all dead.'

'Dead!'

'Yes.'

'Oh!' Raphael took a moment to process this. 'Were they dead when you arrived?' she asked.

'I . . .' I paused. It was an interesting question. I hadn't considered it before. 'I think so,' I said. 'I think they've all been dead a long time, but as I don't remember arriving, I can't be certain. Arriving was something that happened to Matthew Rose Sorensen, not to me.'

'Yes, I suppose that's right. But what do you mean, you take care of them?'

'I make sure they are in good order. As complete and tidy as they can be. I bring them offerings of food and drink and water lilies. And I talk to them. Don't you have Dead of your own in your Halls?'

'I do. Yes.'

'Don't you take them offerings? Don't you talk to them?'

Before Raphael could answer this another thought struck me. 'I said there are thirteen Dead, but that is incorrect. Dr Ketterley has joined their number. I must find his body and make him ready to lie with the others.' I clapped my hands together. 'So, as you see, I have a great many tasks to perform and cannot at the moment think about leaving these Halls.'

Raphael nodded slowly. 'That's OK,' she

294

said. 'There's plenty of time.' She put out her hand and rather awkwardly — but also gently — put her hand on my shoulder.

Instantly, and to my huge embarrassment, I started crying. Great creaking sobs rose up in my chest and tears sprouted from my eyes. I did not think that it was me who was crying; it was Matthew Rose Sorensen crying through my eyes. It lasted for a long time until it tailed off into braying, hiccupping gulps for Air.

Raphael still had her hand on my shoulder. She looked away tactfully while I wiped my eyes and my nose with the back of my hand.

'You will come back?' I said. 'Even though I don't go with you now, you will come back?'

'I'll come back tomorrow,' she said. 'It'll be rather late in the evening. Will that be OK? How will we find each other?'

'I'll wait for you here,' I said. 'It doesn't matter how late it is. I'll wait until you come.'

'And you'll think about what I said? About coming to see your . . . to see Matthew Rose Sorensen's parents and sisters?'

'Yes,' I said. 'I'll think about it.'

Raphael left, disappearing into the Shadowy Space between the two Minotaurs in

295

the South-Eastern Corner of the Vestibule.

My watch had stopped, but I estimated it to be early evening. I was alone, exhausted, hungry and wet. I waded back to the Third Northern Hall. The Water was still a half-metre deep. I climbed up and examined the dry seaweed that I use to build fires. Unfortunately it had been thoroughly wetted by the Great Waves. I could not make a fire. I could not cook anything.

I fetched my sleeping bag — also damp — and took it to the First Vestibule. I lay down on a Dry, High Step of the Great Staircase.

My last thought before I fell asleep was: *He is dead. My only friend. My only enemy.*

I comfort Dr Ketterley

ENTRY FOR THE TWENTY-EIGHTH DAY OF THE NINTH MONTH IN THE YEAR THE ALBATROSS CAME TO THE SOUTH-WESTERN HALLS

I found Dr Ketterley's body in an Angle of the Staircase in the Eighth Vestibule. He had been battered against the Walls and the Statues. His clothes were in rags. I disentangled him from the Balustrade and laid him out straight and composed his limbs. I took his poor, broken head into my lap and cradled it.

'Your good looks are gone,' I told him.

'But you mustn't worry about it. This unsightly condition is only temporary. Don't be sad. Don't fear. I will place you somewhere where the fish and the birds can strip away all this broken flesh. It will soon be gone. Then you will be a handsome skull and handsome bones. I will put you in good order and you can rest in the Sunlight and the Starlight. The Statues will look down on you with Blessing. I am sorry that I was angry with you. Forgive me.'

I did not find the Gun — the Tides must have taken it deep within themselves; but later that morning I found Dr Ketterley's boat, still idling on the Waters in the First Western Hall which were now no more than ankle-deep. It was quite unharmed.

'I wish that you had saved him,' I told it.

I did not feel that it responded in any way. It seemed drowsy, dozing, only half alive. Without the Rushing Waters to animate it, it was no longer the devil that had danced on the Waves, first mocking Dr Ketterley and then abandoning him.

I have been thinking about what Raphael said about Matthew Rose Sorensen's mum and his dad and his sisters and his friends. Perhaps I should send them a message explaining that Matthew Rose Sorensen now lives inside me, that he is unconscious but perfectly safe, and that I am a strong and resourceful person who will care for him assiduously, exactly as I care for any others of the Dead.

I shall ask Raphael what she thinks of this idea.

As the Shadows fell in the First Vestibule Raphael returned

SECOND ENTRY FOR THE TWENTY-EIGHTH DAY OF THE NINTH MONTH IN THE YEAR THE ALBATROSS CAME TO THE SOUTH-WESTERN HALLS

As the Shadows fell in the First Vestibule Raphael returned. We sat on a Step of the Great Staircase as before. Raphael had a shining little device like the one that the Other had. She tapped it and it brought forth a shaft of white-yellow Light to illuminate the Statues and our faces.

I told Raphael my plan to write to Matthew Rose Sorensen's mum and dad and two sisters and friends, but for some reason she did not think this was a good idea.

'What should I call you?' she asked.

'Call me?' I said.

'As a name. If you're not Matthew Rose Sorensen, then what should I call you?'

'Oh, I see. I suppose you could call me

Pir . . .' I stopped. 'Dr Ketterley used to call me Piranesi,' I said. 'He said it was a name to do with labyrinths, but I think perhaps it was meant to mock me.'

'Probably,' agreed Raphael. 'He was that sort of guy.' There was a little silence and then she said, 'Would you like to know how I found you?'

'Very much,' I said.

'There was a woman. I don't suppose you remember her. Her name was Angharad Scott. She wrote a book about Laurence Arne-Sayles. Six years ago, you contacted her. You told her that you were also think-ing of writing a book about Arne-Sayles and the two of you had a long conversation. Then she never heard from you again. In May of this year she called the college in London where you used to work because she wanted to know what had happened about the book — whether you were still writing it. The people at the college told her that you were missing; that you'd been miss-ing pretty much the entire time since she'd first spoken to you. That rang all sorts of warning bells for Mrs Scott because she knew about the people who had disappeared around Arne-Sayles. You were the fourth — the fifth if you count Jimmy Ritter. So she contacted us. It was the first time that we

— I mean the police — knew that there was any connection between you and Arne-Sayles. When we talked to the people who remained of Arne-Sayles's circle — Bannerman, Hughes, Ketterley and Arne-Sayles himself — it was obvious something was going on. Tali Hughes kept crying and saying she was sorry. Arne-Sayles was thrilled by the attention and Ketterley couldn't open his mouth without lying.' She paused. 'Do you understand any of what I'm saying?'

'A little,' I said. 'Matthew Rose Sorensen wrote about all these people. I know that they are connected to the Proph . . . to Laurence Arne-Sayles. Did he tell you where I was? He said that he would.'

'Who?'

'Laurence Arne-Sayles.'

Raphael took a moment to process this. 'You spoke to him?' she asked in a tone of incredulity.

'Yes.'

'He *came* here?'

'Yes.'

'When?'

'About two months ago.'

'And he didn't offer to help you? He didn't offer to take you out of here?'

'No. But to be fair, if he had offered I

wouldn't have wanted to go. In fact, I'm still not sure that I want to go.'

A pale owl glided out of the First Eastern Hall into the First Vestibule. It settled on a Statue high up on the Southern Wall where it gleamed whitely in the Dimness. I have seen owls portrayed in marble. Many Statues incorporate them. But I had never seen their living counterpart until now. Its appearance was, I felt sure, connected with the coming of Raphael and the departure of Dr Ketterley; it was as though a principle of Death had been replaced with a principle of Life. Things, I thought, were speeding up.

Raphael had not perceived the owl. She said, 'You're right. Arne-Sayles told us the truth straightaway. He said you were in the labyrinth. But of course . . . Well, we thought he was just trying to wind us up. Which was right. He *was* just trying to wind us up. My colleagues put up with it for a while, but they gave up on him eventually. I had a different idea. I thought: he likes talking. Just let him. Eventually he'll say something useful.'

She tapped her shining little device. It spoke with Laurence Arne-Sayles's haughty, drawling voice: *You think that all my talk about other worlds is irrelevant. But it isn't. It's absolutely key. Matthew Rose Sorensen at-*

tempted to enter another world. If he hadn't done that, he wouldn't have "disappeared" as you call it.'

Raphael's voice answered him: *'Something about the attempt caused him to disappear?'*

'Yes.' Laurence Arne-Sayles again.

'Something happened to him during this . . . this ritual, whatever it was? Why? Where do these rituals take place?'

'You mean do we perform them on the edge of a precipice and he just fell off? No, nothing like that. Besides, it needn't necessarily have been a ritual. I never use them myself.'

'But why would he do that?' asked Raphael. *'Why would he perform the ritual or do whatever it is? There's nothing in what he wrote to suggest he believed your theories. Quite the reverse in fact.'*

'Oh, belief,' said Arne-Sayles, laying a deep, sarcastic emphasis on the word. *'Why do people always think it's a question of belief? It's not. People can "believe" whatever they want. I really couldn't care less.'*

'Yes, but if he didn't believe, why would he even try?'

'Because he had half a brain and he recognised that mine was one of the great intellects of the twentieth century — perhaps the greatest of all. And he wanted to understand me. So he made the attempt to reach another

world, not because he thought the other world existed, but because he thought the attempt itself would grant him insight into my thinking. Into me. And now you are going to do the same.'

'Me?' Raphael sounded startled.

'Yes. And you are going to do it for the exact same reason that Rose Sorensen did it. He wanted to understand my thinking. You want to understand his. Adjust your perceptions in the way I am about to describe to you. Perform the actions that I will outline for you and then you will know.'

'What will I know, Laurence?'

'You'll know what happened to Matthew Rose Sorensen.'

'It's that simple?'

'Oh, yes. It's that simple.'

Raphael tapped the device; the voices fell silent.

'I didn't think that was a bad idea,' she said, 'to try and understand what you'd been thinking at the point you disappeared. Arne-Sayles described what to do, how to go back to a pre-rational mode of thought. He said that when I'd done that, I'd see paths all around me and he told me which one to choose. I thought he meant meta-phorical paths. It was a bit of a shock when it turned out he didn't.'

303

'Yes,' I said. 'Matthew Rose Sorensen was shocked when he first arrived. Shocked and frightened. And then he fell asleep and I was born. Later I found entries in my Journal that frightened me. I thought that I must have been mad when I wrote them. But now I understand that Matthew Rose Sorensen wrote them and he was describing a different World.'

'Yes.'

'And the Other World has different things in it. Words such as "Manchester" and "police station" have no meaning here. Because those things do not exist. Words such as "river" and "mountain" do have meaning but only because those things are depicted in the Statues. I suppose that these things must exist in the Older World. In this World the Statues depict things that exist in the Older World.'

'Yes,' said Raphael. 'Here you can only see a representation of a river or a mountain, but in our world — the other world — you can see the actual river and the actual mountain.'

This annoyed me. 'I do not see why you say I can *only* see a representation in this World,' I said with some sharpness. 'The word "only" suggests a relationship of inferiority. You make it sound as if the

Statue was somehow inferior to the thing itself. I do not see that that is the case at all. I would argue that the Statue is superior to the thing itself, the Statue being perfect, eternal and not subject to decay.'

'Sorry,' said Raphael. 'I didn't mean to disparage your world.'

There was a silence.

'What is the Other World like?' I asked.

Raphael looked as if she did not know quite how to answer this question. 'There are more people,' she said at last.

'A lot more?' I asked.

'Yes.'

'As many as seventy?' I asked, deliberately choosing a high, rather improbable number.

'Yes,' she said. Then she smiled.

'Why do you smile?' I asked.

'It's the way you raise your eyebrow at me. That dubious, rather imperious look. Do you know who you look like when you do that?'

'No. Who?'

'You look like Matthew Rose Sorensen. Like photos of him that I've seen.'

'How do you know that there are more than seventy people?' I asked. 'Have you counted them yourself?'

'No, but I'm fairly sure,' she said. 'It's not always a pleasant world, the other world.

There's a lot of sadness.' She paused. 'A lot of sadness,' she said again. 'It's not like here.' She sighed. 'I need you to understand something. Whether you come back with me or not, it's up to you. Ketterley tricked you. He kept you here with lies and deceit. I don't want to trick you. You must only come if you want to.'

'And if I stay here will you come back and visit me?' I said.

'Of course,' she said.

Other people

For as long as I can remember I have wanted to show the House to someone. I used to imagine that the Sixteenth Person was at my side and that I would say to him such things as:

Now we enter the First Northern Hall. Observe the many beautiful Statues. On your right you will see the Statue of an Old Man holding the Model of a Ship, on your left is the Statue of a Winged Horse and its Colt.

I imagined us visiting the Drowned Halls together:

Now we descend through this Gash in the

Floor; we climb down the fallen Masonry and enter the Hall below. Place your feet where I place mine and you will have no difficulty keeping your balance. The immense Statues that are a feature of these Halls provide us with safe places to sit. Observe the dark, still Waters. We may gather water lilies here and present them to the Dead . . .

Today all my imaginings came true. The Sixteenth Person and I walked together through the House and I showed her many things.

She arrived in the First Vestibule early in the morning.

'Will you do something for me?' she asked.

'Of course,' I said. 'Anything.'

'Show me the labyrinth.'

'Gladly. What would you like to see?'

'I don't know,' she said. 'Whatever you want to show me. Whatever's most beautiful.'

Of course, what I really wanted to show her was *everything*, but that was impossible. My first thought was the Drowned Halls, but I remembered that Raphael did not love climbing, so I decided on the Coral Halls, a long succession of Halls extending south and west from the Thirty-Eighth Southern Hall.

We walked through the Southern Halls.

Raphael looked relaxed and happy. (I was happy too.) With every step Raphael was looking around with pleasure and admiration.

She said, 'It's such an astonishing place. A perfect place. I saw some of it while I was looking for you, but I kept having to stop at the doors to write out the directions back to the minotaur room. It got very time-consuming and frustrating and of course I didn't dare go too far in case I made a mistake.'

'You wouldn't have made a mistake,' I assured her. 'Your directions were excellent.'

'How long did it take you to learn it? The way through the labyrinth?' she asked.

I opened my mouth to say loudly and boastfully that I have always known it, that it is part of me, that the House and I could not be separated. But I realised, before I even spoke the words, that it was not true. I remembered that I used to mark the Doorways with chalk in exactly the same way that Raphael did and I remembered that I used to be afraid of getting lost. I shook my head. 'I don't know,' I said. 'I can't remember.'

'Is it all right to take photos?' She held up her shining device. 'Or is that not . . . ? I don't know, is that disrespectful in some way?'

'Of course you may take photos,' I said. 'I took photographs sometimes for the Oth . . . for Dr Ketterley.'

But I was pleased that she had asked the question. It showed that she regarded the House as I did, as something deserving of respect. (Dr Ketterley never learnt this. He seemed incapable of it somehow.)

In the Tenth Southern Hall I made a detour to the Fourteenth South-Western Hall to show Raphael the People of the Alcove. There are (as I have explained before) ten of them and the skeleton of a monkey.

Raphael regarded them gravely. She gently rested her hand on one of the bones — the tibia of one of the males. It was a gesture conveying comfort and reassurance. *Don't be afraid. You are safe. I am here.*

'We don't know who they are,' she said. 'Poor things.'

'They are the People of the Alcove,' I said. 'Arne-Sayles probably murdered at least one of them. Perhaps he murdered all of them.'

These were solemn words. Before I could decide how I felt about them she turned to me and said with great intensity, 'I'm sorry. I'm really, really sorry.'

I was astonished, even a little alarmed. No

one has ever been as kind to me as Raphael; no one has ever done more for me. That she should apologise seemed to me inappropriate. 'No . . . No . . .' I murmured and I put up my hands to fend off her words.

But she went on with a bleak, angry look on her face. 'He'll never be punished for what he did to you. Or for what he did to them. I've gone over it and over it in my mind and there's nothing I can do. Nothing he can be charged with. Not without a lot of explanation that literally no one will want to believe.' She sighed deeply. 'I said that this is a perfect world. But it's not. There are crimes here, just like everywhere else.'

A wave of sadness and helplessness washed over me. I wanted to say that the People of the Alcove had not been murdered by Arne-Sayles (though I have no evidence to support that assertion and the probability is that at least one of them was). Mostly I wanted Raphael to come away from them so that I could stop thinking of them the way she thought of them — as murdered — and go back to thinking of them the way I always had before — as good, and noble, and peaceful.

We continued on our way, stopping often to admire a particularly striking Statue. Our hearts grew lighter again and when we reached the Coral Halls, we refreshed ourselves with looking at their wonders.

Though the Coral Halls are dry now, it appears that at one time they were flooded with Sea Water for a long period. Coral has grown there, changing the Statues in strange and unexpected ways. One may see, for example, a Woman crowned with coral, her Hands transformed into stars or flowers. There are Figures horned with coral, or crucified on coral branches, or stuck through with coral arrows. There is a Lion enmeshed in a cage of coral and a Man holding a Little Box. The coral has grown so profusely over his Left Side that half of him appears to be engulfed in red- and rose-coloured flames, while the other half is not.

Late in the afternoon we returned to the First Vestibule. Just before we parted Raphael said, 'I love the quiet here. No people!' She said the last part as if it were the greatest advantage of all.

'Don't you like the people in your own Halls?' I asked, puzzled.

'I like them,' she said, with no very great enthusiasm. 'Mostly I like them. Some of them. I don't always get them. They don't always get me.'

After she had gone, I thought about what she had said. I cannot imagine not wanting to be with people. (Though it is true that Dr Ketterley was sometimes annoying.) I remembered how Raphael had wondered which of the People of the Alcove had been murdered and how the simple fact of her posing the question had made the whole World seem a darker, sadder Place.

Perhaps that is what it is like being with other people. Perhaps even people you like and admire immensely can make you see the World in ways you would rather not. Perhaps that is what Raphael means.

Strange emotions

ENTRY FOR THE THIRTIETH DAY OF THE NINTH MONTH IN THE YEAR THE ALBATROSS CAME TO THE SOUTH-WESTERN HALLS

I once wrote in my Journal:

> It is my belief that the World (or, if you will, the House, since the two are for all practical purposes identical) wishes an Inhabitant for Itself to be a witness to its Beauty and the recipient of its Mercies.

If I leave, then the House will have no Inhabitant and how will I bear the thought of it Empty?

Yet the simple fact is that if I remain in these Halls I will be alone. In one sense I suppose I will be no more alone than before. Raphael has promised to visit me, just as the Other visited me before. And Raphael really is my friend — whereas the Other's feelings towards me were mixed, to say the least. Whenever the Other left me he went back to his own World, but I did not know that at the time; I thought that he was simply in another Part of the House. Believing that there was someone else here made me less lonely. Now, when Raphael returns to the Other World, I will know that I am alone.

And so for this reason I have decided to go with Raphael.

I have returned all of the Dead to their allotted places. Today I walked through the Halls as I have done a thousand times before. I visited all my most beloved Statues and as I gazed on each one, I thought: *Perhaps this will be the last time I look on your Face. Goodbye! Goodbye!*

I leave

ENTRY FOR THE FIRST DAY OF THE TENTH MONTH IN THE YEAR THE ALBATROSS CAME TO THE SOUTH-WESTERN HALLS

This morning I fetched the small cardboard box with the word AQUARIUM and the picture of an octopus on it. It is the box that originally contained the shoes Dr Ketterley gave me. When Dr Ketterley told me to hide Myself from 16, I took the ornaments out of my hair and placed them in the box. But now, wanting to look my best when I enter the New World, I spent two or three hours putting them back in, all the pretty things that I have found or made: seashells, coral beads, pearls, tiny pebbles and interesting fishbones.

When Raphael arrived, she seemed rather astonished at my pleasant appearance.

I took my messenger bag with all my Journals and my favourite pens and we walked towards the two Minotaurs in the South-Eastern Corner. The shadows between them shimmered slightly. The shadows suggested the shape of a corridor or alleyway with dim walls and, at the end of it, lights, flashes of moving colour that my eye could not interpret.

I took one last look at the Eternal House. I shivered. Raphael took my hand. Then, together, we walked into the corridor.

■ ■ ■ ■

PART 7
MATTHEW ROSE
SORENSEN

■ ■ ■ ■

Valentine Ketterley has disappeared
ENTRY FOR 26 NOVEMBER 2018

Valentine Ketterley, psychologist and anthropologist, has disappeared. The police have made inquiries and discovered that before his disappearance he made some unusual purchases: a gun, an inflatable kayak and a life-jacket — purchases that his friends all agree were completely out of character: he had never shown any inclination to be waterborne before.

None of these items has been found in his house or office.

The police think that possibly he used the inflatable kayak to travel to a remote spot and then used the gun to kill himself; but there is one officer, a man called Jamie Askill, who has a different idea. He believes that the sudden and unexpected disappearance of Dr Ketterley must be linked in some way to the sudden and unexpected re-appearance of Matthew Rose Sorensen. Askill's theory is that Ketterley imprisoned Rose Sorensen somewhere, in the same way that Ketterley's one-time supervisor and tutor, Laurence Arne-Sayles, imprisoned James Ritter years before. Ketterley's motive, thinks Askill, was the same as Arne-Sayles's: to manufacture evidence of Arne-Sayles's Theory of Other Worlds. Ketterley became alarmed when the police uncovered the link between himself and Rose Sorensen. Faced with the exposure of his crimes, Ketterley let Rose Sorensen go and then killed himself.

Askill's theory has the advantage of accounting for the reappearance of Matthew Rose Sorensen at the same time — give or take a day or two — that Ketterley disappeared, which is otherwise an odd coincidence. Where the theory falls down is that neither Arne-Sayles nor Ketterley ever used the disappearances as evidence of anything. In fact, for many years Ketterley had been loud in his denunciation of Arne-Sayles.

Undeterred, Askill has questioned me twice. He is a young man with a pleasant, good-natured face, little brown curls all over his head and an intelligent expression. He wears a dark blue suit and a grey shirt and speaks with a Yorkshire accent.

'Did you know Valentine Ketterley?' he asks.

'Yes,' I say. 'I visited him in mid-November 2012.'

He looks pleased with this answer. 'That's just before you disappeared,' he points out.

'Yes,' I say.

'And where were you?' he asks. 'While you were gone?'

'I was in a house with many rooms. The sea sweeps through the house. Sometimes it swept over me, but always I was saved.'

Askill pauses and frowns. 'That's not . . . You're not . . .' he begins. He thinks for a moment. 'What I mean is that you've had problems. A breakdown of sorts. At least, that's what I've been told. Are you getting treatment for that?'

'My family have arranged for me to see a psychotherapist. To which I have no objection. But I have refused medication and so far, no one has insisted.'

'Well, I hope it helps,' he says, kindly.

'Thank you.'

'What I'm trying to get at,' he says, 'is whether Dr Ketterley persuaded you to go anywhere. Whether he kept you anywhere against your will. Whether you were free to

319

come and go.'

'Yes. I was free. I came and went. I did not remain in one place. I walked for hundreds, perhaps thousands, of kilometres.'

'Oh . . . Oh, OK. And Dr Ketterley wasn't with you when you walked?'

'No.'

'Was anyone with you?'

'No, I was quite alone.'

'Oh. Oh, well.' Jamie Askill is slightly disappointed. I am disappointed too, in a way: disappointed that I have disappointed him. 'Well,' he says. 'I don't want to take up too much of your time. I know you've already talked to DS Raphael.'

'Yes.'

'She's amazing, isn't she? Raphael?'

'Yes.'

'I'm not surprised that she found you. I mean if anyone was going to find you, it was probably always going to be her.' He pauses. 'Of course, she can be a little . . . I mean she doesn't really . . .' He fishes in the air with his fingers to catch at the elusive words. 'I mean she's not necessarily the easiest person in the world to work with. And time management? Definitely not her thing. But honestly, we all think the world of her.'

'It is right to think the world of Raphael,' I tell him. 'She is an extraordinary person.'

'Exactly. Did anyone ever tell you about Pinny Wheeller?'

'No,' I say. 'Who or what is Pinny Wheeller?'

'A guy in some city in the Midlands — where Raphael started out. He was an upset sort of person, a troubled person, the sort of person that ends up having a lot to do with us.'

'That's not good.'

'No, it's not. There was this one time something happened to set him off and he climbed up inside the cathedral tower. He got onto a sort of gallery and was shouting abuse at the people inside the cathedral. He had some bales of old, dirty newspaper that he used to take everywhere, and he started setting it on fire and throwing it down onto people.'

'How terrible.'

'I know. Frightening, isn't it? When we — I mean the police — got there, it was evening — all dim and dark with flaming sheets of newspaper floating about and people dashing everywhere with fire extinguishers and buckets of sand. Raphael and another guy tried to get to Pinny Wheeller, but when they were in the stairwell — which

321

was a really tight, confined space — Pinny threw a load more burning newspaper down and some of it wrapped itself around the other guy's face. So he had to go back.'

'But Raphael did not go back,' I say, with great certainty.

'No, she didn't. Technically speaking she probably should have, but she didn't. When she came out onto the gallery her hair was on fire. But, you know, she's Raphael. I doubt she even noticed. The people down below had to shout at her to put the fire out. She sat down with Pinny Wheeller and she got him to stop throwing flaming newspaper everywhere and she got him to come down. Pretty brave, don't you think?'

'Braver than you think. She doesn't like heights.'

'She doesn't?'

'They make her uncomfortable.'

'That wouldn't stop her,' he says.

'No.'

'Thank God, she didn't have to do any of that with you. I mean she didn't have to walk through fire or whatever. She just went to the seaside. That's what I heard anyway — that she found you at the seaside.'

'Yes. I was at the side of the sea.'

'A lot of missing people turn up at seaside places,' he muses. 'It's the sea, I suppose. It has a soothing effect.'

'It certainly did on me,' I say.

He smiles cheerfully at me. 'Excellent,' he says.

Matthew Rose Sorensen has Reappeared
ENTRY FOR 27 NOVEMBER 2018

Matthew Rose Sorensen's mother and father and sisters and friends all ask me where I have been.

I tell them what I told Jamie Askill: that I was in a house with many rooms; that the sea sweeps through the house; and that sometimes it swept over me, but always I was saved.

Matthew Rose Sorensen's mother and father and sisters and friends tell each other that this is a description of a mental breakdown seen from the inside; an explanation they find reasonable, perhaps even reassuring. They have Matthew Rose Sorensen back — or so they believe. A man with his face and voice and gestures moves about the world, and that is enough for them.

I no longer look like Piranesi. There are no coral beads or fishbones in my hair. My hair is clean and cut and styled. I am clean-shaven. I wear the clothes that were brought

323

to me out of the storage in which Matthew Rose Sorensen's sisters had placed them. Rose Sorensen had a great number of clothes, all meticulously cared for. He had more than a dozen suits (which I find surprising considering that his income was not large). This love of clothes was something he shared with Piranesi. Piranesi frequently wrote about Dr Ketterley's clothes in his journal and lamented the contrast with his own ragged garments. This, I suppose, is where I differ from both of them — from Matthew Rose Sorensen and Piranesi; I find I do not care greatly about clothes.

Many other things were delivered to me out of storage, the most important being Matthew Rose Sorensen's missing journals. They cover the period from June 2000 (when he was an undergraduate) until December 2011. As for the rest of his possessions, I am getting rid of most of them. Piranesi cannot bear to have so many possessions. *I do not need this!* is his constant refrain.

Piranesi is always with me, but of Rose Sorensen I have only hints and shadows. I piece him together out of the objects he has left behind, from what is said about him by other people and, of course, from his journals. Without the journals I would be all at sea.

I remember how this world works — more or less. I remember what Manchester is and what the police are and how to use a smartphone. I can pay for things with money — though I still find the process strange and artificial. Piranesi has a strong dislike of money. Piranesi wants to say: *But I need the thing you have, so why don't you just give it to me? And then when I have something you need, I will just give it to you. This would be a simpler system and much better!*

But I, who am not Piranesi — or at least not only him — realise that this probably wouldn't go down too well.

I have decided to write a book about Laurence Arne-Sayles. It is something that Matthew Rose Sorensen wanted to do and something that I want to do. After all, who knows Arne-Sayles's work better than me?

Raphael has shown me what Laurence Arne-Sayles taught her: how to find the path to the labyrinth and how to find the path out again. I can come and go as I please. Last week I took a train to Manchester. I took a bus to Miles Platting. I walked through a bleak autumn landscape to a flat in a tower block. The door was answered by a thin, ravaged-looking man who smelt strongly of cigarettes.

'Are you James Ritter?' I asked.

He agreed that he was.

'I've come to take you back,' I said.

I led him through the shadowy corridor and when the noble minotaurs of the first vestibule rose up around us, he started to cry, not for fear, but for happiness. He went immediately and sat under the great marble sweep of the staircase; the place where he used to sleep. He closed his eyes and listened to the sounds of the tides. When it was time to leave, he begged me to let him stay, but I refused.

'You don't know how to feed yourself,' I told him. 'You never learnt. You would die here unless I fed you — and I can't take on that responsibility. But I'll bring you back here whenever you want. And if ever I decide to come back for good, I promise I will bring you with me.'

The body of Valentine Ketterley, magician and scientist
ENTRY FOR 28 NOVEMBER 2018

The body of Valentine Ketterley, magician and scientist, is washed by the tides. I have placed it in one of the lower halls accessed from the eighth vestibule and I have tethered it to the statue of a half-reclining man. The statue's eyes are closed; he is possibly asleep; thick snakes and serpents entwine themselves heavily with his limbs.

The body is contained in a sack of plastic netting. The mesh of the netting is wide enough for fish to poke their mouths in, and birds their beaks; it is fine enough that none of the small bones will be lost.

I estimate that in six months' time the bones will be white and clean. I will gather them up and take them to the empty niche in the third north-western hall. I will place Valentine Ketterley next to the biscuit-box man. In the middle I will place the long bones tied together with twine. On the right I will place the skull. On the left I will place a box containing all the small bones.

Dr Valentine Ketterley will lie with his colleagues: with Stanley Ovenden, Maurizio Giussani and Sylvia D'Agostino.

Statues again
ENTRY FOR 29 NOVEMBER 2018

Piranesi lived among statues: silent presences that brought him comfort and enlightenment.

I thought that in this new (old) world the statues would be irrelevant. I did not imagine that they would continue to help me. But I was wrong. When faced with a person or situation I do not understand, my first impulse is still to look for a statue that will enlighten me.

I think of Dr Ketterley and an image rises up in my mind. It is the memory of a statue that stands in the nineteenth north-western hall. It is the statue of a man kneeling on his plinth; a sword lies at his side, its blade broken in five pieces. Roundabout lie other broken pieces, the remains of a sphere. The man has used his sword to shatter the sphere because he wanted to understand it, but now he finds that he has destroyed both sphere and sword. This puzzles him, but at the same time part of him refuses to accept that the sphere is broken and worthless. He has picked up some of the fragments and stares at them intently in the hope that they will eventually bring him new knowledge.

I think of Laurence Arne-Sayles and an image rises up in my mind. It is the memory of a statue that stands in an upper vestibule, facing the head of a staircase (the one rising up out of the thirty-second vestibule). This statue represents a heretical pope seated on a throne. He is fat and bloated. He lolls on his throne, a shapeless mass. The throne is magnificent, but the sheer bulk of the figure threatens to split it in two. He knows that he is repulsive, but you can see by his face that the idea pleases him. He revels in the thought that he is somehow shocking. In his face there is mingled laughter and triumph. *Look at me,* he seems to say. *Look at me!*

I think of Raphael and an image — no, two images rise up in my mind.

In Piranesi's mind Raphael is represented by a statue in the forty-fourth western hall. It shows a queen in a chariot, the protector of her people. She is all goodness, all gentleness, all wisdom, all motherhood. That is Piranesi's view of Raphael, because Raphael saved him.

But I choose a different statue. In my mind Raphael is better represented by a statue in an antechamber that lies between the forty-fifth and the sixty-second northern halls. This statue shows a figure walking forward, holding a lantern. It is hard to determine with any certainty the gender of the figure; it is androgynous in appearance. From the way she (or he) holds up the lantern and peers at whatever is ahead, one gets the sense of a huge darkness surrounding her; above all I get the sense that she is alone, perhaps by choice or perhaps because no one else was courageous enough to follow her into the darkness.

Of all the billions of people in this world Raphael is the one I know best and love most. I understand much better now — better than Piranesi ever could — the magnificent thing she did in coming to find me, the magnitude of her courage.

I know that she returns to the labyrinth often. Sometimes we go together; sometimes she goes alone. The quiet and the solitude attract her strongly. In them she hopes to find what she needs.

It worries me.

'Don't disappear,' I tell her sternly. 'Do *not* disappear.'

She makes a rueful, amused face. 'I won't,' she says.

'We can't keep rescuing each other,' I say. 'It's ridiculous.'

She smiles. It is a smile with a little sadness in it.

But she still wears the perfume — the first thing I ever knew of her — and it still makes me think of Sunlight and Happiness.

In my mind are all the tides
ENTRY FOR 30 NOVEMBER 2018

In my mind are all the tides, their seasons, their ebbs and their flows. In my mind are all the halls, the endless procession of them, the intricate pathways. When this world becomes too much for me, when I grow tired of the noise and the dirt and the people, I close my eyes and I name a particular vestibule to myself; then I name a hall. I imagine I am walking the path from the vestibule to the hall. I note with precision the doors I must pass through, the rights and lefts that I must take, the statues on the walls that I must pass.

Last night I dreamt that I was standing in the fifth northern hall facing the statue of the gorilla. The gorilla dismounted from his plinth and came towards me with his slow knuckle-walk. He was grey-white in the moonlight; and I flung my arms around his massive neck and told him how happy I was to be home.

When I awoke I thought: *I am not home. I am here.*

It began to snow
ENTRY FOR 1 DECEMBER 2018

This afternoon I walked through the city, making for a café where I was to meet Raphael. It was about half-past two on a day that had never really got light.

It began to snow. The low clouds made a grey ceiling for the city; the snow muffled the noise of the cars until it became almost rhythmical; a steady, shushing noise, like the sound of tides beating endlessly on marble walls.

I closed my eyes. I felt calm.

There was a park. I entered it and followed a path through an avenue of tall, ancient trees with wide, dusky, grassy spaces on either side of them. The pale snow sifted down through bare winter branches. The lights of the cars on the distant road sparkled through the trees: red, yellow, white. It was very quiet. Though it was not yet twilight the streetlights shed a faint light.

People were walking up and down on the path. An old man passed me. He looked sad and tired. He had broken veins on his cheeks and a bristly white beard. As he screwed up his eyes against the falling snow, I realised I knew him. He is depicted on the northern wall of the forty-eighth western hall. He is shown as a king with a little model of a walled city in one hand while the other hand he raises in blessing. I wanted to seize hold of him and say to him: *In another world you are a king, noble and good! I have seen it!* But I hesitated a moment too long and he disappeared into the crowd.

A woman passed me with two children.

One of the children had a wooden recorder in his hands. I knew them too. They are depicted in the twenty-seventh southern hall: a statue of two children laughing, one of them holding a flute.

I came out of the park. The city streets rose up around me. There was a hotel with a courtyard with metal tables and chairs for people to sit in more clement weather. Today they were snow-strewn and forlorn. A lattice of wire was strung across the courtyard. Paper lanterns were hanging from the wires, spheres of vivid orange that blew and trembled in the snow and the thin wind; the sea-grey clouds raced across the sky and the orange lanterns shivered against them.

The Beauty of the House is immeasurable; its Kindness infinite.

ABOUT THE AUTHOR

Susanna Clarke is the author of *Jonathan Strange & Mr Norrell* and *The Ladies of Grace Adieu and Other Stories.* She lives in Derbyshire.

The employees of Thorndike Press hope you have enjoyed this Large Print book. All our Thorndike, Wheeler, and Kennebec Large Print titles are designed for easy reading, and all our books are made to last. Other Thorndike Press Large Print books are available at your library, through selected bookstores, or directly from us.

For information about titles, please call:
    (800) 223-1244

or visit our website at:
    gale.com/thorndike

To share your comments, please write:
    Publisher
    Thorndike Press
    10 Water St., Suite 310
    Waterville, ME 04901

Jesse Stuart, The Man & His Books

A BIBLIOGRAPHY &

PURCHASE GUIDE

with James M. Gifford

& Jim Wayne Miller

Jesse Stuart,
The Man & His Books

JERRY A. HERNDON
& GEORGE BROSI

THE JESSE STUART FOUNDATION

Contents

Foreword   vii

Preface   xi

1. *Jesse Stuart: A Biographical Sketch*   1

2. *Works by Stuart in Print; An Alphabetical Listing*   13

3. *Out-of-Print Works by Stuart; An Alphabetical Listing*   19

4. *Stuart Studies in Print*   27

5. *Out-of-Print Stuart Studies*   30

6. *Booksellers Specializing in Stuart Materials*   34

7. *Jesse Stuart/W-Hollow Prints: Black Pine Gallery*   39

8. *A Jesse Stuart Film: "Split Cherry Tree"*   41

9. *The Jesse Stuart Foundation*   42

10. *Jesse Stuart Foundation Publications, Prints, and Films*   46

11. *Out-of-Print Works Available from The Stuart Foundation*   51

12. *Jesse Stuart Meetings/W-Hollow Tours*   52

13. *Greenbo Lake State Resort Park/Jesse Stuart Lodge*   55

14. *For the Collector: A Bibliographical Essay, Bibliography, and Price Guide to Jesse Stuart's Books, by George Brosi*   58

On Using the Price Guide   81

A Chronological Bibliography and Price Guide   86

15. *Jesse Stuart's World, by Jerry A. Herndon*   105

16. *Jesse Stuart: A Literary Profile, by Jim Wayne Miller*   121

17. *A Jesse Stuart Chronology, by Jerry A. Herndon and George Brosi*   140

Foreword

Jesse Stuart was a great American, a true ambassador of good will for his Appalachian homeland, and a prolific author of more than sixty books. Some of his books are world-recognized classics which memorably reflect his values—like hard work, respect for the land, belief in education, devotion to country, and love of family. The Jesse Stuart Foundation is working to promote Stuart's literature and to share his values with future generations.

Ever since the Jesse Stuart Foundation was incorporated as a non-profit organization in 1979, the officers have received a steady stream of inquiries about the availability of Stuart's major works. Because of the great number of his publications, it was often difficult to keep an accurate record of which books were in print and where they could be obtained. Questions about the price of Stuart's out-of-print books were equally frequent and even more complex.

Collectively, these inquiries indicated the need for a bibliography and purchase guide that would aid teachers, librarians, collectors, and general readers. For the past two years, Jerry A. Herndon, Jim Wayne Miller, George Brosi and I have been preparing a book to satisfy that breadth of interest and inquiry.

As the project developed, we became increasingly

aware of both the magnitude of the task and of its necessity. Of course, this book is not designed to replace Hensley C. Woodbridge's exhaustive *Jesse and Jane Stuart: A Bibliography,* which lists the whole range of Stuart's publications, including those in newspapers and magazines as well as those in book form. We chose to focus on Stuart's sixty-one major books as well as on significant studies about the late poet laureate of Kentucky rather than on his hundreds of newspaper and magazine contributions.

The result is a book that meets a number of needs. Teachers will find it a useful aid in regional literature classes, because it provides basic biographical facts as well as bibliographic information, and it includes two essays which place Stuart's work in its historical and literary context. The book will also serve, as intended, as a current purchase guide for teachers, librarians, general readers, and collectors.

In the summer of 1985, I suggested the project to Dr. Jerry A. Herndon, a uniquely qualified Stuart scholar, archivist, and bibliographer, and he "took it from there." As the book took shape, the need for a purchase guide became evident, and George Brosi of Berea, Kentucky, a bookseller and specialist in Appalachian books, was invited to join the project. Brosi's bibliographical essay gives helpful information on sources of out-of-print books and valuable advice on evaluating the condition of the books one finds. Additionally, his "Price Guide" will help the collector accurately determine the value of the books in his collection. This guide provides an expert's appraisal of the value of each edition of Stuart's sixty-one major books.

Dr. Jim Wayne Miller, a nationally recognized scholar

who chairs the Jesse Stuart Foundation's Managing Editors Committee, proofread the manuscript and offered information and advice at each stage of the project. The inclusion of his essay on Stuart's place in American literature makes the book a more meaningful aid for any user.

The Jesse Stuart Foundation takes great pride in presenting *Jesse Stuart, The Man and His Books*. We expect it to serve a wide constituency and to prompt continued interest in Stuart's life and works. As the project administrator, I have been fortunate to work with three good men whose unique areas of expertise were complementary. Jerry Herndon's careful attention to detail, George Brosi's vision, and Jim Wayne Miller's perspective combined to produce a solid and much needed book. Special thanks also go to Jesse's brother, James, for the photographs of the books from his collection which appear throughout this work, and to Ashland Oil, Inc., for photographing them.

Finally, in deep appreciation for her support of this work and her contributions to all of Jesse Stuart's literary creations, we gratefully dedicate this book to Naomi Deane Stuart, Jesse's widow.

James M. Gifford
Ashland, Kentucky
March 23, 1987

Preface

Getting this book into publishable form has required frequent updating of the entries and considerable revision in order to make it as accurate and useful as possible. Though much of George Brosi's chronological bibliography and price guide was initially put together in May, 1986, necessary revisions have been made since that time, and as a result, the reader can expect the guide to reflect conditions of early 1987.

The publishing situation with regard to Jesse Stuart's books is a dynamic one, however, and the reader should realize that frequent changes in the status of the titles listed are likely. Some will go out of print, others will be reprinted, and new titles will also appear. As indicated in the last entry in the "Price Guide," for instance, McGraw-Hill will soon be publishing Stuart's *Cradle of the Copperheads,* a previously unpublished book about the year Stuart served as Superintendent of Greenup County Schools, in 1932–33. The Jesse Stuart Foundation is also completing arrangements for the republication of *Kentucky Is My Land, Hie to the Hunters, To Teach, To Love,* and *A Jesse Stuart Reader.* These books should appear in 1987 or 1988. They will be published in attractive, reasonably priced limited editions, and most will be available in both

Man
with
a bull-tongue
Plow

"Jesse Stuart is a rare poet for these times, in that he is both copious and comprehensible. His book ought to be interesting, even to those who think that they cannot read poetry. They can read Jesse Stuart, if they please as auto-biography—and find themselves in the company of a modern American Robert Burns."

MARK VAN DOREN

Jesse Stuart

Bull-tongue plows were used by hill farmers to break ground which hadn't been tilled. This book of 703 sonnets was also a ground-breaking one. It launched Jesse Stuart's commercial publishing career. The book was so popular that it was reprinted the same month it was published, in October, 1934. *(Photo courtesy of E. P. Dutton & Co.)*

hardcover and paperback. The Foundation will also be reprinting a number of other titles over the next several years.

The best way to keep up with the rapidly changing publication situation is to purchase an associate membership in the Jesse Stuart Foundation. These memberships must be renewed annually, but the cost is modest ($15 for an individual, $25 for a family), and the benefits include regular notification, via *Newsletter,* of forthcoming new publications and reprints of Stuart titles. If you use this information to annotate the entries in this bibliography, you can keep the book current, thus extending its usefulness indefinitely.

Jerry A. Herndon
Murray, Kentucky
April 6, 1987

Stuart's first collection of short stories, published in 1936, reveals in its title the true-life setting of almost all of his works, W-Hollow—the Kentucky mountain valley where he lived most of his life. *(Photo courtesy of E. P. Dutton & Co.)*

1.

Jesse Stuart: A Biographical Sketch

Jesse Stuart was a man who knew intimately the life of the rural poor. He was born in W-Hollow, near Greenup, Kentucky, on August 8, 1906, to Mitchell and Martha Hilton Stuart. He was the second of their seven children, and their first son. Mitchell Stuart worked as a coal miner for a time, then as a tenant farmer, moving from place to place in W-Hollow as he tried to make a living for his growing family. Jesse and his brother James grew up helping their father raise the crops which fed them. Two of their brothers, Herbert and Martin, died of pneumonia as children, Herbert at four, and Martin as an infant. During the First World War, Mitchell Stuart got a job as a section hand with the Chesapeake and Ohio Railroad, and he used his wages of four dollars a day to pay for fifty acres of land in W-Hollow, the only land he ever owned. As the family worked together to clear the land and raise crops on it, Mitchell Stuart instilled in Jesse the desire to someday own his own land.

Mitchell and Martha Stuart also instilled in their children the desire to get an education, though Mick Stuart, as Mitchell was known to his friends and family, could not read or write, and Martha had gone only as far as the second grade. Jesse became the first of the family to graduate from high school, in May, 1926, but he had only been able to attend school sporadically, for a total of twenty-two months, prior to taking and passing the examination required for enrollment in Greenup High School. This was the summer of 1922. He had a good job at the time, helping mix the concrete for the crew which was paving Greenup's streets, but he quit to enter high school when the fall term began in September. He had been making three dollars a day, the best wages of his life, but he saw more future in education.

During his high school years, Jesse worked early and late at farm chores to help keep the farm going, and hired himself out on Saturdays when he could, in order to earn the money he needed to pay for his books and clothing. While attending Greenup High, he was encouraged to write by an English teacher, Mrs. R. E. Hatton, who saw promise in the short stories he turned in as theme assignments. With her prompting, he also began to write poems.

After graduating from Greenup High School, Jesse spent some time working for a carnival that had come to town, and he helped in the crops at home until they were laid by. Then he went to work in a steel mill in Ashland. In September, he left his job and went looking for a college that would admit him. He tried Berea College because he could work his way through school there, but there was no vacancy. Advised at Berea to try Lincoln Memorial University at Harrogate, Tennessee, he went there to try his luck. LMU accepted him in September, 1926.

Jesse worked at various jobs on the university campus, and helped harvest the school's crops as well. He also helped dig a water line to the school, and worked

2

in the stone quarry. He received more encouragement to write from Harry Harrison Kroll, one of his English professors, and he published his own material in the campus paper, *The Blue and the Gray*, which he edited in 1928 and 1929. Among his classmates were James Still and Don West, and he received intellectual stimulation from both. Still and West, like Jesse himself, were later to achieve recognition for their literary portrayal of the mountain people. Today, Still continues to be highly regarded for his achievements in both fiction and poetry.

After graduation from LMU in 1929, Jesse began his teaching career at Warnock High School, a one-room country school in Greenup County. He spent one year there. In 1930–31, he was Principal of Greenup High School, from which he had graduated just four years before. The year 1931–32 he spent as a graduate student at Vanderbilt University, where he took classes from Donald Davidson, Robert Penn Warren, John Donald Wade, and Edwin Mims, but he finished the year without taking a degree. His unfinished thesis was lost in the fire which destroyed the dormitory he roomed in, and lack of money made it impossible for him to continue. The year was important to him, however, because of his renewed association with James Still and Don West, who were also there, and because of his contact with the Vanderbilt agrarians, Donald Davidson in particular. Davidson advised him to continue to write about his hill country and its people. He returned home, and in September, 1932, he became Superintendent of Greenup County Schools.

After a year marred by the sniping of political enemies, Stuart stepped down as Superintendent in May, 1933, and accepted the principalship of McKell High

School, a position he held for the next four years. He had recently begun publishing his poems of rural life in several nationally known magazines, including *The American Mercury, Poetry,* and *The Virginia Quarterly Review,* and at McKell he continued to do so. After receiving inquiries from several publishers about a possible book-length manuscript, he submitted *Man with a Bull-Tongue Plow* to E. P. Dutton. When Dutton published the book on October 14, 1934, the event brought Stuart immediate national recognition and acclaim as an authentic American voice. Some reviewers compared him to Scotland's beloved poet, Robert Burns, as a poet expressing the heart and soul of his people.

Stuart also began writing short stories in 1934, and his first three were accepted by major magazines: *Story, The Yale Review,* and *The American Mercury.* They also began to appear in *The Atlantic Monthly* and in *Esquire.* He was prolific, so much so that Dutton was able to put together his first collection of short stories, *Head o' W-Hollow,* in 1936, just two years after he began writing for publication in earnest. In 1937, he was awarded a Guggenheim Fellowship for study abroad, and went to Britain for a year. He traveled in Scotland and England, and in Europe as well. While abroad, he revised the lengthy autobiography he had overwhelmed Dr. Edwin Mims with at Vanderbilt University when Dr. Mims had assigned the class a brief autobiographical paper. When Dutton published this book in 1938 under the title, *Beyond Dark Hills,* it ran 399 pages in print.

Stuart spent the 1938–39 school year teaching Remedial English at Portsmouth (Ohio) High School, but in June of the latter year he decided to leave teaching in order to devote his energies exclusively to writing, farming, and lecturing. Since 1934, he had been speaking from time to time on his works and their background in the life of his mountain people, and he hoped that earnings from regular tours on the lecture circuit would help make it possible for him to depend on writing for most of his income. He had also bought 400 acres of land in W-Hollow by this time. On his birthday, August 8th, he began work on his first novel, and on October 14, 1939, he and Naomi Deane Norris were married. He also began a nationwide lecture tour in October, under the management of William B. Feakins and Company.

Stuart's novel, *Trees of Heaven,* turned out in two and a half months, was published by E. P. Dutton in April, 1940. Dutton also brought out a second collection of his stories, *Men of the Mountains,* in 1941. He continued writing, lecturing, and managing his farm, but spent the 1942–43 school year as Superintendent of the Greenup Independent School District. The Stuarts' only child, Jessica Jane, was born on August 20, 1942. Stuart continued to serve as Superintendent of the Greenup City Schools until he was inducted into the Navy in March, 1944. He had already published *Taps for Private Tussie,* his second novel, in November, 1943, and it had become a best seller, earning him the Thomas Jefferson Southern Award as the best Southern book published that year, and becoming a Book-of-the-Month Club selection. This satirical look at indolent families on relief helped cement Stuart's reputation as a humorist with keen insight into human nature and an affectionate view of its foibles. Another novel, *Mon-*

grel Mettle, appeared in 1944. This fable about a dog's life attested to Stuart's deep feeling for animals, as did scores of his short stories and poems.

Stuart spent his naval service mostly in Washington, D. C., in a unit assigned the task of writing training literature. He also continued to work on his own writing. An important book of poems, *Album of Destiny,* appeared in 1944, and he completed another novel, *Foretaste of Glory,* in 1945. This was published in March, 1946, subsequent to his discharge from the Navy on December 31, 1945. *Foretaste* is a satirical but affectionate portrayal of a community's feverish preparations for Judgement Day when a display of the Northern Lights convinces its people that the great event is at hand.

Dutton brought out a third collection of Stuart's stories, *Tales from the Plum Grove Hills,* in October, 1946. A little less than three years later, in September, 1949, Charles Scribner's Sons published *The Thread That Runs So True,* Stuart's story of his experiences as a Kentucky mountain school teacher and school administrator. This book was an extraordinary success. It was voted "the most important book of 1949" by the National Education Association in 1950, and Scribner's still keeps it in print, to meet a steady demand. The book demonstrated the shortcomings of the public educational system in a rural state, and the thirst of its young people for educational opportunity.

The year 1950 also saw the publication of *Hie to the Hunters,* a very well-received novel about a town boy's introduction to country life, and *Clearing in the Sky and Other Stories.* Both these books show Stuart's humor at its best. The novel portrays a tough country boy who settles disputes by spitting tobacco juice in his oppo-

6

nents' eyes, and the story collection includes the tale of two boys who sober up their drunken father with a wild mule ride and the story of a man who loves machinery so much that he steals a steam shovel, one piece at a time. Dutton published *Kentucky Is My Land*, a popular collection of poems, in 1952, and in 1953 McGraw-Hill, the house which had become Stuart's publisher with *Hie to the Hunters*, brought out another novel, *The Good Spirit of Laurel Ridge*. This is the story of a modern-day Thoreau, a squatter who lives from the land and in harmony with it. Stuart also published his first book for junior readers, *The Beatinest Boy*, the story of a self-reliant boy and his love for his grandmother.

By this time, Stuart had been hard at work as a writer and lecturer for nearly twenty years, but the year 1954, when he was appointed Poet Laureate of Kentucky, brought a crucial event that forced him to slow down and reassess his life. He suffered a massive heart attack in Murray, Kentucky, just after speaking at Murray State College to the First District Education Association, a subgroup of the Kentucky Education Association. As he slowly recovered, Stuart kept a daily journal which became the basis for his book, *The Year of My Rebirth* (1956), a work that many heart patients have found reassuring and therapeutic. It records Stuart's rediscovery of nature's beauty and the joys of existence, including the satisfaction found in a life lived at a pace slow enough to allow one to savor life's simpler joys.

Stuart spent the 1956–57 school year as Principal of McKell High School, and in September, 1958, he published another collection of short stories, *Plowshare in Heaven*. In 1960, he placed many of his papers and manuscripts at Murray State College, preparatory to

7

leaving for Egypt, where he taught at the American University of Cairo for the 1960–61 school year. In November, 1960, McGraw-Hill published *God's Oddling,* a biographical work subtitled *The Story of Mick Stuart, My Father.* Stuart's father had passed away in 1954, his mother in 1951.

In February, 1961, Stuart was awarded the $5,000 Fellowship of the Academy of American Poets, and in May, 1962, McGraw-Hill published another collection of his poetry, *Hold April.* He spent several months in 1962–63 on a good-will tour of the Near, Middle, and Far East for the U. S. State Department. Back home, he continued overseeing the management of his farm, now grown to over 700 acres. He had made the place a model of conservation practices, and, as he had for many years, he continued to write articles on the theme of land and wildlife conservation for such magazines as *Progressive Farmer* and *American Forests.*

In the 1960s and 1970s, Stuart continued to publish both new works and collections of his earlier writings. McGraw-Hill brought out *A Jesse Stuart Reader,* designed for high school audiences, in 1963. This useful book includes the author's introductions to the poems, short stories, and excerpts from longer works included. Six collections of short stories and three novels also appeared in the two decades. The stories, as always, revealed Stuart's characteristic humor and compassion, as well as his ability to seize and portray memorable and significant episodes from life so deftly that the characters come to life on the page and the stories seem to tell themselves. *Save Every Lamb* (1964) and *Dawn of Remembered Spring* (1972)—a book about snakes which includes poems as well as stories—show his love for

8

animals, a theme that runs through all his works. His love for the land and his hill people is memorably expressed in the stories in *My Land Has a Voice* (1966), *Come Gentle Spring* (1969) and *Come Back to the Farm* (1971). The political shenanigans of the hill country are recorded in the stories in *32 Votes Before Breakfast*, which appeared in 1974.

A novel about the mixed-blood Melungeons of East Tennessee, originally written in 1940, appeared in 1965 under the title, *Daughter of the Legend*. This tragic romance about the doomed love of an outsider for a Melungeon girl was followed in 1967 by *Mr. Gallion's School*, a novel based on Stuart's year as Principal of McKell High School in 1956–57. This book emphasizes the need for training in character as well as in the traditional school subjects. Then, in 1973, Stuart published another satirical look at the welfare system, a novel called *The Land Beyond the River*. The book is set in Ohio, and focuses on the abuses of the food-stamp program.

Two representative collections of Stuart's poetry appeared in the 1970s, J. R. LeMaster's *The World of Jesse Stuart* in 1975, and Wanda Hicks' *The Seasons of Jesse Stuart: An Autobiography in Poetry*, in 1976. He also added two more juvenile books to those already published, a series begun in 1953 with *The Beatinest Boy*. These books, which include *A Penny's Worth of Character* (1954), *The Rightful Owner* (1960), and *Andy Finds a Way* (1961), portray traditional moral values and have been consistently popular. McGraw-Hill brought out *Old Ben*, the story of a pet snake, in 1970, and Stuart published *Come to My Tomorrowland* with Aurora Publishers in Nashville, Tennessee, in 1971. This is the story of a

9

This romance was Stuart's first novel, written while he
was courting Naomi Deane Norris and completed shortly
after their wedding. It was published in 1940. *(Photo courtesy of E. P. Dutton & Co.)*

crippled little girl's love for a pet deer. *Dandelion on the Acropolis: A Journal of Greece,* appeared in 1978. This was followed in 1979 by *The Kingdom Within: A Spiritual Autobiography,* and a collection of occasional pieces, titled *Lost Sandstones and Lonely Skies and Other Essays. The Kingdom Within* is an artistic *tour de force,* focusing on Stuart's imagined encounter, when he is near death from a heart attack, with the characters he had created over his long career. This book was published by McGraw-Hill, while Archer Editions Press brought out the essay collection. Archer Editions had also published *The Seasons of Jesse Stuart* and *Dandelion on the Acropolis.*

In 1979, Stuart authorized the formation of the Jesse Stuart Foundation, and in early 1980 he assigned to it the rights to his literary estate, and the responsibility for managing that estate. He and Naomi also presented the Stuart land in W-Hollow to the State of Kentucky as the Jesse Stuart Nature Preserve. The gift was announced at W-Hollow in 1979, with Governor Julian Carroll present for the dedication ceremonies, and on June 25, 1980, the representative of the new governor, John Y. Brown, Jr., came to W-Hollow to present to the Stuarts the State's check for $601,750, representing half the value of the donated 726 acres. This officially completed the agreement entered into by the Stuarts with the Kentucky Nature Preserves Commission.

On August 20th, 1981, Governor Brown presented Jesse Stuart with the Governor's Distinguished Service Medallion in recognition of his contributions to the Commonwealth.

Three collections of Stuart's works appeared in the 1980s. *If I Were Seventeen Again and Other Essays* was published by Archer Editions in 1980, and Jerry A. Herndon's selection of stories and poems for use by junior high and high school students, *Land of the Honey-Colored Wind: Jesse Stuart's Kentucky*, appeared at the close of 1981. This book was published by the Jesse Stuart Foundation with the aid of a grant from the Honorable Order of Kentucky Colonels, and the Foundation then placed copies in the schools of the Commonwealth in 1982. Later in the year, Harold E. Richardson's *The Best-Loved Short Stories of Jesse Stuart* was published by McGraw-Hill. This collection includes an introduction by Robert Penn Warren.

Over the years, Stuart had been plagued by a series of heart seizures after his initial attack in 1954, and in early 1978 he suffered a disabling stroke. Another followed in May, 1982, leaving him comatose. His home was placed on the National Register of Historic Places in June, 1982, and he died on Friday, February 17, 1984. He was buried in his beloved Plum Grove Cemetery, close to his home in W-Hollow, and a granite monument inscribed with lines from his poems marks his grave.

2.

Works by Stuart in Print; An Alphabetical Listing

Clearing in the Sky and Other Stories. Lexington: University Press of Kentucky, 1984. $20 hardcover; $9 paperbound. Order from: University Press of Kentucky, 102 Lafferty Hall, University of Kentucky, Lexington, KY 40506. A collection of twenty-one stories, showing Stuart's characteristic humor at its best. First published in 1950, and out of print for over thirty years until reprinted in 1984. "Foreword" by Ruel E. Foster.

Cradle of the Copperheads. To be published by McGraw-Hill, probably in 1988. Written in 1933 and previously unpublished, this book is the story of Stuart's year (1932–33) as Superintendent of Greenup County Schools. It is being edited by Professor Paul Douglass of Mercer University. The price has not yet been determined.

Dandelion on the Acropolis: A Journal of Greece. Lynnville, TN: Archer Editions Press, 1978. $10. Order from: Archer Editions Press, 318 Fry Branch Road, Lynnville, TN 38472. A travel journal embodying Stuart's reflections on the country, based on a month the Stuarts spent in Greece in 1962 during a tour undertaken for the United States Information Service, U. S. State Department.

Foretaste of Glory. Lexington: University Press of Kentucky, 1986. $19 hardcover; $9 paperbound. Originally published in 1946. Order from: University Press of Kentucky. A satirical novel about the goings-on in a Kentucky community terrorized by a display of the aurora borealis and convinced that the end of the world is at hand. "Foreword" by Robert J. Higgs.

Head o' W-Hollow. Lexington: University Press of Kentucky, 1979. $9 paperbound. Order from: University Press of Kentucky. A reprint of Stuart's first collection of short stories, originally published in 1936. The twenty-one stories include some of his darker portrayals of human nature, and some of his saltiest characters. "Foreword" by Robert Penn Warren.

Hie to the Hunters. Ashland, KY: The Jesse Stuart Foundation, 1988. $20 hardcover; $9 paperbound. Order from: The Jesse Stuart Foundation, P. O. Box 391, Ashland, KY 41114. Add $1 for postage and handling. A reprint of a novel first published in 1950, a hilarious tale about a city boy taken in by a farmer's family, who introduce him to life in the country. Introduction by Jerry A. Herndon.

If I Were Seventeen Again and Other Essays. Lynnville, TN: Archer Editions Press, 1980. $9.95 paperbound. Order from: Archer Editions Press. A collection of sixteen essays on education, the importance of character, freedom, and the meaning of America.

14

Kentucky Is My Land. Ashland, KY: The Jesse Stuart Foundation, 1987. $10.95 hardcover. Order from: The Jesse Stuart Foundation. Add $1 for postage and handling. Originally published in 1952, this collection of poems celebrates Kentucky, the hill people, the poet's domestic life, the beauty of the natural world, patriotism, and love for the land. Introduction by Jim Wayne Miller, a noted Appalachian scholar and poet.

Lost Sandstones and Lonely Skies and Other Essays. Lynnville, TN: Archer Editions Press, 1979. $9.95 paperbound. Order from: Archer Editions Press. A collection of twenty essays on the natural world, conservation, wildlife, and human nature; a number are Stuart's personal reflections about his own life.

Men of the Mountains. Lexington: University Press of Kentucky, 1979. $9 paperbound. Order from: University Press of Kentucky. A reprint of Stuart's second collection of short stories, originally published in 1941. Most of the twenty-one stories focus on the strongly individualized characters among the mountain people. "Foreword" by H. Edward Richardson.

My World. Kentucky Bicentennial Bookshelf Series. Lexington: University Press of Kentucky, 1975. $6.95. Order from: University Press of Kentucky. Stuart's meditations on W-Hollow, Kentucky, the United States, and the foreign countries he had visited and loved.

The Only Place We Live. Illustrations by Frank Utpatel; text by August Derleth, Jesse Stuart, and Robert E.

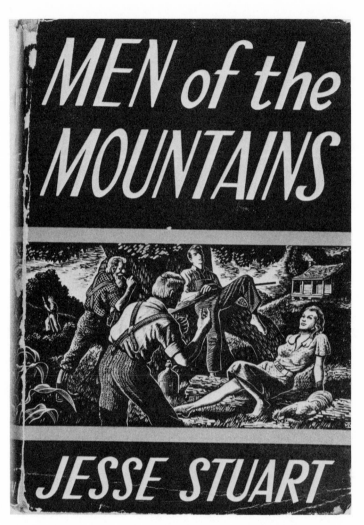

The men and women of the mountains were the subjects of all of Jesse Stuart's fiction, including this, his second short story collection, published in 1941. *(Photo courtesy of E. P.Dutton & Co.)*

Gard. Edited by Mark E. Lefebvre. Madison: Wisconsin House, 1976. $12.95. Order from: Stanton and Lee, 44 East Mifflin Street, Madison, WI 53703. Stuart's contribution consists of twenty poems—or excerpts from poems—illustrated by Utpatel's wood engravings.

The Seasons of Jesse Stuart: An Autobiography in Poetry, 1907–1976. Edited by Wanda Hicks. Lynnville, TN: Archer Editions Press, 1976. $25. Limited edition, $45; deluxe edition, from $150. Order from: Archer Editions Press. An intriguing selection of Stuart's poems, grouped according to the periods of his life portrayed in them, and according to the seasons. The poems included appear both in printed texts and in reproductions of fair copies in Stuart's own handwriting. The limited edition and deluxe limited edition are available in limited quantities. The deluxe edition is leather-bound and each copy includes a handwritten poem by Stuart; the price varies according to the length of the poem.

Songs of a Mountain Plowman. Edited by Jim Wayne Miller. Ashland, KY/Morehead, KY: The Jesse Stuart Foundation and the Appalachian Development Center, Morehead State University, 1986. $10.95 paperbound. Order from: The Jesse Stuart Foundation. This book of poems was originally written by Stuart in 1929–31 and has not previously been published. With an introduction by Professor Miller.

Tennessee Hill Folk. Photographs and captions by Joe Clark; introductory essay by Jesse Stuart. Nashville,

17

TN: Vanderbilt University Press, 1972. $10.95. Order from: Vanderbilt University Press, 1211 18th Avenue South, Nashville, TN 37212. Clark's photographs show hill people engaged in traditional mountain activities in the area near Lincoln Memorial University. Stuart's essay provides insight into his years in the region.

The Thread That Runs So True. New York: Charles Scribner's Sons, 1958. $8.95 paperbound. Order from: Charles Scribner's Sons, 115 Fifth Avenue, New York, NY 10003. Stuart's classic story of his years as a teacher in Greenup County's one-room schools in the 1920s and 1930s, and of his years as Principal and Superintendent in the Greenup City and Greenup County school systems. First published in 1949.

To Teach, To Love. Ashland, KY: The Jesse Stuart Foundation, 1987. $20 hardcover; $9 paperbound. Order from: The Jesse Stuart Foundation. Add $1 for postage and handling. A collection of Stuart's stories and essays on education, originally published in 1970. Introduction by J. R. LeMaster.

Trees of Heaven. Lexington: University Press of Kentucky, 1980. $9 paperbound. Order from: University Press of Kentucky. A reprint of Stuart's first novel, originally published in 1940. A lyrical evocation of country life, portraying a romance between a landowner's son (Tarvin Bushman) and a share-cropper's daughter (Subrinea Tussie). "Foreword" by Wade Hall.

3.

Out-of-Print Works by Stuart;
An Alphabetical Listing

Album of Destiny. New York: E. P. Dutton, 1944. A collection of sonnets following the members of a mountain community through the stages of their lives, from youth to old age and death.

Andy Finds a Way. New York: Whittlesey House, 1961. [Note: Whittlesey House is a McGraw-Hill imprint.] A junior book about a boy finding a way to make it unnecessary for his father to sell his calf; a story of self-help and self-reliance.

Autumn Lovesong: A Celebration of Love's Fulfillment. Kansas City, MO: Hallmark Editions, 1971. A poetic celebration of the joys of maturity.

The Beatinest Boy. New York: Whittlesey House, 1953. A junior book about a self-reliant boy's love for his grandmother.

The Best-Loved Short Stories of Jesse Stuart. Edited by Harold E. Richardson. New York: McGraw-Hill, 1982. A collection of thirty-four stories spanning Stuart's entire career, accompanied by scholarly introductions and a map of W-Hollow keyed to Stuart's writings. Introduction by Robert Penn Warren.

Beyond Dark Hills: A Personal Story. New York: E. P. Dutton, 1938. Stuart's autobiography, embodying the story of his struggles to get an education and his early years as an educator and writer.

Come Back to the Farm. New York: McGraw-Hill, 1971. A collection of sixteen short stories originally published in various magazines over several decades. Most portray the pioneer spirit and self-reliance of the hill people.

Come Gentle Spring. New York: McGraw-Hill, 1969. A collection of twenty short stories published in various magazines over several decades. Seven were published in *Esquire;* most focus on the strong, even ornery, individuals among the mountain people, with a leavening of humor and sentiment.

Come to My Tomorrowland. Nashville, TN and London: Aurora Publishers, 1971. A junior book about a crippled little girl's love for a pet deer.

Daughter of the Legend. New York: McGraw-Hill, 1965. A novel, originally written in 1940, about an isolated people of mixed blood, the Melungeons of East Tennessee, and the love of an outsider for a woman of this people.

Dawn of Remembered Spring. New York: McGraw-Hill, 1972. A collection of fifteen stories and eleven poems about snakes, reflecting Stuart's fascination with these creatures and his interest in their place in nature's pattern.

God's Oddling: The Story of Mick Stuart, My Father. New York: McGraw-Hill, 1960. A celebration of a simple, uneducated man who knew and loved the land, and who taught his values to his children.

The Good Spirit of Laurel Ridge. New York: McGraw-Hill, 1953. A novel about a self-sufficient squatter, a sort of modern-day Thoreau, who lives from the land and in harmony with it.

Harvest of Youth. Howe, OK: The Scroll Press, 1930. Stuart's first book, a collection of imitative poetry published at his own expense. He later destroyed all the copies he could find.

Hold April: New Poems. New York: McGraw-Hill, 1962. A collection of poems expressing Stuart's acceptance of life, with all its beauty and pain, as a divinely ordained pattern.

Huey, the Engineer. St. Helena, CA: James E. Beard, 1960. A reprint in book form of an article about the old Eastern Kentucky Railroad, originally published in *Esquire* magazine in 1937.

A Jesse Stuart Harvest. New York: Dell Publishing Co., 1965. St. Simons Island, GA: Mockingbird books, 1974. A representative collection of eighteen short stories originally published in the 1930s and 1940s, with a lengthy introduction by Stuart. The stories are portraits of self-reliance and human cussedness.

A *Jesse Stuart Reader: Stories and Poems*. New York: McGraw-Hill, 1963. A collection of eighteen stories, twenty-six poems, and excerpts from *God's Oddling, The Thread That Runs So True,* and *The Year of My Rebirth*. Designed for use in the public schools, with Stuart's introduction to each story and excerpt, and his introductory essay on the poems. "Foreword" by Max Bogart.

The Kingdom Within: A Spiritual Autobiography. New York: McGraw-Hill, 1979. A *tour de force,* focusing on the author's imagined encounter at the point of death with the literary characters he had created over his career.

The Land Beyond the River. New York: McGraw-Hill, 1973. A novel satirizing the easy way of life made possible by the food stamp program; set in Ohio.

Land of the Honey-Colored Wind: Jesse Stuart's Kentucky. Edited by Jerry A. Herndon. Morehead, KY: The Jesse Stuart Foundation, 1981. A representative selection of some of Stuart's best work, consisting of twelve short stories and twenty-seven poems, with carefully established texts. Designed for classroom use at the eighth-grade level, but suitable for grades 6–12.

Man with a Bull-Tongue Plow. New York: E. P. Dutton, 1934. Stuart's famous book of 703 sonnets celebrating his earth people and nature. Death and the cycle of the seasons are central themes. An abridged paperbound edition published in 1959 and consisting of 622 sonnets is also out of print.

Mr. Gallion's School. New York: McGraw-Hill, 1967. A novel based on Stuart's year as Principal of McKell High School in 1956–57.

Mongrel Mettle: The Autobiography of a Dog. New York: Books, Inc., 1944. Distributed by E. P. Dutton & Co. A novel, the story of a dog's life, with celebration of America's melting-pot democracy a significant theme.

My Land Has a Voice. New York: McGraw-Hill, 1966. A collection of twenty short stories previously published in various magazines over several decades. They portray the humor, sentiment, pathos, and courage of human life, as well as the ornery side of human nature.

Old Ben. New York: McGraw-Hill, 1970. A junior book about a pet snake.

A Penny's Worth of Character. New York: Whittlesey House, 1954. A junior book about a boy's discovery of the need for honesty.

Plowshare in Heaven. New York: McGraw-Hill, 1958. A collection of twenty-one short stories about the odd, quirky characters among the mountain people.

TAPS FOR
PRIVATE
TUSSIE

•

JESSE STUART

This novel, Stuart's best-selling book, appeared in 1943. While it angered some people because of the way certain characters were portrayed, it delighted thousands more and ended once and for all the financial insecurity Stuart had known since his birth in a one-room log cabin. *(Photo courtesy of E. P.Dutton & Co.)*

Red Mule. New York: Whittlesey House, 1955. A junior book celebrating the virtues of mules in the age of tractors.

A Ride with Huey the Engineer. New York: McGraw-Hill, 1966. Dayton, OH: Landfall Press, 1973. A junior book about a boy's ride with the engineer of a train on the Eastern Kentucky Railroad.

The Rightful Owner. New York: Whittlesey House, 1960. A junior book about a boy learning to respect the rights of others.

Save Every Lamb. New York: McGraw-Hill, 1964. A collection of twenty-five stories and excerpts from longer works focusing on domestic animals and wildlife and man's interaction with the animal world.

Seven by Jesse. Terre Haute, IN: Indiana Council of Teachers of English/Indiana State University, 1970. [This item is volume 5, part 2, numbers 2–4 of the *Indiana English Journal*.] A collection of short stories.

Tales from the Plum Grove Hills. New York: E. P. Dutton, 1946. A collection of twenty short stories illustrating Stuart's love for his land and his people.

Taps for Private Tussie. New York: E. P. Dutton, 1943. A satirical look at the New Deal's relief system and its effects on the character of rural Americans, combined with the story of a boy's love for his grandfather.

Stuart's best-selling novel, *Taps for Private Tussie* has been reprinted many times and translated into several foreign languages.

32 Votes Before Breakfast: Politics at the Grass Roots, As Seen in Short Stories by Jesse Stuart. New York: McGraw-Hill, 1974. [Note: Copies are available at $19.95, plus $1 for postage and handling, from The Jesse Stuart Foundation, P. O. Box 391, Ashland, KY 41114.] A collection of short stories focusing on political skulduggery, as practiced in Kentucky.

Tim, a Story. Cincinnati, OH: 1939. A hilarious short story notable for its earthy realism and humor; published as an issue of *The Little Man* magazine.

Up the Hollow from Lynchburg. Photographs by Joe Clark; text by Jesse Stuart. New York: McGraw-Hill, 1975. [Note: Copies are available at $15, plus $1 for postage and handling, from The Jesse Stuart Foundation.] A book about the country people in the area around Lynchburg, Tennessee, the home of the Jack Daniel's whiskey distillery.

The World of Jesse Stuart: Selected Poems. Edited by J. R. LeMaster. New York: McGraw-Hill, 1975. A comprehensive collection of Stuart's poetry, organized thematically.

The Year of My Rebirth. New York: McGraw-Hill, 1956. The story of Stuart's year of convalescence from his first heart attack, portraying his rediscovery of the simple beauties of life and nature.

26

4.

Stuart Studies in Print

LeMaster, J. R. *Jesse Stuart: A Reference Guide.* Boston: G. K. Hall, 1979. $27.50. Order from: G. K. Hall and Co., 70 Lincoln Street, Boston, MA 02111. Lists "Writings About Jesse Stuart, 1934–1977"; an essential guide to criticism, both brief and book-length. Indexed.

LeMaster, J. R., and Mary Washington Clarke, eds. *Jesse Stuart: Essays on His Work.* Lexington: University Press of Kentucky, 1977. $17. Order from: University Press of Kentucky, 102 Lafferty Hall, University of Kentucky, Lexington, KY 40506. A collection of criticism by ten leading Stuart scholars, treating Stuart's poetry, short stories, and novels, and assessing his place in American literature and his use of the folklife of his region.

Stuart, Jane. *Transparencies: Remembrances of Jesse Stuart, My Father.* Lynnville, TN: Archer Editions Press, 1986. $9.95 paperbound. Order from: Archer Editions Press, 318 Fry Branch Road, Lynnville, TN 38472. Jane's reminiscences, presented as vignettes in poetry and prose.

Woodbridge, Hensley C. *Jesse and Jane Stuart: A Bibliog-*

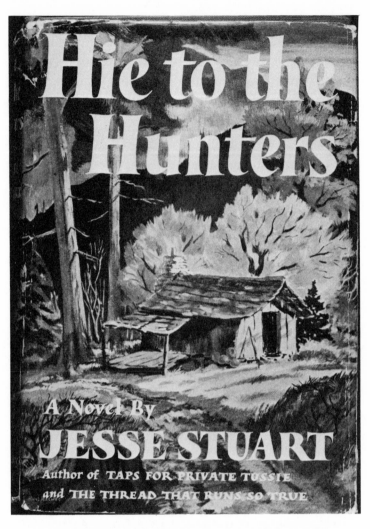

The saying, "Hie to the hunters!", was a wish for good luck called to those who had set out to put meat on the table. This novel, published in 1950, shows a town boy learning the ways of life on a mountain farm. It has been consistently popular. *(Photo courtesy of McGraw-Hill, Inc.)*

raphy. Third edition. Murray, KY: Murray State University Printing Services, 1979. $4.95 paperbound. Add $1 for shipping. Order from: Manager, University Bookstore, Murray State University, Murray, KY 42071. The essential bibliographic guide for the study of Stuart. The first edition, 1960, was the first book-length work on Stuart; the second edition appeared in 1969.

5.

Out-of-Print Stuart Studies

Blair, Everetta Love. *Jesse Stuart: His Life and Works*. Columbia: University of South Carolina Press, 1967. The first major critical study, useful for general information on Stuart's life and his development as a literary artist.

Clarke, Mary Washington. *Jesse Stuart's Kentucky*. New York: McGraw-Hill, 1968. A valuable study of Stuart's use of elements of folklore and folklife in his works.

Foster, Ruel E. *Jesse Stuart*. New York: Twayne, 1968. [Note: This volume is number 140 in Twayne Publishers' United States Authors Series.] A thoroughly informed and critically balanced study of Stuart's achievement as a literary artist; places him in the context of the American literary tradition.

Gilpin, John R., Jr., *The Man . . . Jesse Stuart: Poet, Novelist, Short Story Writer, Educator*. Ashland, KY: Economy Printers, 1977. Includes a very useful essay on Stuart's life, excellent pictures, and a detailed chronology.

Hall, Wade. *"The Truth Is Funny": A Study of Jesse Stuart's*

Humor. Terre Haute, IN: Indiana Council of Teachers of English/Indiana State University, 1970. [This item is volume 5, part 1, numbers 2–4 of the *Indiana English Journal.*]

LeMaster, J. R. *Jesse Stuart: Kentucky's Chronicler-Poet.* Memphis, TN: Memphis State University Press, 1980. The first book-length study of Stuart's poetry, with emphasis on his imagery, themes, and craftsmanship.

LeMaster, J. R., ed. *Jesse Stuart: Selected Criticism.* St. Petersburg, FL: Valkyrie House, 1978. A collection of critical essays by six leading Stuart scholars, including LeMaster.

Pennington, Lee. *The Dark Hills of Jesse Stuart: A Consideration of Symbolism and Vision in the Novels of Jesse Stuart.* Cincinnati: Harvest Press, 1967. A study by a poet who was a student at McKell High School when Stuart was Principal there in 1956–57.

Perry, Dick. *Reflections of Jesse Stuart on a Land of Many Moods.* New York: McGraw-Hill, 1971. An essential tool for understanding Stuart, based on Perry's extended series of interviews with him.

Richardson, Harold E. *Jesse: The Biography of an American Writer, Jesse Hilton Stuart.* New York: McGraw-Hill, 1984. An in-depth biography written with the aid of Stuart's correspondence and extensive interviews with Stuart and his family.

CLEARING
in the SKY

&
other
stories

JESSE STUART

Author of TAPS FOR PRIVATE TUSSIE
and HIE TO THE HUNTERS

WOODCUTS by STANLEY RICE

Short stories in this and other collections give a clear picture of the life of hill farmers during the last generation
that American farms were worked primarily with home-
made implements and the labor of domestic animals.
Clearing in the Sky was published in 1950. *(Photo courtesy of
McGraw-Hill, Inc.)*

Spurlock, John H. *He Sings for Us: A Sociolinguistic Analysis of the Appalachian Subculture and of Jesse Stuart as a Major American Writer.* Lanham, MD: University Press of America, 1980. An attempt to define Stuart's relationship to his mountain culture and to assess his achievement as a major literary artist.

6.

Booksellers Specializing in Stuart Materials

Appalachian Mountain Books
123 Walnut Street
Berea, KY 40403
(606) 986–1663

Bookworm and Silverfish
P. O. Box 516
Wytheville, VA 24382
(703) 686–5813

The Gift Shop
The Jesse Stuart Lodge
Greenbo Lake State
    Resort Park
HC 60, Box 562
Greenup, KY 41144
(606) 473–7324

Glover's Books
862 South Broadway
Lexington, KY 40504
(606) 253–0614

The Ohio Bookstore, Inc.
726 Main Street
Cincinnati, OH 45202
(513) 621–5142

Old Louisville Books
426 West Oak Street
Louisville, KY 40203
(502) 637–6411

Wolf's Head Books
P. O. Box 1020
198 Foundry Street
Morgantown, WV 26507
(304) 296–0706

Appalachian Mountain Books. George Brosi, proprietor. In business since 1979, dealing exclusively in Southern Appalachian Mountain books, both new and used. Free search service. Both in-print and out-of-print Stuart books and studies available. In 1985 began publishing *Appalachian Mountain Books*, a bi-monthly review and catalogue of regional literature. *AMB* ($10 per year) recently did a special issue on Jesse Stuart.

Bookworm and Silverfish. Jim Presgraves, proprietor. In business since 1965, with an experienced full-time staff. Issues catalogues periodically and provides both a search and an appraisal service.

The Gift Shop, Jesse Stuart Lodge, Greenbo Lake State Resort Park. Mrs. Love Conley, manager. Current Stuart materials available, as well as some first editions of out-of-print works.

Glover's Books. John Glover, proprietor. In business since 1978, dealing exclusively in hardback books. Holdings include used, out-of-print, and rare works, including Stuart titles.

The Ohio Bookstore, Inc. James T. Fallon, proprietor. Founded in 1940, now has over 200,000 books and magazines in stock. Holdings cover every subject, but the specialty is Americana, including the Ohio, Indiana, and Kentucky area. Catalogues issued periodically. Maintains selection of out-of-print Jesse Stuart first editions.

Old Louisville Books. Don Grayson, proprietor. In business since 1976. General out-of-print inventory, 15,000 volumes, with emphasis on Kentucky history and literature, including Jesse Stuart's works.

The Good Spirit of Laurel Ridge

JESSE STUART, AUTHOR OF

"TAPS FOR PRIVATE TUSSIE" & "HIE TO THE HUNTERS"

This fascinating novel, published in 1953, was inspired by the life of one of W-Hollow's most unusual residents, George Alexander, whom Stuart described as "a real life Henry David Thoreau." *(Photo courtesy of McGraw-Hill, Inc.)*

Wolf's Head Books. Harvey J. Wolf and Barbara E. Nailler, co-proprietors. Founded in 1980. General inventory, 44,000 volumes, of used, rare, and out-of-print titles. Areas of specialization include West Virginia/Appalachia, juvenile literature, and first editions. Catalogues issued periodically. Search service. Maintains a selection of Jesse Stuart's books, including signed copies, first editions, and signed first editions.

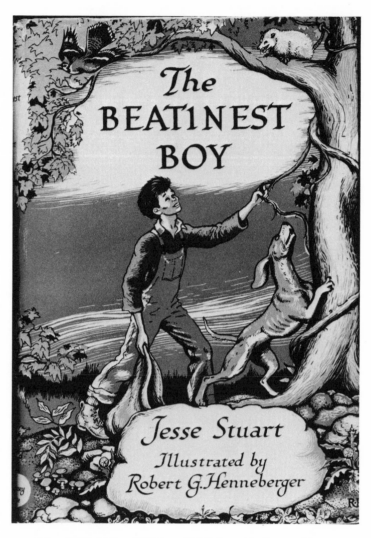

The
BEAT1NEST
BOY

Jesse Stuart

Illustrated by
Robert G. Henneberger

Jesse Stuart's first children's book proudly displayed his
great affection for young people and showed, like his
other books, his respect for the special spoken language
of his people. It was published in 1953. *(Photo courtesy of
McGraw-Hill, Inc.)*

7.

Jesse Stuart/W-Hollow Prints: Black Pine Gallery

The following prints, by Kentucky Heritage Artist Doug Adams, are available at $30 each:

(1) "Plum Grove Church"

(2) "W-Hollow"

(3) "By Sandy Waters"

(4) "The Flower Gatherer"

(5) "The Needle's Eye"

(6) "The Last Leave Home"

(7) "W-Hollow, The Jesse Stuart Homestead"

To order, contact:

Mr. Doug Adams
Black Pine Gallery
P. O. Box 85
Elliottville, KY 40317
(606) 784–5856

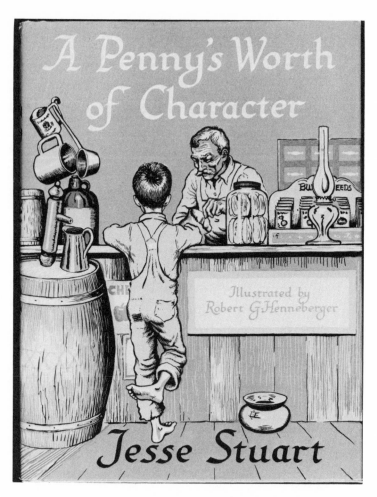

Character must be forged in adversity. This is an important theme not just in Stuart's most popular junior book, but in all his writings. *A Penny's Worth of Character*, published in 1954, is based on an incident in Stuart's own life. *(Photo courtesy of McGraw-Hill, Inc.)*

8.

A Jesse Stuart Film: "Split Cherry Tree"

The film, "Split Cherry Tree," is based on Stuart's short story of this title which originally appeared in the January, 1939, issue of *Esquire* magazine. In 1973, *Esquire's* founder and editor, Arnold Gingrich, called this story his favorite contribution to the magazine, which by then had been in publication for forty years.

The 26-minute film, an award winner at the Birmingham and Midwest film festivals, was produced in 1982 by Learning Corporation of America, and is available on videotape as well as on standard 16 millimeter film. It can be rented for a three-day period for $75, plus $5 shipping. Purchase price is $550 for the film and $425 for the videotape.

Arrangements for rental or purchase can be made through:

> Coronet/MIT Film and Video
> 108 Wilmont
> Deerfield, IL 60015
> (312) 940–1260

9.

The Jesse Stuart Foundation

The Jesse Stuart Foundation was formed in 1979 as a public, nonprofit entity devoted to preserving both Jesse Stuart's literary legacy and W-Hollow, the little valley made famous in his works. The Foundation has control of the rights to Stuart's works, and cooperates with such publishers as McGraw-Hill Book Company and the University Press of Kentucky in keeping them in print. It also publishes occasional new titles under its own name.

The 730-acre Stuart farm in W-Hollow, exclusive of the home place, was turned over to the Commonwealth of Kentucky by the Stuarts in 1980. It is now designated the "Jesse Stuart Nature Preserve" and is part of the Kentucky Nature Preserves System, with ownership vested in the Kentucky Nature Preserves Commission. The Jesse Stuart Foundation has the responsibility of operating the Preserve, and is developing a management plan which will ensure the preservation of W-Hollow. The valley has been made memorable in Stuart's works, and his soil and water conservation practices and protection of wildlife have made it into both a model of fertility and a wildlife refuge. It will now serve permanently as a reminder to visitors of

Jesse Stuart's conviction of America's need to preserve her natural resources. A trail system is also being developed to make it possible for visitors to see the places in the valley which are portrayed in Stuart's stories and novels.

The Jesse Stuart Foundation is governed by a Board of Directors consisting of the presidents of the Commonwealth's universities (or their representatives), members of the Stuart family, and leaders in business, industry, and government. The Foundation also has an Executive Director, who manages the day to day business, plans and schedules events and meetings, coordinates publication projects, and edits a biannual *Newsletter*.

Associate memberships in the Foundation are available to the general public. Associate Members will receive the *Newsletter*, and those who purchase or renew their memberships in 1986 or thereafter will also receive a signed, limited edition print of a Jesse Stuart/ W-Hollow scene. The following categories of associate membership are available, with the annual fees as indicated:

Senior Citizen or Student	$10
Single	$15
Family	$25
Patron	$50
Benefactor	$100

A *Life Membership* is also available at a cost of $500. Those who donate $1,000 or more to the Foundation are designated "Guardians of a Storied Past."

JESSE STUART

The Year of My Rebirth

The dramatic story of a man's struggle back to life from a near-fatal heart attack

Jesse Stuart's first heart attack, on October 8, 1954, came approximately midway in his publishing career. His subsequent writings carried less of a sense of struggle of the earlier works and expressed a spirit of reconciliation. *The Year of My Rebirth* was published in 1956. *(Photo courtesy of McGraw-Hill, Inc.)*

For more information, contact:

Dr. James M. Gifford
Executive Director
The Jesse Stuart Foundation
P. O. Box 391
Ashland, KY 41114
(606) 329–5232

10.

Jesse Stuart Foundation Publications, Prints, and Films

PUBLICATIONS

Hie to the Hunters. Ashland, KY: The Jesse Stuart Foundation, 1988. $20 hardcover; $9 paperbound. Add $1 for postage and handling. The lighthearted, comic story of a town boy learning the ways of the people who live on the land. Introduction by Jerry A. Herndon.

Kentucky Is My Land. Ashland, KY: The Jesse Stuart Foundation, 1987. $10.95 hardcover. Add $1 for postage and handling. This collection of poems celebrates Kentucky, the hill people, the poet's domestic life, the beauty of the natural world, patriotism, and love for the land. Introduction by Jim Wayne Miller, noted Appalachian scholar and prize-winning poet.

Songs of a Mountain Plowman. Edited by Jim Wayne Miller. Ashland, KY/Morehead, KY: The Jesse Stuart Foundation and the Appalachian Development Center, Morehead State University, 1986. $10.95 paperbound. Add $1 for postage and handling. A previously unpublished book of poems written by Jesse

Stuart between 1929 and 1931. With an introduction by Professor Miller.

To Teach, To Love. Ashland, KY: The Jesse Stuart Foundation, 1987. $20 hardcover; $9 paperbound. Add $1 for postage and handling. A collection of Stuart's essays and stories about education. Introduction by J. R. LeMaster.

PRINTS

(1) A montage, "Jesse at His Typewriter" (1986), with a W-Hollow scene as a backdrop. Painted by Stan Nossett, a former illustrator for *The Saturday Evening Post.* Available at $20 each.

(2) "The Thread That Runs So True" (1986). A picture of Stuart with a one-room schoolhouse in the background. The picture is enhanced by a quoted statement by Stuart expressing his faith in the dedicated teacher's influence for good in the lives of his students. Painted by Jim Marsh. Available at $20 each.

FILM

"Jesse Stuart Remembered" (1986). A 57-minute videotape of reminiscences by Stuart's brother, James, and his sisters, Sophia Keeney, Mary Nelson, and Glennis Liles. Produced by Morehead State University's Office of Television Productions and available from the Exec-

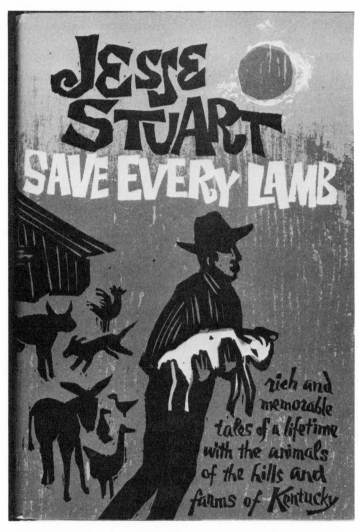

One of Stuart's greatest gifts was writing passionately and precisely about the complex and awe-inspiring relationships between people and animals. This collection was published in 1964. *(Photo courtesy of McGraw-Hill, Inc.)*

utive Director of the Jesse Stuart Foundation at $26.95 per copy.

Note: Additional publications, prints, and films will be available from the Foundation from time to time. For current information, contact the Executive Director's Office.

Also of interest is the 30-minute documentary, "Jesse Stuart," produced by Kentucky Educational Television (KET) and broadcast on August 7, 1986. For further information, contact:

> Kentucky Educational Television
> 600 Cooper Drive
> Lexington, Kentucky 40502

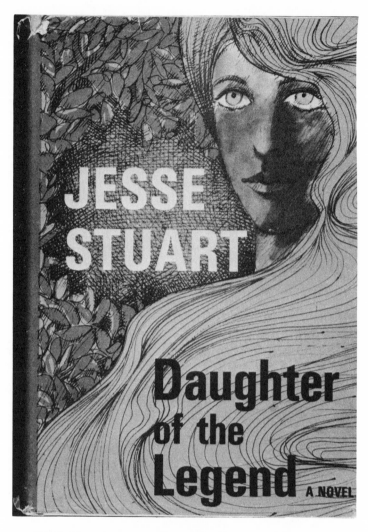

While Stuart was a student at Lincoln Memorial University near Cumberland Gap, he learned of the Melungeons, a racially distinct clan of mountaineers of unknown origins. This romance, begun decades before its publication in 1965, is set among the Melungeons in East Tennessee. *(Photo courtesy of McGraw-Hill, Inc.)*

11.

Out-of-Print Works Available from
The Stuart Foundation

Head o' W-Hollow. Facsimile reprint of the 1936 edition. Freeport, NY: Books for Libraries Press, 1971. $40. Add $1 for postage and handling.

32 Votes Before Breakfast: Politics at the Grass Roots, As Seen in Short Stories by Jesse Stuart. New York: McGraw-Hill, 1974. $19.95. Add $1 for postage and handling.

Up the Hollow from Lynchburg. Photographs by Joe Clark; introduction and text by Jesse Stuart. New York: McGraw-Hill, 1975. $15. Add $1 for postage and handling. This book is about the country people in the area around Lynchburg, Tennessee, the home of the famous Jack Daniel's whiskey distillery.

12.

Jesse Stuart Meetings/W-Hollow Tours

MEETINGS

On May 22–25, 1980, the Jesse Stuart Foundation hosted a retreat for Stuart scholars, students, and the general public at Greenbo Lake State Resort Park. This event, called "Jesse Stuart: The Greenbo Sessions," served as the occasion for presentation of lectures and papers on Stuart's works, and for exhibition of manuscripts, books, photographs, paintings, and handicrafts related to Stuart's works and Appalachian culture. Tours of W-Hollow and Greenup County were also provided.

From 1981–1985, a Stuart meeting, the "Jesse Stuart Symposium," was held annually at Morehead State University, in connection with Morehead's Appalachian Celebration. This two-day event was well attended by teachers, professional people, retirees, and other persons interested in Stuart's writings. The first day of each symposium was devoted to presentation of papers and lectures on Stuart's works and to panel discussions. Audience participation was encouraged. The second day was devoted to a day-long bus tour of W-Hollow. Tour guides were Jesse's brother, James, and his sisters, Mary Nelson and Glennis Liles.

W-HOLLOW TOURS

In 1985, the Stuart Foundation and the Stuart family began a tradition of biannual tours of W-Hollow in April and September. These day-long bus tours are conducted by members of the Stuart family, and provide the opportunity for participants to visit Stuart's home place and grave site as well as the places in W-Hollow made memorable in his works.

The total cost is $15 and covers Greyhound bus transportation, tour guides, and lunch. Reservations are taken on a first-come, first-served basis until the seats are filled.

For tour information, contact the Executive Director, The Jesse Stuart Foundation, P. O. Box 391, Ashland, Kentucky 41114. Phone: (606) 329–5232.

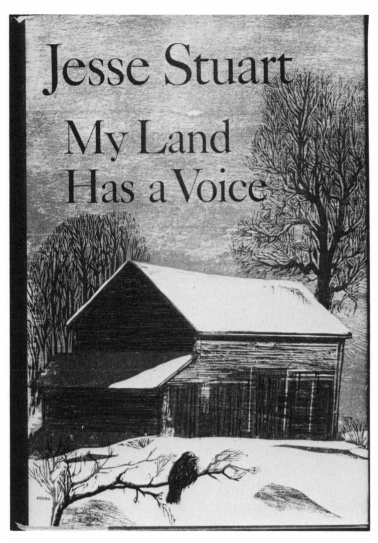

Jesse Stuart

My Land
Has a Voice

Stuart's land does, indeed, have a voice. Through his
writing and through the acquisition, preservation and donation of his large farm to the Commonwealth of Kentucky, subsequent generations will always be able to listen to the voices of the Kentucky hills. This book was
published in 1966. *(Photo courtesy of McGraw-Hill, Inc.)*

13.

Greenbo Lake State Resort Park/ Jesse Stuart Lodge

Greenbo Lake State Resort Park is located on Highway KY-1, eight miles southwest of Greenup, and about eight miles from the Jesse Stuart Nature Preserve in W-Hollow. Highway I-64 is the most convenient east-west approach.

The 36-room Jesse Stuart Lodge overlooks 225-acre Greenbo Lake, which offers good fishing for bass, bluegill, and channel catfish, and accommodations for boaters. A marina located a mile from the lodge provides open slips, a launching ramp, and boat rentals. There is also a bathhouse complex for swimmers. A privately-owned stable operating adjacent to the park offers horses for hire in season.

There is a campground in the park, set up to accommodate recreational vehicles, and there are several miles of hiking trails. The 25-mile Michael Tygart Trail joins the Jenny Wiley Trail, which runs from Jenny Wiley State Resort Park into northern Greenup County.

The gift shop in the Jesse Stuart Lodge contains a collection of Jesse Stuart books and memorabilia, and the manager, Mrs. Love Conley, keeps current Stuart titles available. She also tracks down first editions on request.

Jesse Stuart reveled in his favorite season, the time of rebirth. He often expressed his love for spring in short stories like these, as well as in his poetry, essays, and novels.
This collection was published in 1969. *(Photo courtesy of
McGraw-Hill, Inc.)*

For more information, contact:

Mrs. Love Conley
Manager, Gift Shop
Jesse Stuart Lodge
Greenbo Lake State Resort Park
Greenup, KY 41144
(606) 473-7324

14.

For the Collector: A Bibliographical Essay, Bibliography, and Price Guide to Jesse Stuart's Books / by George Brosi

Collecting Jesse Stuart books is a lot of fun! It has the excitement of a real literary treasure hunt, and when the chase is over, and you bring home the prize, you can curl up by the fireplace and enjoy it time after time. The books you collect may be cherished for generations, giving your descendants great pride in their heritage and a deep understanding of old-fashioned virtues.

Anyone can collect Stuart books. Sure, it is quicker and easier to make a good collection if you happen to be a millionaire who is free to travel anywhere at anytime to get books, but some of the nicest collections are in the hands of retired people living on social security. Read on, and you will learn of some inexpensive ways to acquire these books.

One of the things that makes collecting Stuart's books so enjoyable is that there are many different goals that you can accomplish as you go along. You can feel a great pride in having copies of all of Stuart's novels long before you have copies of each of his poetry books. You may have reading copies of each Stuart short story collection before you acquire first editions of all of them. The satisfaction of achieving many significant goals is yours as you build your collection.

There are only a handful of people who have ever had or who will ever have signed first editions in mint condition of each of Stuart's works, but the difficulty of achieving the final goal only makes it that much more exciting. Anybody who really tries can obtain a collection of Jesse Stuart books which will be a source of deep personal pride.

ACQUIRING JESSE STUART BOOKS

New Jesse Stuart Books. There are two kinds of books for sale, those "in print" and those "out-of-print." Books "in print" are still in stock at their publishers, available for book stores to reorder whenever they need more copies. There is a list of the Jesse Stuart books which are still in print now elsewhere in this book. When this list gets out of date, you can consult the reference book, *Books in Print,* at your local library to see which of Stuart's books are currently being offered by publishers. Only a very few retail booksellers make a point of keeping all of Stuart's books in stock, but most of them will special-order any book which you request.

Used Stuart Books. Considering how long ago most of the Stuart books were written, it is amazing that so many of them are still in print. However, of the more than sixty Jesse Stuart publications, the vast majority are no longer in stock at any publisher. In other words, they are out of print.

Like cars or furniture or any other valuable items which are no longer available from the retail new merchandise trade, used books are sold in a wide variety of ways and sometimes pass through several hands before they are ultimately sold to the customer. The following sections will give you some idea of how used books are sold so you can decide what are the best ways for you to acquire them.

Used Book Stores. The book stores listed in this book all try to keep a good stock of Jesse Stuart books—including out-of-print titles—at all times. You are more likely to find just the book you are looking for in one of these stores than anywhere else. But there is always the chance that *any* used book store might have YOUR book. Check the yellow pages of the phone book under "Book Stores—Used," but don't stop at that. There are many book dealers not listed in the yellow pages, but they aren't always easy to find. Ask at antique shops, new-book stores, and at the used book stores you do find. You can't expect a professional book dealer to give away a secret source of inexpensive books, but you can try!

Many book dealers work out of their homes, but do allow retail book customers to look at their books by appointment. Browsing around old book shops is delightful. As you think about all the interesting people and places represented by the old books which surround you, often you run into some pretty fascinating real-life characters as well!

Book Fairs. A "Book Fair" is an event where a number of book dealers put the books they have for sale on display. Attending these fairs gives you the opportunity to actually meet book dealers you have heard about and to "discover" new dealers. A book fair is also a good place to meet other book collectors and compare notes. Perhaps the most useful such event for Jesse Stuart collectors is the Ohio Valley Book Fair, held in Louisville each spring. It is sponsored by the Friends of the Louisville Free Public Library, and you can call or write this library to find out the exact time and place it will be held each year.

Book Sales. A variety of non-profit groups hold book sales to raise money. Individuals donate books they no longer want to such an organization and receive certification that a donation of the appropriate monetary value has been made. This certification can be used to claim a tax exemption. Then, usually once a year, the books are brought together and a sale is held. Most books at these sales range in price from ten cents to a dollar each, so it is not surprising that there is often a long line at the door an hour ahead of time for the sale to begin. (If there is not, you may be in worse trouble. One year I drove almost 200 miles to a sale and was overjoyed to see no lines at all—until I went up to the door and saw the notice that the sale began the next day!) Actually, when there is a line, it seldom makes sense to be more than a half-hour early. Those first hundred die-hards at the front of the line will rush in awfully fast, and you won't be more than a couple of minutes behind them. On the other hand, some people prefer to be on hand earlier, because they look forward to renewing old friendships on the book sale line.

Don't get your hopes up that you are likely to really

61

expand your Jesse Stuart collection at one of these sales. There probably won't be many Stuart books there, and there will be plenty of competition for them. But these sales are a great source for gift books, useful household books, children's books, and perhaps even books you can trade to book dealers to get that special Jesse Stuart book you have wanted for a long time. You can count what you save on your Christmas shopping by going to the book sale on the plus side when you figure out the expenses of your book collecting habit.

Libraries often hold book sales where they offer both donated books and books from their own holdings which are seldom checked out. In the early 1980s the Louisville and Dayton library sales have been the biggest in Jesse Stuart country. Among the non-profit organizations having significant sales have been the Dayton Planned Parenthood Association; the Louisville Friends of the Opera; the Huntington Galleries; and the Cincinnati Area Brandeis University Alumni.

Book Dealer Catalogs. There are hundreds of used book dealers in the United States who issue catalogs. Some charge a regular rate for keeping names on their list. As a paid subscriber, you avoid being arbitrarily cut off, and you can be confident that the book prices do not reflect an extra mark-up to meet printing costs. Other book dealers send their catalogs out free. It is great fun to scan the entries, just as it is to scan bookstore shelves. You always learn a lot of incidental information, and it is a thrill when you finally find something you are looking for! The more quickly you can scan a catalog after it arrives, the better. It usually makes sense to go ahead and phone immediately to reserve an item you want. Almost all catalog entries are one-of-a-kind books, and if you miss a book, you may not see it listed again in another catalog for years. Books offered for sale by mail are usually returnable within ten days for any reason, so there is very little risk in ordering them.

Book Collecting Periodicals. Professional book dealers often find trade publications to be one of their best sources for used books. These magazines act as a kind of exchange, bringing together book dealers who have books they don't think their customers would be likely to buy with book dealers who may specialize in the exact area that the other dealer has no customers for. You don't, however, have to be a book dealer to subscribe to and utilize these trade periodicals.

The leading trade journal in the out-of-print book business is *AB Bookman's Weekly,* out of Clifton, New Jersey. Most of this magazine consists of ads from scores of dealers listing both books for sale and books wanted, but it also has interesting display ads and feature articles and news. Perhaps the best periodical source for Jesse Stuart books is the *Tri-State Trader,* an antique magazine published in Knightstown, Indiana. It prints ads of books for sale, and there are almost always a dozen or so Stuart books for sale in each issue. By subscribing to any trade publication you will learn about other book-business magazines, about book sales and book fairs, and about many book dealers whom you may some day get a chance to visit. You will also find a number of bargain books, some of which you will phone too late to get, and a few of which your mailman will bring right to your mail box.

Book Searches. Each of the previously mentioned ways of obtaining Jesse Stuart books involves you, the customer, in actively looking for your books. Another approach allows the book dealer to do the hunting for you. Many, but not all, book dealers offer a book search service. All this means is that customers can tell the dealer the titles of particular books they want to purchase, and the book dealer will try to find a copy of each and let the customers know when they arrive. Some dealers charge a fee or request a deposit, while others don't.

The more the book dealer knows about the book—or books—you want, the better off both of you are. Are you only interested in a specific edition, or are you willing to buy the book only in a particular condition? What is your price range? If you can pin down your expectations, you will expedite matters greatly. You can request a book search in person or by mail, and nobody expects to be the only dealer searching for your book. If you have the time and money, go ahead and have as many dealers as you like looking for your book or your "want list" of several books.

Contrary to the belief of some cynics, "letting on" that you want a particular book does not necessarily increase its price. Actually, most dealers will be happy to make much less profit on a book which has a sure buyer than they will expect on one which will go to the shelf and perhaps sit there for years. Also, a dealer who knows the customer's price range is in a position to purchase an occasional book which is priced too high for regular stock. In that way, the customer will get a book that the dealer would otherwise never offer for sale.

In order for a book dealer to search for your books effectively, you must provide the titles and the authors' names, and you should get back in touch every three to six months to update your list or to reaffirm that you still want the particular book or books you originally requested. It won't work to simply ask the dealer to let you know about each Jesse Stuart book which comes in. There is no way that you can receive what amounts to your own constantly updated personal catalog, with complete descriptions and prices. There is plenty of other work to be done in a book shop!

Flea Markets, Antique Malls, Yard Sales, and Auctions. In addition to the sources which specialize in books, there are sales outlets for a variety of used merchandise, any of which may at times have used books for sale. Yard sales, auctions, flea markets, and antique malls can all be checked for used books. Doing this is very time-consuming, and prices are sometimes too high; but, if you know what you are doing, and if you enjoy checking out these events and places, you can often find bargains.

BOOK VALUES

To me, the true value of a book is measured by how much it enriches a person's life, not by how much it can be sold for. But there are times when I do like to know how much a book usually sells for, especially if I am buying or selling.

The whole idea of a guide to used book prices has to be viewed very cautiously and skeptically, and any price guide has to be used with plenty of common sense. A book's price depends on many different factors. Among them are its condition and the edition, where it is sold, when it is sold, why it is being sold, and who is selling it.

Yet, despite great variation in book prices, there is something constant about book value. A book's value is based on how the number of copies of the book for sale compares to the number of people prepared to buy it. When the demand is greater than the supply, the price rises, and when the supply far exceeds the demand, the price falls.

WHAT BOOK IS IT?

The First Printing. A first printing of a book is simply a copy of that book which was part of the first order for books which the printer received from the publisher and subsequently delivered. The second printing is a book from the second batch run off by the printer, and so on.

There is no universal way that the printings of a book are designated. Anybody who wants to publish a book can do it, and a printer is free to print it up however the publisher wants it printed. As a result, the printings of some books are carefully indicated, while other books give no clue to which printing they are from.

However, most publishers who want to follow the conventions of the trade have a title page in their books. That title page gives the name of the book, the author's name, the publisher's name and place of publication, and sometimes the year the particular book is being printed. On the other side of the title page is the "copyright page," or "verso." On that page is the copyright date (which is usually the date of the first printing, but it occasionally designates the year preceding that in which the book actually got printed), and ordinarily it is on this copyright page that the printing of the book is either clearly named or indicated. It can be indicated by the words, "First Printing" or "First Edition," or by a series of numbers, or by the presence or absence of the publisher's logo (known in the trade as the colophon), or it may be designated somewhere else—as in books which indicate the printing by a number in parenthesis after the last word in the book—or not designated at all. Not only are there cases where all the printings look alike, but there are also cases where a book has been reprinted but neither the publisher nor the printer has deleted the words "First Edition" or "First Printing." The result is a book stating that it is a first printing, but which really isn't. You have to know the book or at least the publisher to be sure which printing of the book you have!

The Dropped Number System. One of the greatest expenses in making books is producing the "plates" which are put on the presses to print the book. To add anything to a page, a whole new plate has to be laid out and made, but it is possible to alter an already manufactured plate by deleting something without making a new plate. That is why many book publishers use the "publisher's keyline" or "dropped number system" for denoting the printing of a book. In this system, there is a "keyline"—a line of numbers from one to nine (and later from 10 to 19, and so forth, as necessary), followed customarily by some letters and then more numbers. For the first printing, all the numbers to the left of the letters are there, but for the second printing the number "1" is blocked off on the plate so that the row of numbers begins with "2." Additional printings are denoted the same way, so that a keyline containing "56789" would be the fifth printing, or a keyline containing "13141516171819" would be the 13th printing. Bear in mind that the numbers on the other side of the letters have nothing to do, one way or the other, with designating which printing it is, whether or not they end or begin with "1." Sometimes they are in ascending or descending order because the right-hand side indicates the decade on the left end, and the year on the right end. That still has nothing to do with which printing the book is. Also remember that the keyline can begin with a "1" when the printing is anywhere between the 10th printing and the 19th printing. Only when the "1" on the left-hand side is followed by a "23456789" does it mean that the book is a first printing. Some books contain a row of numbers on the copyright page which has nothing to do with designating the book's printing. Carefully check any row of numbers to be sure they are in numerical order. If they are not, then the printing of the book you have is not designated by the dropped number system.

Actually, there are a few publishers who use the right-hand side of the numbers to designate first editions, but the publishers of Jesse Stuart books that used the dropped number system always used the left-hand side.

Another variation which can be found, though it was not done with any Jesse Stuart book, is for the publisher to identify the book as a first edition, and then start the line of numbers with "2," so the "1" won't have to be deleted when "First Edition" is erased from the plate. Be sure to read everything on the title page and verso before coming to a firm decision about the printing of your book.

First Editions. An edition of a book is simply all of the copies of the book published by the same publisher from the same plates and bound in the same way with none of the pages changed (except possibly the copyright page to indicate which printing of this edition it is). If the same book is republished by another publisher, or if illustrations are added, taken away, or changed, or if the introductory material or afterwords are altered, it is a new edition of the book.

If minor corrections of typographical errors are made while the book is still being printed, subsequent copies are called the "second state" of the first edition. And if the binding is altered in the course of putting out the first edition, it can be called a "variant" of the first edition. Whenever the text of the book is altered, the books that are then printed are part of a "revised" edition.

A "limited" edition of a book is simply any edition limited by its publisher before the printing begins to a certain number of copies. Sometimes a publisher will simultaneously release a fancy edition limited to a certain number of copies and an ordinary edition. When this is done, the regular edition is called the "trade" edition, and if the book has never been printed before, it is called the "first trade edition."

As a rule, the edition of any book which is worth the

least is the "book club" edition. Book clubs are simply businesses which reproduce current books inexpensively and send them out to all their members, typically once a month. If club members want to keep the book that comes in the mail, they pay the enclosed bill. If they don't want it, they reseal the package and mail it back. It is a nice way for lots of people to keep up with current books. Book club editions are less valuable than "trade editions" sold at bookstores, because they are manufactured more cheaply, and because most book club members eventually pass on most of their book club books, thus overloading the used book market with them. Many book club editions of books are not clearly marked as such and can be confused with other editions.

The terms "printing" and "edition" are sometimes confused and even turned around. But it is customary to use the term "first edition" only to mean "the very first printing of the first edition," not to designate even a "variant" or a later "state." It is usually considered unethical for a person to describe any but the first printing of the first edition as a "first edition," unless it is noted that the book is a later printing or state or variant. However, it is wise, before you make a major purchase, to be sure that any "first edition" you are getting is also definitely a "first printing."

All of this is important because in book collecting the "first edition" is almost always more valuable, other things being equal, than later printings. A genuine first edition of a book can easily be worth ten times as much as a later edition or even a later printing. Beware of paying high prices for later printings of any book unless you know the real first edition is very rare. Most collectors are after the first editions, and another reprint of the book might appear at any point, quickly reducing the demand for any reprinted copy.

Dust Jackets. The dust jacket of a book is simply the paper cover which is ordinarily issued with a hardback book, and occasionally with a paperback book as well, to protect the book's cover and improve the book's appearance relatively inexpensively. It is the part of a book which is most likely to be thrown away, torn up, or damaged. Yet, if a book is issued with a dust jacket, it looks very different without it. Sometimes jackets have important information or pictures on them, and sometimes the jacket is by far the most attractive part of the book.

The presence of a dust jacket, especially if it is well preserved, almost always increases the value of any book. Beware of paying a high price for a hardback book without a dust jacket unless you know the book was issued without a jacket or unless it is extremely hard to find in jacket.

THE BOOK'S CONDITION

A book that is exactly as it was when it came off the press is considered to be in "mint" condition. A book which has been read or leafed through very carefully without leaving any traces and which has been completely protected from any deterioration is considered in "fine" condition. Some book dealers use other terms to describe the books they are selling, terms such as "excellent," "good," and so forth, but the meaning varies from dealer to dealer, so the best way to describe the condition of a book is to describe the "defects" or ways in which the book differs from the way it looked when it came off the press.

Dust Jacket Defects. The dust jacket is the part of the book most likely to receive noticeable wear, and it is the edges which are the most vulnerable. Little tears and "chips"—actual pieces missing, of any size—can quickly and easily appear, and just by taking a book out of a book shelf and returning it, the jacket, like the book cover itself, can become noticeably "rubbed." Another common dust jacket defect occurs on the jacket flap. When a book is given away, or when the price is raised by the publisher, the corner of the jacket flap where the price usually appears is often "price clipped" with scissors.

Book Defects. Perhaps the most common book defect, and certainly the most understandable one, is the appearance of the name of the previous owner in the front of the book, often with a date, place, or even a message from whoever gave the book to the owner. This makes a book much less desirable for another person to own than a book with no writing in it. A less damaging defect is the appearance of a previous owner's bookplate, especially a small, attractive one, because the next owner can simply center a new bookplate on top of the old one without tearing up the book.

The spine of the book is its most vulnerable part. It can be unnaturally darkened or lightened by the sun shining on it, and the top of the spine can be torn or chipped by improper removal from the shelf. The book's pages may also be marked by "browning." This term refers to the little brown dots on the paper which sometimes grow larger and larger with age, especially on the outside pages, or end pages, of older books. When you open up the cover of a book, the two pages you see are the "end pages"—front or back. The end page which is pasted to the cover is known as the "pasted end page," and the one which is not pasted down is called the "free end page" or "free end paper." Most other terms used in describing the condition of a book are self-explanatory. There are books which go into this subject deeply and your librarian should be able to help you find them.

Only the rarest of books have value in terrible condition, and the value of any book in poor condition has got to be only a small portion of the value that book would have in fine condition.

Perhaps the defect which most deflates the value of a book is for it to be an ex-library book. Millions of books have been sold by libraries themselves after they have been given library markings. Sometimes these books are stamped "withdrawn" to show they weren't stolen, but at other times libraries sell their books without indicating that they have been officially disposed of. Some book owners try to remove the library markings of a legitimately withdrawn book in order to make it look nicer. Thus, just as it is impossible to tell if any other book was ever stolen, or stolen before it was last sold, it is impossible to tell if an ex-library book was stolen. Although ex-library books do offer an inexpensive way to expand your collection, it is important to be wary of them in two ways. First, if your source of books seems to have lots of ex-library books and hardly any that aren't, perhaps you should be suspicious. Also, you need to beware of paying very high prices for ex-library books, because they are seldom worth even half as much as books with the same defects inflicted on them by individual owners.

Signed Books. The only mark on a book which doesn't make it worth less is the signature of its author! The author's signature almost always makes a book more valuable than it would be without the signature. Some people joke about how fond Jesse Stuart was of signing books, saying that a book *not* signed by him should be worth more, not less, but these are only jokes. Any book signed by Jesse Stuart, unless seriously damaged, is more valuable than the same book unsigned. The author's signature is more valuable if it is dated the year of the first printing of the book, still more valuable if it carries a message of significance revealing something of import about the book or the author, and even more valuable if the book is inscribed specifically to a noteworthy person. Theoretically, any book "inscribed" to any particular person is more valuable in the out-of-print book business than a book simply signed. Actually, if the person the book is inscribed to is not very noteworthy and the inscription not very significant, many buyers would prefer a signed book not personalized to an unknown person.

WHERE THE BOOK IS SOLD

The price of a book is affected not only by its edition and condition, but also by the circumstances of the sale.

When you emerge covered with dust from hours spent sorting through boxes in a back-lot storage room, you don't expect to pay the gruff man smoking the cigar at the cash box as much for your book as you would gladly pay the knowledgeable sales person at a nicely appointed and neatly organized shop in an attractive business district. There is a kind of natural trade-off. If you want to be able to browse comfortably and to have a good selection to choose from, you expect to pay a little more than you do when sloshing through the mud at an outdoor flea market. But beware: Sometimes the prices at a low overhead operation are higher than at a really nice shop. Don't pass the nice shops up.

You don't expect to pay as much for a Jesse Stuart book in Miami or Milwaukee as in Huntington, West Virginia. But again, beware. Because the supply of Stuart books can be greater closer to his home, prices can be more reasonable here, and a faraway book dealer who has heard that it is okay for Stuart books to carry high prices may not realize that a particular book is especially common.

SUPPLY AND DEMAND AND OTHER FACTORS

Like the prices of stocks or bonds or any type of merchandise, the prices of Jesse Stuart books do have trends. The trend was upward as long as Stuart was able to actively promote his books. Since about 1979, however, when he was forced by poor health to decline public engagements, the values of his books have ceased to increase and actually have gone down a little. This trend could easily continue, accelerate, or reverse itself at any moment, driven by all kinds of factors. If one of Stuart's books is made into a movie (like the TV version of *The Dollmaker* by Harriette Arnow, first published in 1954, but first aired in 1985), or if Kentucky spends a million dollars on its W-Hollow land, or if a major critical study very complimentary to Stuart comes out, any of these things could affect the drift of Stuart book values overall.

Volatile factors can express themselves even more quickly and easily on particular books, affecting not only demand, but supply. When the University Press of Kentucky reprinted *Clearing in the Sky* in 1984, the value of that book changed. Until then, only one printing of one edition had ever been done, so anyone who wanted a copy had to buy one of those few first edition copies. Now anyone who wants the book can order a reprint in hardback or paperback from the University Press of Kentucky. The only people now interested in buying a first edition are first edition collectors, so the demand for first editions, and thus the price, has declined. In the 1970s some people bought up several cases of Jesse Stuart's books when they were first published, figuring that because the prices of Stuart books had been going up so fast, a case of books would be a good investment. Occasionally, a batch of cases of a Stuart first edition can hit the market, driving down the value of that particular book.

WHEN A BOOK IS SOLD

The time a book is sold affects the price, too. Most book businesses do a very high percentage of their gross sales during the Christmas season—especially in November and December—and most such businesses have a really tough time after Christmas and in the middle of the summer. Try going to the same store in November and again in February. If your book is still there, you are likely to get a better deal on the second trip!

WHY A BOOK IS SOLD

That last comment leads right into the next basic consideration affecting price—why a book is sold. The shopkeeper who sells for gravy in November and for biscuits in February is a victim of this important price determinant. The hungrier, or more anxious, the seller is, the more fortunate the buyer is. On the other hand, a book dealer may be quite proud to have a copy of a particular book in his locked case, and may have very little inclination to sell it. The price will probably reflect that attitude, too.

WHO IS SELLING THE BOOK

Another important consideration is the seller himself. One of your kinfolks or neighbors may charge too little or too much for that book you covet, and it may have nothing to do with any of the other factors we have mentioned here!

Another thing to consider is the whole question of bargaining. Some book dealers refuse, on principle, to go down on their prices. They take it as an insult that anyone who would not ask Visa or Master Charge to lower their interest rate would ask them to lower their prices. Other dealers, however, really enjoy a good bargaining session. Nobody is going to mind a polite inquiry, but you are more likely to get a price reduction for several books than for just one or two.

SELLING JESSE STUART BOOKS

Buying and selling Jesse Stuart books isn't a good way to make money. Those which are rising in value simply aren't going up fast enough to make speculating on them worthwhile. Furthermore, Stuart's books are difficult to find, and when you do find one, it is likely to be priced at least as high as you would want to sell it for anyway. There is no way anybody except a professional book dealer, for whom Stuart books are only a small part of a much larger business, can possibly make enough money buying and selling these books to justify the time and money spent in locating and acquiring them. There are, however, two good reasons to *sell* Jesse Stuart books. One concerns the collector who is committed to spending all the time and money it will take to find all of Stuart's books anyway, and who will most likely find lots of duplicates before finding a copy of every book published. If a duplicate is very inexpensive, the collector should consider buying it for resale or trade, simply to have a positive as well as negative cash flow for a time-consuming hobby. The other good reason to sell Jesse Stuart books is to transfer Stuart books which one doesn't want to the hands of someone who would really appreciate having them.

Selling To Book Dealers. There are so many book dealers and so few book customers that hardly any of the dealers can average as much as $1,000 worth of sales a week all year long in order to gross as much as $50,000 a year. When the gross sales of any business are that small, it almost always has to spend more than a third of its gross income on overhead and at least another third on salaries. That means that less than a third is left for purchasing books for resale, which in turn means that, unless the book dealer is doing you a personal favor, she or he cannot afford to give you any more than a third at the very most of the price that will be put on the book for retail resale. So, if you are using the price guide that follows to estimate what a retail book dealer should give you for your collection, figure the total value of your books for sale—bending over backwards to evaluate their condition fairly, as explained in the section, "On Using the Price Guide"— and then expect to get less than one third of that figure. Of course, if you do have a figure you absolutely HAVE to get from your books, go ahead and try your favorite book dealer. If the dealer just happens to have customers lined up waiting for each book you are offering, maybe your price will be acceptable.

If you are selling to a wholesale book dealer who isn't set up for retail sales, but is expecting to pass the books on to a retail bookseller, figure ⅓ of the initial ⅓ or ⅑ of the price-guide value. Again, if you have a favorite book scout and a predetermined price, it won't hurt to give it a try.

Selling To Another Individual. If you are selling to a friend who has no business overhead or payroll, you and your friend will have to decide what is fair to both of you. In my opinion, a person who is not in the business should expect to charge a friend about half of the retail price. But that kind of sale is strictly a matter between friends!

DONATING JESSE STUART BOOKS

One of the best uses for the following price guide is in estimating the retail value of collections being donated to a worthy nonprofit organization. Many public and school libraries can use extra copies of all of Jesse Stuart's books, both to have plenty of circulating copies and to place at least one copy in a special collection which is made available for use only inside the library. Sometimes libraries accept extra duplicate books and trade them to book dealers for other books they wish to acquire, thus improving their collection without increasing their budget.

When thinking of donating books, don't forget the Jesse Stuart Foundation, which is always willing to accept donations of Jesse Stuart books in order to utilize them to further its important work.

If you are having a donation appraised to determine its value for tax purposes, be sure to give your appraiser a copy of this book so that you can get as large a tax break as you deserve! Those who have a large enough income and few enough dependents to have to pay income tax will notice that half the value of a donation to a nonprofit organization will qualify as a deduction. If a book dealer is only offering you ⅓ of the value of the books in cash, then making the donation looks pretty attractive if you can wait until April 15th for your "payoff."

ON USING THE PRICE GUIDE

Before using this price guide, please read the preceding discussion on book values. It will clarify many terms used and will explain why you can't use this guide as some kind of final authority for all transactions. Also, for the considerations involved in donating or selling either a collection of Stuart books or a single book, see the sections immediately preceding this one.

The Purpose of this Price Guide. This guide gives a range of prices for Jesse Stuart books which meet a particular description, as you are likely to encounter them in a typical bookshop. You can use the guide to get some idea of what you should expect to pay for any Stuart book you hope to buy. It can also be useful in evaluating your collection of Jesse Stuart books for insurance or tax purposes.

Price Ranges. No matter how carefully you use this price guide, it is not an acceptable substitute for a professional book appraisal. A qualified person has to examine each book carefully in order to make an accurate assessment of its condition and value. This cannot be done by an amateur with any price guide. I realize this is frustrating because it makes a difference to anyone whether a book costs or sells for $100 or $200. But there is just too much involved in book pricing for anyone to be able to say that a particular used book ought to carry a particular dollar figure. That is why I give a price range, rather than a particular price, for each book I have listed. The price range given for each book is for a "fine" copy in dust jacket (when the book was issued with one) without any noticeable defects in condition and without any repairs to either the book or the jacket. These ranges are not meant to account for the same book in different conditions or different editions. I use them to indicate that the very same book could easily and fairly be offered for sale at prices anywhere in the indicated range.

The Price Guide's Time Frame. This price guide reflects an estimate of the values of Jesse Stuart books in early 1987. As noted earlier, the value of both Stuart books in general and of specific Stuart books can easily change in the future. The figures given for each book represent the range of prices you are likely to find in a retail book shop in Kentucky. As indicated previously, prices vary according to the geographic area in which the book is purchased, and according to the kind of book business the dealer is involved in.

USING THIS GUIDE FOR DETERMINING PRICES OF BOOKS OTHER THAN FINE COPIES IN JACKET

Books Signed by Jesse Stuart. As a general rule, any Stuart book signed by Jesse Stuart is worth approximately half again as much with his signature as the same edition of the book in the same condition without it. For example, if you figure that a fine copy of *Mongrel Mettle* is worth $75.00, then a signed copy of this book in fine condition in a fine dust jacket would be worth about $75.00 plus half again that much, or about $112.00.

Books Without Jackets. As a general rule, similar copies of these books without a dust jacket are likely to be priced at about half the price of the same book with a dust jacket which itself has no defects. For example, a fine edition of *Tales from the Plum Grove Hills* in a fine dust jacket might be priced at $195.00. The same book, without a jacket, would be likely to be priced at $95.00.

Used Books with Defects in Condition. Some of Jesse Stuart's books are so hard to find that they have considerable value in any condition, so long as all the pages and the covers are intact. Most books in poor condition, however, cannot be priced over $10.00. Figuring the value for a book which is not in fine condition is a matter of judgement, but if you figure the book is worth half the value listed in the price guide without a dust jacket, and $10.00 in terrible condition, that gives you a range of prices. Within this range, you just have to judge whether the book is almost "fine" or almost "terrible," or about how far along on the scale to place it. For example, you might figure that a fine copy in dust jacket of a first edition of *Foretaste of Glory* would be worth about $60.00; a fine copy without jacket about $30.00; and a copy in awful condition about $8.00. Your copy without a jacket and with a previous owner's name might be worth about $20.00. If the cover has some marks, and the cover edges are beginning to fray, it might be worth about $15.00, and with some inside pages torn or marked, you might figure its worth at $10.00 at the most.

Like fine copies of Stuart books, his books in inferior condition, but signed by Stuart, are worth about half again as much as they would be unsigned. Thus, in the example above, a first edition of *Foretaste of Glory* without the jacket and with a previous owner's name in ink, would be worth about $20.00. That same book, signed, would be worth about $30.00. Any signed Stuart book, with the covers and pages intact, is worth at least $25.00—even a book club edition of *Taps for Private Tussie*.

To figure the value of a book with a tattered jacket, you have to figure the value of the book with a fine jacket and with no jacket, and simply estimate where your book falls along that scale. Using our previous example of the first edition of *Tales from the Plum Grove Hills*, worth $195.00 fine in a fine jacket and $95.00 fine without a jacket, a copy with a price-clipped dust jacket with several tears and chips along the edges, but with none reaching to any print, somewhat spine-darkened, might be worth about $145.00.

WHAT'S INCLUDED IN THIS PRICE GUIDE

What follows is a list of Jesse Stuart's separately published works. It includes the books Stuart wrote, co-authored, edited, and co-edited. It does *not* include the "appearances" of his writings in magazines or newspapers or in books which include the work of other authors as well as Stuart and which were edited by someone else.

All of Stuart's separately published works are included, paperback as well as hardback—even those paperbacks which some people would call "pamphlets." However, "broadsides"—one-page prints of Stuart's works intended to adorn walls—are not listed.

Only American editions are included and only those editions in printed English. Excluded are Braille editions and audio recordings.

THE FORMAT OF THIS PRICE GUIDE

The books are listed by year of publication in the first edition. Subsequent editions of these books are listed immediately after the first edition, in the order of their publication. These later editions then do *not* appear along with the first editions of other books for the year they were released. Titles which appeared in the same year are listed alphabetically. I have attempted to list all editions of each book, but I have *not* listed all the printings of each edition.

First, the title of the book is listed, then the year of publication and the publisher and the place of publication. Then I list the number of pages in the book and state whether it is hardback or paperback. Unless I specify to the contrary, it is assumed that all paperbacks are issued without a dust jacket and all hardbacks are issued with a dust jacket.

Next, I mention how the first edition is determined and give a range of values for the first edition. For example, if the words, "First Edition," appear on the copyright page, I will indicate this by saying: "First edition so stated." Other methods of determining the first edition will be similarly explained.

If the first edition went through more than one printing, I next give values for a reprint of the first edition. Since it has little effect on the value, I do not give separate values for the different reprintings, nor do I state how many times each edition was reprinted, or when.

Later editions of the same book, when noted, are given the same number and the following letter. I do not repeat the title when I am listing a later edition of the same book. No mention is necessarily made of whether or not later editions of a book were reprinted.

Once I have listed a publisher and its place of publication, I do not repeat the place of publication when I list that same publisher again.

A CHRONOLOGICAL BIBLIOGRAPHY
AND PRICE GUIDE

1a. *Harvest of Youth.* 1930, The Scroll Press, Howe, Oklahoma. An 80-page hardback issued without a dust jacket. It does not state that it is a first edition, but there was only one printing. $1,500–$2,500.

1b. ———. 1964, The Council of the Southern Mountains, Berea, Kentucky. An 80-page paperback issued with a dust jacket. Only one printing was done. $75–$125.

2a. *Man with a Bull-Tongue Plow.* 1934, E. P. Dutton, New York, New York. A 361-page hardback. First edition so stated. $350–$450. Reprints: $175–$225.

2b. ———. 1959, E. P. Dutton. An abridged edition, a 320-page trade paperback. $15–$25.

3a. *Head o' W-Hollow.* 1936, E. P. Dutton. A 342-page hardback. First edition so stated. $300–$350. Reprints: $100–$150.

3b. ———. No date, but probably in the 1940s, Editions for the Armed Forces, The Council on Books in Wartime, New York, New York. A 383-page paperback measuring 4½" × 6½". $40–$50.

3c. ———. 1971, Books for Libraries Press, Freeport, New York. A 342-page hardback issued without a dust jacket. Available for $40 from the Jesse Stuart Foundation.

3d. ———. 1979, University Press of Kentucky, Lexington, Kentucky. A 342-page paperback with new introductory material. In print at $9.

4a. *Beyond Dark Hills: A Personal Story.* 1938, E. P. Dutton. A 399-page hardback. First edition so stated. $175–$200. Reprints: $100–$125.

4b. ———. 1972, McGraw-Hill, New York, New York. A 328-page hardback. Deluxe signed edition limited to 950 copies. $40–$60.

4c. ———. 1972, McGraw-Hill. When the publisher printed copies of the previously-listed 328-page limited edition as first planned, the people at McGraw-Hill were not satisfied with it and stopped the presses.

Some of these preliminary copies, different from the Deluxe Edition as it eventually appeared commercially, and different from the regular trade edition of the book, did get into circulation. They have oxblood endpapers and the extra page for the author's signature, but were not signed at the time of publication. $45–$75.

4d. ———. 1972, McGraw-Hill. The regular trade edition of this 328-page hardback with brown endpapers. $20–$40.

5a. *Tim, a Story.* 1939. *The Little Man Magazine,* Cincinnati, Ohio. A 20-page paperback. First edition not stated, but determined by the date and publisher. Limited to about 500 copies. $350–$400.

5b. ———. 1958, Robert Lowry, New York, New York. 13 mimeographed pages stapled together, limited to 25 signed and numbered copies. $75–$125.

5c. ———. 1967, W-Hollow Harvest, Cincinnati, Ohio. A facsimile reprint of the 1939 edition, with original front and back covers reproduced. Published by David and Phyllis Brandenburg. A hardback with a foreword by Jesse Stuart and a text of 17 unnumbered pages, issued without a dust jacket and limited to 100 copies. The copyright page reads, "First Edition, Hardback," which is literally true, although this is actually the third edition of the book published, since paperback books do count as "first editions," unless they are published simultaneously with a hardback edition. $125–$145.

5d. ———. 1968, Harvest Press of the Kentucky Writers' Guild, Cincinnati, Ohio. A hardback with a 34-page text; a reprint of the above item, including the foreword by Stuart. $125–$145.

6a. *Trees of Heaven.* 1940, E. P. Dutton. A 340-page hardback. First edition so stated. $125–$175. Reprints: $50–$75.

6b. ———. 1980, University Press of Kentucky. A 340-page hardback with new introductory material. $20–$30.

6c. ———. 1980, University Press of Kentucky. A 340-page paperback. In print at $9.

7a. *Men of the Mountains.* 1941, E. P. Dutton. A 349-page hardback. First edition so stated. $300–$350. Reprints: $125–$150.

7b. ———. 1979, University Press of Kentucky. A 349-page paperback with new introductory material. In print at $9.

8a. *Taps for Private Tussie.* 1943, E. P. Dutton. A 253-page hardback. First edition so stated for both variants: Trade edition, $125–$175, known by the salmon color of its covers. Library variant, $50–$75, known by the red color of its covers.

8b. ———. 1943, E. P. Dutton. A 303-page hardback edition illustrated by Thomas Hart Benton. Those with Dutton indicated as publisher were printed by the

Kingsport Press, Kingsport, Tennessee. Those printed by the Montauk Book Manufacturing Co. of New York City indicate Books, Inc., of New York as the publisher; Dutton is indicated as the distributor. [This book has been reprinted more times by more publishers than any other Jesse Stuart book. Among these publishers were the Garden City Publishing Company, The Sun Dial Press, and the Book of the Month Club. The latest and most attractive reprinting was brought out by the World Publishing Company of Cleveland, Ohio, in 1969.] $5–$25.

8c. ———. No date given, but assumed to be in the 1940s. Editions for the Armed Services, New York, New York. A 318-page paperback measuring 3¾″ × 5⅜″, with an "Author's Note." On the cover: "This is the complete book—not a digest." $25–$45.

8d. ———. 1946, Pocket Books, New York, New York. A 248-page paperback. $10–$15.

8e. ———. 1962, Paperback Library, New York, New York. A 192-page paperback. $5–$10.

8f. ———. 1967, Harvest Press. A limited edition (25 copies, lettered A-Y) of Dutton reprints specially leather-bound by David Brandenburg to commemorate Stuart's sixtieth year. $40–$60.

8g. ———. 1973, Mockingbird Books, initially an imprint of Ballantine Books, New York, New York, presently an independent publishing firm of St. Simons Island, Georgia. A 214-page paperback. $5–$10.

9. *Album of Destiny.* 1944, E. P. Dutton. A 255-page hardback. First edition so stated. $175–$200. Reprints: $75–$100.

10. *Mongrel Mettle: The Autobiography of a Dog.* 1944, Books, Inc., New York, New York; distributed by E. P. Dutton. A 201-page hardback. First edition so stated. $75–$100. Reprints: $30–$50.

11a. *Foretaste of Glory.* 1946, E. P. Dutton. A 256-page hardback. First edition so stated. $50–$75. Reprints: $25–$50.

11b. ———. 1974, Mockingbird Books. A 214-page paperback. $5–$10.

11c. ———. 1986, University Press of Kentucky. A 264-page hardback with new introductory material. In print at $19.

11d. ———. 1986, University Press of Kentucky. A 264-page paperback. In print at $9.

12a. *Tales from the Plum Grove Hills.* 1946, E. P. Dutton. A 256-page hardback. First edition so stated. $175–$225. Reprints: $75–$100.

12b. ———. 1974, Mockingbird Books. A 181-page paperback. $5–$15.

13a. *The Thread That Runs So True.* 1949, Charles Scribner's Sons, New York, New York. A 293-page hardback. The first edition is indicated by the appearance of the capital letter "A" centered under the paragraph which starts, "All rights reserved . . ." on the copyright page. $50–$100. Reprints: $20–$30.

13b. ———. 1958, Charles Scribner's Sons. A 293-page hardback, a new edition with a preface by the author. $25–$45.

13c. ———. 1958, Charles Scribner's Sons. A 293-page trade paperback with the author's preface. Still in print at $8.95.

13d. ———. 1963, Charles Scribner's Sons. A 361-page hardback school edition with a new preface by the author, and issued without a dust jacket. Study guide by Albert K. Ridout. $20–$40.

13e. ———. 1968, Charles Scribner's Sons. A 361-page paperback. The school edition, with author's new preface and Albert K. Ridout's study guide. $10–$15.

13f. ———. 1974, University Press of Kentucky. A 313-page boxed hardback celebrating the Centennial of Eastern Kentucky University; limited to about four or five hundred copies, all distributed without charge to friends of E. K. U.. Contains a "Foreword" by Kentucky's distinguished historian, Thomas D. Clark, and an "Introduction" by highly-regarded Appalachian novelist Wilma Dykeman. $25–$45.

13g. ———. 1974, University Press of Kentucky. A 313-page hardback in dust jacket, the trade edition of the previous entry. $25–$35.

14a. *Clearing in the Sky and Other Stories*. 1950, McGraw-Hill, New York, New York. A 262-page hardback. $150–$250. Never reprinted by McGraw-Hill.

14b. ———. 1984, University Press of Kentucky. A 262-page hardback with new introductory material. In print at $20.

14c. ———. 1984, University Press of Kentucky. A 262-page paperback. In print at $9.

15a. *Hie to the Hunters*. 1950, Whittlesey House of McGraw-Hill. A 265-page hardback. First edition indicated by the absence of any statement of a later printing on the copyright page. $75–$100. Reprints: $40–$60.

15b. ———. 1951, Harcourt Brace, New York, New York. The high school edition, a 273-page hardback issued without a dust jacket. Contains a preface by Stuart, and study materials by J. Arthur Ferner. $20–$40.

15c. ———. No date, but known to be 1968, Ace Editions of Scott, Foresman and Company, Chicago, Illinois. A 143-page paperback. $10–$20.

15d. ———. 1988, The Jesse Stuart Foundation, Ashland, Kentucky. A 265-page hardback. Introduction by Jerry A. Herndon. In print at $20.

15e. ———. 1988, The Jesse Stuart Foundation. A 265-page paperback. In print at $9.

16a. *Kentucky Is My Land.* 1952, E. P. Dutton. A 95-page hardback. First edition so stated, but assured only by the presence as well of a salmon-colored cover, since the book was reprinted without the words, "First Edition," being deleted. $125–$175. Reprints from Dutton of the salmon-colored book with "First Edition" deleted, $45–$65. Reprints from Economy Printers, Ashland, Kentucky (known by their brown or green covers and/or by the words "Author's Edition" pasted over "First Edition," and/or by the name of the reprinter on the bottom of the front jacket flap), $25–$45.

16b. ———. 1987, The Jesse Stuart Foundation. A 95-page hardback, with an introduction by Jim Wayne Miller. In print at $10.95.

17. *The Beatinest Boy.* 1953, Whittlesey House. A 110-page hardback. First edition indicated by the absence of a publisher's keyline (the line of numbers which is used to indicate a first edition by the dropped number system). $50–$75. Reprints (indicated by use of a publisher's keyline): $25–$45.

18. *The Good Spirit of Laurel Ridge.* 1953, McGraw-Hill. A 263-page hardback. First edition indicated by no later printing being stated on the copyright page. $100–$150. Reprints: $60–$90.

19. *A Penny's Worth of Character.* 1954, Whittlesey House. A 62-page hardback. First edition indicated by the absence of a publisher's keyline. $50–$75. Reprints (indicated by the dropped number system): $25–$50.

20. *Red Mule.* 1955, Whittlesey House. A 124-page hardback. First edition indicated by no later printing being stated on the copyright page. $45–$65. Reprints: $20–$50.

21. *The Year of My Rebirth.* 1956, McGraw-Hill. A 342-page hardback. First edition indicated by no later printing being stated on the copyright page. $25–$45. Reprints: $15–$35.

22. *Plowshare in Heaven: Stories.* 1958, McGraw-Hill. A 273-page hardback. First edition so indicated. $50–$90. Reprints: $30–$50. Note: The second printing states, "First edition, second printing," which is technically correct, but it is not to be confused with the book which states simply, "First Edition."

23a. *God's Oddling: The Story of Mick Stuart, My Father.* 1960, McGraw-Hill. A 266-page hardback. First edition so stated. $40–$70. Reprints: $30–$50.

23b. *Strength from the Hills: The Story of Mick Stuart, My Father.* 1968, Pyramid Books, New York, New York. A 127-page paperback. A "Ladder Edition" of *God's Oddling* at the 1,000 word level, adapted for the beginning reader by Elinor Chamberlain. $10–$20.

24. *Huey, the Engineer.* 1960, James E. Beard, St. Helena, California. A 50-page hardback issued without a dust jacket. First edition not stated, but this is a rare Stuart hardback never reprinted or reissued in a different edition. Limited to 585 copies, it is probably the Stuart

book with the fewest copies printed, considering all printings and editions of each book. $450–$550.

25. *The Rightful Owner.* 1960, McGraw-Hill. A 110-page hardback. First edition indicated by no later printing being stated on the copyright page. $40–$60. Reprints: $20–$40.

26. *Andy Finds a Way.* 1961, Whittlesey House. A 92-page hardback. First edition indicated by no later printing being stated on the copyright page. $35–$55. Reprints: $20–$40.

27. *Hold April: New Poems.* 1962, McGraw-Hill. A 114-page hardback. First edition so indicated. $75–$125. Reprints: $25–$50.

28a. *A Jesse Stuart Reader: Stories and Poems Selected and Introduced by Jesse Stuart.* 1963, McGraw-Hill. "Foreword" by Max Bogart. A 310-page hardback. First trade edition indicated by the absence of a publisher's keyline and by the number of pages. $45–$75. Reprints: $30–$45.

28b. ———. 1963, McGraw-Hill. "Foreword" by Max Bogart; commentary and questions by Ella DeMers. The text edition, a 342-page hardback. $30–$60. Reprints: $25–$40.

28c. ———. 1966, The New American Library, New York, New York. A 255-page Signet paperback. $5–$15.

29. *Save Every Lamb.* 1964, McGraw-Hill. A 278-page hardback. First edition so stated. $25–$50. Reprints: $20–$40.

30. *Daughter of the Legend.* 1965, McGraw-Hill. A 249-page hardback. First edition so stated. $50–$90. Reprints: $30–$50.

31a. *A Jesse Stuart Harvest.* 1965, The Laurel-Leaf Library of Dell Publishing Company, New York, New York. A 288-page paperback. $15–$25.

31b. ———. 1974, Mockingbird Books. A 288-page paperback with a new author's introduction. $10–$15.

32. *My Land Has a Voice.* 1966, McGraw-Hill. A 243-page hardback. First edition so stated. $25–$40. Reprints: $20–$35.

33a. *A Ride with Huey the Engineer.* 1966, McGraw-Hill. A 92-page hardback. First edition not designated, but never reprinted by McGraw-Hill. $30–$50.

33b. ———. 1973, Landfall Press, Dayton, Ohio. A 92-page paperback. $5–$10.

34. *Mr. Gallion's School.* 1967, McGraw-Hill. A 337-page hardback. First edition so stated. $30–$50. Reprints: $25–$40.

35. *Rebels with a Cause.* 1967, Murray State University, Murray, Kentucky. A 12-page pamphlet, a Commence-

ment Address delivered at Murray State University. First edition not stated, but never reprinted. $45–$75.

36. *Stories by Jesse Stuart.* Adapted by Lawrence Swinburne. 1968, McGraw-Hill. "Reading Shelf I: A series of books adapted for easy reading." An 83-page paperback, including five stories and nine poems. First edition designated by the presence of the number "1" on the publisher's keyline on the copyright page. $40–$60.

37. *Come Gentle Spring.* 1969, McGraw-Hill. A 282-page hardback. First edition so stated. $25–$40. Reprints: $20–$30.

38. *Old Ben.* 1970, McGraw-Hill. A 92-page hardback issued without a dust jacket. First edition so stated. $45–$75. Reprints (indicated by the dropped number system): $20–$40.

39. *Seven by Jesse.* 1970, Indiana Council of Teachers of English, Terre Haute, Indiana. A 42-page paperback. First edition not indicated, but never reprinted. $45–$75.

40a. *To Teach, To Love.* 1970, World Publishing Company, Cleveland, Ohio. A 317-page hardback. First edition so stated. $30–$50. Reprints: $20–$30.

40b. ———. 1973, Penguin Books, Baltimore, Maryland. A 315-page paperback. $5–$15.

40c. ———. 1987, The Jesse Stuart Foundation. A 315-page hardback. Introduction by J. R. LeMaster. In print at $20.

40d. ———. 1987, The Jesse Stuart Foundation. A 315-page paperback. In print at $9.

41. *Autumn Lovesong*. 1971, Hallmark Publishing Company, Kansas City, Missouri. A 44-page hardback. First edition not stated, but not reprinted. $25–$45.

42. *Come Back to the Farm*. 1971, McGraw-Hill. A 246-page hardback. First edition so stated. $25–$40. Reprints: $20–$30.

43. *Come to My Tomorrowland*. 1971, Aurora, Nashville, Tennessee. A 195-page hardback. First edition so stated. $75–$90. Reprints: $45–$75.

44. *Dawn of Remembered Spring*. 1972, McGraw-Hill. A 179-page hardback. First edition indicated by the absence of the publisher's keyline. $30–$45. Reprints: $20–$40.

45. *Tennessee Hill Folk*. Photographs and captions by Joe Clark, with an essay by Jesse Stuart. 1972, Vanderbilt University Press, Nashville, Tennessee. A hardback of 96 unnumbered pages, 9½" × 12". First edition indicated by the absence of a stated later printing. Still available in its first printing at $10.95.

46. *The Land Beyond the River*. 1973, McGraw-Hill. A 380-page hardback. First edition indicated by the pres-

ence of the number "1" in the publisher's keyline on the copyright page. $20–$35. Reprints: $15–$30.

47. *32 Votes Before Breakfast: Politics at the Grass Roots, As Seen in Short Stories by Jesse Stuart.* 1974, McGraw-Hill. A 349-page hardback. First edition indicated by the presence of the number "1" in the publisher's keyline on the copyright page. The Jesse Stuart Foundation has first editions for sale for $19.95, plus $1 for shipping and handling. Reprints: $10–$15.

48a. *My World.* 1975, University Press of Kentucky. A 96-page hardback issued without a dust jacket. First edition indicated by the $3.95 price printed on the back cover. $10–$20. Still in print at $6.95.

48b. ———. 1975, University Press of Kentucky. A limited edition of 1,000 copies of the same 96-page hardback bound in blue (rather than the green of the trade edition) and given to Alumni of Murray State University who contributed over $100 to a Library Construction Fund. $25–$45.

49. *Up the Hollow from Lynchburg.* Photographs by Joe Clark; text by Jesse Stuart. 1975, McGraw-Hill. A 128-page hardback, 8″ × 10″. First edition indicated by the presence of the number "1" in the publisher's keyline on the copyright page. The Jesse Stuart Foundation has copies of the first edition for sale for $15, plus $1 for shipping and handling. Reprints: $10.

50. *The World of Jesse Stuart: Selected Poems.* Edited by J. R. LeMaster. 1975, McGraw-Hill. A 309-page hardback.

First edition indicated by the presence of the number "1" in the publisher's keyline on the copyright page. $40–$60. Reprints: $20–$40.

51. *The Only Place We Live.* By August Derleth, Jesse Stuart, and Robert E. Gard. 1976, Wisconsin House, Sauk City, Wisconsin—formerly an independent publisher, now an imprint of Stanton and Lee, Sauk City, Wisconsin. A 186-page hardback. First edition so stated. Still in print at $12.95.

52a. *The Seasons of Jesse Stuart: An Autobiography in Poetry, 1907–1976.* Edited by Wanda Hicks. 1976, Archer Editions Press, originally of Danbury, Connecticut, presently of Lynnville, Tennessee. A 229-page hardback, 12″ × 9″. The Deluxe Edition, leather-bound and limited to 145 signed, numbered copies, was originally priced according to the length of the poem, varying from one to eleven pages, which Stuart inscribed in each copy. Still in print at $150.

52b. ———. 1976, Archer Editions Press. The same 229-page hardback, bound, in this edition, in beige linen, and limited to 489 signed copies. Still in print at $45.

52c. ———. 1976, Archer Editions Press. The trade edition of the same 229-page hardback, bound in brown cloth. First edition not stated, but still in print at $25.

53. *Honest Confession of a Literary Sin.* 1977, W-Hollow Books, Detroit, Michigan. A 24-page hardback issued without a dust jacket. First edition not stated, but there

To Teach, To Love

What Teaching Means To A Famous American Teacher-Writer

Jesse Stuart

"First, last, always," said Jesse Stuart, "I am a teacher. I love the firing line of the classroom." He began his teaching career in 1924 before he had graduated from high school. His last full teaching year was 1956–57, when he returned to again be principal of a high school he had served twenty years before. His earnings from writing make it clear that his decision to take this job, and many subsequent short-term ones, was based solely on his desire to teach. This book appeared in 1970. *(Photo courtesy of World Publishing Co.)*

has been only one printing, limited to 350 signed and numbered copies. $45–$75.

54a. *Dandelion on the Acropolis: A Journal of Greece.* 1978, Archer Editions Press. A 167-page hardback, the Special Collector's Edition, limited to 250 signed and numbered copies. $40–$50.

54b. ———. 1978, Archer Editions Press. A 167-page hardback. First trade edition, so stated. Still in print at $10.

55. *The Kingdom Within: A Spiritual Autobiography.* 1979, McGraw-Hill. A 168-page hardback. First edition indicated by the presence of the number "1" in the publisher's keyline on the copyright page. $30–$45. Reprints: $20–$35.

56a. *Lost Sandstones and Lonely Skies and Other Essays.* 1979, Archer Editions Press. A 176-page hardback. First edition so stated. $20–$30. Reprints: $15–$25.

56b. ———. 1979, Archer Editions Press. A 176-page paperback. In print at $9.95.

57a. *If I Were Seventeen Again and Other Essays.* 1980, Archer Editions Press. A 137-page hardback. First edition so stated and never reprinted in hardback. $20–$30.

57b. ———. 1980, Archer Editions Press. A 137-page paperback. In print at $9.95.

58a. *Land of the Honey-Colored Wind: Jesse Stuart's Kentucky.* Edited by Jerry A. Herndon. 1981, The Jesse Stuart Foundation, Morehead, Kentucky. A 168-page hardback. Only one printing done. $20–$30.

58b. ———. 1981, The Jesse Stuart Foundation. A 168-page paperback. $15–$20.

59. *The Best-Loved Short Stories of Jesse Stuart.* Selected and with commentary by H. Edward Richardson. 1982, McGraw-Hill. A 406-page hardback. First edition indicated by the dropped number system. $20–$30.

60. *Songs of a Mountain Plowman.* Edited by and with "Introduction" by Jim Wayne Miller. 1986, The Jesse Stuart Foundation and Morehead State University's Appalachian Development Center. A 162-page paperback. In print at $10.95.

61. *Cradle of the Copperheads.* To be published by McGraw-Hill, probably in 1988. Pagination and price not yet set. Edited by Paul Douglass of Mercer University.

15.

Jesse Stuart's World[1] / *by Jerry A. Herndon*

Ruel Foster has called Jesse Stuart an "elegist of a lost world."[2] In many ways, this is an accurate assessment. Stuart's world is the slower-paced agrarian America which has been mechanized almost out of existence, and speeded up almost past our recognition. His people live in interdependent rural communities, yet they are also independent, self-reliant individuals. Their interdependence is a result of a sense of community values, of a moral code, which gives stability to their world.

Their lives are also attuned to the rhythms of the natural world and the inexorable cycle of the seasons. They are aware of their dependence on the natural world for the elements of life, and their sense of reverence for the mystery of life is sharpened by this sense of dependence. Their love for the earth which gives them life is extended to the animals which serve as their partners in wringing sustenance from the soil.

In 1942, Whit Burnett asked Jesse Stuart for a contribution to an anthology to be called *This Is My Best*. Burnett, editor of *Story* magazine, was soliciting representative samples of their best work from established writers throughout America. Stuart chose a new story,

This essay was first printed in *The Journal of Kentucky Studies*, 1 (July 1984), 119–128. Reprinted by permission.

"Another April," to typify his art. His instinct served him well. Forty years later, this story still seems to reveal the essence of Stuart's world, and in terms of point of view, presentation, and character portrayal, it is one of the finest examples of Stuart's art in the short story. It has stood the test of time.

The story concerns an old man's first walk outdoors in the spring. It is presented through the eyes of his little grandson, who sees the humor but not the pathos of his mother bundling her ninety-one year old father up like a little child to keep him from catching cold. The pathos is achieved through the mother's comments on how strong this feeble old man once was, and her comment that he will not see many more Aprils. From the window the child watches the old man's brief ramble, noticing but not understanding his Grandpa's interest in the redbud and dogwood blossoms, and in an empty butterfly cocoon. The reader understands, however, that Stuart is presenting the contrast between the brevity of man's life and the eternally recurring cycle of the seasons. Finally, the old man kneels down by the smokehouse to talk to an old friend, a terrapin. He has been talking to the old terrapin every spring for eleven years, perhaps feeling a kinship with this creature of the natural world. The terrapin has the date 1847 cut on its back, and is even older than Grandpa.

Stuart's comments in the prefatory material he prepared for Burnett's anthology are instructive, not only in regard to this story, but in regard to the world portrayed in all his writings. He writes that his subject matter, "man's associations with earth and the living creatures upon the earth and his fight with the elements—his cutting trees, plowing the rugged soil for a

106

scanty livelihood—these are enduring things."[3] It is these enduring things which make up Stuart's artistic world.

As for the pathos of the situation portrayed in "Another April," Stuart comments, "this sort of . . . thing haunts me [,] when a . . . dynamic sort of a human being, who has been as tough as the tough-butted white oaks on the rugged mountain slopes, is calmed enough by the passing of time to sit down and talk with a . . . terrapin. . . ."[4]

Stuart's characters—his people—care enough about the animals which help them earn their bread with their sweat to see them as individuals and to shed tears when the animals die. Such tears are shed for a prize rooster in "Nest Egg" and for a superb working mule in "Old Dick." The men who dig "Old Dick" a grave do it out of respect, affection, and gratitude. They are indignant when a neighbor thoughtlessly suggests that they sell his carcass for fertilizer. "Old Dick" would break their ribs or try to kick their heads off if they hitched him up wrong, but if they harnessed and worked him correctly, he put his heart into his work and never quit. He was their partner in helping them live, and he was worthy of their respect.

It seems fitting for the portrayal of this lost world of the small farmer of the pre-automobile and tractor age to fall to the lot of Jesse Stuart. It was the world he grew up in, and the car, the truck, the tractor and the machinery associated with them did not come to his isolated section of Kentucky until fairly late. Stuart himself, as I recall, did not learn to drive a car until 1942, when he was thirty-five years old. And, in looking back on that world when the farmer was connected to the living earth which fed him through a living creature whose cooperation he had to have, Stuart writes, in an unpublished essay, "Animal Personalities," that "Each horse and mule had a personality. He or she was a living animal." Then he goes on to reflect, "Cars and trucks do not have personalities. They are not living things. They are dead [,] mechanical things."[5]

Stuart's people pull together to endure hardship and overcome it, as the Powderjay/Stuart family does in "Spring Victory." To get enough money for food and stock feed to get them through the bitter winter of 1917–18, when the father is in bed with the Spanish influenza, the mother makes baskets from the white oak saplings her son cuts and drags to the house for her. He sells them to neighbors and buys provisions and feed. When spring comes and the snow melts, the father is on his feet again, and his self-reliant wife and son have earned enough money to pay the doctor for delivering the new baby.

Sometimes Stuart's people need the perspective an outsider can give them before they properly appreciate what they have. In "This Farm for Sale," for instance, Richard Stone does not fully appreciate the beauty of his farm, the independence its fertility gives him, or its ties with the pioneer past, until a real estate man describes them for him in print.[6] Thinking of his rich bottom land, giant virgin timber, and the four generations his family has lived in the great log house, built more than a century before of "giant yellow poplar logs with twenty to thirty-inch facings," he takes his farm off the market and decides against moving to town for an easier way of life. He decides to preserve, in the real estate man's words, an example of "a way of life, [of the] richness and fulfillment that [made] America great, that put solid foundation stones under America."

Stuart's people are believers. In "Walk in the Moon Shadows," the narrator, a child, and his sister are taken by their mother to sit in the moonlight outside an old house where friends of her youth had lived before they died in the flu epidemic of 1917–18. The mother believes so strongly in the spiritual world that she thinks it is possible for her old friends to appear to her. She wants to present her children to them, and she is newly pregnant, carrying another child. This strange story, Stuart told me in 1975, is based on fact, and it clearly affirms a belief in the reality of life after death and in the continuity of life and death. It takes place, appropriately, in the spring, the season of rebirth.

The belief in a spiritual world's existence, in God, if you will, is also affirmed comically in "Rain on Tanyard Hollow." Sweeter is helping his wife and son pick strawberries during a terribly dry summer when a blacksnake bites him. He kills the snake and hangs it on the fence to "make it rain." Lizzie scoffs, telling him that only God can make it rain, and that prayer, the only available tool, is useless for Sweeter, an ungodly man whose prayers won't be listened to. Sweeter is so insulted that he gets down on his knees in the strawberry patch after his wife goes to the house and prays for rain—for a real frog-strangler and gully-washer. He asks for the Lord to "wash Tanyard Hollow clean," to send a storm that will "make the weak have fears and the strong tremble," that will "wash rocks from these hillsides that four span of mules can't pull on a jolt wagon," and that will "wash trees out by the roots that five yoke of cattle can't pull." He asks for darkness so thick "a body can't see his hand before him," and for "a mighty river" of water flowing out of the hollow "faster than a hound dog can run." In short, he asks the Lord to "show . . . [His] might," and "skeer everybody nearly to death."

The Lord complies, detail by detail. There is a hell of a storm, with terrifying wind, thunder, and lightning, and Tanyard gets drenched, drowned, and washed out, losing most of its topsoil in the process. Sweeter's family, along with the mooching in-laws who have overstepped the bounds of reasonable hospitality and have overstayed their welcome, are forced by the rising floodwaters to abandon the first floor of their house for the upstairs. Lizzie, now impressed by the power of Sweeter's faith, begs him to pray to the Lord to turn the tap off. But he refuses, saying he is not "two-faced enough to ast the Lord fer somethin' . . . and atter I get it—turn around and ast the Lord to take it away." Adding to Sweeter's satisfaction at the proof of his faith is the departure of the moochers after the storm. In their terror they had promised the Lord they would leave the hollow forever if He would only spare their lives. They had been eating Sweeter out of house and home, and as they leave with their fifteen children Sweeter counts his blessings: "Tanyard Hollow is washed clean of most of its topsoil and [has] lost a lot of its trees. But it got rid of a lot of its rubbish and it's a more fitten place to live."

Some of Stuart's protagonists also violate community mores or accepted ethical standards themselves, but they get their comeuppance, too. In "As Ye Sow, So Shall Ye Reap," the young narrator helps his cousin sow grass seed, including Johnson grass, in a neighbor's

110

strawberry patch. They are trying to get even because the neighbor's boys have given the cousin a whipping, and the neighbor, Jeff Skinner, has refused to let the narrator see his pretty daughter, Martha. The boys get the patch sown with grass seed after working hard nearly all night to do it, but their reward is to be chased home at full speed by Skinner's watchdog. They suffer the terrors of the damned, because they think it is that terrifying nemesis of rural life, the mad dog. But when they reach the supposed safety of the narrator's house, the father identifies the dog and tells them it has been trained to watch the strawberry patch. The Skinners, he says, will be along shortly. The boys, as the story ends, are envisioning themselves on their knees in the grassy patch during the long, hot summer days, performing the laborious task they had meant for others.

In "Hot-Collared Mule," Pa sets out to "skin" a neighbor by trading him Rock, a cold-shouldered mule that will not work until he gets a sweat up. Just before the trade, Pa runs the mule til he gets hot, knowing the fault won't show up until the trade is over and it is too late for the neighbor to back out. His wife warns him that this kind of trading isn't right, and that sooner or later he will get "a good swindlin'" himself. But Pa thinks he is too smart to get caught. When he and his son take the load of melons to market, using Rye, the mule Pa swapped for, however, he finds justice overtaking him. Rye is the exact opposite of the mule unloaded on the neighbor. He will work *until* he gets hot, then he balks. When they try to make him "get up" he goes backward, throwing the melons out of the wagon and ruining them all. People on the way to town stop and eat the melons and have a good laugh, while an old man tells Pa what is wrong. After pouring water from the nearby creek over the mule's shoulders to cool him down so they can go back home, an embarrassed Pa tells his son ruefully, "I'll haf to do some more swappin'. Yer mom was right."

So, this is the kind of world Stuart presents in his writings—a stable world in which people live close to the earth, and according to their community's received traditions and moral standards. He does portray people who seriously violate the standards, as in the case of his story of a murderer's hanging, for instance, and in his story of a man who poisoned his wife and was lynched for it, but these characters do not damn the standards: They knowingly damn themselves. Stuart's characters either accept or reject the moral code; they do not agonize over its validity. Stuart's perspective is clearly indicated in his comments on the graves of his parents in *God's Oddling*. "Their graves lie," he says, on the "very spot where ... the old Plum Grove school once stood," and within a hundred and fifty feet of the church where they met and in which they were married. They took their children to the same church, and sent them to the school a stone's throw away.[7] This set of facts serves to illustrate Stuart's acceptance of his family's and community's belief in religion and education.

This traditional attitude, an optimistic one, led Dick Perry (in his *Reflections of Jesse Stuart* [1971]) to compare Stuart to Walt Whitman, the pre-eminent celebrator of American democracy and the American people. Perry went on to ask Stuart, "Do you feel sometimes like writing something which *doesn't* celebrate?" He tells us that Stuart only smiled in reply.[8]

112

This acceptance of traditional values helps give Stuart's writings their characteristic tone of good humor. It also helps explain why many see his writings as quaint and old-fashioned today. It is not just agricultural change, technological change, and sociological change which have put his world at a distance from us. This distance is also a result of a change in mental outlook.

In an unpublished essay written in 1970, Stuart expresses his fears that this country may become so overwhelmed by human population that the natural world and its creatures will disappear and his works may, as a result, become "archaic and lost."[9] But two recent events indicate that a change in mental outlook is also a factor to be considered. In 1974, a controversy over textbooks used in the public schools erupted in Charleston, West Virginia. At issue were not only the readings about contemporary life which presented whores and pot-smoking with gentle understanding, but also Jesse Stuart's *A Penny's Worth of Character*. In this famous child's story, a boy cheats a storekeeper of a penny, then repents and makes up for his dishonesty, earning, as the title suggests, "a penny's worth of character." But the story, as used in a D. C. Heath third grade reader, had been edited, or rather, guillotined, without Stuart's permission or knowledge. The story ends where the boy runs out of the store after deceiving the storekeeper. The helpful editor then presents a question to the little third-graders: "Most people think that cheating is wrong, even if it is only to get a penny. . . . Do you think there is ever a time when it might be right?"[10]

Stuart was furious. The butchering of his story and

the question, taken together, indicated an intent to subvert the traditional values which his story actually affirmed. This episode also illustrates an irony. Stuart, as teacher and educator, has always believed in the value of education and has consistently held that improved education is essential to the good health of our democracy. But he has always assumed that education would incorporate and express traditional moral values. In at least one letter I have seen, he does not leave this to inference: He states explicitly that education, to be worthwhile, must always be a moral education. In other words, a valid education, for Stuart, must also be, in part, an education *in* morality.

Ironically, the very thing Stuart advocated, an extension of education—especially higher education—as broadly as possible among the American people, has led to the challenging of traditional values rather than to their affirmation. The sufferings and upheavals of the Second World War led many intellectuals to believe that man is trapped by historical forces beyond his control. This gave rise to the doctrines of existentialism, which holds that man is on his own, with no *a priori* values to sustain him. As far as the existentialists are concerned, man has no past—and no tradition—at his back. He starts with a clean slate, on his own responsibility, and must form his own values from scratch. The implications of science's discoveries, especially the development by science of the horrendous possibilities for nuclear destruction of the civilizations on our planet, moved in the same direction: Man is environed by forces beyond his control.

The Second World War resulted in a tremendous influx of millions of veterans into America's higher educational system via the G. I. Bill. Thus, the extension of educational opportunity Stuart advocated came to pass. But many—perhaps most—of the educators in both science and other disciplines had abandoned traditional values under the influence of scientific discovery, world events, and changes in philosophical perspective. These educators necessarily exercised a profound influence on many of the millions of students they taught. This helped continue and accelerate the shift of the intellectual climate of the nation in the direction of rationalistic humanism and secularism. An explosion of creature comforts with the turning of industry and business enterprise from war production to production for domestic consumption helped even more to produce a secular viewpoint. Life began to seem so easy that the traditional virtues of the past, once held to be necessary for survival, seemed not only quaint but absurd. Life was not to be given to self-restraint and moral struggle, but to self-release and enjoyment. Morality became a museum piece, a psychological aberration practiced by those benighted, "unprogressive" people who did not understand that pleasure is the reason for existence.

Stuart was one of those left behind. His characters, as previously indicated, do not agonize over the validity of the traditional value system. They accept it. Robert Penn Warren is in this sense a more "modern" writer. In his novels he presents protagonist after protagonist who endures agonies of self-doubt and alienation because he feels unable to accept the values of the past. The thrust of these works is the protagonist's movement toward a re-definition of his "self" and his values. The result is usually a reorientation of the character in his world so that he can accept his life—or his death, as the case may be.

Walker Percy's novels also have a pronounced pattern of alienation and reorientation. His perspective is explicitly existential, and his characters, having rejected all traditional values, including love, typically find themselves again through rediscovery of love and its meaning. Binx Bolling, the protagonist of *The Moviegoer* (1961), for instance, decides love is the only way from his existential island back into the human community. In *Love in the Ruins* (1971), a shattered community begins to come back together in a Christmas Eve mass which takes place at the end of the book. With their civilization—their community—crumbling into "ruins," the characters move beyond the illusive "freedom" of sensuality, and make a rediscovery of the validity of love and self-denial, the central values of the past. The sense of community is reborn, in Christian terms.

Jesse Stuart's characters don't need to rediscover the validity of traditional moral and religious values, because they never abandoned them. For this reason, his fictional world looks "quaint" and too innocent for belief to many of our intellectuals who are acutely conscious of recent philosophical trends. For many readers, unless a character is skeptical of traditional values, oblivious of them, or at least engaged in agonizing reappraisal of them, the character does not seem "real." He is only a cardboard figure, if he is not burdened with an analytical intellect directed inward.

The broadening of the intellectual base which Stuart championed has helped produce this state of affairs.

John Stuart Mill warned that "moral associations . . . of artificial creation, [as] intellectual culture goes on, yield by degrees to the dissolving force of analysis. . . ."[11] That is, the cultivation of the reason has a tendency to erode away the basis of religious faith. Both Dostoevsky and Tolstoy proclaimed the same thing, and Dostoevsky predicted that intellectuals who had abandoned belief in God would deluge the world in blood. Walt Whitman, the celebrator of democracy, worried, in *Democratic Vistas* (1871), that intellectual culture in America was "rapidly creating a class of supercilious infidels, who believe in nothing."[12]

Modern education is oriented toward the questioning of traditional values. In Wallace Stegner's novel, *Angle of Repose*, published in 1971, the protagonist thinks about his "liberated" hippy secretary:

> Somewhere, sometime, somebody taught her to question everything—though it might have been a good thing if he'd also taught her to question the act of questioning. Carried far enough, as far as Shelly's crowd carries it, that can dissolve the ground you stand on.[13]

The change in mental outlook among the arbiters of current literary taste, and the effect of this change on Stuart's position in the literary scene, cannot be better illustrated than by looking at the "Publisher's Page" article by Arnold Gingrich in the 40th Anniversary issue of *Esquire* magazine, published in October, 1973. Gingrich had welcomed Stuart to *Esquire*'s pages, first publishing him in 1936. By 1973, even though he had appeared only infrequently in the previous ten years, Stuart was "the magazine's champion contributor," with seventy-nine stories and poems printed. Yet, in spite of this, not one piece by Stuart appeared in the 40th Anniversary issue, devoted to *Esquire*'s best.

Gingrich says he would have liked to see his favorite contribution, Jesse Stuart's "Split Cherry Tree," included, but he had turned full control of the issue over to the editors, and had stayed out of the selection process. Gingrich notes that Stuart's story, which appeared in the January 1939 issue, had been anthologized "many more times" than Hemingway's "The Snows of Kilimanjaro"—in fact, over 150 times. But he goes on to say that "Jesse Stuart's regional stories are . . . out of synch with our current and recent New Fiction policies. . . ."

Esquire's editors refuse to define those "New Fiction policies" when requested to do so, so one must make one's own assessment. Stuart's stories are not sophisticated enough for either the arbiters of literary taste at *Esquire,* or for the sophisticated reading public the magazine caters to. Times have changed, and one of the most significant changes has been the raising of the level of education of millions of Americans since 1945. A more sophisticated, more analytical reading public demands a more sophisticated, more analytical literature, with characters plunged into the well of consciousness and/or sensuality, in the context of an urban/technological society. At the very least, this literature must show characters who are trying to orient themselves to a constantly changing environment with value assumptions shifting like kaleidoscope images.

Will Jesse Stuart's world remain available to us, or will it be lost? I think the efforts of The Jesse Stuart Foundation to keep representative examples of Stuart's

118

work in the public schools of the State, and the reprinting by the University Press of Kentucky of some of his most characteristic collections and longer works, will help to keep Stuart's world in the public consciousness. I also think that a major role must be played by the use of his works in university-level literature classes. To the extent that a consuming market for his works is kept active, his works will survive. This survival may be helped along by the developing trend of a population shift from cities and towns back to the country. Stuart's works will seem more relevant to Kentuckians living in the country, even in the midst of the technological change that is the context of our lives. Nostalgia for an earlier, simpler time will obviously be a factor in keeping alive public interest in Jesse Stuart's world.

Finally, the drifting from moral and ethical moorings of the past may become unsettling enough to cause many people—Kentuckians included—to rediscover the validity of traditional values. They may discover, as William Faulkner predicted in 1958, that, drift away as they will from these seemingly "irrelevant" values, these are truths which are not relative to one's viewpoint, but *realities* which, if not acknowledged or at least respected, will "knock [their] brains out."[14] As they reach back for these values, they may see Jesse Stuart's works with new eyes, because those works deal with real people in a real world, in which *everything* matters.

NOTES

[1]This paper was originally delivered as an address to a meeting of the Louisville Arts Club, on October 23, 1983. Reliable texts of the stories dis-

cussed herein can be found in Jerry A. Herndon, ed., *Land of the Honey-Colored Wind: Jesse Stuart's Kentucky* (Morehead, KY: The Jesse Stuart Foundation, Inc., 1981).

²This is the title of the concluding chapter in Foster's *Jesse Stuart* (Boston: Twayne, 1968).

³Whit Burnett, ed., *This Is My Best* (New York: Dial Press, 1942), p. 407.

⁴*Ibid.*

⁵*Source and Substance,* pp. 1091, 1094. This unpublished typescript is in the Jesse Stuart Collection, Forrest C. Pogue Special Collections Library, Murray State University. Quoted by permission.

⁶I am indebted to Professor Jim Wayne Miller of Western Kentucky University for this insight, provided me by Dr. Miller's stimulating paper, "Jesse Stuart: Builder with Words." This paper was delivered as part of the Jesse Stuart Symposium held at Morehead State University in June, 1981.

⁷*God's Oddling* (New York: McGraw-Hill, 1960), p. 253.

⁸*Reflections of Jesse Stuart* (New York: McGraw-Hill, 1971), p. 159.

⁹"Fifty-Four Years From Now," *Source and Substance,* p. 1413.

¹⁰W. Robert Weller, "300 Different Books in W. Va. Controversy," Ashland (KY) *Daily Independent,* Sunday, Dec. 15, 1974.

¹¹From an excerpt from Mill's *Utilitarianism* (1897), reprinted in Ethel M. Albert, *et al.,* eds., *Great Traditions in Ethics,* 4th ed. (New York: D. Van Nostrand, 1980), p. 271.

¹²John Kouwenhoven, ed., *Leaves of Grass and Selected Prose by Walt Whitman* (New York: Modern Library, 1950), p. 488.

¹³*Angle of Repose* (Garden City, NY: Doubleday, 1971), p. 513.

¹⁴"A Word to Young Writers," April 24, 1958, in Frederick L. Gwynn and Joseph L. Blotner, eds., *Faulkner in the University: Class Conferences at the University of Virginia, 1957–1958* (Charlottesville: University of Virginia Press, 1959), p. 244.

16.

Jesse Stuart: A Literary Profile /
by Jim Wayne Miller

An early description of life in Kentucky, published in
Lexington in 1812, begins:

> 'Twas late in autumn, and the thrifty swain
> In spacious barns secur'd golden grain.

These lines were written by Stephen Theodore Badin,
who was born in France and who came to the United
States as a Catholic missionary. Badin wrote his poem
about life in Kentucky first in Latin, then translated it
into English.[1]

For the remainder of the 19th century, and for about
two decades of the 20th, writing having to do with the
lives of ordinary people in Kentucky tended to be produced by people who knew that life only from the outside, as tourists or reporters. Inevitably, their writing
could be only a report on what they saw, and often,
because they had only a superficial understanding of
what they observed, it lacked depth and could not convey the feel of life in all its intimate detail. It would be
more than a hundred years after Badin wrote before
Kentuckians would begin to tell their own story.

But in 1934, with the publication of Jesse Stuart's
Man with a Bull-Tongue Plow, a collection of 703 sonnet-
like poems,[2] we see Badin's "thrifty swain," or at least

121

a descendant of this proud, independent yeoman farmer, begin to speak of his own life, in a much different voice and accent, and with a different viewpoint. *Man with a Bull-Tongue Plow* begins: "I am a farmer singing at the plow." The difference between Badin's description of a "thrifty swain"—an outsider's arm's-length view—and Stuart's presentation of *himself* as the farmer "singing at the plow" indicates something about the history and development of literature in America, and about Jesse Stuart's contribution to American literature and his place in it as well.

Among literary historians, it is a generally accepted notion that American literature was old before it was new. It began imitatively, as a reflection of the literature of England and Europe, and seemed at first like a periwigged old gentleman, a bit hard of hearing, speaking in English accents and peering at the American wilderness through opera glasses. Early American writers often could not even see the American landscape except in terms derived from European culture and civilization. Washington Irving, writing about a tour of the American prairies in 1835, compared the virgin forests to the great cathedrals of Europe. He compared the trees to cathedral columns, and the sunlight slanting through the trees to stained glass windows. The wind in the trees he likened to organ music.[3]

Then, at mid-century, American literature achieved a new voice and a new perspective in the poetry of Walt Whitman. Whitman heard America singing, and in his poems American writing grew young and open-collared, and took to the road "afoot and lighthearted." Our writing began to reflect the vigorous, varied life beyond the settled areas of the east, life which Emerson, lamenting the lack of a truly American poet while sitting in his parlor in New England, could only point to: ". . . our log-rolling, our stumps and their politics . . . the wrath of rogues . . . the pusillanimity of honest men. . . ."[4] Our problem in the 19th century, Emerson said, was that we derived our sense of culture from one place (the Old World) and our duties (building a country, exploring and clearing the land) from another, our own continent. Our problem was to give literary expression to our own American experience, in uniquely American terms. As our writers found ways to do this, our literature stopped being old and started being new.

The growth and development of American literature can be viewed, therefore, as a process in which writers have discovered the land and life of different geographical and cultural regions—New England, the South, the Midwest, the Far West. The writers and their works have then been discovered by the country, with the result that the country has come to know itself better. Jesse Stuart belongs to a group of writers who discovered a better way of writing about the Appalachian South, one of the country's oldest cultural regions.

Of course, Kentucky and the Appalachian South had been written about before Jesse Stuart embarked on his career. In the late 19th century the entire South was a favorite subject of the writers known as "local colorists." They emphasized the peculiarities of landscape and local character, but, as a literary historian points out, their writing

> was sometimes severely undermined by bathos [excessive sentiment] and by characters too predictable and stereotyped to come alive as individuals. . . . place

123

and span of time were presented for their own sake, the result being that vivid characterizations and strong themes were often overshadowed or neglected.[5]

These local colorists, such as George Washington Cable in Creole Louisiana, Mary Murfree (writing under the pseudonym, Charles Egbert Craddock) in east Tennessee, and John Fox, Jr., in the mountains of east Kentucky and southwest Virginia, emphasized the picturesque and exotic features of people and places. Often considered an American form of pastoral literature,[6] the work of the local colorists also provided Northern readers of the post Civil War era with a picture of a quaint and docile South that could no longer be considered a threat to national unity.[7] The South was already perceived as a distinct region, so the local colorists writing about the South came to be thought of as regional writers.

But during the 1920's and 1930's and thereafter native writers began to produce work which placed emphasis on the peculiarities and uniquenesses of their place, and stress on the importance of ordinary folk and commonplace events, without sacrificing wholeness and depth of characterization. These writers were capable of looking long and hard at human nature at its best and worst, and they avoided subordinating life to landscape. Among the Kentuckians in this group were Elizabeth Madox Roberts, James Still, Harriette Simpson Arnow, and Jesse Stuart. Donald Davidson, Stuart's teacher at Vanderbilt University, understood the difference between the older local color writing and Stuart's work. Davidson considered Stuart to be the first real poet, aside from the ballad-makers, to come out of the Southern mountains, because he portrayed the life of his people as a living reality rather than as something quaintly eccentric and picturesque.

The shift from the late 19th century's superficial and stereotyped local color writing to a more valid literature capable of emphasizing both the uniqueness and universality of human experience in a particular locale was a significant development. It is part of the process by which American writing everywhere, at first imitative of Old World modes, gradually found ways of giving genuine expression to life in various parts of the country. Kentucky writing, as evidenced by Stephen T. Badin's 1812 poem, was born genteel and overly mannered, wearing a ruffled collar and lace cuffs. By referring to a Kentucky settler of the early 19th century as a "thrifty swain," Badin mistakes frontier Kentucky for a manicured English province. His poem gives one the impression that he had glimpsed the people and the land of early 19th century Kentucky from the window of a touring coach. Though more than a century would pass before the change came, Kentucky writing would grow muscular and young. Like Whitman, Jesse Stuart had eyes to see, ears to hear, and the literary ability to portray and interpret his own land and people. When he published *Man with a Bull-Tongue Plow* in 1934, it was as if Badin's thrifty swain, in a sweat-soaked shirt, had undertaken to write his own dispatches in the rough-and-ready verses that begin: "I am a farmer singing at the plow." In this opening poem Stuart announces that he does not write to please an audience ("I do not sing the songs you love to hear") but rather to be true to life as he knows it:

> My basket songs are woven from the words
> Of corn and crickets, trees and men and birds.
> I sing the strains I know and love to sing.[8]

125

The very stereotypes long associated with the South, stereotypes established by the 19th century local colorists, have proved an obstacle to understanding Stuart's work in its relation to Southern literature and to American literature generally. Because his work shares some of the characteristics of the local colorists who preceded him, it has sometimes been considered nothing *but* local color. Yet the freshness and immediacy of his writing, together with the amount of work he produced, caused him to be thought of by many as a gifted naif without precedent. Stuart was often considered a phenomenon apart from literary influences or traditions, an artist difficult to categorize. But Stuart's preoccupation with a particular place—the hill country of eastern Kentucky—caused even those who considered his work to be superior to that of the local colorists to think of him as a regionalist.

But we are beginning to see beyond this inadequate view of Stuart and his work. Stuart's contemporary and one-time teacher at Vanderbilt University, the poet and novelist Robert Penn Warren, writing in a foreword to the reissued collection of Stuart's stories, *Head o' W-Hollow,* acknowledges Stuart's literary gift. He says Stuart has "a rattrap memory for turns of speech," and has "given a sociohistorical record of daily life in his remote world—now so much less remote and more changed." *Head o' W-Hollow,* Warren insists, is a work of "true literary talent." Stuart succeeds at one of the most difficult things a writer can achieve, which is to convey "the sense of language speaking off the page . . . a gift based on years of astute listening and watching."[9]

While stressing Stuart's literary talent, Warren also indicates that he is not an isolated phenomenon, but

stands in a literary tradition—that of Southwestern humor—which began about a generation before the Civil
War in the area now called the Southeast. This movement produced such drolly comic works as George
Washington Harris's *Sut Lovingood,* Augustus Baldwin
Longstreet's *Georgia Scenes,* and *The Autobiography of Davy
Crockett.* The humorists of the Old Southwest were in
many respects the forerunners of the later local colorists, sharing with them an emphasis on the peculiarities of local character and custom. To see Stuart's work
as part of a larger literary context in no way detracts
from that work. On the contrary, one is better able to
appreciate Stuart's achievement and grasp the significance of his work by seeing it in relation to the work
of others.

Warren is also insightful when he describes Stuart,
as a young man at Vanderbilt University, as "already a
compulsive writer, as though all the life he had absorbed was struggling to find a way out, and perhaps
to achieve its meaning."[10] For Jesse Stuart's poems,
novels, short stories, essays, and autobiographical accounts are not just his own personal expression. The
poet, as Emerson points out in his famous essay, "The
Poet," is the "representative" person, and in his role
as "Sayer," gives expression not merely to his own
thoughts, feelings, and aspirations, but to those of others as well. He may also express the experience of a
whole country and its people. This is especially the
case with Jesse Stuart, for he began to write at a time
when the entire Appalachian South was beginning to
"say" itself, as Emerson would put it, and to express its
meaning, its identity, through its literature.

Jesse Stuart's work belongs to a widespread literary

127

quickening which first manifested itself in the South during the late 1920's and early 1930's. In the Appalachian South, this quickening had been anticipated. Emma Bell Miles, in her book, *The Spirit of the Mountains,* published in 1905, spoke of the people of southern Appalachia as "a people asleep, a race without knowledge of its existence." But a literary awakening would come to the Appalachian region, Miles believed, once mountain people were awakened to "consciousness of themselves as a people."[11] Several years later, in 1913, Horace Kephart made a similar observation in his book, *Our Southern Highlanders.* Kephart saw mountain folk as a "people without annals"[12] who awaited their artist.

Kephart wrote on the eve of a period of great change, beginning with the entry of the United States into World War I and continuing into the years of the Great Depression. During this time economic and political events and technological change broke down the isolation of both lowland and upland South, bringing increased self-awareness and creating conflicts in values which caused people to feel the need to reexamine, defend, or perhaps redefine the traditional life of their region. This cultural shock released creative energy and imagination throughout the South and resulted in a Southern literary renaissance. In the upper South, including the Appalachian region, this period produced not one literary artist but several, including North Carolina's Thomas Wolfe and the Kentuckians Elizabeth Madox Roberts, Caroline Gordon, Allen Tate, Robert Penn Warren, James Still, Harriette Simpson Arnow, and Jesse Stuart. Stuart belongs with this group as one of the first generation of native voices from the Appalachian South.

Stuart's ability to convey "the sense of language speaking off the page," Robert Penn Warren points out, "is a gift that goes far toward creating a world."[13] And more than any other writer of his time and place, Jesse Stuart succeeded in creating a literary version of the world he came from and knew to the bone. For the people of W-Hollow, Stuart's "place," his world, exist not only literally, on the map, but also in the imagination. Like William Faulkner's Yoknapatawpha County, Jesse Stuart's W-Hollow is a reality created through language, a part of the American literary landscape.

Although he is deeply rooted in the oral traditions of his place, and rightly associated wtih the Southwestern humorists, it must be remembered that Stuart is, without contradiction, both a Southern Appalachian and an American writer. Philosophically, Stuart is related to the New England Transcendentalists, of whom Ralph Waldo Emerson is perhaps the chief spokesman. Stuart shares Emerson's understanding of the relationship between word and thing. "Words," Emerson says in his essay "Nature," "are signs of natural facts." The natural facts of W-Hollow are present in Stuart's work in abundance. But just as, according to Emerson, "particular natural facts are symbols of particular spiritual facts,"[14] Stuart's created world is a symbolic embodiment of a tradition, a symbol-at-large, which resonates with very American values and aspirations.

One sees particular natural facts functioning as symbols of spiritual facts in the story, "Clearing in the Sky." Here a father leads a reluctant son up a steep slope, past many paths, each steeper than the last, and finally reveals to the son a plot of "new ground"—land never planted before—where the father has grown potatoes,

129

yams, and tomatoes. As the father and son rest in the clearing and look down at the land below, the father explains that when he and his wife were young, they had cleared and farmed the lower level. Now that he is old, clearing another such spot is a way of returning to his youth, a way of recapturing his past. Earlier, the old man was advised by doctors not to exert himself, "'to sit still and take life easy'." But he found that impossible. Although he was weak, the land called him. In order to clear the new ground on the mountain top, he began by making a winding path up the slope. Walking the path day after day, he gained strength, and, taking a less circuitous route up as time passed, he made steeper paths until he was able to climb straight up the mountain, making the path on which he had just climbed with his son.

The many paths, each one a little steeper than the previous one, are both literal and figurative, that is, both physical and spiritual, in their import. Natural facts, the paths are also a symbol of the father's indomitable, productive spirit. The clearing itself, wrested from the previously uncultivated land, to which no path originally led, suggests that the father's is a pioneering spirit. He is a pathmaker. "'But there's not even a path leading up here,'" the reluctant son says when they begin their climb to the clearing. "'There's a path up there now,'" the father replies. "'I've made one.'" The clearing is a symbol of the American pioneering spirit and experience.[15]

Stuart blends his southern Appalachian background and experience with other strains of American literary tradition and philosophical thought to produce, in the imaginative world of W-Hollow, a place that is expressive of American ideas, attitudes, ideals, and values. In other ways, too—in his person, life, and work—Stuart is representatively American. He is both unique and typical, a dreamer and a doer.

Stuart was not the sort of trendy, fashionable writer, anxiety-ridden and alienated, who fancied himself too deep and sensitive to be understood. Stuart's work is accessible. He did not stand back from the common life; he plunged into it. During his active and productive life, he was a farmer, school teacher, high school principal, and county school superintendent, and, for a time, a newspaper editor. He was active in local civic affairs. A far-sighted conservationist, he planted 22,000 trees on his farm.

Stuart was an outgoing, energetic man interested in everything and everybody, as much at home in a cattle barn or at a tobacco sale as he was in the classroom, lecture hall, or at his desk. He was instinctively positive, an affirmer, as his works suggest. Because he was both a dreamer and a doer, he turned his dreams into deeds and words. He did not tear down. He was a builder—of barns, fences, land. And he was a builder with words.

Jesse Stuart was a common man with uncommon vitality and talent. His works appeared in both popular magazines aimed at mass markets, and in so-called "quality" literary publications. His stories, poems, and essays have appeared in *Reader's Digest, The Saturday Evening Post* and *Esquire,* as well as in *The Saturday Review of Literature* and *The Virginia Quarterly Review.*

Stuart had talent, but he also had genius. With Stuart in mind, the Illinois poet Edgar Lee Masters once explained the difference. "Genius," Masters said, is a bend in the creek where the bright water has gathered, and which mirrors the trees, the sky, and the banks. It just does this because it is there and the scenery is there. Talent is a fine mirror with a silver frame, with the name of the owner engraved on the back.[16]

Stuart's writing is indeed like bright water mirroring the trees, the sky, and the Kentucky life he knew and loved. When we look into it more closely, we discover that it mirrors *us* as well, showing us the gift of our land and its relevance to our lives.

Nowhere do we see this more clearly than in Stuart's short story, "This Farm for Sale," in which Dick Stone decides to sell his farm and move into town. He authorizes Melvin Spencer, a well-known local real estate agent, to sell his place. Spencer is really a poet, whose poetry has been appearing for years in the county newspaper in the form of advertisements describing hill farms being offered for sale. The advertisements are so striking that local people look forward to reading them even when they are not interested in buying a farm. After spending the better part of a day looking over the farm, and taking dinner with the Stone family, Melvin Spencer returns to town and puts his advertisement in the paper. He describes the nuts and berries and other wild fruits growing on the Stone farm—the hazelnuts, elderberries, pawpaws, and persimmons— and the jellies and preserves Mrs. Stone makes from them. He describes the tall cane and corn growing in Stone's rich bottomland beside the river, which is full of fish; the broad-leafed burley tobacco; the wild game in the woods; the house constructed of native timber. When Dick Stone hears his nephew read Spencer's description of his farm, he sees the farm with new eyes. He says to his family: "'I didn't know I had so much. I'm a rich man and didn't know it. I'm not selling this farm!'"[17]

"This Farm for Sale" illustrates the complex relationship between word and thing, the magical power of language, artistically used, to transform and clarify our perceptions and heighten our experience. This story may be taken as a key to the proper understanding of all of Stuart's work—the poetry, the fiction, and the autobiographical accounts. In this celebration of a farm and the life a family lives on it, we have on a small scale what Stuart has written large in all his works. For as creator of W-Hollow, the fictional place, Stuart is celebrator of a land, a people, their way of life, and their values. Stuart is to W-Hollow and to us what Melvin Spencer is to the Stone farm and family.

Stuart's art is a genuine expression of his land and people; through his work, as Robert Penn Warren suggests, his land and people achieve their meaning. He has the power to heighten our awareness of both the uniqueness and the universality of our experiences, to help us appreciate not only who we are as Americans living in the border South, but to appreciate as well the universal element in our experience, the things we have in common with human beings of all times and places. For Stuart is first and last a poet, an artist who has the ability not only to *see* but to "say" what he sees, not only to feel but to express his feelings, and to do so in a way that transcends the limitations of particular times, places, and circumstances.

Stuart is a poet even when he is writing prose, as his story "Another April" makes clear. In this story a

133

young boy, the narrator, watches his ninety-one year-old grandfather, who has been cooped up in the house all winter, venture out into the air and sun on the first day of April. The old man's grandson says of him: "Mom put the big wool gloves on Grandpa's hands. He stood there just like I had to do years ago, and let Mom put his gloves on." Outside, the old man toddles along the path, like a child exploring the world for the first time. He waves his cane at a butterfly, stops to examine dogwood and redwood blossoms, a bumble-bee. The old man's identity with nature is suggested by his encounter with a terrapin, also very old—it has the date 1847 carved on its shell—and like the old man, it is also venturing out on this April day for the first time since last year. The grandson, watching from a nearby window, exclaims: "'Gee, Grandpa looks like the terrapin.'"[18]

Nothing much happens in this story. Incident and event are not as important as the symbolic details—the natural facts which represent spiritual facts. The story is a poem in prose, a poem which takes as its theme the notion that we are all children of the earth, as it were. This is a universal theme which can be appreciated regardless of one's cultural background or nationality.

Like Whitman, Jesse Stuart was engaged throughout his career in writing one book, a book about a "great thought" he had as a boy. Stuart describes his great thought in the autobiographical *Beyond Dark Hills:*

> At an early age on one of my walks in the Kentucky hills I thought a great thought. . . . It was this: People last only a short time. Nature plays a trick on them. She stays young forever. The leaves come forth on the trees at spring's rebirth. They flower during the sum-

mer season. They wither in autumn and they tumble to the ground. Then the trees rest for a night—winter. Again they wake with spring's rebirth and flower in their season. Not so with man. His youth is springtime; middle age his summer. He flowers then. Autumn comes and his flesh begins to wither, his shoulders lower, his beauty decays, and then the winter comes when he sleeps. He awakens to flower no more. His work is done. Night comes when man works no more.[19]

This "great thought" contains Stuart's dominant theme and central metaphor (expressed most memorably in *Man with a Bull-Tongue Plow,* no. 27, "Man's life is like the season of a flower," and in elaborations of this notion in sonnets 671–674 in the same volume). This insight accounts for Stuart's repeated use of the cycle of the seasons as metaphor and organizing principle in his work, whether poetry or prose. The "great thought" suggests what Stuart has to say, and helps determine the way he says it as well. The poems, stories, novels, essays, and autobiographical accounts—more than sixty volumes—are pages and chapters of the one book Stuart was writing throughout his career, all of them parts of it as leaves and branches are parts of a tree.

The content of Stuart's great thought is expressed in the *carpe diem* ("seize the day") and *memento mori* ("remembrance of death") motifs present in his first collection of poems, *Harvest of Youth,* and it can be traced through successive collections of poems, including *Man with a Bull-Tongue Plow* and *Album of Destiny,* as well as through the novels, short story collections, and autobiographical writings, from *Beyond Dark Hills* (1938) to *The Kingdom Within* (1979). The two motifs—the injunction to "seize the day" and the reminder that one must

135

die—while separable in analysis, are inseparable in Stuart's expression, because they function as the opposite poles of his great thought. This age-old insight, which informs a story such as "Another April," with its poignant contrast between nature, which is in the process of renewal, and the ninety-one year-old grandfather, who cannot renew himself as can nature, is indeed a great thought. Thousands of years ago it informed the works of poets in the Graeco-Roman and Hebraic traditions (one thinks of the Old Testament Psalms), which have been influential in our literary traditions. Stuart's "great thought" gives his work a universal dimension.

While Jesse Stuart can be seen to belong to a tradition of Southern writing at the same time that he gives expression to fundamentally American ideas, attitudes, and values, he also deals with universal themes. The fact that we can appreciate his work at all these levels—the regional, national, and universal—is an indication of Stuart's range and scope as a writer. According to the novelist Wilma Dykeman, the literature of the Appalachian region is "as unique as churning butter, as universal as getting born."[20] Again and again Jesse Stuart achieves such a combination of uniqueness and universality. His poems, stories, novels, essays, and autobiographical accounts deal with the particular facts and details of a specific time and place. But his works are finally symbols, too, containing values, ideas, and ideals, abstractions that arise naturally from the details, showing what they ultimately mean. Like all genuine literature, Stuart's work is not a mere transcript of reality. His works are not so much portrayals of facts as

136

they are, in the words of the poet William Carlos Williams, "a vision of the facts."[21]

NOTES

[1]Sister Mary Carmel Browning, O. S. U., *Kentucky Authors: A History of Kentucky Literature* (Evansville, IN: Keller-Crescent Co., 1968), p. 79.

[2]Jesse Stuart, *Man with a Bull-Tongue Plow* (New York: Dutton, 1934). For the Dutton Everyman paperback reprint in 1959 Stuart deleted 81 poems that appear in the first edition. Subsequent reference is to the 1959 reprint.

[3]Washington Irving, *A Tour on the Prairies*, in *The Works of Washington Irving*, New Edition, Revised, Vol. IX: *Crayon Miscellany* (New York: G. P. Putnam, 1861), p. 42.

[4]Ralph Waldo Emerson, "The Poet," in *The Complete Writings of Ralph Waldo Emerson* (New York: Wm. H. Wise & Co., 1929), p. 250. Subsequent reference is to this volume.

[5]Herschel Gower, "Regions and Rebels," in *The History of Southern Literature*, Louis D. Rubin, Jr., Blyden Jackson, Rayburn S. Moore, Lewis P. Simpson, Thomas Daniel Young, eds. (Baton Rouge: Louisiana State University Press, 1985), p. 399.

[6]Merril Maguire Skaggs, "Varieties of Local Color," in *The History of Southern Literature*, Louis D. Rubin, Jr., *et al.*, eds., p. 219.

[7]Gower, p. 399.

[8]*Man with a Bull-Tongue Plow*, p. 7.

[9]"Foreword," *Head o' W-Hollow* (Lexington: University Press of Kentucky, 1979), pp. ix–x.

[10]*Ibid.*

[11]Emma Bell Miles, *The Spirit of the Mountains*, a facsimile edition with a foreword by Robert D. Abrahams and introduction by David E. Whisnant (Knoxville: University of Tennessee Press, 1975), pp. 200–201.

[12]Horace Kephart, *Our Southern Highlanders*, a reprint edition with an introduction by George Ellison (Knoxville: University of Tennessee Press, 1976), p. 429.

[13]"Foreword," *Head o' W-Hollow*, p. x.

[14]*Complete Writings*, p. 7.

[15]This story can be found in *Clearing in the Sky and Other Stories* (Lexington: University Press of Kentucky, 1984), pp. 32–40, and in *Land of the Honey-Colored Wind: Jesse Stuart's Kentucky*, Jerry A. Herndon, ed. (Morehead, KY: The Jesse Stuart Foundation, Inc., 1981), pp. 124–130. It is also included in *The Best-Loved Short Stories of Jesse Stuart*, H. Edward Richardson, ed. (New York: McGraw-Hill, 1982), pp. 378–385.

[16]H. Edward Richardson, *Jesse: The Biography of an American Writer, Jesse Hilton Stuart* (New York: McGraw-Hill, 1984), p. 306.

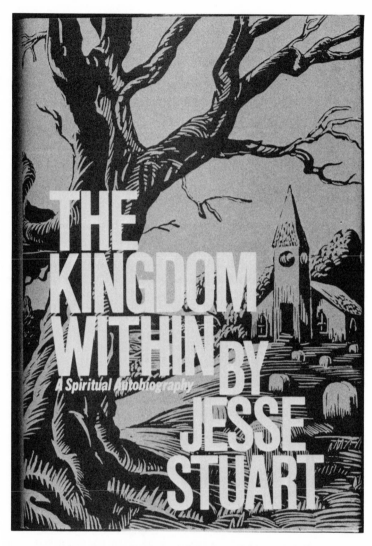

THE KINGDOM WITHIN

A Spiritual Autobiography

BY JESSE STUART

Stuart's last major book, published in 1979, reveals his alter-ego, Shan Powderjay, at the end of his career revisiting his fictional characters who seem to have come to life just as his own flesh and blood is preparing to return to the earth. *(Photo courtesy of McGraw-Hill, Inc.)*

[17]"This Farm for Sale" appears in *A Jesse Stuart Reader* (New York: McGraw-Hill, 1963), pp. 130–140, *Land of the Honey-Colored Wind,* pp. 36–44, and *The Best-Loved Short Stories,* pp. 126–133.

[18]Jesse Stuart, *Tales from the Plum Grove Hills* (New York: Dutton, 1946), pp. 13–21. "Another April" also appears in *Land of the Honey-Colored Wind,* pp. 116–123, and *The Best-Loved Short Stories,* pp. 362–369.

[19]Jesse Stuart, *Beyond Dark Hills: A Personal Story* (New York: Dutton, 1938; reprint, McGraw-Hill, 1972), pp. 20–21.

[20]Wilma Dykeman, "The Literature of the Southern Appalachian Mountains," *Mountain Life and Work,* 40 (Winter, 1964), 18.

[21]William Carlos Williams, *A Recognizable Image: William Carlos Williams on Art and Artists* (New York: New Directions, 1978), p. 255.

17.

A Jesse Stuart Chronology /
by Jerry A. Herndon and George Brosi

1906   August 8: Birth of Jesse Hilton Stuart, the second of Mitchell and Martha Hilton Stuart's seven children, in a one-room log cabin in Greenup County, Kentucky.

1912   Began the first grade at Plum Grove School in Greenup County.

1917   Moved with his family to the first property they had ever owned—a fifty-acre farm.

1921   Took his first regular job for wages, laying concrete streets in Greenup, Kentucky.

1922   Enrolled at Greenup High School.

1924   Taught at Cane Creek Elementary School, Greenup County.

1926	Graduated from Greenup High School and enrolled at Lincoln Memorial University at Harrogate, Tennessee, near Cumberland Gap.
1927	Began publishing poems in a variety of small magazines.
1929	Graduated from Lincoln Memorial University with a Bachelor of Arts degree.
1929–30	Became the Teacher/Principal at Warnock High School in Greenup County.
1930	Published his first book, *Harvest of Youth*, a collection of poems, at his own expense.
1930–31	Served as Principal of Greenup High School, only four years after his own graduation from the school.
1931–32	Did graduate work at Vanderbilt University in Nashville, Tennessee.
1932–33	Served as Superintendent of Schools for Greenup County. At the age of 26, he was the youngest superintendent in the state of Kentucky.
1933	Attracted national attention with the publication of his poems in such re-

spected magazines as *The American Mercury* and *The Virginia Quarterly Review.*

1933–37   Served as Principal of McKell High School at South Shore, Kentucky, in Greenup County.

1934   Published a short story, "Kentucky Hill Dance," in *The New Republic.* This was the first Stuart story published in a major national magazine.

1934   Saw the appearance of his first commercially published book, *Man with a Bull-Tongue Plow,* brought out by the E.P. Dutton Company of New York City and remarkably well received by critics and the public alike. This book established Stuart's reputation as a serious poet.

1936   Published *Head o' W-Hollow,* his first collection of short stories.

1936   Published his first short story in *Esquire.* Eventually 56 of his stories would appear in this magazine.

1937–38   Spent a year in Scotland supported by a Guggenheim Fellowship. Traveled extensively in Europe.

1938   Published his first autobiographical work, *Beyond Dark Hills.*

1938–39	Taught Remedial English at Portsmouth High School in Portsmouth, Ohio, across the Ohio River from Greenup County.
1939	October 14: Married Naomi Deane Norris.
1939–40	Embarked on his career as a public speaker, making appearances in the Midwest and on both coasts.
1940	Published his first novel, *Trees of Heaven*.
1940	November: Moved, with his wife, to the farm in W-Hollow where they would remain throughout their active life together.
1942	August 20: Jessica Jane, the Stuarts' only child, born.
1942–44	Served as Superintendent of the Greenup City Schools.
1943	Published *Taps for Private Tussie*, a novel which sold more copies than any of his other books. It was a Book-of-the-Month Club selection and received the Thomas Jefferson Southern Award as the finest Southern book of that year.
1944	Inducted into the United States Navy,

serving primarily as a writer in Washington, D.C.

1944   Received the first of many honorary degrees, this one a Doctor of Literature from the University of Kentucky.

1944   Published another book of poetry, *Album of Destiny,* on which he had worked for eleven years.

1945   December 31: Discharged from the United States Navy.

1946   Published *Foretaste of Glory,* one of his most respected novels, and *Tales from the Plum Grove Hills,* one of his best-loved collections of short stories.

1949   Published *The Thread That Runs So True,* based on his experiences as a teacher in Greenup County's one-room schools and as County School Superintendent and high school Principal. This autobiographical novel was selected as the best book of the year by the National Education Association, and the NEA President called it "the best book on education written in the last fifty years." The original publisher, Charles Scribner's, still keeps the book in print to meet a steady demand.

1950	Published *Hie to the Hunters*, the first of 29 Stuart titles which McGraw-Hill of New York City released during his lifetime.
1951	May 11: Death of Martha Hilton Stuart.
1952	Published the last of his eleven E.P. Dutton books, *Kentucky Is My Land*, a poetry collection.
1953	Published *The Beatinest Boy*, his first juvenile book.
1954	Designated Poet Laureate of Kentucky.
1954	Published *A Penny's Worth of Character*, his best-known children's book.
1954	October 8: Suffered a severe heart attack at Murray State College in Murray, Kentucky.
1954	December 23: Death of Mitchell Stuart.
1955	October 15: Governor Lawrence Wetherby declared this day, "Jesse Stuart Day," and a bust of Stuart was placed on the grounds of the Greenup County Courthouse.
1956–57	Served for the second time as Principal

of McKell High School. He had been Principal there from 1933–37.

1956	Published *The Year of My Rebirth,* a journal of his convalescence after his 1954 heart attack.
1958	Honored as the featured guest on the popular network TV show, "This Is Your Life."
1958	Taught for the summer in the Graduate College of Education at the University of Nevada, Reno.
1960	Deposited the bulk of his papers and manuscripts at Murray State College in Murray, Kentucky. The Jesse Stuart Collection is housed in the Forrest C. Pogue Special Collections Library.
1960–61	Taught at the American University, Cairo, Egypt.
1960	Published *God's Oddling,* a biography of Mitchell Stuart, his father.
1961	Received the $5,000 Fellowship of the Academy of American Poets, in recognition of his poetic achievement.
1962–63	Toured the Near, Middle, and Far East

for the United States Information Service, U.S. State Department.

1963 Published *A Jesse Stuart Reader,* designed for use in the secondary schools.

1963 August 20: Celebrated the wedding of his daughter, Jane Stuart, to Julian Juergensmeyer.

1964 Served as Chairman of the Kentucky Heart Association Fund Drive.

1964 Co-edited *Outlooks Through Literature,* a textbook which the Scott, Foresman Publishing Company has kept continuously in print ever since.

1965 Published *Daughter of the Legend,* his only novel set in Tennessee, the state where he attended college and graduate school.

1966–68 Served as "Author in Residence" at Eastern Kentucky University, Richmond, Kentucky, for two academic years.

1967 July 21: Birth of Conrad Stuart Bagner Juergensmeyer, his first grandchild.

1969 Toured southern Europe and the African continent.

1969–75 Taught at summer creative writing

workshops named in his honor and held at Murray State University.

1970	November 5: Birth of Erik Markstrom Norris Juergensmeyer, his second grandchild.
1971	Published *Come to My Tomorrowland,* the eighth and last of his children's books to be published during his lifetime.
1972	August: Dedication of the Jesse Stuart Lodge at Greenbo Lake State Park in Greenup County.
1976	Saw the publication of *The Seasons of Jesse Stuart: An Autobiography in Poetry,* the eighth and last volume of poetry to be published during his lifetime.
1978	Suffered a disabling stroke which kept him essentially bedridden throughout the rest of his life.
1978	Published *Dandelion on the Acropolis: A Journal of Greece,* based on the journal he kept during his tour of Greece in 1962.
1979	Published *The Kingdom Within: A Spiritual Autobiography,* the last novel to be published during his lifetime.

1979	Created The Jesse Stuart Foundation to administer his literary legacy.
1980	Published *If I Were Seventeen Again and Other Essays,* the last book he was actively involved in preparing for publication.
1980	The Stuart farm in W-Hollow, less the home place, was presented to the Commonwealth of Kentucky as part of the Kentucky Nature Preserves System.
1981	Saw the appearance of the first book to be published by The Jesse Stuart Foundation, *Land of The Honey-Colored Wind,* a collection of stories and poems intended for use in secondary and middle schools.
1981	August 20: Governor John Y. Brown, Jr. presented Stuart with the Governor's Distinguished Service Medallion.
1982	Saw the publication of *The Best-Loved Short Stories of Jesse Stuart,* selected and edited by Harold E. Richardson and with an introduction by Robert Penn Warren. This was the 17th collection of Stuart short stories and the last book to be published during his lifetime.
1982	May: Rendered comatose by another stroke.

1982	June: Stuart's home in W-Hollow placed on the National Register of Historic Places.
1984	February 17: Stuart's life ends at the Jo-Lin Health Care Center in Ironton, Ohio.